WORTHY

A Pride and Prejudice Variation.

JULIA WINTER

GLASS HAT
PRESS

ISBN: 9798862575842

DEDICATION

For Mum

30 December 1931 – 24 July 2022

With love, always.

I owe eternal gratitude to Claire and Sally, whose advice, comments and criticism helped me make this book halfway decent.

Gratitude too, to Megan, whose patience and wonderful editing skills corrected all those darn errors. Thank you! Also a huge vote of thanks to Doris, who spotted all the new errors I introduced after Megan had finished!

A worshipful genuflection to Miss Austen. I wonder what she would make of the reverence with which she is held by any lover of literature, and if she would be surprised by how many people have agreed with her over the last two centuries, that Elizabeth Bennet is indeed "as delightful a character as ever appeared in print".

CONTENTS

Dedication

Acknowledgments

ACKNOWLEDGMENTS

Editing : Megan Reddaway

Cover Art: Detail from a portrait by Eugen von Blaas. Provenance and whereabouts unknown. Image in the public domain, obtained via ArtVee..

WORTHY

"By you, I was properly humbled. I came to you without a doubt of my reception. You showed me how insufficient were all my pretensions to please a woman worthy of being pleased."

Jane Austen, Ch 38, *Pride and Prejudice*

LETTER: Miss Iphigenia Palmer To Thomas Bennet Esq, December 1810

To Thomas Bennet Esq, Longbourn, Herts

Wenderton Cottage, Wingham, Kent.
This 27th day of December, 1810

Nephew Thomas,

It is with great Trepidation and after much agitated Reflection, yet with Hope we might achieve a true and congenial Accord, that I pen this Missive to you, praying my genuine Desire to heal the grievous Rift in our Families may find an Echo in your own Heart after so many sad Years.

I have long wished to establish a Link with my Sister Eliza's Family—to you—but have been constrained all my Life by the oft-expressed Opinions of my noble Father, gone to his Reward these twenty Years, and the Disapprobation with which he viewed the Marriage of One he once considered as dear as his own Daughters. Though I would have cast aside all Hesitance and sought a Reunion after he entered into Heavenly Bliss, our elder Sister

Cassandra kept alive in her Heart all possible filial Loyalty and Partiality, and would not countenance any lessening of the Respect she believed we owed our Father. She counted it the most impertinent Impiety to countermand even his least Wish. This Devotion and Obedience burned in her all the more fiercely with every passing Year.

Cassandra was a Character of great Uprightness, Strictness and Probity, and I must confess I leaned upon her greatly all our Lives together. Yet Cassandra is gone to our Lord to partake of his Bounty, and I am left alone until I too find His Goodness and Mercy bestowed upon me.

I find I am not made of the same stern Stuff as my dear Papa or Cassandra. I have no personal Injury to resent with regard to my Sister's Marriage to your esteemed Father, no reason for harsh Intransigence against One whom I remember always with the fondest Love.

You will likely know I have no living Brother, and my Cousin James inherited Wingham Hall. His only Child, his Son, is yet full young—being denied his first choice of Bride, James married late in Life to a Lady, now with the Lord, twenty Years our junior. James is a good and kind Man, yet still I think more and more of those far-off Days when your Mother, Cassandra and I were happy Girls together, and my Regrets at our Sundering grow ever deeper.

I am old, and, perhaps, foolish, but I cannot go to my eternal Rest without doing my utmost to mend this sad State of Affairs. Though Eliza is no longer living and is beyond my frail Attempts at Reconciliation, and I must seek her Forgiveness in the Life that is to come, I turn to you, her beloved Son.

My dear Nephew Thomas, I held your Mother, my dearest of Sisters, in real Affection, and my Regret we were parted so long is unassuaged. Can you find it in your Heart to receive these Overtures and allow me to claim you and your Children to be connected to me? That you are Father to five Daughters I know from Eliza's letters, and I am certain they are the Delight of your Heart. I would give much to be acquainted with them.

It would give me great Joy to see you again and spend what Time is left to me in closer Harmony with Family than I have known these many Years.

I await your Reply with Hope,

Iphigenia Palmer

CHAPTER ONE

The Olive In Hand

> I hold the olive in my hand.
> My words are as full of peace as matter.
> – William Shakespeare, *Twelfth Night*

"I suppose," Mr Bennet remarked, "many would consider it a great blessing to gain the acquaintance of a hitherto unknown relative, and hence re-establish family ties."

Elizabeth followed her father out onto the portico, her gaze on the gig turning in at Longbourn's main gate, bearing the Reverend Mr Collins—a stranger, so distant a cousin she must look back to her great-great-grandfather (and his) to find a forebear in common. Because he was a man, Mr Collins would one day inherit her home, despite his own grandfather having married an heiress and taken her name to claim, and subsequently lose, her fortune. He was not even a Bennet.

But all she said aloud was, "From his letter to you, the relative in question believes it, I think. It must be our consolation, Papa, that one of the party is satisfied. Although we may only hazard a guess at his expectations."

"He has offered his olive branch, Lizzy. We must hope he is a better man than his father, although that is no great accomplishment. Had he outlived me, the elder Collins would have turned you all out of Longbourn before I was cold. For myself, I have great hopes of the man. He wrote such a delightfully absurd letter inviting himself here." Papa turned as the bustle at the door announced Mamma and Elizabeth's younger sisters had joined them.

He ceased the conversation, offering Mamma his arm and patting her hand when she took it. It would not do to agitate her into greeting Mr Collins with a demonstration of distempered irritation, a state for which she had both great talent and many years' experience in honing the performance. Mamma found the entail making Mr Collins Papa's heir an incomprehensible mystery, and was beyond the reach of reason on the subject. She saw only the cruelty of settling Longbourn away from her five daughters.

Elizabeth was seldom in sympathy with her mother, but this grievance she could understand. Mamma would not readily forgive Mr Collins the sin of being Papa's heir.

The gig bowled up to the house, gravel spitting out from beneath the horse's hooves, and Papa stepped forward. "Mr Collins, I deem, sir? I am Thomas Bennet. Welcome to Longbourn!"

Mr Collins stepped down from his hired gig and swept Papa a bow. "I am happy to be here, cousin."

"I hope you had an uneventful and easy journey." Papa indicated his waiting wife and daughters, gathered on the portico steps to greet their guest. "Come in, and meet my family."

Mr Collins, murmuring something about being all agog to meet his lovely cousins, bowed and smiled and simpered throughout the introductions. Once he reached Lydia and the end of the welcoming line, he burst out with, "Oh, how delightful is the renewal of old, severed connections! I am glad, Cousin Bennet, I overcame all my filial scruples and sent my little epistolary dove of peace to begin the task of healing the breach between us, despite all my late father... Well, enough of that. It becomes us as Christians to forgive all offences against us, does it not? Blessed indeed are the peacemakers and how beautiful upon the mountains are the feet of him that publisheth peace!" His smile widened a mouth crowded with too many teeth. "What a day for your dear family, to know they are no longer sundered from your heir! It must fill you all with grateful joy!"

Papa's answering smile betrayed his delight at this absurdity. "In truth, I cannot articulate my emotions on this occasion, Mr Collins. They are quite indescribable."

While no woman would call Mr Collins excessively handsome or charming, he was a tall, well-set-up young man of about twenty-five and by no means ill-looking. He had the added advantage of both a good competence and good prospects. By his own account, chance had brought him into an excellent living in the parish of Hunsford in Kent, near Westerham in the west of the county, a rich farming area generous in tithes. And, of course, he would one day own Longbourn, though he had sufficient tact not to mention this above three times an hour in the hearing of its current owner. His elevation to the Hunsford living and the munificence of his noble patroness, however, could not be discussed enough.

Papa's right eyebrow winged upwards, mirrored in the quirk of the right-hand corner of his mouth, conveying his opinion of his cousin with great eloquence.

He kept Elizabeth near him, all the better to murmur in her ear. "It appears to me, my Lizzy, that early preferment and the condescension of the owner of a living are a danger to those whose minds are not of a strong constitution. Such fortune risks instilling an air of pompous pride. It may not be sound to theorise on merely one such specimen, but I think I am right."

Elizabeth pressed her lips together hard to prevent her smile. She leaned back in her chair to return a whisper, while the object of their discussion sat in a place of honour beside her mother, intent on glorifying his patroness and not perceiving that two of his unwilling flock had strayed. "Such pride may be forgivable in an archbishop, but it sits uneasily on the shoulders of a cleric barely a year or two beyond his deaconship. A man should serve his parish a few years longer before assuming such elevated ecclesiastical airs."

Papa's mouth twitched. "He is his father's son."

Before Elizabeth could respond, Papa took base advantage of a slight pause in Mr Collins's oration—the cleric had raised his teacup to his lips and had, perforce, to stop speaking—to rise and excuse himself.

"A small matter of business," Papa murmured, and left before Mr Collins could swallow his tea, or Elizabeth give him anything other than a speaking look.

A very speaking look. In any other man, it would have engendered guilt and, one hoped, some measure of contrition. In Papa's case, it merely earned her another quirk of his mouth.

Forced into civility, Elizabeth pretended an interest in Mr Collins's descriptions of his parish, inviting him to continue his oration. "For, indeed, it is most interesting, sir."

Mr Collins believed her, which must be her punishment for dissembling. Her sisters—barring Mary, who listened eagerly to Mr Collins—promised retribution by means of glares and impatient sighs, and her mother allowed her eyes to close. Mamma would deny dozing, of course, but from many sleepy Sundays in church, her daughters were familiar with her beatific expression. For herself, Elizabeth allowed Mr Collins's voice to wash over her like the tide, ebbing and flowing, but having less impact upon her than the sea did upon the sand, and leaving a smooth stillness in its wake.

Despite his long conversations since his arrival, Mr Collins was still in fine voice when everyone assembled for dinner. Though he sat at Mamma's right hand and Elizabeth was at the other end of the table, seated at her father's left, she was in a prime position to enjoy Mr Collins's company and share her enjoyment with Papa.

Mr Collins was full of happiness and praise.

He praised the house—

"Such noble proportions! How cleverly the true classical front has contrived to hide the ungainliness of the older portions of the place and lend the whole a pleasing unity of form! I am reminded of the south face of Rosings Park, the seat of my noble patroness, which is an architectural wonder and a monument to Lady Catherine De Bourgh's excellent taste. A commodious and appropriate dwelling for an estate of Longbourn's importance, I deem. Yes, indeed. Quite fitting."

— the furniture and furnishings —

"What excellent drawing and dining rooms! Whose artistic eye has been at work here? Yours, of course, Mrs Bennet! What taste and ingenuity are displayed in all your contrivances! I am sure your lovely daughters have inherited your sensitivity and refinement. A lovely room... Why, I am again reminded of Rosings, and the third parlour in the east wing... Ah, you shake your head, but you must understand that Rosings is very grand, and Lady Catherine De Bourgh, my most revered patroness, is one of the noblest ladies in the land. Her taste is incomparable, but I dare to say that she would not find fault with your arrangements here. Not at all! She would approve them, I have no doubt, as being most appropriate to your condition in life."

— the excellent dinner provided by Mamma, who was famed as the leading hostess in the district —

"I have never tasted such magnificent potatoes! And the sauce, so rich and yet piquant! Why, I might almost suppose myself to be dining at Rosings. Lady Catherine has a French chef... Oh no, Cousin Bennet. I am certain employing him cannot be improper, despite our holy war against the Tyrant. His loyalty to Lady Catherine is unquestioned. Which of my fair cousins is responsible for this wondrous feast... Ah, Mrs Bennet, forgive me! I meant no offence! You keep a cook? How splendid! Longbourn is profitable indeed."

— and the daughters he had traduced by assuming their domestic duties included drudgery in Longbourn's kitchens —

"I had heard you had five lovely daughters, Cousin Bennet, and rumour does not lie in this case. I am sorry Cousin Jane is in London with Mrs Bennet's brother Gardiner, since she is the eldest... Her absence is a great pity, as I am sensible of the hardship to my fair cousins when one day I must supplant them." Another smile full of teeth. How did any man have voice enough to be forced past such a barricade? "I will say no more at this juncture. I do not wish to appear precipitate, though I am come at the direct behest of the noble Lady Catherine, whose beneficence extends to all in her purview! With her sanction in mind, and her kind generosity in encouraging me to marry and promising to acknowledge my wife, I am prepared to admire my fair cousins with every fibre of my being! I anticipate deepening our acquaintance. It will be a joy to consider how I may make amends..."

Elizabeth looked up sharply from the magnificent potatoes, her suspicions confirmed as Mr Collins made this pronouncement. Mr Collins stared at each of them in turn, his intent unmistakable. He had the air of a man weighing up which juicy apple to buy at market: which had the shiniest skin, which had the shape that most pleased his eye, which would best suit his palate and gratify his taste.

Lydia could never respond with propriety. Her expression showed affronted astonishment, and he looked quickly away from her unforgiving stare. Elizabeth wished her own sense of civility allowed her to display honest emotions, but she was more than sixteen and must show a good example. Not that Lydia was prone to following one. Mr Collins was not to know Lydia and Kitty—next up from Lydia in years if not in maturity and who would not look at their cousin at all—were wholly taken up with the company of militia infesting the area. Even if he wore a red coat, Elizabeth would hazard nothing on the chance of Mr Collins making amends in their direction. Mary, though... serious, devout Mary was flushed, and the pink in her cheeks was pleasing and becoming. It was inconceivable she should like Mr Collins... But she had both the temperament and a sincere piety that would become a clergyman's wife.

Elizabeth glanced back at their cousin. Had he had noticed? Could he share Mary's interest? But no, he was staring at Elizabeth herself. When she caught his gaze with hers, he smirked and simpered.

Good heavens, no!

Too busy hiding his smile with his napkin, Papa offered no help. Her mother, not slow to understand an opportunity to disposing of one of her daughters, narrowed her eyes at Elizabeth and pursed her lips, before nodding. Always alive to the advancement of her own interest, Mamma's face brightened like a sunrise.

No.

Elizabeth returned the man's stare with a raised eyebrow and lifted up her chin to convey her disinterest. She withdrew her gaze and turned her attention to her father, ignoring Mr Collins for the rest of the meal.

Never!

Papa sent for Elizabeth not long after returning to his library. He had excused himself from the drawing room, leaving his ladies to entertain the heir. Elizabeth, who had waited until Mamma and the other girls were seated before insinuating herself onto a small sofa with Mary and leaving Mr Collins no space to sit beside her, was delighted when Mrs Hill brought Papa's summons. Mamma had been winking and nodding all evening, and her expression on hearing Mrs Hill's message was inimical. Her heavy frown followed Elizabeth all the way to the door.

Elizabeth darted across the library to Papa's desk, to deposit a smacking kiss on his brow. "Bless you, Papa! You have always been my refuge!"

He quirked an eyebrow at her. "Come, Lizzy. You are not fleeing our new cousin's company already, are you?"

"I am a lady, sir, otherwise I would tell you what I think of Mr Collins. You will have gathered the nature of his olive branch, I am sure."

Papa smiled. "I suspect he intends to marry one of you."

"It will not be me, sir."

"He gives you the preference, Lizzy."

"He may give it. I will not accept it. Or him. Oh, how glad I am Jane is safe in London with Aunt Gardiner!"

"Very wise, child. I would not have you wasted on a Collins, even to secure Longbourn. However, put our enthralling cousin aside. I wish to discuss another family conundrum. If familial reunions are indeed a joy, then to regain two long-sundered relatives brings me to a level of felicity that creates havoc with the balance of my humours. Joy and indigestion are indistinguishable."

"I have every sympathy with your humours, Papa. Another long-sundered relative?"

Papa tapped a small pile of opened letters, four or five, lying upon his desk, before thrusting them into a drawer which he locked with the tiny key hanging from his watch-chain. "We will speak of these in a moment. Run and fetch a bonnet and pelisse, Lizzy, and come and walk with me. It is too close indoors. Does not the atmosphere fit over you like a clammy glove? We need air, to clear our heads."

She frowned at him, but it would be an hour at least before the arrival of the tea tray would recall her to the drawing room. She duly ran and fetched. The late-April evening was cool, and she was not surprised, on her return, to find Papa shrugging into his greatcoat before venturing out.

Despite the closed door to the drawing room and the long hallway, Mr Collins's droning voice emanated like a verbal miasma. It was usually Mamma's voice to be heard, talking of their neighbours' doings (scandalous), or lace (an expensive necessity), or the difficulty with servants (ungrateful creatures) or the marital prospects of her daughters (poor). How Mamma must resent being outdone by the man she declared would one day toss her into the hedgerows to starve! It was more fodder for the strain on her nerves.

Papa paused when the monotone drone was pierced by Lydia's voice expounding on some incident to do with the militia regiment currently imposed on the local town, Meryton, followed by a raucous laugh. A fainter echo sounded like Kitty.

He chuckled. "Lydia and Kitty are showing their mettle, I see. They must be the silliest girls in the county. That should be enough to frighten off Collins."

"They are heedless," Elizabeth ventured. "And all too entranced by the militia officers."

"Surely they are not spending that much time in the redcoats' company? More silliness. They are children yet, and hence absurd and foolish. Enough of them now, Lizzy. I wish to walk, and to speak with you on more important matters where we may not be overheard."

Elizabeth pressed her lips together hard. She had spoken to him before of the wild, unconstrained behaviour of her two youngest sisters, and each time he would not listen. How she wished it were just childish silliness!

She feared it was the sort of folly that would lead to infamy. She could not laugh at that.

CHAPTER TWO

What's Past Is Prologue

> to perform an act
> Whereof what's past is prologue
> — Shakespeare, *The Tempest*

Elizabeth and Papa used a side door to reach the garden. For a few minutes they walked the paths in restful silence, wandering without conscious direction until they reached the corner of the house. The gravel sweep to the gates lay before them. To their left, Longbourn's long Palladian frontage glowed pale gold in the last rays of the westering sun. They sat together on an old stone bench under an arbour that in summer would be sweet with climbing roses, out of sight of the drawing room windows.

A long sigh from Papa, and finally he came to business. "Did my mother ever mention the Palmers to you, Lizzy?"

"Her mother married into the Palmer family, did she not? I recollect Grandmamma always seemed sad when she mentioned them."

"It grieved her. Her own father died when she was still a babe-in-arms, and within a year or two, her mother remarried a widower who had issue of his own. Sir Thomas Palmer, a baronet whose seat, Wingham Hall, is in Kent—"

"Kent! A curious coincidence, sir."

"A small one. Most of the county lies between our cousin's rectory at Hunsford and Wingham Hall. Now, then. Palmer brought up my mother with his children, and I believe treated her as one of his own daughters. Until she disobliged him by eloping with your grandfather, that is. The ensuing breach was never healed, though she named me for her stepfather. They visited once when I was a boy, but if they intended rapprochement, they failed."

"Do you remember the visit?"

"Very well. When I received the first letter, I calculated with exactness. It was the summer of sixty-seven, shortly before my eighth birthday, some two years after my father died. Forty-four years since the Palmers descended on us in a caravan of three coaches, each one—even the lesser vehicle bearing the servants—pulled by four matched horses. They rolled up to the front door in great state. And what does that tell you?"

"With a dozen prime horses at their command, the Palmers were very rich."

The drive now was empty. The gig Mr Collins had hired to convey him from the coach stop in Stevenage had returned whence it came, leaving nothing but ruts in the gravel to mark its passing. Not even a ghost of those grand coaches remained in the dusk.

Papa nodded. "Very rich indeed. They all came. Sir Thomas and my grandmother, his daughters, and a young man who watched my mother a great deal. Sir Thomas's heir, but not his son, who had died years before." He half turned on the seat to stare at the house. "I am the fourth generation trapped in this entail, Lizzy. Our misfortune is not the lack of connection to the Palmers, but the lack of a son. With no son to follow me, that mutton-headed cleric boring your sisters to death will one day stand in my shoes and feel all the satisfaction and pleasure of ownership. After three centuries, Longbourn will pass out of the hands of the Bennets."

"Oh Papa." She put her hand into his.

"It is a hard truth to swallow, my Lizzy, and grieves your mother greatly. It is not helped by my laxity in providing for my family in the event of my death. I have been remiss there. But perhaps... Well. The Palmers may have a role to play after all. I received a letter last Christmas."

"From the Palmers?"

"From one of the daughters. Iphigenia. I was astonished. My mother persisted in writing, sending a letter to her step-father and family every Christmas until she died in the year two. But after the death of her mother—oh, it must be forty years now—no reply ever came. Your grandmother said her step-father would never allow it. My only firsthand knowledge of him is from that visit. He seemed a most difficult and arrogant man." Papa shook his head. "I do not doubt my memory is tainted by knowing he hurt my mother, but he was not all a doting grandfather."

"He does not sound a pleasant man."

"He was not. According to my mother, he never forgave anything he deemed an injury to his consequence. Your grand-aunt Cassandra, his daughter by his first wife, was of similar bent. Your grandmother always said a more fitting classical name for her was 'Alecto'."

"After the oldest of the Furies? Well, that gives a keen impression of Miss Cassandra."

Papa squeezed her hand. "I am pleased you have retained some of my teaching, Lizzy! Well, to return to my tale, they took offence at your grandmother's choice in the matter of your grandfather, and they never forgave her. She wrote principally to the younger Palmer sister, this Iphigenia who now writes to me, whom she loved a great deal. As I said, she had no response. The Palmers did not even acknowledge the notice I sent them of her death."

"That was cruel."

"Indifference often is." He glanced around. "It grows cold. Come, let us return to the library. I would like your opinion of the Palmer correspondence."

Elizabeth being eager to assuage her curiosity, they hastened indoors. Mr Hill, their butler, greeted them with candles lit against the encroaching night. Elizabeth plumped down into her favourite chair, while Mr Hill set the candelabrum in place and Papa poured himself a glass of port.

Papa opened the desk drawer, removed the batch of letters he had locked away earlier, and handed one to Elizabeth as soon as Mr Hill had left and closed the door behind him. "This is the first letter I received. I have had others since, but this first was a trifle disconcerting."

Disconcerting? Papa seldom admitted to any such emotion. Adept at finding amusement in the quirks and follies in others, he was usually loath to reveal such qualities in himself.

Elizabeth accepted the two sheets of good-quality parchment and turned her attention to the fine, old-fashioned script in which Miss Iphigenia Palmer made the first approach to the Bennet family in forty years.

Here, with Papa the sole witness, Elizabeth did not need to wear the polite face Society demanded of young gentlewomen. She could allow her expressions to convey all she felt: astonishment, sympathy, curiosity. And at the last, sadness. "She is old, I think, from the penmanship. She is one of Grandmamma's step-sisters?"

"Her half-sister through the same mother, your great-grandmamma. She was several years my mother's junior, and must be near seventy now. She never married. Nor did Cassandra, the daughter from Sir Thomas's first wife. In my mother's opinion, Sir Thomas kept them by him for the convenience of ordering them about. This Iphigenia appears to have been well named, if she were bred to be sacrificed on the parental altar. Should I employ that stratagem, Lizzy, and command your obedience in every particular?"

"I doubt its efficacy, Papa. I am far too stubborn a creature to be a willing sacrifice."

"Yes. You inherited more of my mother than her name and looks." He nodded at the topaz cross she wore around her neck. "Along with her mother's trinket. The Palmers sent it after your great-grandmamma died, as a token of remembrance. Then, as I say, silence."

Elizabeth touched the old cross, the smoothness of each stone familiar to her fingers. It had been hers since childhood, gifted by her grandmother. She had never before considered the link to the Palmers in Kent. It had belonged to the grandmamma she had loved, not the shadowy great-grandmother of whom not an iota else remained. "Miss Palmer seems sad and lonely. Her sister Cassandra... well, I understand the point about Alecto."

"She seems to have kept Miss Iphigenia cowed and obedient. Miss Cassandra remains in my memory as a figure stiffer and less kind than the fireside poker, while Miss Iphigenia seemed a gentle, unassuming soul." Papa looked through the other letters while he spoke. "Your grandmother remembered her younger sister with great affection. Now, then. I responded to that letter in the New Year. We have exchanged letters in the months since, to allow her to understand who we all are."

"I expect you enjoyed delineating our characters to her."

"I did, indeed. I told her of each of my girls. Of Jane's beauty and gentle nature, your impertinence—" Papa smiled and shook his head when Elizabeth laughed. "She knows, of all my daughters, you are the one most like my mother in looks and temperament. I mentioned Mary's desire to do good and to learn accomplishments, Kitty's... well, Kitty's character is a little indeterminate at present, but I hope she will grow. And I felt constrained to tell her of Lydia's precocity."

"Oh dear. She will have an exact picture of us."

"I also explained how we are circumstanced. I hesitated at first, because the Palmers are rich and I did not wish to appear grasping."

"Their riches cannot be anything to us, surely? Grandmamma was but Sir Thomas's stepdaughter. We can have no claim." Elizabeth smiled at him. "We have riches of our own, do we not, of the kind this poor lady seeks? We may be able to do much good with her, and relieve some of the loneliness imbuing her letter. She wishes for company, Papa. For girls."

"Of which I have a surfeit, to be sure."

"Will you offer her Lydia? Miss Palmer may welcome precocity after what appears to have been a dull life."

Papa smiled. "Oh but Lizzy, consider. You are the image of my mother, and Miss Palmer knows it!"

"Well, I am the only one who favours the Bennets, to Mamma's chagrin. She despairs about this—" Elizabeth tugged at her unruly brown curls—"and that I have none of her own looks."

"Your mamma was a great beauty in her day. She is a very pretty woman still, though perhaps I do not tell her often enough."

Elizabeth grimaced at the flutters and agitation such a compliment would cause, and from the glitter in Papa's eyes, he was relishing a similar image.

Mamma had aged gracefully, and though her youthful beauty was fading, she was indeed still very pretty. Each of Elizabeth's sisters had, to a greater or lesser extent, inherited something of Mamma's looks: they were all fair-haired and blue-eyed, all with a measure of her great beauty. Even Mary, deemed the plainest Bennet, would in most other company be considered a pleasant-featured girl. As for Elizabeth... well, she had oft studied the marriage portrait of Elizabeth Beeching, known as Elizabeth Palmer, in its place of honour over the drawing room fireplace, and seen herself. Of all the Bennet girls, only she had Grandmamma's rich, brown curls and dark grey eyes.

"No, it was your grandmother who excited Miss Palmer's love and sympathies when they were girls together, and it is your grandmother's image who has attracted her now." Papa took back the first, tentative letter, and offered another. "It is not Lydia she wants, child, or any of the others. This is her latest letter, which arrived a few days ago. Read it. She wants you."

CHAPTER THREE

Our Maladies Unseen

With eager compounds we our palate urge,
...to prevent our maladies unseen
— Shakespeare, *Sonnet 118*

Doctor Rhys-Griffiths closed the door to Georgiana's room behind them, ushering Darcy away. Darcy stumbled as he went, his feet oddly heavy, as if Harris, his valet, had filled his Hessians with lead. His toes caught on the hallway carpet.

Rhys-Griffiths put one hand under his arm, supporting him. The other touched him on the brow, palm lying flat against his skin. "No fever, thank heavens, but I judge you are weary to the bone. You must rest."

"I may be able to sleep, now."

Rhys-Griffiths had been the Darcy family doctor since before Georgiana's birth, and had seen her through every small ailment from her babyhood. Darcy would entrust his young sister to no other, and in the darkest hours of this most dreadful illness, he had put all his faith in the old man.

"Yes. She is safe." Rhys-Griffiths was kindness itself. "She does well, and we are over the worst. She is no feeble miss, the Lord be thanked, and her strong constitution has carried her through. She is out of danger, although I suspect she may have a long road to recovery. She will need careful nursing for some weeks yet."

The muted sounds of London outside the house, the rolling wheels of coaches and carts on Brook Street and the occasional voice of a passer-by, came to Darcy through the buzzing in his ears. The cold fist that had been clenched in his chest for the last week slowly unfurled, the loosening grip bringing a warmth with it.

Darcy conceded his sister's breathing seemed easier.

"It is. Do not fear a relapse." Rhys-Griffiths's sharp gaze appraised Darcy, who lifted his chin to meet it. "When did you last eat, sir?"

Darcy shook his head. He could not recall.

"Mmn." Rhys-Griffiths gestured to his assistant and spoke in the young man's ear before turning back to Darcy. "I have sent for your valet, sir, and for a tray to be brought to you in your own rooms. I suggest that you sleep for a few hours. I will return this evening."

Darcy nodded and took another two or three leaden steps towards his own rooms. Harris appeared in the corridor ahead of him.

Rhys-Griffiths put his hand under Darcy's arm again. "I will accompany you, if you will permit. Miss Darcy does not need me now."

Rhys-Griffiths was right. Darcy could sleep, and it was not a dereliction of duty to leave her for a few hours. She was safe, and well cared for. If only half the tales of drunkenness and debauchery were true, nursing was not the most genteel of occupations, but the two women Rhys-Griffiths had provided were sober and grandmotherly.

He nodded, and stumbled along beside the doctor until Harris came to his other side, and instead of lurching along the corridor like the veriest swill-tub befuddled by too much brandy, he was falling and falling until his mattress caught him in its feathery embrace, and all was dark and quiet.

Rhys-Griffiths came back as evening drew in, looking fresher. Rejuvenated.

Darcy himself had slept for most of the day and had bathed since wakening, but his rest had been little more than a drop of water to a man dying of thirst. He had had no real repose for more than a week, and while the edge of his weariness was blunted, it was still sharp enough to wear on him, honing him to sinew and bone. He felt hollowed out.

Not at all like the master of Pemberley should feel.

He greeted the doctor and added, "I looked in on Georgiana, but she is asleep and the nurse chivvied me out with as little ceremony as if I were a schoolboy she had caught in mischief."

"My nurses know their work." Rhys-Griffiths looked him over. "You appear better, although I suggest you do not sit with Miss Darcy tonight but try to sleep more. She no longer needs you to be constantly at her side. She will not slip away while you are sleeping, you may be sure of that, and the night nurse will send for me at need."

"I have slept all day." Darcy picked at the food on the tray Harris had brought to his study, where the doctor had found him after a preliminary visit to Georgiana.

Rhys-Griffiths had refused a meal but accepted a glass of Madeira. "You have repaid a little of your debt to Morpheus, but my strong advice is that you rest again tonight. I will rely upon the nurses to continue to chivvy you out of Miss Darcy's chambers."

Darcy's laugh surprised him perhaps more than it did the doctor. "The lady who refused me entrance this evening reminded me forcibly of my mother's sister."

"Lady Catherine?"

"The same. You could not guard Georgiana better if you had procured a flight of Welsh dragons for the task."

Rhys-Griffiths smiled and sipped his wine. "Let us consider where we stand, then, now we are protected by dragons. My assistant and I have examined everyone in the house, and no one else has taken the illness."

"The Lord be thanked."

"Indeed. The precautions we put in place to limit those entering Miss Darcy's room and for scrupulous cleanliness, have both been most efficacious. Your staff are to be commended for their diligence."

Darcy nodded. He did not employ fools who would risk taking infection. Besides, Rhys-Griffiths had ruthlessly enforced constant hand-washing, and had permitted only his nurses to touch Georgiana directly.

Rhys-Griffiths smiled. "It irks you still, I see. Well, sir, dirt is no friend to the sick. Mayhap it feeds the noxious miasmas that carry disease... who knows? I have found the cleaner we are, and the cleaner a sick person's bedlinen and surroundings, the weaker the hold of illness. Hand in hand with that, the fewer people allowed into the sickroom, breathing the same miasmic air, the lower the risk the sickness will spread to others. As for allowing only my nurses to tend to her physical care, it would do her no good to be pulled and tugged hither and yon, and the nurses know how best to manage her whilst she is in this helpless state. She needs peace and quiet, and as little disturbance around her person as possible."

Darcy himself had been the one exemption from the injunction against touching Georgiana, but was allowed to do no more than hold his sister's hot, damp hand in his while remaining at arm's length. For the last three days and nights, he had not left her side as the crisis approached. He had sat at her bedside, helpless against her pain and suffering, agonised that she did not see him, did not know him. Once he had held the bowl as Rhys-Griffiths bled off the fever, nose wrinkling against the hot, metallic stench, before resuming his seat and enclosing her limp hand in his to hold it tight. Another time he had sat in resentful silence as Mr Hodgson, rector of nearby St George's, read the prayers for the visitation of the sick. And all the while, silently for the most part, he had prayed for her life with such fervency, he had no room for any other thought.

"Your instructions were hard to obey." Darcy met the old man's gaze. "I understood your reasoning, but the heart protests mightily at the necessity of keeping a distance at such a time."

"You would do her no good to take the disease yourself. It *is* hard, but I did what I must to preserve Miss Darcy, and prevent anyone else succumbing to the same sickness."

"I cannot fathom how she took the illness."

"Cases of putrid sore throat are not uncommon. The weekly tallies reported by the parish authorities show it sweeping through the areas in the north of the metropolis. Miss Darcy was at school in Barnet, I believe? The authorities reported cases there."

"At Miss Ryder's Seminary, yes. I took her from school a month ago. She had need of more sophisticated masters, those who consider themselves too dignified to travel out of Town to their pupils." Darcy plucked at his cravat. "I intended she have a few weeks tuition before we retired to Pemberley for the summer. Music is her delight, and the master I found for her is eager to teach her."

"A month? Well, that seems too a long a period before the onset of her illness. I would not have thought her able to keep it at bay for so long." Rhys-Griffiths shook his head. "We can but speculate. Man knows too little, even in all these centuries since Hippocrates gave us the notion about bad air bringing contagion with it. No man is able to see what atomies ride on such air to afflict us."

"Georgiana and I hardly live in such squalid conditions as breed miasmas and foetid odours. And we are barely into May… too early in the year for such vile contagions, surely? The summer heat is not yet here to breed them."

"True. But this is a big city, full of want and disease. You can walk to the rookeries of St Giles's parish from here, do not forget. We cannot escape rubbing shoulders with it."

Darcy nodded, rubbing a hand over his face. "I suppose you are right. London has ever been unhealthy and unsanitary. I shall take her back to the clean air of Pemberley as soon as I may."

"A wise decision, though it will be some weeks before she regains enough strength to travel. As to her future care, she will sleep a great deal in the next few days. When she wakes, the nurses have their instructions concerning medicines to give her, and I have left your estimable housekeeper a recipe for bone broth to strengthen her. She should be left to sleep—it is the sovereign remedy. Your part will be to calm and cheer her when she is awake and keep up her spirits, and, in due course, when she is stronger, to ensure she neither tries to do too much and rises too early from her bed, nor yet languishes in an invalidish state too long. I will visit again in two days, and we will review her progress. Send for me if need be, but in truth, Mr Darcy, I do not anticipate you will have cause."

"Thank you. May others visit? Her companion thinks to help keep Georgiana cheerful as she convalesces. Reading to her, that sort of thing."

"Yes, as long as she is careful to maintain a little distance and will follow my rules on cleanliness. Do not allow too many visitors. Your cousin Colonel Fitzwilliam shares guardianship with you, I believe. His company may cheer her. Other than those two, none else for a week or two."

"He is in Portugal with his regiment, but Lady Ashbourne, his mother, might visit in his place. She is fond of Georgiana and of all the ladies in Georgiana's life, she is the most like a mother, and will bring great comfort to all of us here."

"I see no difficulty if our rules are followed."

"I will write to her tomorrow and arrange it."

"Excellent. Shall you and I brave the dragon and visit Miss Darcy? Afterwards, perhaps you will be reassured enough to return to your bed until morning. You will be the better for it."

Rhys-Griffiths was the most obstinate of obstinate old men! Darcy suspected he would be allowed a few minutes with his sister, then the doctor would shepherd him back to his own rooms, and doubtless try to tuck him into bed himself.

Darcy smiled for the first time in days. He was weary enough to allow the doctor his way. Other than tucking him up in bed, of course.

As they left his study to climb the stairs to the family rooms, the footman admitted Georgiana's new companion to the house. Darcy caught a brief glance of the street outside as the large door swung closed behind her. Twilight thickened the shadows, and the lamplighter, perched on the top of his ladder, trimmed the wick of the oil-lamp swinging on its bracket at the top of the iron post in front of the house. His apprentice stood below him, holding up a bottle of oil. When Darcy had been a boy, it had been one of his delights, he and cousin Edward together following the lamplighters around as they worked to push back the night and light the great city from one end to the other. The warm, rich, waxy smell of the oil was the very scent of nightfall.

The companion looked up. She seemed a little conscious, the reddening of the skin over her cheekbones visible despite the obscuring qualities of the light veil she had thrown over her bonnet. She put back the veil, and bobbed a low curtsey. "Mr Darcy. Doctor. It is excellent news about Miss Darcy's improving health. I am sure all in Pember House are giving thanks." She glanced at the book in her hand as she spoke. Small and bound in white leather... ah. A prayer book.

She had no need to be embarrassed at his finding she had left the house for a while. Indeed, she could do nothing for Georgiana's comfort; no reason to expect she should remain indoors. She had not been allowed in Georgiana's room for well over a week: she had but taken up her duties when his sister fell ill, and had not that depth of intimacy and friendship to give her entry when others, more familiar, were denied. It showed her good heart, that she had taken a few moments to walk to St George's and give her thanks in a proper setting. Darcy expected such correct, Christian behaviour of a clergyman's relict.

Darcy allowed his approbation to warm his voice. "It is indeed good news. Doctor Rhys-Griffiths tells me we may allow Georgiana more visitors as she grows stronger. We must work together to keep her amused as she recuperates. Thus in a day or two, as the doctor allows, you may start reading to her. She will welcome that, I am sure, and you and she will become better acquainted."

Her returning smile was bright, her eyes crinkling. "Oh, excellent news. I mean to be of great use to Miss Darcy, and nothing will give me more pleasure!"

"Excellent. Thank you. Excuse me..." Darcy nodded, and he and Rhys-Griffiths started up the stairs. He glanced back from the landing, as he turned to climb the flight to Georgiana's suite of rooms.

She stood in the hall watching them, her head tilted to one side and her relieved smile enlivening her narrow face. When she caught his gaze, Mrs Younge inclined her head, and dropped him another curtsey.

CHAPTER FOUR

A Hey Nonino

It was a lover and his lass,
With a hey, and a ho, and a hey nonino
— Shakespeare, *As You Like It*

Mr Collins proved to have a greater tenacity of purpose than Elizabeth had anticipated. Her hopes of indicating to him through her chilly behaviour that she did not welcome his suit came to nothing. He appeared wherever she turned, his round face wreathed in smiles, ever ready with tributes to her beauty, vitality, wit, understanding... In short, every quality she possessed came in for its allotment of praise. He must have spent many hours composing and arranging elegant little compliments to pay, while attempting, not quite successfully, to give them an unstudied air when he delivered them.

"I have hidden in Papa's library for hours. I leave the house to walk before even the maids are astir, to avoid his company. I ensure there is never a seat beside me at meals or in the drawing room in the evenings. I have barely evaded outright incivility. All to no avail." Elizabeth pulled at the front of her gown to settle it into place. Several of the neighbourhood families were invited to dine at a formal reception for the Bennets' guest, and Mamma had insisted on her daughters wearing their prettiest dresses. "He does not appear to understand I do not welcome his attentions."

"You are cold in the face of his advances." Mary sat on the bed behind Elizabeth, resting from her labours. In Jane's absence, she had taken on some of their elder sister's habit of assisting everyone as they dressed. Lydia and her echo, Kitty, had repulsed Mary's efforts. Elizabeth had welcomed her. Mary tamed Elizabeth's curls with a far more ruthless hand than Jane's, but with pleasing effect. She had a good eye for such things. Odd that she refused to use it for herself.

"Again, Mary, to no avail! Most men of discernment would be discouraged."

"I agree. He is not a man of great perception, and cannot comprehend you might not find him eligible."

"I am left to contemplate a kind of brusque, uncivil honesty on the matter."

"You have brushed the edges of it more than once, Lizzy." Mary's reflected expression lost not one ounce of its reproof as their gazes met in the looking glass.

"I am never outright rude, I hope!"

"No. But he is not quick, as you are. We are told, are we not, that the ideal conversation should in both matter and manner, appear most graceful, being tempered by courteousness and modesty, and seasoned with wisdom and discretion."

Ah, the Reverend Fordyce delivering one of his famous sermons, using Mary's voice and manner.

Elizabeth grimaced. While she had little patience with Fordyce, she had indeed sported with Mr Collins's inability to understand even when she was at her most pointed. It had not been well done of her. She sighed, and turned away from the looking-glass to join Mary. The bed frame creaked and the mattresses dipped under their combined weight. "It is unfortunate Mamma has taken it into her head to encourage him towards me. If she would but take a moment to consider, she must realise I will not accept him, and to raise his expectations will increase his chagrin when he is refused. That will not sweeten relations between him and the family."

"I do not believe Mamma can comprehend any of her daughters refusing an eligible match."

Snorting was unladylike. Elizabeth did it anyway. "Mamma and I have different notions of eligibility. She does not think beyond fortune. I do not mean she deliberately seeks out rich men for us, but any man with enough of a competency to take a wife and support a family is in her sights, and our cousin's current position as rector in a rich parish is comfortable, even without his inheriting Longbourn one day. She does not consider eligibility of character, or humour, or shared ambitions, interests and values. She does not look beyond her frantic desire to marry us off as quickly as may be while Papa is still with us."

"She fears the future."

"I know, and I do understand. But I cannot allow Mamma's fears to govern my future. Marriage to Mr Collins! No, that is something I cannot contemplate. I would be exceedingly unhappy."

Mary kept her attention on her skirts, fingers picking at the soft folds of embroidered muslin. For once she had eschewed the drab colours she usually favoured, donning instead an old evening dress of Jane's. Lydia had complained loud and long that the dress had gone to Mary and not to her, but Elizabeth was pleased Jane had ignored their youngest sister. The soft blue of the dress became Mary very well indeed.

"Lizzy, surely you must give greater weight to duty and what is owed your family? Insisting always on what you want, and what you will allow... forgive me, but does not Fordyce remind us a woman's place is to seek her happiness in performing her duty?"

Elizabeth bit back a sharp retort, and instead spoke with care and deliberation, determined to appeal to Mary's pious, moral sense. "We all have many duties, do we not? I owe duties to our parents and to you as my sister, but I also owe duties to myself, to preserve my own happiness and peace of mind. Which do I obey? Consider that a woman is subject always to the authority and whims of another—her father, while she is unmarried, and then her husband. We cannot choose our parents, but we must be careful when it comes to our husbands. Marriage is for life, Mary! If we choose ill, it cannot be rescinded or escaped, except by death. I cannot and will not marry any man without great care and consideration. We must choose husbands with more thought than choosing ribbons for our bonnets. That is the greatest duty, to treat the wedded state with the due reverence it deserves."

"And yet we must marry. If we do not, we shall be terribly poor after… well, you know. After Papa."

"Unmarried women are often poor, but marrying prudently with an eye to a man's ability to support his family is far different than marrying for mercenary reasons. If it is folly to marry a gentleman with insufficient income and poor prospects, it is equally foolish to marry solely for money. To accept Mr Collins without respect and some element of affection, because he is the heir to Longbourn, is mercenary. In all conscience, I could not vow before God to love and honour a man, when in essence I am marrying him in order to pick his pocket. I would be speaking an absolute untruth at a moment when I should be at my most pure and honest."

"I suppose…"

"I do not dislike Mr Collins, but I have not one jot of admiration for him. He is not for me." Elizabeth regarded this quiet, neglected, least-noticed of her sisters. "Would you consider him, Mary?"

"He is a good match for a lady of our circumstances—that is, of little fortune, and without the sort of connections valued by those in Society. We cannot offer grand relations or social position to counteract our small dowries. Mr Collins is not a bad man. I have seen no tendency in him towards viciousness or evil of any kind. I cannot imagine him being cruel or violent."

"I agree. He is none of those things, and seems no worse than many men of our acquaintance. He appears to be moderate in his habits. While he eats heartily, I have noticed he is restrained in his consumption of wine at dinner. He played at cards at Aunt Phillips's house the other night, but to oblige our aunt, and for low stakes. He accepted his losses with good humour and resignation. All that is to his credit. I do not think he would ever hurt his wife, but would he listen to her views and accept her advice? Would she be first in his mind, and valued? Or is that respect all given over to Lady Catherine De Bourgh?"

Mary pulled her bottom lip between her teeth, frowning. "Lady Catherine has a profound influence upon him, but the right wife might eventually replace her in that regard."

"I would be the wrong wife. I do not have the patience needed to win such influence over him, and I would chafe at giving Lady Catherine undue prominence in my marriage. Mary, speak plainly. Are you interested in him as a potential husband?"

"I would consider him. I am not romantic, you know, and I do not wish for Society and grandeur. I seek to live a life of… of quiet usefulness. Mr Collins's position as rector appeals to me. I think I may do a great deal of good in a country parish, helping the villagers lead better and more Christian lives, teaching them and their children, and providing an example. Those are circumstances to which I am suited, and I would be very happy serving God so."

"I agree. Such a situation corresponds exactly to your character and interests."

"But he is fixed on you, Lizzy, like the needle on a compass."

"Then we shall have to point him towards his true north. We will do our utmost to put you before him, and I will slip into the background, and hope Mamma will see you are a better match than I. And if she cannot, then I will accept an invitation that came to me a few days ago, to visit our grandmother's half-sister—"

"Truly? I had no notion any of our grandmother's family were yet living."

"No more did I! However, Papa is considering how the visit may be encompassed, and I have written to her so we may not be complete strangers when we meet. If I am removed from Longbourn, you will have your chance. If I am not here and Mr Collins's attention is turned upon you, Mamma will willingly lend you her aid."

"I would not have you chased from home, Lizzy."

Elizabeth smiled, and pressed her cheek against Mary's. "It will be an adventure, and I would brave far more than a comfortable month or two with an old lady, if it helps you win a situation in life that will suit you. Although in truth it is little more than an airy plan at the moment and it is doubtful my removal can be arranged for some time. So, we must instead act to turn Mr Collins's attention where it will be best received, and trust Mamma will not interfere."

"She will not care if it is you or I, as long as one of us secures him. We are neither of us a favourite."

Elizabeth embraced her. It was true. "Nevertheless, let us direct Mr Collins towards you tonight. I will ensure you are seated beside him at dinner. Be sure to engage him in conversation. Be brave, Mary. You have much to win, if you will but dare to try it."

After all, what was life but a game of Hazard? One must throw the dice, and pray to roll the main. Nothing ventured, after all, is truly nothing gained.

"What are you about, Eliza?" Charlotte Lucas, a dear friend, and the only person to still call her by the pet name her grandmother had used for her, nudged Elizabeth. Hard.

Elizabeth rubbed at her ribs, meeting Charlotte's saucy smile with one of her own. "I do not comprehend you."

Charlotte cocked her head, eyes bright with mischief. "I am familiar with the notion that sisters pass down dresses from elder to younger. It is a matter of prudence and thrift, after all, and practised in most families of sense and respectability. Mary, by the by, looks very well in that cornflower blue. It became Jane, too." Charlotte's smirk grew wider. "I am not aware, though, of a similar tradition of passing down gentlemen with the same insouciance as one would a ribbon or a bonnet. If this is indeed the practice in the Bennet family, I wish I were one of your sisters!"

"You are in all but name. But we are not as practical as that, I assure you."

"Nonsense. I have seen you in company with Mr Collins four times since his arrival. He has been inclined towards you. Tonight, though, you leapt up from your place beside him and almost pushed Mary into your chair. It was most unsubtle of you."

"Subtlety would be wasted on such a man."

"I do not doubt it. So, here you are at the other end of the table, far out of his reach. He and Mary, in consequence, appear to be comfortable. If I were not such a desperate old maid, I should not mind it half so much."

Charlotte's tone had enough of an edge to give Elizabeth a sharp pang under her breastbone. Regret, perhaps? She would not permit it to be pity. Since Harry Goulding, Charlotte's betrothed, had died in the battle of Maida in Italy, no one had presented himself as a suitor. Charlotte had turned twenty-seven on her last birthday, and many in the district deemed her at her last prayers.

Elizabeth made her an apologetic little grimace. "It is true I am attempting to give his inclination a new direction. He is not the sort of lover to appeal to me, and I am not his lass. Mary is the most suited to him, and will not dismiss his attentions."

"As you do." And Charlotte sighed.

For a few moments they were silent, both of them looking the length of the table to where Mary listened patiently as Mr Collins talked on some matter or other. Mr Collins's mien towards Mary was respectful and not once did his gaze stray to seek out Elizabeth. Now they had turned his attention to Mary, it seemed he preferred his audience to be captive, rather than expend energy on the hunt.

Elizabeth glanced at her mother. Mamma's gaze was as focused on Mary as Elizabeth's own had been, and she nodded, satisfied.

Excellent. It all boded well.

Mary might yet be the first Bennet daughter to be led to the altar, and Elizabeth could relax her guard.

CHAPTER FIVE

The Parfit, Gentil Knyght

In al his lyf, unto no maner wight,
He was a verray, parfit, gentil knyght.
— Chaucer, *The Knight's Tale*

"Darcy! My dear man, I have not seen you this age. A month, at the least!" Galahad Palmer bounded forward as Darcy entered the Small Drawing Room at Brooks's. He grasped Darcy's hand in both of his, shaking it with all the hearty goodwill of a man working the parish pump. "Miss Darcy is better, I hope?"

Charles Bingley, a dear friend to them both, came to join them. "Darcy! Well met! Miss Darcy?"

"She is better, I thank you both. Recovering well, our doctor says, though too slowly for my comfort. It has been five weeks. However, she is no longer confined to her rooms. Indeed, she ventured out to the garden this morning for the first time." Darcy dropped his hand to his side and flexed it. Bingley's grip had been unusually strong, as enthusiastic as Palmer's. Handshakes conveying manly sympathy were wearing on the fingers.

Darcy allowed them to steer him to the table set in the window overlooking St James's Street. His shepherds' dogs chased his sheep up and down the Derbyshire hillsides in similar manner, although perhaps with more barking and lolling of tongues. Bingley in particular had the same amiable characteristics and determined helpfulness of the herding dog: friendly, a happy nature, and a little too biddable. Palmer, a year or so older and much wiser than Bingley, was more like those less good-natured dogs suspected of nipping at a ewe's heels to send her in the direction he wanted.

Palmer gave Darcy a devilish grin. "I am particularly relieved at your good news. M'father is talking of grandchildren again."

Darcy frowned. "That will never concern my sister, Palmer! You are so very far from your namesake's purity of thought, any man of sense would baulk at consigning a lady to your care."

Palmer claimed his unusual Christian name arose from his father's relief at finally having a son, making the old man indulgent of Lady Palmer's romantic fancies. Given that one day, he would wear a baronet's title, Palmer himself deplored those same fancies: living as Sir Galahad would be a heavy burden to bear. "I am no perfect knight, and am well aware I do not live up to the standards of chivalric romance. I should not know what to do with the Holy Grail, were it presented to me, and I am far more enamoured of the romance than the chivalry!"

Darcy could not pretend surprise at this assertion. While not a rake, Palmer was a charming flirt, and many a Society matron eyed him askance, while shepherding her daughters out of harm's way. He gave Palmer a flat look in response, and his friend laughed.

"You may keep Sir Galahad's purity. I would not have it as a gift." Palmer waved at the waiter in a complicated series of signals to indicate the requirement for Madeira and glasses. Darcy glowered, until Palmer tugged at his cravat. "You are a damned intimidating fellow. Is he not, Bingley?"

"I know of no more awful object than Darcy, on particular occasions and in particular places." Bingley's smile widened. "Balls come to mind. Or evening soirées. Or dinners. Or card parties. Or Sunday evenings when he has nothing to do. Or—"

"Yes, indeed! He is the most unsociable creature alive. It is a sad thing, all these long years later, I am reminded of him as our praeposter, lording it over we lesser boys and threatening us with a caning for our transgressions. Why does any man look back on his schooldays with nostalgia? They were brutish in the extreme, and best forgotten." Palmer let loose a generous laugh. He leaned in a little closer and tapped Darcy on the arm in what may have been an effort to convey earnest gravity. "In all seriousness, I am not seeking a bride from the schoolroom. How old is Miss Darcy? Thirteen? Fourteen? I am no cradle robber, not yet a fortune hunter. I was teasing in the hope of lifting your mood."

"Fifteen. No matter her age, she will always be too young for a man of your stamp. You flirt too much."

"All nonsense, as you know. If it were not, I doubt you would recognise my acquaintance. If ever there was a 'parfit, gentil knight', 'tis you, Darcy, not I!"

Darcy permitted his smile to show. "You have faults enough, I am sure. Not least, you still cannot distinguish Malory from Chaucer—"

"Hence those threatened canings," sighed Palmer. "I was an indifferent scholar."

"You were, but I acquit you of worse sins, at least. You are no villain. A flirt, but an honest one."

"It is my father's fault. He presses me to marry, and as long as I am able to tell him I am considering Miss A or Lady F, he is content I am at least making some small attempt to carry on the family name. A little light flirting allows me to survey the marriage mart, that is all." Palmer laughed again.

"I have met your father. Sir James must have wed late himself."

"He was fifty. I am but six-and-twenty. You would think he would not expect more of me than he was willing himself, but hey-a-day, I must do as he says, and not as he did." Palmer brightened as the waiter approached with a laden tray. He paused to allow their glasses to be filled and once they each held one, and the waiter had retreated beyond hearing distance, he went on, "Once, in his cups, he told me the lady he had loved eloped with another, leaving him repining, and she would not have him even when left a widow. He must have nursed his broken heart for nigh on thirty years before Mamma and Cupid together planted him a loving facer, so to speak."

Bingley leapt on that as a drowning man clutched a straw bobbing past him on the waves. "If it is a facer you need to make you marry, Palmer, may I bring my sister to your notice? She has a stronger fist than Tom Cribb, and brings with her twenty thousand sweeteners to soften the blow. She is yours!"

Palmer snorted. Miss Bingley was fixed upon marrying into the first circles, and a man would need to be fleet of foot to escape with a mere flirtation. Palmer was an athletic sort of man who displayed to advantage at Jackson's Boxing Academy, but was rather too heavy-footed to be a runner. Consequently, he steered clear of Caroline Bingley, using a hard rudder and crowding on sail to bring himself steady on a course out of dangerous waters; so reserved in her company, no woman alive could suspect him of flirtation.

Bingley chuckled. "Content yourself, man. I will not force her upon either of you. Neither will I tell her about Miss Darcy daring to leave her chamber, Darcy, lest she be at your door demanding entry. I would not wish to provoke a relapse."

Darcy did not allow the prospect to alarm him. "The knocker remains down. No one will enter."

They laughed, and something inside Darcy lightened. Only in this trio of close friends—the closest!—would Bingley speak of his sister so, or Palmer express his exasperation with his father's exhortations to marry. Darcy's reserve was greater than theirs, but he shared their confidence in each other's loyalty and discretion. He had few enough friends of whom he could make that claim.

Palmer, still chuckling, replenished their glasses. "Tell me, Bingley, if we are to be romantics, who has you all-a-mort these days? I cannot believe you are not languishing at the feet of some goddess or other. I have never known a man more prone to standing in the way when Cupid seeks a target. You must bristle with more love arrows than a hedgehog has spines."

"Pffft! I appreciate a lovely lady when I see one, that is all."

"And yet Darcy considers me to be the flirt." Palmer attempted a sorrowful look, using his forefingers to pull his smiling mouth down at the corners and making his chin wobble.

"Odd, is it not?" Darcy replied, and Palmer laughed.

"I am a susceptible man." Bingley smirked with pardonable pride in this achievement. "Mine are eyes that must slake themselves on beauty."

Palmer was not to be diverted. "And the beauty's name?"

"Miss Jane Bennet. An angel sent to this Earth to bedazzle men with her beauty. Such hair and eyes—"

"Golden hair and blue eyes, of a certainty." Palmer favoured Darcy with a sidelong glance.

Darcy smiled. "They always are."

"True, she is blonde, tall and elegant, and surpassingly beautiful. Her figure... well, clouds could not move with more grace! I have never seen a lovelier woman. I met her three weeks ago, at a ball given by the Lord Mayor at Mansion House. We danced twice, and I have called upon her since."

"A Cit." Darcy did not hide the grimace.

"I am one myself, Darcy. As you know." Bingley's smile did not waver.

"You are no such thing. You are within an ames-ace of buying your estate and raising yourself into the gentry."

"My father made his fortune in trade, and I owe every penny I have to the mills and looms of Yorkshire. But for the friendship you have both offered me, and the influence you have brought to bear, I would have fared badly at school and at Cambridge. The smell of the shop is still on me. Miss Bennet, however, is the daughter of a landed gentleman, though the relations who brought her to the ball are in trade."

Darcy grimaced again.

"You and Caroline are of like mind. Miss Bennet is not rich or highly-born enough for Caroline, who makes no allowance for Miss Bennet being of the gentry, or for the fact that the uncle in trade is a warden of the Mercer's Company and will be an Alderman one day. He is greatly respected—and respectable, although that is not at all the same thing."

Darcy acknowledged this with a slight inclination of his head. "I have no doubt the gentleman is indeed a City grandee, or one in the making. Nevertheless, such a lady can do little to help raise you further."

Bingley shook his head. "Darcy, why do you think I can be raised? The daughters of dukes and earls do not fight over the privilege of being my wife, not even those whose fathers are drowning deep in River Tick. Most barely acknowledge my existence, other than as one of your friends. Oh, do not frown so! I am content with what I have achieved. A member of Brooks's and friend to you and Palmer... such social success is beyond my father's wildest dreams. I am too practical to aspire to more. A daughter of the gentry—and mind, I do not say it will be Miss Bennet! I do not know her well enough. But someone of her birth and breeding will be as high as I dare aspire."

This thoughtful Bingley was a stranger; all those puppyish tendencies gone in the instant, leaving a jaded practicality in their wake. Darcy opened his mouth to say something, to extol Bingley's worth both as a gentleman and for his estimable character and qualities, but he closed it again, the words unsaid. In truth, Bingley's acceptance in Society would never be unquestioned. If he married well and bought his estate, then his children—or their children—would have a place by right. Not so for Bingley himself, who would always be accepted on sufferance, eyed with condescension, and spoken of, in supercilious terms, as being 'tolerably gentlemanlike, for one of his breeding'. Steps to more social prominence would hinge upon his making a good marriage, and yet here he was accepting his achievements and talking, in essence, about being content to consolidate his gains.

A silence followed; a heavy silence, thick with all the unpleasantness of being forced to take a step or two in another man's Hessians, the unfamiliar leather tight enough to bite. Darcy had never before considered Bingley's precarious social position in such depth, and privilege weighed on him where he stood in his own assured place.

When Palmer laughed, Darcy jerked out of his introspection.

"Yes." Palmer's tone was light. "I will be content with a gentleman's daughter, when I must settle."

Darcy snorted. "I do not boast the affection of dukes' daughters myself! I have a good estate and I am a wealthy man, but I am untitled without even a baronetcy like yours to aid me. I am no more than a country gentleman."

Bingley eased their discomfort. Always the most cheerful of souls, his manners and disposition were such that he wanted always a pleasant, comfortable ambiance, free of conflict or ill-temper. "Come! This began as a merry talk about Cupid's blows. We should not end it in such disquiet. It remains that I have met a lady—"

"Another lady." Palmer smirked.

Bingley inclined his head. "Another lady who is more beautiful than the sun, and kinder than... than... well, I confess a simile escapes me. I am content with the acquaintance for now. If it deepens and we suit... well then, that will be time enough to consider the weighty matter of Society's expectations. Speaking of which, June is upon us and the Season is coming to its end. Are you both for the country soon?"

"There is little to keep me here. I shall be glad to return to Kent's cleaner air, and Wingham in summer is a delightful place." Palmer clapped a hand over his mouth with a dramatic flourish Sarah Siddons might envy. "Did I say that aloud? Do not tell my father, I pray you! Though I must confess it is true. What of you, my friends? Do you retire to the country?"

"I am yet to find an estate." Bingley spoke without rancour. "I may rectify the lack this year. Or next."

"I had intended to take Georgiana to Pemberley as soon as I was confident I could remove her from our doctor's care." Darcy frowned, reminded of his current dilemma. "But her companion suggests a course of sea bathing will help restore her health. Our doctor agrees, hence I must set my people to discover from the land agents any houses to let at the resorts. I fear, though, 'tis late in the year to find anything suitable. The best houses will already be let for the summer."

"Perhaps I can help," Palmer said.

"But you live in Kent." Bingley frowned.

Palmer snorted. "Which has a coastline, Bingley."

"Ah." Bingley was unrepentant. "I was never an aficionado of geography."

"We shared a classroom for many years, my boy. That assertion is no surprise! I will forgive your lack of cartographical knowledge since you were unable to join us when Darcy visited Wingham."

"It was the year my father... I was much occupied."

"I am sorry to raise sad memories." But at Bingley waving a forgiving hand, Palmer went on, "Well, since you have not yet visited us, Bingley—though I hope you will soon!—I will tell you that Wingham is in the east of Kent. Indeed, were we any farther east, we would wet our toes in the Dover Strait each time we stepped out of doors. We are situated within fifteen miles of the coast, and for many years we have had a summer cottage at Ramsgate." Palmer turned to Darcy. "The cottage is fully staffed, and stands on the outskirts of the town, overlooking the sea. We do not use it ourselves a great deal these days—my father bought for it my mother's benefit, when she was ill, and since her death we have leased it on occasion. Allow me to enquire of our steward whether it is free for Miss Darcy's use. I would be delighted to offer it to aid her recovery."

"My dear Palmer, that would be kind of you! It sounds a perfect situation for my sister." Darcy smiled, the tension in his shoulders easing with a rush of relief. "I accept with pleasure. Georgiana will be delighted!"

CHAPTER SIX

The Business Of Man

Reflection is the business of man;
a sense of his state is his first duty:
but who remembereth himself in joy?
— Dodsley, *The Oeconomy of Human Life* (1765)

Bingley left Brooks's early to meet his sisters and escort them to some gathering, leaving Darcy and Palmer to essay more of the excellent Madeira.

"Bingley is seldom so serious," Palmer remarked.

"He is one of the more blessed children of Gelos."

Palmer's sidelong glance was amused, despite the wrinkling of his brow. "Gelos? Oh! The spirit of laughter?"

Darcy chuckled. "Not so dull a scholar, after all."

"I could never be as dull as you suspected me! Yes. Bingley is one of those pleasant, amiable characters forever caught on the cusp between one burst of laughter and the next, always pleasant and cheerful, light-hearted and enthusiastic."

"I am sorry he was cast down over our conversation."

"I thought him but open-eyed about his position. His wealth sweetens the circumstances a little—though for many in Society, the only evil more dire than no money is new money—but he is not mistaken when he speaks of how high he might reach. He is clear on the limits upon his sisters' ambitions, even if they are not." Palmer paused, then added, his tone reflective, "The lady he spoke of... You were dismissive of her suitability."

"She has family in trade."

"So does Bingley. He is from trade. If she is indeed a gentleman's daughter, she would be a gain for him."

"What she brings in one hand of gentle birth, she takes away in the other with the ties to her uncle, the Cit."

"Did you not hear Bingley say the man is a warden in the Mercers' Company? They are all rich as Croesus. She is not a step down for Bingley, though you consider her one. On the contrary, a gentleman's daughter confirms his place."

On his way to Brooks's, just after he turned from Berkley Street into Piccadilly, Darcy had wrinkled his nose against the stench from the open mouth of a narrow alley, little more than a gap between the houses. God alone knew what hellish rookery was down there. No wonder Georgiana had fallen ill. Rhys-Griffiths had the right of it: they all lived cheek-by-jowl with noxious miasmas.

A man must do his best to avoid contagion of every possible kind. When it came to that of blood, it was not an odious top-loftiness. It was proper caution, and the least Darcy owed his name. His mother had been a sister of the Earl of Ashbourne, and even disregarding this unimpeachable connection, Darcy was a man of wealth and consequence, and the owner of extensive properties and estates. It was his duty to Georgiana and to his noble relatives—what he owed to his position in the world—to marry well, to promote the prosperity and reputation associated with the name of Darcy. He was obliged always to improve the family's circumstances, and never act to its detriment. His wife, the mistress of his home and mother of his children, must enhance his position. The niece of a Cit would be detrimental, a contagion that would weaken his status. No one could argue otherwise.

Bingley had a freedom he did not. He could almost envy him.

"Darcy?"

"I was reflecting on Bingley's words. For you and I, the requirements of eligibility in marriage are strict. We must marry well, to a lady from a class at the least equal to our own, with impeccable family connections and a good dowry. Bingley has far fewer constraints, with fewer dire consequences if he chooses ill." Darcy forced a smile. "Lady Catherine—my mother's sister—hints often I should marry her daughter, who is something of an heiress."

"Ah yes. George Wickham spoke of it once."

Darcy rolled his eyes. Wickham always pretended a closeness to the family that he yearned for in that envious heart of his, but did not have.

Palmer laughed. "I remember your travails with him at Cambridge. Do you see him these days?"

"Not at all for… oh, it must be three years. I have heard little of him, and, this last year at least, I have not had to cover one of his debts. That, I assure you, is a welcome development. He has leeched upon me for years." At Palmer's quirked eyebrow, Darcy added, "I have felt some obligation, you see. My father was very fond of him—he was his godfather—and made an effort in his will to preserve the connection to my family. He desired Wickham be considered for preferment to a family living, if he took orders. Orders! The furthest thing from Wickham's mind. Five years ago when my father died, he took three thousand in exchange for resigning all claim to the bequest. He came back within two years, having spent every penny. He bemoaned his poverty and begged me for the living. I refused, of course. Not least because he had not taken orders, and is most unfit to be a priest."

"That chimes with my memories of him. Something of a rogue, but with a great deal of charm."

"He was always so, from childhood. We were friendly enough as boys, but our paths sundered as we grew older. Mine led to Pemberley, and he had no inheritance to speak of, other than that my father bestowed. The gulf was too wide, and he has not been a friend these many years. I have not seen him since the day I refused to renege on the agreement over the living."

"No great loss, I imagine. He was smug and amused at your aunt's ambitions for your marriage, I remember. I take it your cousin does not meet the criteria you listed?"

"I have considered Anne, I confess, but her health is poor, and, like any other man, I hope for an heir. I made my debut more than eight years ago, and yet still I have not met the woman I would wish to make mistress of Pemberley."

"There are well-bred ladies enough, paraded before potential husbands every season with the same bloodless practicality with which the sellers parade mares before the buyers at Tattersalls."

"I would hope a gentleman would spend more time and effort choosing his wife than he does his horses."

Palmer snorted. "You may indeed hope, but many of our peers take a narrow view of eligibility and look no further than the lady's bloodline and dowry. No thought is given to character or to compatibility of temperament, and even less to where incompatibility might rub more painfully than saddle sores."

Darcy glanced away. Was that meant for him? Of course he looked beyond bloodline and dowry. Eight years, and being still outside of parson's mousetrap proved it. Resistance to Lady Catherine's demands proved it.

Palmer went on as if he had not noticed Darcy's discomfort. "A man may sell a mare he tires of, or that proves too hard in the mouth to respond well to the bit. A gentleman, though, cannot sell his wife, much as he may wish to. They are one flesh until death parts them. And that, Darcy, is an awful prospect! Too many ladies are taught that to make a good match, they must be bland and vacuous and deny the good Lord granted them intelligence—"

"Some men would deny He had."

"Some men wish that to be true, I suppose, but I do not want a stupid wife whose only thoughts are of balls, gowns and jewels. I would die of boredom." Palmer cocked an eyebrow in Darcy's direction. "I suspect you are of a similar opinion. We must balance our duty and our inclinations. If I could but find a lady I could tolerate for more than a half hour, even I might consider matrimony."

When had Palmer developed this depth of character? Darcy was fond of him, but Palmer had always appeared to be a touch worldly and shallow; more interested in enjoying the delights of Society than in deep thinking. This more thoughtful Palmer was as unfamiliar a creature as Bingley turned serious.

Darcy, too, wanted a wife of intelligence and charm, good character and moral virtue, along with the sterling, more worldly qualities he had already considered. He doubted the perfect wife existed. Or that he was formed for happiness.

He blinked. Where had that thought come from?

By June, Parliament had risen and many of the best families had already left London for their estates, eager to leave the humid stench of the city for the cleaner air of the country. Company at social gatherings grew thin, and audiences were sparse even at the Theatre-Royal, Covent Garden—to distinguish it from that in Drury Lane—despite its boast of possessing the finest company of actors in the world.

"I undoubtedly will have seen better," Palmer predicted, as they settled into Darcy's box. A waiter followed, bearing the bottle of champagne and the hamper of the delectable pastries Palmer claimed were essential to sustain him against his exposure to High Art. "I expect the principals have already deserted Town for their country retreats, and this will not be a top-notch performance."

"If an actor can afford a country retreat, then I ought to give up farming and take up the stage."

"You do not have the talent for it." Palmer alleviated this flat criticism with the broad smile that was his best feature.

Darcy laughed. "Did you hear from Bingley?"

"I did. He has hired a box for the evening. His guests are the young lady he admires and her family. He said he will not impose them upon us unless we seek an introduction."

Darcy grimaced. "For his sake, I will accept the acquaintance if we meet during the interval."

"There he is. Do you see? One level down, to our right." Palmer sighed. "Oh lud, his sist— Good Lord, Darcy!"

Darcy, startled, turned.

Palmer leaned forward, his hand on the front edge of the box, tense as a hunter sighting his prey. "Look at the beauty with him! If that is the lady he spoke of, she is a diamond of the first water. She certainly puts the other ladies in the party in the shade."

The young lady sitting on Bingley's right was indeed very lovely, the epitome of Society's notion of true beauty. Even Darcy, whose taste did not run to golden-haired goddesses of the type Bingley always admired, blinked. Bingley stared at the lady with such an expression of slack-faced adoration, Darcy blushed for him. His entire attention on his companion, Bingley had not noticed Darcy and Palmer.

On Bingley's other side, his sister Caroline sat with the pinched, stony expression of one who had inexplicably found herself at Billingsgate market surrounded by rotting fish. Mrs Hurst, his other sister, and her husband sat in the seats behind with another couple, strangers to Darcy. Mrs Hurst had tilted her face upwards, appearing to survey the ornate, gilded carvings decorating the box's ceiling. Perhaps she had developed an interest in architecture. Hurst was already asleep. The unknown couple were both dressed with sober elegance. At a glance, Darcy would have taken them for gentry.

Palmer let out a long breath, his gaze on Bingley's box rather than the stage where, five minutes late, Leonato welcomed Don Pedro and his victorious forces to Messina.

Within a few moments, Palmer's prediction came to pass. The finest company of actors in the world? Not that evening. Darcy would prefer a company that did not treat Shakespeare as if it were the farce and did not send forth all the second-raters and understudies, several of whom paid more attention to the prompter in the wings than to his or her performance.

"Oh, it is of no account," was Palmer's impatient response when Darcy complained. But Palmer's rapt attention was on the girl Bingley had declared an angel.

Darcy turned his gaze back to the stage. He could not escape the introduction. Palmer would insist upon it. Not that he suspected Palmer of an ulterior motive—he was too honourable to poach on any man's game preserves, particularly in matters of the heart. But that Palmer was interested in at least meeting the girl could not be denied.

Palmer gave him an apologetic glance as soon as the curtain fell on the first act, and nodded towards the box door. "Shall we?"

Darcy blew out a sigh. "For Bingley's sake. I would not have him think…"

"I agree. It meets entirely my own intention to support Bingley."

Of course it did.

In truth, Bingley seemed delighted to see them, and could not beam more brightly if a small but vigorous sun had appeared in the theatre box. Quite blinding. At Darcy's reluctant request, Bingley introduced the Cit and his wife, a Mr and Mrs Gardiner, and their niece, Miss Jane Bennet.

Miss Bingley's being afflicted with a raging toothache would explain her pained expression as Darcy gave a polite bow, judged in its depth to an absolute nicety, and murmured something correct and cool. She turned her head to give her brother's guests the information that "Mr Darcy, you must understand, owns the largest and best estate in Derbyshire. It is a great honour to make his acquaintance."

Darcy felt the heat rise in his face. Did she think he needed to have his consequence puffed to all and sundry? "The Duke of Devonshire would disagree, Miss Bingley. I am proud of Pemberley, but it does not stand comparison with Chatsworth."

"Pemberley is very fine," Mrs Gardiner said, smiling. "I do not suppose the Duke would disdain it, Mr Darcy."

Darcy doubted she had ever seen Pemberley. Typical toadying behaviour, to be expected from a Cit. He merely bowed.

Palmer commented his own estate—"my father's, really"—was in Kent, and in as fine a country as could be imagined. Miss Bennet greeted this news with a serene smile, and the assertion that her family's estate in Hertfordshire lay in beautiful countryside.

She anticipated with pleasure her return the following week for a few days, for a sister's wedding.

An estate of no great note, Darcy assumed. The young lady was elegantly and fashionably dressed, but her gown did not come from the finest modiste. Being the custodian of his sister's purse, he had, perforce, developed an eye for such things. He waited for Miss Bennet to realise that he and Palmer were worth more than Bingley, landed gentry opposed to a man still making his way from trade, and hence much better prospects. How long would it take for her to turn her attentions to them, instead of landless Bingley?

But Miss Bennet, though she smiled a great deal, offered no more than the ordinary civility one granted to strangers. She did not give Darcy and Palmer any preference. Odd. But who could tell what lay behind that façade of beauty and the air of serenity? Miss Bennet was a very handsome woman indeed, but gave no indication of the real character beneath the civil, courteous, proper exterior.

Perhaps it was a case, as the old proverb had it, of 'better one byrde in hande than ten in the wood'. She may well have calculated to a nicety which of them was the most likely to succumb to her charms. With Bingley already in her net, what need to throw it wider and risk losing her conquest?

Palmer fell into easy conversation with Bingley and the Gardiners, drawing the smiling Miss Bennet into their ambit and leaving Miss Bingley to Darcy. The Hursts stayed in the background. Indeed, Hurst looked to be half asleep again, hiding a yawn behind his hand and regarding the world from behind drooping eyelids.

Miss Bingley's eyes were glassy with some indefinable emotion. Taking care to turn until her brother's guests could not see her face, she spoke in a low, urgent voice, not to be overheard. "I am mortified beyond endurance to have such people introduced to your acquaintance, sir. I hope you can acquit me of desiring such a thing, at least. I do not know how to turn my brother from his current fascination. It is not to be borne."

Darcy would like to agree, but propriety would not allow him to gossip with Miss Bingley. Besides, apart from Mrs Gardiner's absurd pretension about Pemberley, the Cits did not thrust themselves forward.

"One must make many acquaintances if one is to have any sort of public life." He bowed and joined the main group, to tap Palmer on the shoulder. "The bell will sound in a moment. We had better return to our box."

"Yes, yes." Palmer took a step away.

A few bows and polite compliments from all present, and Darcy escaped.

Palmer followed with many a backward glance over his shoulder. "What a diamond, Darcy! Do you not agree? The most beautiful creature I ever beheld."

"A handsome woman. But she smiles too much."

CHAPTER SEVEN

Nature's Children

All dear Nature's children sweet
Lie 'fore bride and bridegroom's feet
— Shakespeare, *Bridal Song*

The eighteenth of June arrived, bringing Mary's wedding with it. She made a happy bride. Her sallow skin was flushed a soft rose, and her eyes were bright. She had been persuaded to leave off her spectacles—"You only wear them to look learned and wise," Elizabeth told her, "and all you need to look on your wedding day is triumphant"—and allowed Jane, who had an eye for such things, to style her hair under her wedding bonnet. Elizabeth tied the bonnet ribbons in a large bow, becomingly set under Mary's right ear, despite Mary's faint protest that to tie the bow under the exact middle of her chin was more modest and seemly. Wearing the cornflower-blue dress Jane had given her, refurbished with new ribbons and lace by Kitty, who had clever fingers for fine needlework, and with Elizabeth's best lace shawl held in the crook of her elbows, Mary looked bridal indeed. They all said so, as they pressed around her and kissed her.

All except Lydia. She stood back from the embraces, crossed her arms under her ample bosom and heaved out a disgruntled "Hmmmph!" to signal her disfavour for all the attention paid to Mary.

Elizabeth, who was to stand with her sister as bridesmaid, took a step away from Mary to survey her, before giving a decided nod. "Mr Collins will be dazzled, Mary."

Lydia hmmmph-ed again. "I cannot believe Mary—Mary!—is marrying before me. Before any of us! Even Jane. I cannot fathom being Jane's age and an old maid. I vow I would be ashamed to be still unmarried!"

If Jane felt any aggravation over Lydia's brash malice, she did not show it. She treated their little sister to a serene smile. "You are not yet sixteen, Lyddie. You have plenty of time."

Elizabeth, though, was happy to be aggravated on Jane's behalf. Lydia stood near the door, and it was the work of an instant to bundle her out of it. Lydia might be taller than Elizabeth, but she was taken by surprise and found herself halfway down the stairs before she realised it. When she squawked in protest, Elizabeth overrode her with a harsh, "And were I you, I should be ashamed of being so spiteful and vicious!"

They had reached the landing where the stairs turned to descend into the downstairs hall. Lydia tried to stand her ground, but Elizabeth gave her a little push to persuade her to continue.

"Not now, Lyddie. Go to the drawing room and keep Aunt Gardiner and her children company until it is time to leave for church, and endeavour to be the sweet and polite young lady we all wish you were. Do you think she will be happy to host you in London this coming winter if you cannot control that mischievous tongue of yours? Behave, or I will tell her you are not worthy of such a treat, and only Kitty should go."

"You would not!"

"Do not test me. This is Mary's day, and I will not allow you to spoil it."

"Mary! How did she manage to be first of us all to the altar? A dull mopsy is still a dull mopsy, even when she is wearing one of Jane's dresses!"

It seemed Jane's giving the dress to Mary still rankled. Elizabeth took a deep breath in lieu of boxing Lydia's ears for her unkindness.

"Oh, are you disappointed, Lyddie? Did you wish for Mr Collins yourself? You poor dear, to be so forlorn! I must tell Kitty and all your friends. They will have great compassion for your broken heart—"

Lydia's jaw dropped. "I? Marry him?"

"Quite. And yet, by wedding him, Mary is making sure Longbourn remains in Bennet hands. Any of us still at home when Mr Collins inherits can expect his kindness and generosity. You should be grateful. Go to Aunt Gardiner, please. And watch your tongue!"

Lydia sniffed, and bridled in the theatrical manner so reminiscent of their mother dealing with an imagined slight that Elizabeth's ire cooled into a wry amusement. Mrs Jane Bennet would always live on in her youngest daughter.

"Go, Lyddie. We will join you soon."

"Hmmmph!" But Lydia obeyed.

Elizabeth oversaw her sulky progress to the drawing room and returned to Mary's room after the door had closed. "What a little beast Lydia can be! She is all unkindness."

Jane smiled. "She does not mean it."

"Oh, yes, she does." Mary glanced up from the task of tucking a sprig or two of lavender between the pages to mark her place in the bible she intended to carry with her to church. "But truly, Jane, Lydia is not someone whose views and opinions matter one jot. She is without charity. As this says"—she lifted the Bible in her hands—"such people become as sounding brass or a tinkling cymbal. She makes no harmony, no pleasing music. Give no heed to her. I do not."

Kitty looked up from making final tweaks to Mary's finery. "She wanted to be the first of us to marry."

Elizabeth snorted, most inelegantly. "Did she indeed? I cannot fathom who might wish to marry such a brazen-faced sauce-box! If such a man exists, he cannot possibly be a sensible one. Lydia cannot become many degrees worse without her bad behaviour brings shame on all of us."

A bright scarlet stained Kitty's cheeks. "She is lively and merry, and the gentlemen all notice her. Mamma says that is the way to catch a husband!"

"We will talk about it later, Kitty." Jane, tucking Kitty's hand under her arm, tugged her towards the door. She paused by Elizabeth and kissed her cheek. "A little more charity yourself would not go amiss, dearest! Kitty and I will go downstairs. It must be time to leave for church."

Mary released a small, displeased huff of air when they had gone. "Jane's goodness is, on occasion, a little too... too..." She made a whirling motion with her free hand, and shook her head. "I have not the words. Lydia can be quite reprehensible, but Jane refuses to acknowledge it."

"Yes, but I am grateful to have Jane's forbearance bestowed on me when I least deserve it! She is the best of us."

"Indeed." Mary heaved out a sigh. "Lizzy, am I selfish to admit I am glad I will be gone before Lydia—or Kitty, for she follows wherever Lydia leads—ruins us?"

"Not selfish at all. It concerns me too. Oh, here is Mamma, to see you all bedecked in your finery. Does not Mary look the most perfect summer bride, Mamma?"

Mamma bustled in, ribbons and lappets aflutter, and a handkerchief clutched in her hand, presumably to capture those bitter-sweet maternal tears expected of her at the first wedding in the family. Her gaze raked over Mary from head to toe.

"You do look well!" And Mamma's voice held a note of unflattering surprise. "Did Jane do your hair? It is very becoming."

"Fine feathers," said Mary, in repressive tones.

"And a very fine bird beneath them. Do not denigrate yourself, Mary." Elizabeth smiled as her mother came forward to put her imprimatur on Mary's appearance.

Mamma twitched Mary's broad sash a mere quarter of an inch lower, and tweaked the matching ribbon bow on the bonnet. She reset the angle at which Kitty had placed the pearl brooch loaned for the day out of Mamma's jewellery box, draped the shawl more becomingly, and generally set her to what Mamma considered to be 'rights'. She nodded and stepped back, dabbing the ridiculous scrap of laced-edged linen at the corner of one dry eye. "Well, it is the best we can do, I suppose. You will never be the match of Ja—"

"Mamma!" Elizabeth protested.

Mamma sniffed, giving Elizabeth a sidelong glare, and conceded. "You look very nice, Mary."

Mary's blush deepened. "Thank you, Mamma."

"Mary always looks nice." Elizabeth caught her sister's hand. Mary's fingers tightened on hers. "Pretty, but modest, as becomes the bride of a clergyman. She will be an exemplary wife in a country parsonage."

"Did I say anything to the contrary? And as for you, Miss—" And here Mamma broke off and gave Elizabeth the same raking stare poor Mary had endured. "You are not half as pretty as Jane, nor half as lively as Lydia. You can ill afford to hand off suitors to your sisters. Just as well for you that Mr Collins decided to offer for Mary, when you turned him away—"

"I did no such thing, Mamma. Mr Collins saw which of us would suit him best, and acted in his own interest." It was Elizabeth's turn to squeeze Mary's hand for comfort.

Mamma laid the backs of her fingers against her brow. "I shall not allow you to discompose me, Lizzy. My nerves will not withstand your contentious nature today, of all days. I cannot at all understand why you wish to take my attention from Mary, whose due it is." She looked them both up and down again. "I am very pleased with you, Mary. Though I never thought you would be the first to marry, you have chosen well."

And at the sound of Papa's call from the foot of the stairs, and, without another word, Mamma fluttered out as swiftly as she had fluttered in.

"Well." Even after twenty years of familiarity with her mother's nerves, Elizabeth was uncertain as to how she had garnered Mamma's displeasure this time. And poor Mary! Could not Mamma praise her once, unstintingly, without odious comparisons to her favourites?

Mary, though, smiled. "Do not fret, Lizzy. Nothing we can say or do will change her. You are too like Grandmamma to be a favourite, and I am too plain."

"You are not plain!"

"I daresay in other company, I may not be counted so. Forgive me, but that is another reason I am pleased to be going into Kent. There I shall not be compared to Jane, or you, but may establish myself on my own merits. There is a great deal of pleasure to be gained from anticipating such a state."

"It grieves me that our mother should be so blind, and so partial. She cannot know how much pain she inflicts."

"We are told we must honour our parents, but I will confess that though her words sting at times, I will not allow them to affect me in any material way. Were you to say such things to me, it would hurt all the more because yours is an opinion I value. Mamma is another sounding brass."

"Our family," said Elizabeth, hearing her father's tread on the staircase, "has rather too many brasses and cymbals, and all too few harmonies. There you are, Papa! Has everyone gone to church? Is it time?"

"Almost. Your mother and the other girls are boarding the coach now, and as soon as it returns, we will leave. I wanted a moment with you first, Mary-child... and see! My little sparrow has very fine plumage, after all." Papa's eyes were bright, and Elizabeth took a few steps away to give him a moment with his middle daughter. Papa's hand wavered as he raised it to rest it against Mary's cheek. "I doubt we have done our best by you, but Collins, I hope, will do better."

Disregarded by their mother, and her literal, moralistic bent being as far from Papa's sardonic quickness as could be imagined, Mary was easily overlooked. Neither of their parents had attention to spare for their middle daughter. That Papa realised it, did not surprise Elizabeth; that he should regret it, did.

Mary's eyes, however, were on the future. "He is a respectable man, Papa. I am content with my choice."

Papa smiled. "You reassure me, Mary. You will be a blessing in his home." He pressed his lips against her forehead and stepped back. Mary, rosy with blushes, looked pretty indeed, and so he told her, finishing with a more cheerful, "Come then. Let us get you to church, and see you married!"

The wedding had gone very well, despite their mother's threatened fit of hysterics in the church porch, handily averted by Papa with the judicious use of sal volatile. He had secreted her vinaigrette in his pocket for just such an eventuality. Many neighbours attended, and later converged on Longbourn for the wedding breakfast, eager to wish the new couple every happiness. And, of course, eager to partake of the Bennets' hospitality: Mamma's fame in the Meryton area as an excellent hostess was well deserved.

During the wedding ceremony itself, Mr Collins's loquacious tongue had, perforce, been limited to the age-old responses dictated to him by the Book of Common Prayer. It must have chafed him, to be restrained. He burst his bounds the moment he entered Longbourn's dining room, his new wife on his arm.

"Oh, what bounty! What munificence! I am sure, Mrs Bennet, that nothing could hold a candle to this magnificent feast. I might justly compare it to Rosings, and the offerings of my noble patroness's superb chef. Such lavish, noble hospitality, such a splendid— What, my dear?" He inclined his head to Mary, who said something softly. "Oh. Oh. Quite right. So inconsiderate of me, to block the entrance! Shall we go in, Mrs Collins?"

And thus naming his wife for the first time, Mr Collins blushed and simpered, threatening to burst out his tight-buttoned coat with obvious pride. He led Mary into the dining room, looking around and smiling his happiness, which thankfully reduced his raptures to a beaming silence. The neighbours shared his contentment, relieved to follow the happy couple, and fall upon the proffered feast; while Mamma gleefully repeated, several times, "Mrs Collins! How well that sounds!" until Papa distracted her with some question about hot chocolate, and she hurried off to find Mrs Hill to remedy whatever was amiss.

In keeping with Mary's noted modesty and restraint, the breakfast was not as elaborate as Mamma had wanted. Still, Cook had provided plenty of everything good: a great dish of ham and eggs and a side of beef formed the main portion of it, with hot rolls and many smaller delicacies to tempt the appetite and tickle the palate: devilled kidneys, mounds of buttered toast, a dish of pork and mustard among many others. Longbourn's cellars had been plundered to make a powerful punch bowl. Tea and chocolate were supplied for those who could not face brandy and arrack so early in the day.

Mamma had been allowed free rein with the wedding cake. Thick with dried fruit and liberally soaked in brandy—along with the punch, a sacrifice Papa had made with a wry grimace at the empty bottles—it had been covered in a marchpane icing. It was delicious. Lydia and Kitty had two pieces each, and were eyeing the remainder. The little gluttons.

"And I say that because I should like to emulate them." Elizabeth tucked her hand under Jane's elbow as the noon bells rang at church, and, it being time for Mary and Mr Collins to depart for London where they would stay one night before pressing on to Kent, the company crowded out of Longbourn's front door.

Jane laughed. "There is cake to spare."

"Not if our sisters are to be relied upon! They are conscienceless."

And not merely for taking all the bridal cake, either. Lydia paraded onto the gravelled sweep before the house clutching the arm of one of the militia officers. Her face glowed pink with too much punch and too much unrestrained laughter. Her fichu was missing, and the officer was privy to far more of her bosom than was seemly.

Mary's fears about Lydia's behaviour could not easily be dismissed. Mamma smiled at Lydia being the centre of the young officers' attention, and would see no ill in it. Papa... well, he frowned, but Mamma plucked at his sleeve until he looked the other way and went to escort Mary to the carriage.

It seemed a hopeless case.

The company farewelled Mary and her new husband with many kisses and cheers, calling good wishes and "Goodspeed!" with bright, happy faces. Mary seemed both surprised and pleased. How dreadful she should be astonished at such ordinary loving attentions from her family!

Mary paused by Mamma and said something Elizabeth could not hear. Mamma gave a great start and stared at Mary with her mouth hanging open, her face crumpling like a child's about to cry. Mary nodded, her smile shy and uncertain, and turned away to allow Papa to hand her into the carriage. But Mamma stopped her, and kissed her with a fervency that must have been as novel an experience for Mary as it was for those of her watching sisters. Tears rolled down Mary's cheeks as the carriage pulled away.

Whatever was that about?

Elizabeth waved her handkerchief around her head until the coach rolled out of the front gates and turned the bend in the road for Meryton, and the London road far beyond. If Mary should chance to look back—though Heaven knew she would be better employed looking forward—she would see that one sister, at least, shared her happiness and sincerely wished her joy.

And, though she did not regret resigning all interest in Mr Collins, Elizabeth could not but know, deep in herself, she envied Mary's venture into a new life.

She was ready for change and adventure. Perhaps Kent would offer it.

CHAPTER EIGHT

A Secret To Your Ear

> …durst commend a secret to your ear
> Much weightier than this work.
> — Shakespeare, *Henry VII*

"You may be sure I have said nothing to Mamma." Now most of the guests had left, Elizabeth drew Jane away into the rose garden for their first real talk since Jane and the Gardiners had come from London the day before. With many final details to settle before the wedding, she and Jane had been too weary the previous evening to do other than fall into bed, worn out with Mamma's fretful demands. "Papa was sly, and gave me my post privately to prevent Mamma's demanding I read your letters aloud. She knows nothing of this Mr Bingley of yours."

"I do not know that he is mine. He is a gentleman-like man, and I find his acquaintance pleasing. Thank you for preserving my privacy, Lizzy."

Their mother's laments and her fractious complaints to Aunt Gardiner the previous evening had been heard around the house, singing a tune of "And Jane is returned unbetrothed! Surely she is too beautiful not to catch the eye of some great gentleman or other! Oh, why cannot she capture a husband? No one knows what a trial that is to me, sister, for those who do not complain are seldom heard and understood, and we must go on uncomforted."

Safe in the arbour in the garden, Elizabeth and Jane could speak undisturbed.

"Well," Elizabeth admitted, "I have confided in Charlotte, but you will not mind that. She keeps our confidences, and has naught but good wishes for you. I daresay even the French would not winkle out a secret from her!"

"No, indeed, I am not troubled about Charlotte's knowing. She is sensible and kind. I must try to spend some time with her before I return to London."

"Perhaps tomorrow we shall go to Lucas Lodge for a comfortable coze. Now, Jane, tell me more!"

"He is a handsome young man," Jane began, and smiled when Elizabeth interrupted her with a laugh.

"As a young man ought to be, if he can!"

"Oh, certainly! He must be a pattern card gentleman, then, for he is very handsome!" Jane laughed with her, and went on, "He is five-and-twenty, and, following his father's death, the head of his family."

"You mentioned in your letters that he has two sisters, but you were very discreet about them."

"The elder is married to a gentleman, a Mr Hurst. The younger lives with him and is mistress of his household. They are fashionable and take part in many of the amusements offered by the Season."

"Come, Jane, do not prevaricate! Is their acquaintance as pleasant as their brother's?"

Jane hesitated, but true to her character, sought to present the Bingley ladies in the most generous light. "They are not his equal in ease of manner. But they have received me with civility."

But not with warmth: Elizabeth could discern Jane's meaning well enough. Should Mr Bingley pursue Jane's acquaintance, his sisters would have to accept his choice. A man of twenty-five and the head of his family had authority enough to do as he wished.

"So, Jane, though the Season is over, you are to return tomorrow with the Gardiners for another three months complete? Do you expect to be frequently in the gentleman's company?"

"Mr Bingley has no estate yet in which to spend the summer, although he has mentioned he intends to buy one in the near future and thus meet the dearest wishes of both his father and his sisters." Jane's blush deepened. "Although the events of the Season have come to a close, Town is still busy. There are galleries and lectures and so forth, and the Haymarket theatre has its summer season offering performances enough to meet any taste. We may still have some engagements in common and I hope to be able to continue our acquaintance."

Elizabeth nodded approval. The purchase of an estate would signal Mr Bingley's elevation into the gentry, and loosen the ties to trade. He had all the appearance of good prospects and comfortable circumstances, should he and Jane come to an understanding.

"And now, Lizzy, I have some news that will astonish you. A few days ago we were Mr Bingley's guests at Covent Garden. At the first interval, I was introduced to two of his close friends. A Mr Darcy, who is a wealthy landowner from Derbyshire—"

"Oh, did Aunt Gardiner know him?"

"Only by repute. His estate, Pemberley, is the great house near Lambton, where she lived as a girl. But she says the Darcys are far above her father in consequence. The Darcys do not attend church in Lambton but in Kympton, in which parish Pemberley lies, although as rector of All Saints, her father has some business with the great house when it comes to charitable endeavours. Mr Darcy was civil when introduced, but somewhat reserved. I think, though, the other gentleman would interest you more. A Mr Galahad Palmer"—Jane quirked an eyebrow at Elizabeth—"of Kent."

"Indeed!"

"It was not the place to discover if he is a connection to our grandmother's family, and make myself known to him in that particular. We had time for no more than a conventional greeting before he and Mr Darcy returned to their box. Is he a nephew or great-nephew of Miss Palmer's?"

"Grandmamma was the only one of her sisters to have a family. Mr Galahad is her cousin's son, and the heir to the baronetcy. Papa and I did chuckle over the poor young man's high-flown name. From her letters, I deduce Miss Iphigenia is very fond of him."

"You maintain a regular correspondence with her?"

"We have exchanged several letters since Papa first told me of her. She seems to be a dear creature, and I think I will like her a great deal."

"It must be strange to meet her after so long a gap in intimacy between our families."

"Yes, but she has been a faithful correspondent and she is eager for us to meet. I have written about all of us and our doings—maintaining a discreet silence about your Mr Bingley, of course! She knows you are my most particular sister"—Elizabeth squeezed Jane's arm—"and she bid me tell you that you would always be welcome if you wished to come to Wingham."

Jane nodded, but demurred. "I would prefer to remain in London for the present, Lizzy. You are for Kent next week?"

"Yes. Papa and I will leave early on Friday morning, and will be with you in Gracechurch Street before noon. We intend to stay the night in Westerham, before going on to Wingham in the east of the county. We will arrive in Canterbury on Saturday and will stay with an old university friend of Papa's, a Mr Harding, who is something to do with the cathedral. We will not reach Wingham until the following Monday."

"Mary mentioned she hopes she and Mr Collins will join you for supper at the Westerham inn. I believe it is but two or three miles from Hunsford?"

"So I understand. We would not agree to stay with them in the rectory, although our new brother offered to host us. They will have been married only ten days, and visitors so soon are not to be countenanced. Mary should not be put to such trouble while she is yet adjusting to being a wife."

"That is very considerate."

"I thought so, though Papa is grumbling a little about the discomfort of beds at an inn. He will stay with Mary on his return. He intends to spend a week with Miss Iphigenia—though I shall remain until autumn—and to his mind, that extra se'ennight is more than enough time to inure Mary to married life and be ready to welcome him. He is incorrigible." Elizabeth smiled and sighed together. "I look forward to this visit with great anticipation, Jane. I am all agog to meet Grandmamma's half-sister and see the house where she grew up. What adventures await me!"

Ten days after Mary's wedding, John Coachman brought the Bennet family coach around from the stable yard to the front door. Elizabeth had risen before dawn. She and her father ate a hasty breakfast alone—none of the rest of the family would rise so early, and their farewells had been made the night before at supper. Kitty and Lydia were largely indifferent to Elizabeth's departure, their minds fixed on their own concerns: viz, the militia officers. Mamma viewed the temporary loss of her second daughter with tolerable composure. No flutterings about opportunities, no exhortations about marriage and eligible gentlemen, no orders to find and marry any gentleman who offered himself... Elizabeth had bidden her mother farewell in some consternation at this odd change in behaviour.

At a quarter to six, the coach bowled out of the gates and onto the London road. Jack Hill, son of the couple who were housekeeper and butler to the family, sat beside John. Miss Palmer would provide Elizabeth with a maid, but Jack would remain in Kent as footman and guard. Though barely a year Elizabeth's senior, Jack showed the same steady temper and deep loyalty as his parents, and would offer stalwart protection. He was a large young man. A very large young man. As Papa had remarked when deciding on this arrangement, "A species of young Goliath, indeed. He must be twice my width. What does Mrs Hill feed the boy?"

Now settled in the coach, Papa yawned widely. "I detest starting out at such a ridiculous time of day. I should sleep all the way to your uncle's house and gather my strength, if I am to face the hordes of children we shall find there."

"The Gardiner children are very well behaved."

"Do you think so? I seem to recall that when they were here for Mary's wedding, they had but one mode of perambulation. They gambolled out of rooms in the same pell-mell fashion as they gambolled into them, tumbling everywhere as if they were circus acrobats. I spent a great deal of my time with at least one child attached to each leg, clinging to me like young gibbons."

"I have never seen a gibbon, Papa."

"Nor have I, but it seems my imagination is stronger than yours. I had no notion I was so popular with the young ones as to be their tree to clamber upon!"

"You are a master story-teller, Papa, as you know very well, and hence beloved by children, your own and our relations'. I have lively recollections of Kitty and Lydia dealing with you so. You have such patience with little ones."

Papa gave her a smile, both bitter and sweet. "Ah, my Lizzy. It is easy when they are small. It is as they grow I lose my ability to talk to them or deal with them. They grow so far away from me. All my girls have. You are the one exception to that rule."

"It is not a rule, Papa. You may still reach them, if you attempt it. Indeed, they need it. Two of your girls, at least, would benefit from your attention." She leaned forward to touch his arm, gently, to escape a rebuff. He had come close to recognising his failure with Mary. So close. And Mary, if she had lacked guidance, was so moral in herself she could come to no real harm. The same could not be said of their two youngest sisters. "Kitty and Lydia need a stronger hand than Mamma can wield. They are far too familiar with the militia regiment, too forward in general company, and too impatient of restraint. Remember Lydia at the wedding breakfast last week. She was wild and improper, as she and Kitty all too often are. In truth, Papa, they risk more than their own reputations."

"They are silly. That is all." But he turned his head to stare out at the passing scenery and would not meet her gaze.

"Oh, Papa. Where does silliness end and real mischief begin? They teeter on the knife-edge, but they are worth your effort, if you will make it."

"She was silly." He was stubborn to the end. "Childishness."

"You will not think so when she presents you with your grandchild."

He stared, his shock showing in the way his face paled, leaving spots of bright colour on his cheekbones. "Lizzy!"

"I am not jesting, sir. She is more circumspect in your company, for she does not wish you to curtail her freedom and her amusements. If you wish to view her at her worst, go unannounced and unexpected to a monthly assembly in Meryton. Observe her and Kitty and see how they act when they believe themselves safe from your eyes. I do not think you will be so sanguine then regarding childishness."

"You are serious."

"I could not be more so. I cannot tell you how pleased I am for Mary that she is safely wed, but if you do not check Lydia, I venture to predict no other of your daughters will marry well. We will be shunned. We have little enough to offer a gentleman, and if we cannot even give him a good and virtuous name, our poor prospects dwindle to nothing."

The spots of colour faded, leaving him ashen. "Lizzy, I... I do not know what to say. You truly believe this."

"Mamma is so anxious about our futures, she has filled their heads with the idea that they must marry quickly. It matters not who they marry, or if he has competency enough to support a family, for she thinks any husband is better than none." Elizabeth allowed her mouth to twist into a wry smile. "I was astonished not to receive her usual admonishments last night to do my utmost to catch a husband in Kent."

"You may thank Mary for that. She promised that your mamma would always have a home at Longbourn and need never fear for the future."

"Indeed? Well, I do thank her if her marriage to your heir has eased Mamma's fears, but Mamma's fixation on marrying us off has had its effect. Jane is above reproach, but the younger two!

Lydia's head is full of nothing but officers and flirting, and Kitty follows her every footstep. Please, Papa. Take the time to truly look at them and act to stop their ruin. Our ruin."

He stared at her for a few moments, and, eventually, nodded. "Very well. I will do as you ask. But I will have no peace if I curtail their pleasures."

"Better that, than no peace because of the infamy, and the wreck it shall make of our family."

Papa looked heavenward. "Your grandmother must be laughing to know her image is as relentless as she was."

"We Elizabeths are all wise women. You should heed our advice, before it is too late."

He grunted. "I will think on it. Enough. I will sleep now, so no more prattle, my girl." He stretched out his legs, tilted his low-crowned 'Eccentric' hat until the wide brim covered his eyes, and crossed his arms over his chest. He gave out a defiant, if unconvincing, snore.

Elizabeth hoped his eyes were a little more open to their danger. She forbore to vex him further. It would achieve nothing.

CHAPTER NINE

An Age Of Discord

For what is wedlock forced, but a hell,
An age of discord and continual strife?
— Shakespeare, *Henry VI*

The first day of their journey to Ramsgate, Darcy and Georgiana travelled only to Rosings, to allow her to rest overnight in the greatest comfort. When planning their journey, Darcy had told her they could not travel into Kent without stopping to visit Aunt De Bourgh.

"I have decided we should travel in easy stages." He had spread an atlas over the table beside her couch so she could trace their proposed journey over the post roads of Kent. "To Rosings, first."

Georgiana's expression could not have shown more dismay if he had promised her they would stay overnight in the Castle Udolpho, with veiled skeletal horrors hidden in every room in the house. "Must we stay with Lady Catherine?"

Darcy pressed his lips together hard to prevent a laugh escaping them. "Lady Catherine may seem a little formidable, Georgiana, but she has our wellbeing at heart. We will stay one night, then travel to Canterbury. Another rest there, and we will go on to Ramsgate."

One night at Rosings would be enough for both of them. His aunt was formidable indeed. Georgiana, naturally shy and reserved, was even more subdued in the lady's august presence, and Darcy himself would be more at ease if his aunt did not continually push him to marry her daughter.

Who might have lineage and wealth, but assuredly lacked every other quality Darcy would like to see in his wife.

"I am much improved," Georgiana told him. "I am sure it need not take three days to travel to Ramsgate."

She had been obedient to the good doctor's instructions to rest daily after noon, a shawl cast over her legs, and plump, feather-filled cushions behind her head. She was stronger, more her old self, yet Darcy would not wager with her health by journeying too hard.

"We could travel to Ramsgate more quickly, yes—"

"The mail coaches do it in a day." Georgiana should not pout so. She was fifteen, not five. "The guidebooks tell us so. Mrs Younge has been reading them to me while I rested. She has visited Ramsgate and says it is a very pleasant place, where the air and sea bathing will do me a great deal of good. It seems to me, since that is the case, we should delay our arrival as little as possible so I derive the greatest benefit."

She had the grace to blush when Darcy raised an eyebrow at her, then laughed. He laughed along with her.

"A good attempt at an argument, Georgiana. But such a journey would be long and hard. A good fourteen or fifteen hours, even if I could be assured of obtaining changes of horse at every post house along the way. No, my dear. We will make an easy journey of it, and halt at Rosings."

"But Aunt De Bourgh is always so severe! I am almost grown, am I not? Mrs Younge is preparing me for my come-out, after all, and is teaching me what I must learn to take on a woman's role and responsibilities. She tells me always I must act as—and be!—a full-grown lady."

"She is succeeding." Darcy showed the approval she looked for, because it was true. Georgiana was growing older, and showing more maturity. Mrs Younge had helped in a myriad of ways, aiding her in learning the duties and responsibilities of the lady of the house.

"But Aunt De Bourgh still treats me as if I were a small child barely out of the nursery. It will be mortifying. I will be quizzed on my deportment lessons, and told to practise my music more, and she will demand to inspect my sampler..."

Darcy sympathised with his sister's complaints of his aunt's officious nature, but remained obdurate. They would rest overnight at Rosings.

"Very well. I shall have to feign a fainting fit when we arrive, and hope she will excuse me from attending her." And Georgiana had practised languishing, the back of one hand pressed to her brow.

Darcy had laughed. But since he knew his duty, he perforce had reminded Georgiana of hers.

"Well, if you say so, brother. I will try to welcome the opportunity to spend time with our family." Another little grimace. "I do not suppose Cousin Anne will wish to share her fainting couch, anyway."

"You are unkind, Georgiana. Anne's health is indifferent, but after your own experience these last weeks, you should have some compassion for her."

Georgiana had blushed and apologised, and meekly acquiesced to his plans for their journey, but now, ensconced in one of Rosing's opulent sitting rooms, Darcy's eye was drawn to his sister and cousin sitting together on the sofa in front of Lady Catherine's chair. He understood Georgiana's comment about Anne.

Despite her protests that she was well recovered, Georgiana's weariness from their short journey showed in her pallor and lack of energy; but for all that, she improved in strength and vitality daily, looking healthful and vibrant in contrast to their cousin. Poor Anne! So small and shrunken in on herself, frailty made manifest in a sad young woman whose restricted life must excite the deepest pity.

Lady Catherine, perhaps, did not see it. Darcy saw Anne only when visiting Rosings, and the changes in his cousin were more noticeable to him. He had last seen her at Easter, and she had continued to fade. For Lady Catherine, there was no such shocking revelation. For her, Anne's deterioration must have come on so gradually she could not discern it clearly. Or she saw what she wished to see. Certainly, her complacent glances between him and her daughter spoke of her undimmed ambition to unite Rosings and Pemberley. She would not wish to acknowledge any impediment arising from Anne's health.

She talked incessantly over dinner on matters to do with Rosings and the surrounding parish, pausing for an instant when Anne rose to her feet and hurried out with her hand pressed against her mouth. Mrs Jenkinson, Anne's companion, dropped a hasty curtsey and followed. Georgiana stared. Darcy leapt up, as any gentleman should, to be waved back into his chair by his aunt. Lady Catherine's mouth tightened as her daughter left, but this was evidently so common an occurrence that she returned to her discourse before the door had closed again, telling them of troubles with an obdurate tenant farmer, the perfidy of a neighbouring estate over a disputed boundary, and the recent marriage of Hunsford's rector.

Anne did not return.

At the end of the meal, Darcy excused Georgiana and sent to her room to rest. She scurried away before Lady Catherine could protest, and whatever objection their aunt might raise was choked when Darcy escorted the lady into the drawing room, took a seat beside her and said he wished to talk about Anne.

"At last! I feared you would neglect your duty to your family for ever!" Lady Catherine's smile was brilliant, hinting at the handsome woman she must have been in her youth.

"You are mistaken, Aunt, if by that you mean marriage to Anne." He shook his head. "You must see it is impossible."

"Impossible! How is it impossible, pray? You have been intended for each other from your infancy. Your mother and I planned the union while you were in your cradles. It was her favourite wish, Darcy! It is a fixed thing. You cannot renege on it!

You have delayed far too long, and now you will do as you are told and as your family expects. You will do your duty."

"My duty is to my name and the Darcy family, ma'am. I will do what I must to enhance both and ensure Pemberley prospers. I am very aware of the sort of lady I must marry—"

"No lady can be a more fitting a wife than Anne! There is none so eligible, so suitable as Anne!"

Darcy shook his head, and she made a strange growling, noise.

"You would break Anne's heart? She has been brought up to expect this marriage. It is her right, her heritage!" Lady Catherine breathed so hard, her nostrils flared like that of a threatened horse; her head thrown back, eyes glittering. "Are you intending to offer to someone else?"

"I am not, at this time. But that changes nothing. I will not offer for Anne."

"You must. You have been betrothed since infancy—"

"I have not, madam. A fancy between two fond mothers is not reality. No legal documents have been signed, no promises or contracts made. There is no betrothal and there will be no betrothal. I am grieved to disappoint you."

"How dare you! The entire family expects this union. I am disgusted by your ill-conduct, and your mother would be utterly ashamed of you!"

"Aunt, my mother spoke only to me of how happy she would be if, when we were grown, Anne and I found we were suited. That is not a marriage contract."

"How can you be otherwise than entirely suited? Tell me! Explain to me what possible objection you could have! Your lineage, and Anne's, are both impeccable. You share the same noble blood on your mother's side and mine; your fathers were gentlemen of the most respectable, honourable and ancient families. Anne brings you Rosings. Rosings! What other bride could bring you half as much? Her fortune combined with yours and Pemberley... Good Lord, few indeed in the land can transcend—"

"Anne's dowry and holdings will not entice me into matrimony. I am not a fortune hunter. Nor will consanguinity prove an effective argument." He held up a hand in a sharp gesture of negation as she opened her mouth to continue. "No, aunt. I am sorry I have delayed speaking this clearly. I should not have allowed you to continue to hope for a union between Anne and me. The fault is mine. I was not resolute enough in denying your misapprehension, and I regret distressing you. For that, I pray your forgiveness."

"Better you pray for Anne's!" she spat back at him, her colour alarmingly high.

Well, he preferred to eschew that conversation. He had raised no expectations, and it was not his duty to depress those raised by others. He caught both his aunt's hands in his. "Aunt. Listen to me. Anne is weaker, more frail. She is not fit for marriage. I am concerned for her—"

"She is perfectly well!" But Lady Catherine's fierce hawk-gaze dropped.

"No. She is not. You must see it. Remember her sitting with Georgiana, earlier? Could you not mark the contrast between them? My sister is thinner than she should be, but Anne is gaunt. Georgiana is still too pale, but Anne is ashen. She looks very ill. She is not well enough to marry anyone. How could she bear a child? Even the most healthy of women may be lost in childbed. In Anne's case, the risks are immeasurably greater, as anyone can see. I would never risk her health and happiness in such a manner."

"She is not so ill as that—"

"And yet she runs from the table, to cast up her accounts—as she did when I visited at Easter."

Lady Catherine turned away.

Darcy swallowed a sigh. She knew. Poor Aunt. She knew.

He squeezed her hands. "Georgiana's illness has made me more anxious for the health of those I care for. Georgiana, of course. Our Fitzwilliam family. You and Anne. She is my dear cousin, and though she shall never be more than that, I am yet concerned about her."

Lady Catherine did not speak. Her mouth trembled a little, and she set it, raising her chin.

"What does your physician say?"

She shook her head. Pride, likely, kept her upright and stiff. In her place, he would have sagged where he sat. "It is some disorder of the blood. Purges and leeches do not help, nor bleeding. He has suggested blistering and fomentations, but neither have had a good effect. She eats but little, and cannot tolerate anything but the simplest of foods."

He gentled his tone, softened it. "What might I do to help?"

"You know what you should do! Obey your mother's dying wish!"

He remained silent. Waited.

"She must marry," Lady Catherine said at last. "She must. It is the only protection a woman has. What will happen to her if she does not? I cannot watch over her forever and she cannot live in Rosings alone. She will be prey to every passing fortune hunter, with no one to prevent an assault or a compromise intended to take control of her fortune."

"She is not friendless. The Fitzwilliam and Darcy families will protect her."

She huffed out her displeasure. "Not so well as a husband. Besides, apart from you and the colonel, who of her family chooses to visit Rosings or is truly acquainted with Anne? I doubt my brother has seen her these five years."

Darcy could not deny that the Fitzwilliam side of the family could be closer, but Lady Catherine expected always they should come to Rosings, supplicants approaching the family altar. She and Anne rarely went to London. Perhaps that could be one thing to change.

His aunt heard him out in silence, but shook her head. "Anne cannot tolerate London's airs and miasmas."

He inclined his head. He would say no more, but considered another possibility.

Colonel Edward Fitzwilliam.

The younger son of Darcy's uncle the Earl of Ashbourne, Edward always joked that, not having Darcy's resources, he must be inured to self-denial and dependence. "You are a luckier fellow than I, William," he had said once, but with great cheerfulness and a lack of real rancour. "Unlike you, I suffer from want of money.

Do not laugh! I do indeed mean 'suffer'. Oh, not in daily life, but younger sons cannot marry where they like." He had paused, taking a moment to appreciate the superlative port Darcy had poured for him. "Unless where they like women of fortune, and while I do like them, I am saddened women of fortune rarely return the sentiment. A younger son's habits of expense make us too dependent, it seems, and I am looked on with suspicion rather than fondness. My own fault, doubtless. You always tell me I should practise to be more subtle than a cavalry charge."

Edward and Anne dealt together well. He treated her with the same gruff kindness that he would a child or some other helpless creature exciting his protective nature. Whenever he and Darcy visited Rosings together, he would sit with Anne for hours at stretch. Darcy suspected his restless, war-bruised spirit welcomed the quiet peace, allowing him to rest and recruit his strength. Anne seemed to exert herself more with Edward, too. A companionable marriage might suit them both.

Well, it bore consideration. With his regiment in Portugal, Edward's return home was uncertain. In the meantime, Darcy resolved to speak to his uncle and depress whatever expectations the earl might harbour with regard to Darcy and Anne, while reminding him of his son's need for a wealthy wife. Lord Ashbourne often regretted the necessity of his son's seeking a military career that had, more than once, put Edward in harm's way. Darcy might mention the convenience of Anne's great fortune meeting Edward's lack of the same commodity. It provided a solution everyone in the family would welcome.

"You may cease the pretence of caring about Anne's future." His aunt's harsh tone broke into his thoughts. "I had not considered you this perfidious, but I see I am vastly mistaken. I am most seriously displeased."

Well, perhaps not everyone.

CHAPTER TEN

The Heavens Themselves

The heavens themselves, the planets and this centre
Observe degree, priority and place
— Shakespeare, *Troilus And Cressida*

On the last Saturday of June, Darcy's travelling coach rolled into
Canterbury as the evening bells tolled from the many church
towers. Darcy had bespoken rooms at the Falstaff on St Dunstan's
Street, a few yards from an interesting old city gate that must have
stood there for centuries, and near the High Street and the cathedral
close.

Palmer met them at the inn, greeting them with careless good
humour. "Oh, I am not showing you any particular courtesy, old
friend! The compliment is all for Miss Darcy. I am eager to
welcome her to my part of Kent." Palmer bowed over Georgiana's
hand, smiling at her blushes.

Indeed, Georgiana, coaxed out of her habitual reserve with
reminders of the times they had met previously (a dozen, perhaps),
showed an alarming tendency to blush whenever Palmer glanced at

her. Darcy was pleased to see her relax her guard until she could join the conversation freely. She was, perhaps, at last losing some measure of the shyness she had shown since childhood.

Greetings completed, and established in a comfortable chair with a cup of tea in his hand served by Georgiana under Mrs Younge's tutelary gaze, Palmer confessed, "In truth, I am here at my father's behest, to carry out a commission on his behalf. He, I am sorry to say, is too occupied by a dispute with my Aunt Iphy to conduct this business himself."

"Oh dear." Georgiana glanced at Darcy, her expression showing mischief in equal proportion with lively alarm. "Your aunt is disputing with her brother? Goodness! Is this a common state of affairs, sir?"

"I confess myself astounded, Miss Darcy, though I must explain she is in truth my father's cousin, and hence my cousin once removed, but of such an age with him that she and her sister have been honorary aunts since my childhood. Aunt Iphy—her name is Iphigenia, and as you comprehend, our family is all too fond of fantastical names! My father owns to a workaday 'James', but he, I am sad to say, is the exception. However, as your brother will tell you, Aunt Iphy is the gentlest and sweetest of souls. I had never thought her able to, as they have it, say 'shoo!' to a goose. Mind you," Palmer went on, in ruminative tone, "I remember one old gander on our home farm when I was a boy which I held in the deepest respect, not to say terror. I would never have dared 'shoo!' that bird myself!"

Georgiana laughed merrily. Darcy rejoiced to see her old cheerful disposition unaffected by their journey. She must not have been too wearied by it. Palmer regarded her with patent satisfaction, and winked at Darcy. The man loved an appreciative audience, and he was kind to set out to amuse Georgiana.

"If it had been her sister, the late, lamented Aunt Cassandra… well, she could have turned the Gorgon to stone, and I vow the entire population of Wingham, up to and including the fearsome old gander, conducted themselves most unobtrusively to avoid catching her attention. Aunt Iphy's discovering firmness of mind and purpose, is therefore surprising to us all. But I must not be giving you ideas, Miss Darcy, or your brother will forbid you my acquaintance!"

Darcy shook his head. "Georgiana, you should cover your ears. The intransigence of sisters and cousins is not for you to heed."

"I shall be good," Palmer promised, smiling at Georgiana's giggles. "I have completed most of my father's business but for a social engagement this evening. Dean Andrewes at the cathedral holds a summer reception tonight, Darcy, and you and I are invited to attend the dinner beforehand. I hope you will agree."

"But I do not know the dean."

"That is of little consequence. He told me earlier today he would be delighted to host you at dinner, before *hoi polloi* arrive for the reception afterwards. Given the lack of entertainments offered me in the country, and since you insist on resting here rather than carry on to Wingham, I have bespoken a room, and will travel with you to Ramsgate on Monday— No, no, Darcy. I do not complain. I fully understand you do not wish to tax Miss Darcy's strength with an extra stage to your journey and I do not decry your thoughtfulness! However, since we are in the city, I thought we might attend the dinner—the dean has a fine wine cellar—then grace his reception for an hour or two and enjoy ourselves." Palmer smirked at Darcy's frown. "Well, I shall enjoy myself. You will enjoy disapproving of everything and everyone."

Palmer was the most annoying, persistent fellow when he took a notion into his head. Every obstacle thrown in his way was brushed aside as if he were clearing away gossamer. Georgiana met Darcy's finest argument—that she was not out and could not attend—with disappointment. Not to say more pouting.

"I am almost out. May I not go? It sounds eminently respectable, and, you know, Mrs Younge says a lady grown must learn to be gracious and sociable in all circumstances. How shall I achieve if I am not allowed to practise?"

Darcy glanced at Mrs Younge, who looked both a touch self-conscious and exasperated at her charge's obstinacy. "You are not 'almost out', Georgiana. Not for at least two years, which will give you plenty of time to practise. You will stay here and rest, if you please."

Georgiana opened her mouth, but caught Mrs Younge's eye. Her preceptress shook her head, and Georgiana said, gaily, "I will be gracious, as Mrs Younge advises, and obey."

"Good girl. You see, Palmer, I should not go, but remain with Georgiana."

Georgiana countered this argument herself, maintaining that if all she would be doing was rest in her room, her brother need not be confined to the inn with her. "You should indeed go, brother, and bear Mr Palmer company. Indeed, between Mrs Younge and the two footmen, not to mention my maid and your valet, I will be well taken care of. If I may not go with you, I will retire early. Do go with Mr Palmer"—a glance at that gentleman was accompanied by another alarming blush, raising fears of Georgiana's susceptibility to a charming rogue, as well as gratitude her come-out was indeed still two years away—"and amuse yourself at the reception. I depend upon you to tell me all about it over breakfast."

Darcy was left defenceless. He could no longer protest, without appearing churlish. If he had not known Georgiana to be the most guileless and sweetest of obedient, biddable sisters, he might have suspected her of exacting retribution for the overnight stay at Rosings and his refusal to allow her to attend the dean's reception. Perhaps she had taken Palmer's raillery a little too literally.

"A clever little maiden, Miss Darcy," Palmer said an hour or two later as they walked through Canterbury's quiet streets to the deanery, situated in the cathedral precincts. "Left you without a shot in your pistol, did she not? Canterbury is a prosperous city, Darcy, full of gentry-folk. The dinner itself will be one to savour, and although the reception will be a crush, it will mostly be the lesser local gentry. There will undoubtedly be a sprinkling of the middling sort with some of the upper tradespeople, but do not forget that with the cathedral, we have a goodly population of respectable clergy and the legal classes. You need not fear pollution."

"I do not fear pollution. I fear boredom." Darcy followed Palmer into the deanery, a most commodious, if ancient, house. "I am not at home at such occasions."

"Or anywhere where there are people." Palmer flashed him a smile over his shoulder as the butler announced them in mellifluous tones.

Darcy sighed, and followed him to his doom.

Gerrard Andrewes, dean of the cathedral, was an undoubted gentleman, urbane and intelligent. Like Palmer and Darcy, he had taken his degree at Cambridge. That gave them common ground in the pre-dinner conversations, and the dinner itself had been, as Palmer had promised, excellent. Darcy had enjoyed the dinner, despite finding himself escorting the dean's eldest daughter into the dining room. She was an educated lady, and his struggles to find topics of conversation were less overwhelming than usual.

The reception, however, was something to be endured.

An hour after dinner ended, the guests for the evening reception arrived. The dining table had been cleared and relaid for a supper to be served at around ten. The deanery staff had thrown open all the doors into the spacious grounds, where gardeners had hung dozens of lanterns from the trees. The lanterns lit a dusky purple twilight, casting shadows under the scattered trees and, here and there, illuminating the heavy-headed roses filling the gardens with their rich scent: a demure, ecclesiastical version of Vauxhall, with more lemonade and far less impropriety.

A charming scene, if one did not consider the guests who, while not of the meaner sort, were also not of Darcy's usual circle. Gentry, yes, but none held estates and incomes that could compare with Pemberley. Or Wingham. He privately acknowledged they at least had made an attempt at refinement. The ladies' dresses were as fashionable and decorative as a provincial city could provide, but, with the exception of the dean's silk-clad family, predominantly of mull or jaconet, and with few feathers and even less good jewellery on display. The sparkling rivière clasped about the neck of the most gorgeously-attired damsel there was certainly paste.

Palmer knew many of the gentry, and tugged Darcy along with him to make their acquaintance. It was some moments before Darcy was able to drift away and take up station in the shadows of a rose arch, from whence he could scrutinise the crowds and catch his breath. Only a country assembly could be more insupportable. Here he would have to listen to innumerable young ladies warbling Italian love songs—one was already at the piano, if the sounds coming from the open music-room windows were any indication— but at least he did not have to dance.

His respite did not last long. Palmer sought him out and with his usual raillery, attempted to persuade him into more sociability.

"Come! Have you not hidden in the shadows long enough? Surely you wish for more conversation than this!"

"Here? It would be punishment."

Palmer would have none of this, pointing out a nearby group and claiming one of them to be an acquaintance of his father's. He spoke with enthusiasm of the young lady in the group, declaring her to be a very pretty girl.

"Whom do you mean?" Darcy turned and regarded the small group gathered in chairs near a magnificent weeping willow. The girl Palmer admired was simply dressed and had no claim to extraordinary beauty. He had no doubt her conversation would be as unremarkable and as insipid as her appearance. He did not trouble to lower his voice. "Pretty-ish, I suppose, but hardly tempting enough for me to give consequence to a provincial nobody."

CHAPTER ELEVEN

Speaking Poniards

She speaks poniards, and every word stabs
— Shakespeare, *Much Ado About Nothing*

Elizabeth enjoyed her journey into Kent, and the opportunity to travel through unfamiliar towns and countryside. As she and Papa agreed, the more they saw of the world, the greater the opportunities to laugh at it.

On that first day, they had called on the Gardiners for a nuncheon and a short rest—although Papa had been besieged by the children from the outset and bought his rest at the price of a story bearing more resemblance to the Iliad than to Tommy Thumb's Pretty Little Songbook—before continuing on to Westerham where Mary and Mr Collins met them for supper at the George and Dragon.

Mr Collins looked well. Whenever his gaze fell on Mary, his contented expression softened into one of fondness and respect. Mary herself was blooming. She smiled more readily than Elizabeth could remember her doing since childhood. Even Papa remarked upon the couple's felicity after supper, when they had bidden the newlyweds farewell.

"Do you know, my Lizzy, I think this marriage will be the making of both Mary and Collins. He is already less silly, and she less righteous. I may not regret leaving Longbourn in their care." Papa gave one more desultory wave as the gig carrying Mary and Collins turned a bend in the road and was lost from sight in the gathering twilight. "I will go to my eternal rest with a lighter heart."

"Not for many years yet, I hope." Elizabeth hooked her arm through his. They entered the inn together. "And certainly not before we reach Wingham. You are far too indulgent a parent to cut short my amusements in such an offhand manner."

They arrived in Canterbury not long after noon on Saturday. Though Wingham village was but an hour's travel farther on, Papa kept to their plan of staying in the town until Monday, when Miss Palmer expected them. The postillion took them to Northgate and the Mill Inn, opposite the small house attached to Boys's Hospital where Papa's old schoolfellow, the Hospital's Warden, was to be their host.

Mr Harding had a faint air of shabbiness: his clothing was well cared for by his housekeeper but showed signs of age along the hems and seams, and his hair, greyer and more abundant than Papa's, stood on end, as if in defiance against his mild countenance and gentle manners. He had walked across to the Mill to greet them, shaking Papa's hand and helping Elizabeth down from the coach. A moment later, John Coachman backed the coach into the small cart house off the Mill's stable yard, getting it into place without jostling the old two-horse gig stored there.

The house Mr Harding enjoyed as Warden of the hospital and guardian of the twenty souls who dwelt within the almshouses, was large enough to provide shelter to Elizabeth and Papa, but Jack Hill and John Coachman would sleep in a room at the Mill.

Elizabeth's room was tiny, with just enough space for her bed and her trunk. She refreshed herself at the basin provided by the housekeeper, and went downstairs to find her host and Papa. Those two were already at hammer and tongs in the small parlour, reminiscing about their youth at Oxford and catching up on their lives since in a spate of words. Elizabeth occupied herself with the tea tray until the floods abated somewhat and the two remembered her presence.

Papa gave her an apologetic look when she presented them with their tea. "Well, my Lizzy, there you are! Shall we enjoy the rest of today as visitors on pleasure bent, explore the town and cathedral and see everything there is to be seen? We might attend the services at the cathedral tomorrow, too."

"I would like that, Papa."

"You will enjoy the services," Mr Harding put in. "I and the alms-brethren who live in the hospital are bound by the founder's statutes to attend divine service every Sunday morning at the cathedral in our habits—long, black cloth gowns, Miss Elizabeth, unchanged from mediaeval times. You will admire the spectacle, I am sure!"

"I look forward to it sir."

"Shall we play at pilgrims today while I show you my city? This evening, I have a special treat for you. Dean Andrewes holds his summer fête in the deanery gardens, with music and supper, and we are invited to attend. When I mentioned I could not leave you alone here after dinner, Bennet, the archdeacon assured me you and Miss Elizabeth would be welcome guests. You understand that for the clergy attached to the cathedral, it is most impolitic not to attend. I was quite at *point non plus* about it! He was all graciousness and spoke to the dean, although I doubt the dean will notice one or two extra guests amongst the crowd." Mr Harding added, in apologetic tones, "I do not think there will be dancing, but Mrs Andrewes will provide ices and all manner of good things to eat, and I believe the dean's gardeners have put forth every effort to ensure the gardens will show to their best advantage. They are very fine gardens indeed."

Mr Harding promised his housekeeper would furbish up their evening clothes whilst they explored Canterbury, adding that "She is already anticipating helping you prepare, Miss Elizabeth. A crusty old widower like myself cannot offer her many such opportunities, you know."

Papa stared in patent dismay and sighed with as much drama as Kemble himself might show—or, for that matter, Lydia, who may not have inherited her love of histrionics solely from Mamma. But this little moment of pique behind them with Papa accepting the invitation with all the grace he could muster, the three enjoyed several hours rambling about the town and the cathedral. Mr Harding's knowledge was vast, and he was able to show them parts of the great church closed to all but its officers and clergy, a circumstance that appeased Papa mightily.

So it was with good-humoured resignation that Papa and Mr Harding, both spruce in black silk breeches and formal tail-coats—although rather out of the current fashion—escorted Elizabeth to the cathedral close at the appointed time. Elizabeth wore her best evening gown of embroidered jaconet, and the housekeeper had helped tame her curls into an elegant, unostentatious style suitable for such an ecclesiastical occasion.

The deanery was properly Gothick in appearance, being of an age with the cathedral itself, but inside it had been modernised and stylishly fitted out, lit by chandeliers and crystal wall sconces. It was very elegant. The gardens were delightful.

"Ah, here is the archdeacon," Mr Harding said as they passed out of wide, full-height windowed doors, and emerged on the terrace. "Archdeacon, allow me to present my old friend Bennet from Oxford—like you, a Brasenose scholar—and his daughter, Miss Elizabeth. Bennet, Miss Elizabeth, this is the Reverend Houstonne Radcliffe, our archdeacon."

Mr Radcliffe, an elderly gentleman with an air of great dignity, appeared to have taken their new Prince Regent as his model: while his coat and breeches were of a dark, clerical hue, his scarlet brocade waistcoat, embroidered with gold thread, was possibly the eighth wonder of the world. Given how his mid-section creaked and grated when he bowed to Elizabeth, he shared Prinny's appreciation of the benefits of a strong corset in controlling his generous figure. He was gracious and welcoming, however, and Elizabeth forbore to return Papa's teasing glances. Within a few moments, Mr Radcliffe had introduced Elizabeth and Papa to his unmarried sister, who was so neatly the antithesis of her brother in figure, she had no need of the services of a corset-maker at all, being as lean as the Clerk of Oxford's horse. Pepper-and-salt curls beneath a voluminous lace cap softened Miss Radcliffe's thin face into kindly interest, and she was as affable and welcoming as the archdeacon. She took Elizabeth under her wing, declaring herself happy to act as chaperone, and encouraged Papa and Mr Harding to leave Elizabeth in her charge and take themselves off to the library where they would find other gentlemen eager to join in scholarly debate. Papa obligingly departed, his arm through Mr Harding's.

Elizabeth settled in to enjoy Miss Radcliffe's solicitous care. She and Elizabeth wandered the gardens while she chattered away on any number of subjects, requiring little in return other than a willing ear, with an occasional diversion into asking her new charge about herself. Amused, and liking the lady, Elizabeth happily satisfied her temporary chaperone's curiosity.

"We are to visit some connections in Wingham, ma'am. Our hostess is indeed one of the Palmer family, but she does not live at the Hall and has a cottage in the village nearby...

"Yes, Miss Iphigenia. How pleasant that you are well acquainted with her! She is a connection of my grandmother's, you see. Of course I will convey your compliments, and I, too, look forward to your weekly meetings with her on market day. It is delightful to meet one of Miss Iphigenia's friends. I shall feel at home in no time...

"My mother and two of my sisters remain in Hertfordshire, ma'am... I have four sisters... I daresay my mother would agree that she is indeed in a constant state of nervous exhaustion on our behalf... Papa? Oh, he is more stoic in that regard...

"Only my next youngest sister, Mary, is married, earlier this month to the incumbent of the parish of Hunsford, near Westerham. Ours is a small district with few eligible gentlemen... Mary was indeed fortunate. How right you are! In the circumstances, one must travel to larger towns and widen the scope... My elder sister Jane—I am the second of the five, you understand—is visiting family in London. They have a wider social circle...

"No, ma'am, I am unacquainted with any gentlemen in this part of the country, in particular single gentlemen of good fortune... I have not heard that view expressed with more happy precision, ma'am! Such a gentleman usually *is* in need of a wife, and why not one such as I, if the chance presents itself...?"

And so on, until Elizabeth's cheeks ached from smiling. By this time, they had established themselves in wrought-iron seats set near a magnificent weeping willow to one side of the lawn, beside an ornamental pond and fountain. Papa's appearance at her side with Mr Harding had her turning to them in relief at the opportunity to rest her face for an instant.

"Are you enjoying yourself, Papa?"

"The gentleman are disputing a reading of Aeschylus, my dear, and I find I have not the patience to bear with their folly." His chuckle was echoed by Mr Harding. "Have you had a pleasant time?"

"Very pleasant. Miss Radcliffe is well acquainted with Miss Iphigenia, and she and I have amused ourselves very well indeed— have we not, ma'am? We have been considering the lack of single gentlemen, both as a commodity in themselves, if you will, and, at the more philosophical level, the lack of a good wife from which they suffer."

"The two, my dear, are inextricably linked." Miss Radcliffe spread her fan, raising it to cover her mouth, and dropped her voice. "Now that is a fine gentleman! By the rose arbour, to our right."

The young man in question stood but a few yards distant, and Miss Radcliffe had been wise in the cautionary use of her fan to cover their notice of him, and in lowering her tone. His serious and unsmiling expression marred an otherwise handsome face. He was taller than the average, and fashionably dressed. Unlike the other young men present, whose clothes were likely tailored locally, the gentleman's evening attire showed both the influence of Brummell's penchant for expensive, simple elegance and the quality only a London tailor could bestow.

Elizabeth responded in a similarly low tone. "He seems very fine."

"He may be a perfect example of the kind of young man we were discussing. Well, we must not sit here and do nothing! Shall I summon the archdeacon to make the introduction?" But before Miss Radcliffe could do more than shut up her fan with a practised flick of her wrist, a second young man joined the first.

The newcomer was as well-dressed and gentlemanly in appearance as the first. He wore a broad smile, giving his expression a cheerful and open quality that was more attractive than his companion's brooding mien, though an impartial eye might judge him the less handsome of the two. His pleasant temperament and sociable manners showed in his greeting. "Come! Have you not hidden in the shadows long enough? Surely you wish for more conversation than this!"

"Here? It would be punishment."

"Nonsense. A friend of my father's is there, in the seats by the willow. Mr Harding is the best of good fellows, and a scholar whose mind and conversation should impress even you. I do not know the gentleman with him, but a very pretty girl is sitting beside them. The archdeacon's sister too, so they must be acceptable."

"Whom do you mean?" The dour man sent a glance Elizabeth's way.

She returned it.

He turned away, but did not trouble to lower his voice. "Prettyish, I suppose, but hardly tempting enough for me to give consequence to a provincial nobody."

"Oh!" said Elizabeth.

Miss Radcliffe gasped, and clutched Elizabeth's hand. Beside her, Papa stiffened and beyond him, Mr Harding made a sound of distress.

The dark gentleman's affable friend was a study in astonishment, his lower jaw dropping and his eyes widening. "Darcy!"

Elizabeth glanced at the two gentlemen; one refused to look at her at all, his chin lifted into the air in disdain, and the other could not appear more agonised if he were dancing a jig in boots five sizes too small for him.

She raised her voice, employing a cloying, sweet tone. "Goodness! Do you think that gentleman can be royalty, Papa?"

Papa—dear, clever, sardonic Papa—responded without an instant's hesitation. "I doubt it, my dear. He does not have the look of Farmer George about him."

The gentleman spun on his heel to face them, and stared in affronted amazement. In the deepening dusk, his face reddened visibly. Anger, or embarrassment at his crass rudeness being overheard? Who could tell?

Elizabeth swallowed against the sudden lump in her throat.

She would not quarrel with being called 'provincial', because she was. Even in Meryton, where the Bennets had been the local squires for generations and were of some importance, no one would claim they were more than minor gentry. They *were* provincial. The sort of gentry who were the backbone of England, and proud of it.

But 'not tempting'. A nobody.

Mamma had said worse. Elizabeth was all dark-haired Bennet with nothing of the fair Gardiner colouring, and hence, in Mamma's eyes, unfit to be compared to Jane's golden loveliness. Mamma would shake her head, with many a "She will be an old maid, that one. No man wants tart impertinence, without a tenth of Jane's beauty to sweeten it." Elizabeth was used to such opinions on her appearance.

Still. Not tempting.

She would not look away from him, but resolved to remain dignified and appear undaunted by insults and rudeness. If she could seem unmoved whenever Mamma complained about her, she could do so now. She was no timid mouse to fall into a quake at a stranger's disapprobation. "Perhaps a duke travelling incognito, then?"

"Sadly, child, there are very few dukes in the kingdom. The chances are not high."

"Oh, Mamma will be disappointed. She quite depends upon one of her daughters marrying one."

The affable gentleman closed his sagging jaw with a snap. His lips tightened until they were white, but he appeared to struggle to contain his laughter, the skin beside his eyes crinkling and dimples making an appearance at the corners of his mouth. His rude companion, however, was as scarlet as the archdeacon's splendid waistcoat, and his jaw set hard. Cold eyes raked Elizabeth up and down.

She lifted her chin and said to Papa, "Shall we go into the music room? I cannot hear clearly from here."

Miss Radcliffe seemed struck dumb, poor lady, staring with as much astonishment as the gentlemen. Her lips parted to emit a faint squeak before she could say, in an anguished whisper, "But that is young Mr Palmer! Of Wingham Hall! Miss Iphigenia's relation... Oh dear! Iphy will be so unhappy..."

Elizabeth lowered her voice again to match that of her temporary chaperone. "Which is Mr Palmer? The proud gentleman?"

"The other. Oh dear. I do not know what the dean will say to such a scene happening at one of his receptions. I do not, indeed! He will... I do not know. Oh, poor Iphy!"

Elizabeth pressed the old lady's hand. "Mr Palmer has conducted himself well. Miss Iphigenia need not repine his behaviour."

Miss Radcliffe's answering smile was tremulous and watery.

"Palmer, eh?" Papa, too, had lowered his voice again, but those two young men could have no doubt but they were under discussion. "Well, this is not an opportune time to introduce ourselves, Lizzy, but it will add some zest to our stay."

"Perhaps, sir."

Papa arched an eyebrow at her, with a swift flicker of his eyes towards the gentlemen. "Do you wish me to speak to that young blade?"

"I must speak." Mr Harding wore a pained expression. "Such incivility is unbearable."

Elizabeth shook her head, and raised her voice, loudly enough to be overheard, "It is of no consequence."

Papa's mouth twitched. "Quite so, my dear."

Elizabeth leaned across her father to touch Mr Harding's arm. "I am not discomposed by such paltry things, Mr Harding. I pray you, ignore it. There is nothing to be gained by remonstration, other than a scene distasteful to all."

He patted her hand, but nodded. "I will pray for the gentleman."

Which seemed as close to damning the gentleman's behaviour as the mild warden could manage.

"Well, I think the entertainment is over for the nonce." Papa rose and offered Miss Radcliffe and Elizabeth a bow. "Please join us, Miss Radcliffe. You will be more comfortable away from here when you have taken a little wine to compose you." He helped her rise, and tucked her arm through his.

Elizabeth took her father's free arm and they walked away, bearing Miss Radcliffe with them. Mr Harding followed, looking as though he had witnessed the thunders and earthquakes of Armageddon rather mere unconsidered incivility. Aware the two gentlemen stared after them, Elizabeth made a point of keeping her carriage upright, and attempted to display a graceful air in the manner of her walking. Given that she was more used to brisk healthful exercise than a smooth, elegant gait, she was uncertain of her success.

"Miss Radcliffe, do you know the other gentleman?" she asked.

"Not at all." Miss Radcliffe fluttered her fan vigorously with her free hand, her colour returning. "He is a stranger."

Papa chuckled. "Well, Lizzy, that explains everything. He guards his consequence here so jealously, because he has none to spare. You must not blame yourself."

Oh, how dear Papa was! How very dear! The hard lump melted away. Still, provincial nobody, indeed! Not tempting enough! Heavens, what a story to share with Charlotte when she returned home. How they would laugh together over it!

And with a glance behind her to where the two gentlemen stood, to be certain they were still watching, Elizabeth threw back her head and duly laughed.

CHAPTER TWELVE

Mockable At Court

...the behavior of the country is most mockable at the court.
— Shakespeare, As You *Like It*

What had happened?

Darcy had not spoken with the intention of being overheard, and might have been too forceful in rebutting Palmer's insistence that he be more sociable. He had not intended the girl hear him, but her response— That such a girl— That any girl dared! She had mocked him. Mocked him! In public! What a harridan! Impertinent jade!

"Badly done, Darcy!" Palmer's normally cheerful face was dark with disapprobation, his mouth drawn down at the corners. "I knew, from our discussion of the lady in whom Bingley is interested, that you were uncomfortable around people of lower consequence... No. I shall be honest. I knew, as I have always known, that you can be odiously top-lofty, but I never thought you would insult a lady so."

"Lady!" Darcy scoffed.

"Yes, a lady. What else could she be? She is here as a guest of the dean, in the company, as I told you, of an acquaintance of my father's and the sister of the archdeacon. Good Lord, Darcy, have you no conception of cathedral life? Those are unimpeachable connections. She is a lady, a member of the gentry. Not as high as you, perhaps, but a lady all the same."

"What lady would respond so? What—"

"One who is both intelligent and has her own pride, perhaps? She certainly had your measure! Well, I applaud her for showing you how little she cared for your disdain. It was masterful. To put a lady in the position of having to defend herself so, however, was badly done on your part. Very badly done."

Darcy's face burned. "I had no conception of being overheard. I merely wished to stop you importuning me."

"So I gathered. It is perfectly possible for you to say that you do not wish to pursue an introduction, without delivering an ungentlemanly insult. I had not realised you had grown this proud. I will leave you to your own company, since none other here is high enough to merit the honour."

"Palmer—"

"No, Darcy. Please reflect upon what has happened tonight. I will find you in an hour or so, when my temper has cooled."

And Palmer, his mouth a hard line, departed, leaving Darcy staring after him.

What in heaven's name had happened?

The rose arch was blessed with a wooden seat, along with welcome shadows in which to hide his burning face. Darcy collapsed onto it, needing to regain his equilibrium. He had never before been taken to task in such a manner. Whatever could Palmer mean by it?

He had only a small circle of friends and family with whom he was at ease. The rest of the world? Well, no sensible man would do other than regard the world's venality, its grasping greediness, as worthy of caution at the least. Where was the blame in treating with reserve those people who were, no matter how one regarded it, beneath one's own position in life? They were out for what they could get, like so many of their class, and itching for advancement.

He had a proper pride, that was all, and he kept it under good regulation. But odiously top-lofty? Palmer exaggerated.

A murmur of voices recalled him to his surroundings. A new group of people took the seats formerly occupied by the impertinent young lady's party. He shifted in discomfort. The unyielding wooden seat could not be more penitential in its effects if the dean had labelled it for use 'for reflection and contrition'.

He did not regret his caution in mixing with people who were so far beneath him, but he should have moderated his tone and not have spoken loudly enough to be heard. That was rag-mannered. He should find Palmer and beg his pardon, then find the young lady and offer his regrets. To humble himself in such fashion! It was intolerable, but still… still, he should not have been so intemperate in public. The fault was his, and so must the remedy be.

A gentleman could do no less.

It took him a good half hour to find Palmer, who, for once, had sought a quiet, shadowy place of his own in which to recover his usual good humour.

Palmer accepted Darcy's halting apology with a nod. "I understand your discomfort with strangers, Darcy. You have a limited circle with whom you feel comfortable, I know, but you must disabuse yourself of the notion that everyone outside it is unworthy of entry." He softened this with a smile. "I am pleased you wish to seek out Mr Harding's party."

"I must make restitution for my ill manners. I should have spoken more quietly, and I do regret causing offence. I am grateful for your indulgence, Palmer."

"Come. Let us find the offended young lady and get ourselves out of the basket, if we can. Look. There is the archdeacon's sister. She may know where Mr Harding and his guests are to be found."

Miss Radcliffe, however, caught sight of their approach. She whisked herself off to join the group of upper clergy gathered around her brother and the dean, from which haven she frowned and bristled at them. Palmer and Darcy came to a halt.

Palmer winced. "I would prefer not to explain myself to the dean. He would probably practise a sermon upon us."

Perhaps content to have made plain her disapprobation, Miss Radcliffe seemed most determined not to see them, if the way her gaze continually passed over them was any indication.

Darcy grimaced. "She cannot more clearly signal her disinclination to speak to us. She will not acknowledge us."

"Well, you are a tall, imposing fellow, and your expression is forbidding and haughty to keep the unworthy at bay. I suspect you intimidate her."

"Yes, yes," Darcy said, tetchy with discomfort, "I understood your earlier strictures, Palmer. Besides, you are as tall as I am."

"Very true, but my mien is pleasant and cheerful. I have practised to make it so, and I recommend the discipline to you. Shall we look for Mr Harding and his company?"

Darcy agreed, but they found no sign of Harding or of the young lady and her father anywhere in the gardens or the deanery's public rooms. Darcy was almost grateful for the reprieve, were it not for the uneasy notion that Palmer had the right of it. Perhaps he did need practice.

Georgiana was eager to see the amenities of Ramsgate as they drove through the town two days later, charmed by every elegancy and amusement on offer: the confectioner's shop advertising its iced creams with gloriously bright paintings hanging from stanchions above its windows and swaying in the brisk sea breeze like frantic inn signs flapping in a gale, another confectioner's many-paned windows heaped with delicate pastries and sweets, shops selling shells and other maritime curios, milliners' shops, the small theatre and the circulating library.

"Ramsgate is not as grand or fashionable as Hove or Brighton but I believe it can boast most of the amenities one looks for in a seaside place. As a staging post for the military, the town is accustomed to a lively population." Palmer caught Darcy's gaze, and smiled reassurance. "The troops were shipped to the continent in the spring to supplement the Peninsula army in this year's campaign, though a small contingent of military remains. It is likely, however, that the Admiralty has all the admiration and glory at the moment, thanks to those two frigates." And he pointed to the two vessels anchored offshore.

Georgiana granted the ships no more than a glance, but exclaimed over the bathing facilities as the coach passed them, and she listened avidly as Palmer described his own experience of sea bathing in a graphic account of the shock of cold water and how it made one shiver and shake, and "My teeth positively rattled in my mouth, Miss Darcy. Most invigorating!" Georgiana laughed and looked apprehensive in equal measure, glancing at Mrs Younge. Her companion smiled, and spoke some words of reassurance and encouragement, while Palmer, chuckling, talked of waves splashing up into a man's nose to make him sneeze while the crabs were nibbling at his toes.

"You have much to anticipate, Miss Darcy! Though I am sure the crabs would not dare assault a lady so. No, indeed. Only the finest of lobsters are fit for that occupation." Palmer made biting motions with his fingers. "Bigger claws."

Georgiana let out a breathy laugh, and Darcy left her to Palmer to amuse. He allowed his attention to wander to the frigates instead, admiring the brave show made by the pennants on the mastheads snapping against the brisk wind. Surely ships of the line should be huge and imposing, bristling with cannon? The frigates were small and cramped, and yet were England's last—and first!— bulwark against the Corsican. The courage shown by the men crowded onto those narrow decks was sobering. Humbling. The navy's habit of distinguishing its officers as gentlemen was meritorious, even if many of them were not of a rank most would consider... No. It was meritorious. The officers earned the approbation Society gave them.

The carriage came to a halt. They had arrived at the 'cottage', a substantial house set on the East Cliff with panoramic views over the sea and the harbour, shielded from the neighbouring houses by neat gardens. Altogether, a commodious place to shelter Georgiana for a few weeks while the fresh air and sea bathing brought her back to full health.

Palmer did the honours with the servants, introducing the housekeeper and staff. Georgiana performed prettily, greeting them with smiles and kindness. She did not cavil at Darcy's orders that Mrs Younge must be deemed mistress, but, delighted with the house, flitted from room to room exclaiming over the views or the decor. She professed herself perfectly satisfied with the arrangements, and Darcy considered his four guineas a week well spent. He and Palmer remained long enough to drink tea before leaving her to her new independence and taking the coach inland to Wingham Hall.

He had not quite regained his usual easy relations with Palmer. Though they had spent the previous day together exploring Canterbury with Georgiana and attending Sunday evening services at the cathedral, they had found little opportunity for serious conversation.

Darcy coughed, glanced sidelong at his friend's profile, and turned his attention to the passing scenery outside. The coach had already left the confines of Ramsgate and was rolling back west through the lush summer countryside. "Will my faux pas at the deanery cause difficulty for your father and you with the cathedral people, Palmer? Would you prefer me to return to Town?"

Palmer turned to him at once. "Of course not, dear fellow! It was unfortunate, but do not let us dwell on it. I have been distracted, I know, but not because of that. My mind was on my father and Aunt Iphy, and wondering if they have resolved their quarrel. You have met my Aunt Iphy. She is the gentlest of souls, and it astonished me beyond measure that she stood up to my father with such determination. I rather thought the Gorgon Cassandra had browbeaten it out of her when they were girls. I would not wish their dispute to cause discomfort for everyone. I hope they will bury their differences for the sake of a guest."

"Does Miss Iphigenia live at the Hall, following her sister's death?" Darcy remembered the old lady from his previous visit, recalling her gentle, inoffensive character. He agreed with Palmer's less happy estimation of the late Miss Cassandra Palmer.

He had met the lady but once, but she was indelibly impressed on his memory. 'Gorgon' was not the half of it.

"No. She remains in the house in the village, just outside our gates. It was hers and Cassandra's outright, and now is hers alone. She did not wish to leave it, though we provide whatever help she needs. Our head gardener considers her gardens to be an extension of our own, and one of the grooms goes every market day to hitch up her little gig and drive with her into Canterbury. Also, since Cassandra died, Iphy often comes up to the Hall in the evenings to drink tea and soothe Papa's temper by allowing him to win at backgammon. I suspect he will be unwilling to lose her companionship, and will reconcile himself to her hosting some unwelcome guests."

Darcy raised an enquiring eyebrow.

Palmer smirked and chuckled. "These guests are the cause of my father's discontent but until Aunt Iphy announced their coming, I was unaware of the whole tale, although I had some notion of parts of it."

"If this is a delicate family matter—"

"Not delicate, but the usual tale of alliances and disagreements, such as any family boasts of. Where to start.... Well. You might recall my father inherited from my grandfather's brother, my grand-uncle Thomas, the fifth baronet. What you may not know is that old Thomas married twice. His first wife had given him Cassandra as one token of affection—which in itself does not suggest theirs was a felicitous union—and then died birthing his son. He remarried a few years later to a gentleman's widow. She brought a little daughter, Eliza, into the marriage. My grand-uncle brought Eliza up as his own, alongside Aunt Iphy, the only child of that second marriage, and the two offspring from his first. When Thomas junior died, my grandfather was heir, but he did not live to inherit. The Hall and the baronetcy came to my father."

"A sad circumstance for your grand-uncle, though a fortunate one for you."

"Yes, indeed. A story that could be told of dozens of families such as ours. The male line is attenuated, dies out, and a side-shoot takes its place. Our families need infusions of stronger and earthier blood to improve the stock." Palmer lolled back against the seat squabs, getting himself more comfortable. "Well, on with my tale! It seems my grand-uncle was eager to match my father with one of his daughters and keep the Hall in the family, as it were, but Papa says Cassandra was too acid for any man to swallow without severe damage to his innards, and Iphy was too young for him, in manner if not in years. More to the point, his heart was given to Eliza, the adopted daughter. I cannot be surprised my father had interests in the petticoat line before he married my mother. I told you once he was fifty when he married. While I do not doubt he held Mamma in affection, it would be folly to pretend he was unstruck by a female until he met her."

"I take it nothing came of his interest in Miss Eliza?"

"No. She threw off the gilded Palmer shackles as soon as she was of age, and eloped with some Hertfordshire landowner. Gentry, at least, but his estate was nothing to Wingham. Grand-uncle Thomas, who was a most resentful and cantankerous man, cut Eliza off. He never spoke of his adopted daughter, and banished her portrait to such an obscure attic that I do not recall ever seeing it. We shall have to hunt it out, when next it rains. The search will prevent us from succumbing to boredom."

"All family history is an amalgam of such human tales."

"Indisputably! Well, to continue this one, even when my grand-uncle died, no one attempted a reconciliation with Eliza. Aunt Cassandra would not permit it." Palmer laughed. "Pure jealousy. My father told me Cassandra threw such a tantrum when he wished to marry Eliza, one would think a storm laid waste all of east Kent. That he never turned to her in his disappointment engendered deep resentment—she was indeed her father's daughter and the essence of formidability—and she was adamantly opposed to any reconciliation. Few dared stand against her."

Darcy smiled a little at Palmer's eager expression. "Have you finally discovered a love for history? You are relishing this tale."

"Ah well. It is easier, is it not, when the history involves one's own people, and not distant kings and battles from centuries ago?"

"Far more interesting." Darcy glanced out of the coach window as it lurched to the left. They were leaving the main Canterbury road for the smaller, less travelled lanes leading to Wingham. "Miss Palmer has reestablished contact with Eliza's family?"

"Eliza's son and one of her granddaughters arrive today, the granddaughter to stay with Aunt Iphy for some months. Papa is… disconcerted. As am I, Darcy. When Aunt Iphy announced their coming, I learned their name is Bennet."

Palmer imbued his tone with such emphasis he clearly expected the name should have some significance for Darcy. It did not. Darcy awaited enlightenment.

Palmer obliged. "The young lady with whom Bingley is currently besotted is a Miss Bennet. We met her at the theatre."

"The Cit's niece?"

"Yes. That is the lady. Do you not recall she told us her father had an estate in Hertfordshire? If I am distracted, Darcy, it is because, well, they may well be connected. It seems incredible that two families of the same name have estates in the same county." Palmer paused, frowning.

"If so, would she not have said something when we were introduced?"

"It was a public place. The conversation would have been most awkward."

"Palmer, the Miss Bennet we met was of the lower gentry at best, with regrettable connections. If this is the same family, then I would view with suspicion any renewal of relations with them. As descendants of a mere adopted daughter, the relationship is weak and they, like so many of their ilk, will be out to lift their standing in Society by improving their wealth, position and connections by any means possible. They will make the most of any opening, you may be sure. If Miss Palmer owns the house you mentioned, she must have some fortune and thus be an object of their plans. I hope she may be convinced to be cautious."

Palmer nodded, but said only, "I cannot help but wonder if the granddaughter she is to host is the same Miss Bennet. She was very lovely."

"Was she? All I recall is she smiled too much."

CHAPTER THIRTEEN

Giving Joy

You must come home with me and be my guest;
You will give joy to me
— Percy Bysshe Shelley

Elizabeth was on the *qui vive* for the first signs of Wingham from the moment the coach turned off the coast road. The village did not disappoint.

Larger than she expected, with many cottages grouped around an ancient church, Wingham still wore an air of having been left behind by the bustling world despite boasting two inns and at least one shop. Most cottages were straw-thatched, and many showed their extreme age in their weathered, wooden frames inset with decorated plaster, their frontages broken here and there by small, diamond-paned windows. They reminded Elizabeth of the portion of Longbourn built during the time of Henry Tudor.

"Older." Papa, when she mentioned this, looked over the cottages with a dispassionate eye. "And by a century or two. This is a very old settlement, I believe, but I hope Wendover Cottage is not quite so picturesque. Small, poky rooms with little light may appeal to romantics, Lizzy, but are inconvenient to live in."

Wendover Cottage, however, was a more modern construction and built of a rosy-red brick under a clay-pantile roof. They had passed almost entirely through Wingham on a road leading north up Preston Hill when the wide gates of Wingham Hall came into view. Opposite the gates, the last house before open fields and woods, Miss Palmer's cottage—a substantial house set in an acre of gardens—stood well back from the dusty road, and at such an elevation on the hill that it afforded lovely views of the soft, green Kentish countryside.

"Well," said Papa, as the coach came to a halt. "At last we meet long-sundered family. We must be brave, Lizzy."

They were watched for, it seemed. They had but drawn up at the gate when the front door was flung wide open and an elderly lady hurried along the path between the long, beautiful parterres separating the house from the road. She had both hands outstretched as Papa helped Elizabeth from the coach, but her words of welcome died unspoken. Elizabeth dropped a curtsey, but the old lady did not respond. She stood mute, staring, her hands still stretched out towards them.

"Elizabeth is the image of my mother, as she was when I was a boy." Papa's voice so lacked his normal tone of sardonic amusement that Elizabeth cast him a flickering sideways glance.

Miss Palmer drew a hitching breath. Her eyes, the same clear grey as Elizabeth's own, were wet. "Yes." She took a step or two forward, and laid a hand against Elizabeth's cheek. "Yes."

"I am so very glad to meet you." Elizabeth did not flinch from the soft hand trembling against her face.

Papa, always uncomfortable in moments of high emotion, returned Elizabeth's glance with a little grimace but remained kind. He bowed to Miss Palmer. "Shall we go in? We have much to talk about, I suspect."

"Oh, by all means! Forgive me... I ... Oh, how rude of me! Forgive me, please." Miss Palmer's face grew rosy. It appeared no matter how old one grew, one could still blush.

"There is nothing to forgive. The surprise has you a little overset." Papa's smile held nothing of its usual mocking humour, and Miss Palmer put her hand onto his arm.

Elizabeth went swiftly to her other side. When Miss Palmer turned to her, Elizabeth smiled and offered her arm as additional support. "I am strong, you see, and most willing, should you like to lean on me a little."

The old lady managed a smile, and laughed, shaking her head. "Oh no! You should not indulge me so! I am surprised, but am otherwise quite well and not nearly so foolish as I must appear." She had stopped on the path and turned to Papa, putting both her hands on his arm. "Nephew, you are very welcome here. Your arrival gives me a great deal of happiness. I am sorry our family was sundered for so long, but now you are here... well."

Papa nodded, his face grave. "Thank you, Miss Palmer."

"Miss Palmer? No! I am your aunt, and I would like it very well if you would call me so."

"Aunt Palmer, then?"

"Oh, my sister Cassandra was always Aunt Palmer! I am Aunt Iphy, if you please. It is what Galahad, my cousin's boy, calls me." She turned back to Elizabeth. "I cannot tell you what joy it gives me to see you... Elizabeth? Eliza?"

Elizabeth smiled, and chose her words with care. "The rest of our family calls me Lizzy, Aunt. I would like it if you did, too."

Miss Palm— Aunt Iphy's smile would have lit up a starless night. "Thank you, child. Come in, come in, both of you! It is time to get acquainted"—here the smile wavered a little—"and I have waited more than fifty years. I find I am too impatient to wait any longer."

Elizabeth had been twelve when Grandmamma had died, and the images living in her memory were strong and clear. From the first, she noted Aunt Iphy's resemblance to Grandmamma, and, for that matter, she saw herself in the thick, curling hair and grey eyes: the three shared a family resemblance that Grandmamma had said came from her and Aunt Iphy's mother. But it was all softened in Aunt Iphy's case; quieted, mellow and sweet. Grandmamma had not worn Aunt Iphy's air of fragility, or shown the lack of robustness or the delicacy that was a sense of... of fluffiness, like an old woollen shawl grown downy with age and many washings. That was it. Eliza Bennet's character had not been sweet, or velvety, but one of great spirit, and a sharpness that invigorated with the same fresh verve as the suddenness of a snowball to the nape of the neck. Grandmamma's determination and strength were the qualities Elizabeth both remembered best and hoped she had inherited.

Still, she could not help but be drawn to gentleness, the way she was drawn to Jane, to try and temper her own quickness by learning tolerance and patience. Aunt Iphy already gave her the same sense of mild kindness familiar from being at Jane's side these twenty years. It would do Elizabeth good to spend time with her. After all, not everyone relished cold, tingling snow.

Aunt Iphy took Elizabeth to her room. She left Papa to the ministrations of young Jack Hill, and did not appear to give him a thought beyond "The gentlemen always contrive, my dear." She settled into the chair set before the bedroom window while Elizabeth and a maid unpacked. She did not chatter a great deal, seemingly content to sit and watch, perhaps unwilling yet to allow this image of her sister out of her sight. Every time Elizabeth glanced at her, the old lady was smiling, her expression one of deep content.

When they were all settled in a sitting room overlooking the gardens, and Elizabeth had taken on the duty of serving the tea and little cakes Aunt Iphy had prepared for them, the old lady spoke in earnest.

"You are aware, Thomas, that Eliza's marriage caused the breach between our families." Aunt Iphy sighed. "My father was not an easy man, and not in the habit of brooking disappointment. He preferred she marry cousin James, you see. James wished for it, too."

"Your cousin came with you all when you visited Longbourn, did he not, after my father died? I was but a child, but I remember it well. Did he attempt to put it to the touch again?"

Aunt Iphy nodded. "With as little success as the first time."

Elizabeth glanced at her father. "I hope your cousin is not a resentful man, Aunt, who will cavil at having a reminder of his romantic failures residing under your roof!"

"Oh no! James has mellowed with the years. He is a good man and a good landlord, and has made Wingham more prosperous than ever." Aunt Iphy looked around rather furtively, as if expecting someone to jump at her from behind the bow-front sideboard to chide her for speaking out of turn. "In truth, that aggravated my sister Cassandra. She preferred to think our father the apotheosis of masters, and she did not at all approve that James has surpassed him." She flushed. "I do not mean... I have no right... Cassandra was so very good, you know, and such a noble spirit, and her ideals were very superior. No one could be more correct than Cassandra, more alive to what is upright and proper. Such a model of feminine delicacy and decorum! Though I cannot approach her goodness, she is quite a pattern for me to follow."

Elizabeth suspected Aunt Iphy had been checking to be certain it had not been the redoubtable Cassandra hiding behind the sideboard to disconcert her. Elizabeth's first impression was that Aunt Iphy lived up to the promise of her letters: she was a dear soul, but heavens! She had not an ounce of steel in her.

Still, Elizabeth smiled, and reassured her new aunt that she, too, had the advantage of an elder sister of unparalleled goodness—although, out of consideration for Aunt Iphy's sisterly feelings, she did not mention that dear Jane also had healthy measures of sweet temper and innate kindness—adding she was sure her aunt missed Miss Cassandra most dreadfully. "Though I must say, Aunt Iphy, that while I love Jane dearly, I fall short of her virtues in every way and am daily reminded of my shortcomings! It is a most lowering reflection."

"Oh, you do remind me of Eliza! That is exactly something she would say to Cassandra, and with just such a light in her eyes and the same little quirk of her mouth to show she was funning. Cassandra did not always see the joke..." Aunt Iphy's smile wavered, and she hastily turned away to look at Papa. "We have issues of some delicacy to talk about while you are here, Thomas, much of it for you and me to discuss in private."

Papa bowed his head.

Elizabeth had no time for more than a momentary chagrin at being left out of interesting conversations, because Aunt Iphy turned back to her.

"Your letters gave me much happiness, Lizzy. You are a lively correspondent, with news of Longbourn and the wedding and all you had to tell me of your sisters. I hope I may meet them one day." She took Elizabeth's hand. "But, most of all, our correspondence allowed me to know you. I am happy to see you in the flesh, child. You are all I imagined you to be. To have Eliza's grandchild here with me! I cannot tell you what it means."

For all the old lady's comfortable means and way of life, for all this pretty cottage and its grounds, Elizabeth suspected Aunt Iphy's had been a lonely existence under her sister's repressive thumb. She smiled and pressed the old lady's hand.

"I am glad to be here with you. We shall be great friends, I think."

It was nothing but the truth.

Elizabeth got Papa alone the next morning. They explored the village together before breakfast, leaving Aunt Iphy to an hour's quiet repose and her usual morning occupations.

Elizabeth was particularly pleased that one of the public rooms at the Dog Inn, reached by a discreet side door, had been given over to a small circulating library. Papa bought her a three-month subscription.

"Aunt Iphy's library will not to be to your taste, Lizzy, from what I saw of it yesterday evening. I suspect it is more to the late Miss Palmer's inclination than anyone's." Papa tucked her hand under his arm and they started back along the little High Street towards Preston Hill. "So, do you think you will be content here?"

"I can always make myself content, Papa. I like Aunt Iphy a great deal, and I am sure I will find enough amusement here."

"Good. Good. I expect you to be here three months complete. Or longer, if you and Aunt Iphy wish it."

Elizabeth shot him a sharp glance. He and Aunt Iphy had talked after Elizabeth had retired, she knew. "I am not anticipating a longer stay."

Papa countered with a nod, and "Nor, at the moment, is one mooted. However, I do counsel you... " He paused, wincing as though a tooth nagged at him. "Lizzy, listen to me carefully. Miss Palmer is a little dazzled by your close resemblance to my mother, that is plain. But I think she will come to love more than that, and appreciate those qualities I most prize in you: your quickness of mind, your kind heart, your principles. You are honest and true, child, and I am prodigiously proud of you. I leave you here for you two to learn to know each other, and, if she wishes you to stay longer, please consider her request. She is hungry for family, for the connection through you to your grandmother."

Papa paused, drawing Elizabeth into the shade of a large oak. "My mother took umbrage at the Palmers—and indeed, I do not blame her for that—and she would not soften beyond sending them a yearly letter to which she expected no reply. I suspect she did so to irk them by reminding them of her existence, as much as for any other reason. But consider that the Palmers have held this baronetcy for six generations. We are gentry, Lizzy, but not of any consequence. That proud young buck at the dean's house... well, his views are those of Society in general. To have the Palmers acknowledge us as family, however remote, may not give us any great advantage in the world, but I am inclined to believe it does us no great harm, either."

"I understand the value of family, Papa, and for that reason I am happy to spend time with Aunt Iphy. I like her, and I would relish a deeper connection and better understanding of her. But I do not wish to search for a worldly value to be had there. I would not use her for those reasons. It would be too mercenary to grasp for any advantage."

Papa laughed. "Honest and true, indeed! And I agree. I would never ask such a thing of you and I am not suggesting any scheme to cozen or deceive our new aunt—heavens forfend! I am merely thinking... Well, Lizzy, I have not done enough to ensure your futures, and we are lucky indeed that Mary made the match with Collins and secured Longbourn. He may yet prove to be a less objectionable son than I first feared, but still I doubt you, in particular, will thrive under his roof. If other possibilities are open to you, do not allow your pride to prevent you nurturing them."

Elizabeth raised her free hand to rub lightly over her mouth, an odd, hot fluttering in her stomach, as if she had swallowed a guttering candle flame. "Are you ill?"

"What? No! No, I promise you. I am very well. But Collins's appearance brought me up short against my own dilatory habits, reminding me I had not made provision enough for your Mamma and you and your sisters. Mary saved us, through no effort on my part. I cannot say your being here will mean anything tangible in the future, but I wish you to have the opportunity to find an alternative source of aid if ever you should need it."

"My uncles—"

"Both will help, naturally. But your uncle Gardiner has children of his own, and your uncle Phillips's resources are limited. This is all airy speculation, and I expect you will be married to some good man who will strive to deserve you, long before I go to meet my Maker. But if you are not, and if our aunt is able to be a refuge for you, however temporary... well. That is all I mean. Build your relationship with her based on the best of reasons, those of family, and liking, and even affection one day. Do not repine if it brings some benefit. Do not seek it actively for those reasons, but be open to it."

"It had not crossed my mind."

"Do not dwell on it. Strive to know your aunt, and be the bridge between her part of the family and ours. Whatever follows is as the gods decide." Papa leaned in and dropped a hasty kiss on Elizabeth's forehead, having to crane to get under her bonnet frame to do it. "Enough of this now, Lizzy. Time to return to the house. I find all this exercise and discussion early in the day leaves me eager to break my fast. Our aunt has a fine sense of hospitality and I daresay her breakfasts are to be savoured. Let us go and put that to the test."

CHAPTER FOURTEEN

The Cheated Eye

> … catch the cheated eye in wild surprise,
> — Keats, *Endymion*

Sir James Palmer was in excellent health for his age, still active and busy about his estate though he must have been more than five-and-seventy. Darcy had met him several times, both in Town and here in Kent, it being Darcy's second visit to Wingham. He had a strong liking for the older man.

Since Darcy's arrival, he and the two Palmers had had several excellent conversations. These had ranged from the efficacy of nostrums to eradicate powdery mildew in barley to Morrice's translation of Homer, taking in, en route, the role of Bow Street's mounted Robin Redbreasts in keeping down highwaymen, and the *on dit* that Beau Brummell had made his rustic brother walk the quiet back streets of London where the brother would not be seen, until his new clothes arrived and he was deemed a fit companion for the kingdom's best-dressed man. No matter the topic, Sir James had joined in with relish. He had a lively and enquiring mind, undimmed by age, and held opinions on every issue of the day. An affable, cheerful man, his spirits and good humour had been bequeathed to his only child in full measure. Every conversation ended in laughter and amusement, and Darcy had seldom been so well entertained.

After dinner on Darcy's third day at the Hall, the three were savouring Sir James's fine port. A bachelor household had no need to delay rising from the dining table for the greater comforts of the drawing room, and Darcy sank into a comfortable armchair, to enjoy both the wine and the conversation.

Sir James cleared his throat. "I sent down to your Aunt Iphy's today, Gal. I told her to bring the Bennets to drink tea this evening and be introduced. I have come round to the view that we should not have another division in this family. Cassie is not here to oppose it, and in truth there are not enough of us to support schism." He raised his free hand to rub at the back of his neck. "Iphy... Miss Palmer, Darcy, as you will recall? Iphy has some connections of ours staying with her. Closer to Iphy as family than to us, but still they are connected. Deuced awkward, but perhaps we should acknowledge 'em."

Palmer grimaced. "I related some of our family history to Darcy, sir."

"But not all, I wager."

"I may have glossed over some parts of it. The tale was not all mine to tell."

"You are a good lad," his father said, approval in his tone. "Very good. You know, then, Darcy, these visitors are the family of my uncle's adopted daughter?"

Darcy nodded. "Yes. Palmer told me of the relationship."

"I loved Eliza very dearly." The old man spoke with gruff, simple honesty. "I wanted to marry her, but she met Henry Bennet and wed him instead. He died young and I made another attempt to persuade her into marriage, but she did not wish to move her son from his estate or leave him to be raised by his trustees. She remained in Hertfordshire, and I returned alone to Kent." He smiled at his son. "This does not slight Gal's mother in the least, for there were nigh on five-and-twenty years between my love for her and for Eliza, but it is God's truth that once I loved my uncle's ward most ardently."

Palmer returned the smile and nodded. "Hence your long bachelorhood."

"Women are credited with the ability to love faithfully without hope of requitement, but men can love as deeply and truly. We are no more likely to be inconstant and forget those we love, or have loved, than are women. Our feelings are as strong and can be immutable."

Darcy inclined his head. "I could not agree more. My father was never the same after my mother died."

The old man gave him a smile, both understanding and rueful. "We men are oft taught to hide what we feel, and to shake off disappointment as if it were nothing; encouraged to think one woman is much the same as another, and so long as Society's demands for birth, beauty and wealth are satisfied, then we should care for naught else. Love is for callow fools and poets, is that not so? Well, I would argue that any man of heart and honour would seek for more. Until I met your mother, Gal, I met none I considered Eliza's equal. Your mother broke through some high walls to reach me."

Palmer smiled back. "Planted you a facer on behalf of Cupid and darkened your daylights with love."

The old man let out a short crack of laughter, laced with as much pain as amusement. It died into a sigh. "So, I am beset with a past I had thought long behind me and if I am somewhat distracted, I crave your pardon. There is little of joy for me to recollect about that time, and I fear these Bennets will be a hard reminder. This Mr Bennet is her son."

"I can well believe their approach after all these years is disconcerting, sir," Darcy said.

"Oh, Iphy went to them. I have not heard anything from Bennet since… since Eliza died in the year two, and though I might have answered then, well…"

"My mother was very ill," Palmer put in, quietly.

His father swallowed, and nodded. "It was not the time, and there has been no favourable circumstance since. In any event, they did not make the first approach."

That was a surprise. Darcy had assumed the Bennets, being lower gentry, must have contrived to bring themselves to the notice of their higher, richer connections, and would seek to turn it to their own advantage. Well, even so, doubtless the Bennets had seized on the opportunity offered them by Miss Palmer's kindness. But before Darcy could voice this opinion, a stir and noise in the hall beyond the door told them Miss Palmer and her guests had arrived to spend an hour or so before tea. He had no time to sound a warning.

The three rose, all eyes turning to the door.

The butler announced the newcomers: Miss Palmer, Mr Thomas Bennet, Miss Elizabeth Bennet.

The silence was thick. Heavy with anticipation. Miss Palmer fluttered in first, her soft voice making no headway against the quiet expectancy that cloaked the room, clutching the arm of a gentleman who kept a silence of his own behind the wry smile twisting his mouth. He was familiar. Darcy had seen him before.

She entered behind them. Head held high, face framed with dark curls, eyes bright, and a knowing smile all the more mocking because of its sweetness.

The impertinent girl from the deanery garden.

"Oh, Lord," Palmer breathed, voice choked with... something. Apprehension? Amusement? Probably both.

Darcy was not to discover which, because Sir James gasped, and took a step forward, stretching out a hand.

"Eliza!" Then, a hushed, wondering, "Eliza."

CHAPTER FIFTEEN

Gentle Rain

The quality of mercy is not strained.
It droppeth as the gentle rain from heaven
— Shakespeare, *The Merchant of Venice*

This was unendurable. How could Darcy tolerate such an awkward situation? How could anyone? What would she say? What would she do? He saw that Palmer glanced at his father, his cheerful expression wiped away. How... how impossible it would be if she and her father were to say something to Sir James!

Darcy waited for her to expose him, for her to use the tone of false sweetness and sheer impudence she had employed in the deanery garden.

She did not acknowledge him. One swift look from bright eyes under arching brows, and she turned her attention to Sir James, who had grasped both her hands and stooped to stare into her face. Would even Sir James be exempt from her so-called wit? Yet all she said, with a quiet, gentle simplicity, was something about her strong likeness to her grandmother.

To Sir James's lost love, although she had enough of a sense of propriety not to say as much, at least.

Sir James, still pale, looked shocked and disconcerted. He glanced at Miss Palmer. "Iphy, I cannot believe how close the likeness is. You must agree."

"I do indeed, James. As if Eliza returned to us."

"In spirit too, I hope." Sir James rallied, and straightened. "She had a rare, sportive nature, did Eliza."

The girl smiled. "Papa will tell you, sir, that I have all my grandmother's impudent ways." Her tone was confiding, but laughter thrummed underneath it all. "I can promise you I am not one to hide candles under bushel baskets."

Sir James's smile had an element of sadness to it, a wryness. "I look forward to it, my dear." He raised her hand and kissed it, and finally the formal introductions were performed.

Darcy bowed to the hoyden known as Miss Elizabeth Bennet, hoping his expression signalled his indifference. Her curtsey was exact in cold civility, and she offered not an iota more. Not a look beyond politeness, no hint of being conscious of who he was. She gave him back his indifference in full measure.

Mr Bennet nodded and quirked an eyebrow in Darcy's and Palmer's direction. His mouth curved into a smirk that had Darcy wishing politeness did not demand he hide his discomfort in public. Miss Iphigenia fluttered in the way reminiscent of a wing-shot partridge, giving Palmer a wounded look that had Darcy's friend wincing and mouthing "She must know!" at him. But if Miss Iphigenia intended to remonstrate, the moment was past: Sir James spoke up to call the Bennets "cousins". Darcy supposed they were, of a kind. Distant ones, and not of blood, but mere faint ties to a marriage made more than three quarters of a century earlier. Barely any connection at all.

Sir James escorted Miss Bennet to a sofa. He gestured to Palmer before taking Miss Iphigenia and Mr Bennet off a little to one side, presumably for some private conversation. Palmer proved equal to the occasion, employing a natural charm to smooth over awkwardness. A few moments of courteous greetings, social nothings, and polite offers of refreshment, and he presented Miss

Bennet with the requested glass of ratafia before taking the chair set opposite her sofa.

"I am very happy to obey my father, Miss Bennet, and welcome you as a cousin. My family, you see, is small, and all additions to it are to be celebrated. But, as I think you will agree, we must have a conversation."

Miss Bennet smiled. "I believe we must. Should we make it a philosophical one? You are an educated gentleman, and I am sure your friend is also?"

She still did not look at Darcy. The heat of discomfort tightened in his belly, and he ran a finger under the constriction of his neckband. He felt the same sensation of faint vertigo he would experience if he had stood too swiftly and his vision had whitened for an instant.

"Cambridge." Palmer gave Darcy a glance in which alarm and amusement were at war.

"I may have absorbed my father's prejudices since he is an Oxford man, but even Cambridge is better than the opportunities afforded we poor females. Still, Papa is an indulgent teacher who taught me many things. We have been considering a philosophical question, these last few days. Is it better to be gratuitously insulted by a… a gentleman whilst among people one knows and who can then provide comfort, or amongst strangers who will not care two straws whether one is hurt or not, but who will not remember one's name—and therefore one's humiliation—when they wake the following day?"

Darcy choked. He had obviously not only stood too quickly, but had cracked his head against an iron bar on the way up. The faint vertigo became mortification, an icy trickle down the nape of his neck, seeping under his cravat. He hunched his shoulders against it and sat, heavy and graceless, in a nearby chair.

Palmer's jaw dropped. He closed it with an audible clack. "And what did you conclude, Miss Bennet?" His voice was several notes higher than usual. Perhaps his cravat had him in a stranglehold, too.

"That I should endeavour to consort only with true gentlemen who would scorn to insult a gentlewoman on no provocation whatsoever." The vixen turned to look at Darcy at last. "Would you not agree, sir? Or do you have some other point of argument to advance in the debate?"

Darcy stared. Whatever the chill sweat under his cravat was doing, it was not cooling the volcano heating his face.

Bless him, but Palmer leapt to his defence. "We looked for you and the rest of your party to ask your forgiveness... erm... You must have left, for... erm... We could not find you. It was an unconscionable scene, Miss Bennet. My regret and, I assure you, my mortification are most sincerely felt."

"You did not offend me, sir."

Darcy swallowed a lump in his throat the size of the Hall itself. Good God, but he had never—*never*—come across a woman... a lady... with such biting fire. He swallowed. "That was my office, I am aware." He inclined his head in a sharp jerk. "I am not proud of my conduct, madam. I was unpardonably rude and should not have spoken so in a public place. I do not deserve your forgiveness, but I do beg for it."

She regarded him for a long moment, with an air of waiting for something. What, he could not fathom. When she tired of waiting, she graced them with the wry smile he had seen more than once, and nodded. "We are enjoined always to exercise forgiveness for those who trespass against us, are we not? You have my pardon, for what it is worth."

Darcy, with all the awkwardness of a man caught in transgression, murmured his gratitude for her forbearance. He must be red as fire, the way his face burned.

"It was in part my fault, and I, too, beg forgiveness," Palmer said. "Darcy here is not comfortable in public gatherings, and I pressed him too hard to be sociable when it is not in his nature. Pardon me, too, I pray."

The smile she turned to Palmer was far less mocking. "If a gentleman ventures out of his doors, Mr Palmer—"

"Cousin. If you please."

"Cousin." She inclined her head, making a graceful arc of her neck. "As I was saying, if a gentleman ventures out into Society, it behoves him to practise to attain at least some proficiency in its manners." She primmed up her mouth into a little moue. "Oh dear. I make a poor Portia, do I not? I sit in judgement, but lack mercy. Very well. We shall say no more about it."

"You are very gracious," Darcy managed.

"I do not believe I am, sir."

A moment passed, where none of them would meet the gaze of the others. Palmer took a large gulp of port from his glass, Miss Bennet took delicate little sips of ratafia, and Darcy looked at the door. It would be heaven indeed to be on the other side of it.

Miss Bennet broke the silence. "You have, I take it, both lately come into the country from Town?"

Palmer's easy smile appeared. "I came down two weeks ago. Darcy and I met in Canterbury last Sat—" He winced and his voice petered out.

It seemed every conversational gambit was fraught with peril. Palmer had flung himself into the breach once. It was Darcy's turn. "My sister was gravely ill earlier this year, Miss Bennet. She has gone to Ramsgate, to a house I have rented from Palmer here, to improve her health with the sea air. He met us to escort us the final stage."

"Oh. I hope she is recovering?"

"Yes. More slowly than I would like, but yes. Thank you for your concern."

"I am pleased to hear it. You must have been very anxious. I intended to ask if you had enjoyed the Season. My oldest sister is living in Town at present, and attended many events there."

"I believe we met her at the theatre." Palmer brightened so vividly, Darcy was tempted to shield his eyes.

Miss Bennet's answering smile was as bright. "You did! She told me a fortnight or more ago, when she returned to Longbourn for our sister Mary's marriage. A most curious coincidence."

"She did not mention your visit to Miss Palmer." Darcy considered such reticence odd.

"No, but how could she? In such a place and amongst mere acquaintances, to claim any sort of connection, or speak of Aunt Iph... Miss Palmer's invitation or the possibility of our meeting here, would have been presumptuous. Let me assure you, that is far from Jane's character." She gave Palmer a sweet smile. "Which is as beautiful as she is."

"She is all loveliness," the poor fool sighed. He had been smitten at the theatre by the lady's face and manners, and had not, it seemed, recovered.

"Most people think so. My sister is accounted the great beauty in our neighbourhood, and rightly so."

"She would be accounted a great beauty anywhere." Palmer's attempted gallantry was irksome.

Miss Bennet beamed. Odd. Most girls did not care to sit in another's shadow. "It is, I assure you, more than skin-deep. Jane unites a calm disposition and strong principles with a sweet temper, and you will seldom find a more upright character. I confess I regret my own failings in comparison."

Darcy could resist no longer. He allowed a cynical tinge to his tone. "Does she have any faults?"

He ignored Palmer's hissed, "Darcy!" and waited for Miss Bennet's response.

She smiled. "Of course. She is but human, after all! I would say her principal failing is her wish to believe the best of all people, often despite the evidence to the contrary they themselves provide by their actions. She will always try to find a way to think disputes are mere misunderstandings, and the failings in others are to be pitied, but not condemned."

"But that is admirable!" Palmer protested.

Darcy inclined his head in agreement. He supposed it was. "But it is also a form of blindness. Benign, but still blindness. She must risk continual disappointment. People do not usually merit such faith."

"I agree. But her kindness is less reprehensible than its opposite. A little cynicism may be useful, but an excess?" Miss Bennet's smile widened. "I am myself too much my father's daughter, I fear."

Palmer, his voice once again a note of two higher than normal, burst in to ask if this was her first visit to Kent, and she graciously allowed him to turn the conversation.

"It is. What pretty country! I hope to see more of it. My younger sister Mary married a clergyman in west Kent last month, and I hope to have the opportunity to visit her…"

Bless Palmer. He and Miss Bennet were alike in taking amusement in discussing Kent, and they talked of the sights of Canterbury without the conversation degrading into embarrassment or acrimony.

Darcy sat silent, allowing their inconsequential chatter to wash around him without touching him until a familiar word jerked him back into taking note of his company. "Hunsford?"

Miss Bennet seemed startled at his interruption, but she smiled and nodded. "My father's heir, a very distant cousin, is also my new brother. He is the rector of Hunsford. His preferment allowed him to marry my sister. He is most fortunate to have been presented to a parish at his young age, thanks, I believe, to the kind notice of its patroness."

"Lady Catherine De Bourgh."

It did not seem possible she could arch those eyebrows any higher, but she succeeded. "Are you acquainted with the lady, sir?"

"She is Darcy's aunt." And Palmer made the sort of grimace Darcy associated with the advent of the four horsemen of the Apocalypse.

"My late mother's sister." Darcy cleared his throat. "And sister to the Earl of Ashbourne."

"Oh." Miss Bennet went on with an innocent-sounding, "Mr Collins—my new brother—speaks highly of your aunt, sir. I gained the impression she is very active in the parish."

Not so innocent as she appeared, then. Darcy allowed his mouth to twitch in silent acknowledgment of that gentle barb. His aunt's interference in all aspects of life in the district around Rosings was an infliction better imagined than experienced. Miss Bennet's sister would learn this for herself.

Still, it cemented the Bennets in their place as minor gentry at best. Sister to his aunt's rector, who was also her father's heir—whatever estate Bennet had could not be used to the benefit of his wife and daughters. Minor gentry, and, from her showing so far in the area of clothing and jewels, not particularly wealthy.

Darcy glanced at her as she and Palmer resumed their conversation, and gave himself over to considering her in detail.

He had been right, in the deanery garden, with his assertion about her looks. Yes, a pretty sort of girl, but no great beauty— certainly not compared to the sister they had seen in London. Those eyes under their arched brows, though! An unusual grey, sometimes darker and sometimes more silvery according to the light, and rimmed with long dark lashes... he would allow those to be an outstanding feature, dancing with a life and vitality that lifted her above mere bland prettiness.

Her manners were not those of the *bon ton*. She did not strive to present the icily regular façade to the world demanded by fashion, nor show the cool perfection that valued moderation and conformity to an ideal propriety above a more individual character. If he cast an inner eye over the ladies of the *beau monde*, he could recall few for any distinguishing feature. Oh, some stood out as great beauties, and others as sweet singers or talented painters of screens and tables; but a lady was schooled to display little more than these shallow accomplishments in the hope she would net herself a husband with the same ease that she netted a purse. Her true nature, beneath the Society mask, was a mystery. No, Miss Bennet's manners were not tonnish, and sometimes she showed an impudence he could not find pleasing... yet she also displayed an educated, quick and playful mind. She was more colourful than the generality of girls in Society. He was unconvinced it was a virtue. He was not used to it. Would he countenance such natural openness in Georgiana?

She caught him staring. He turned his head quickly, to glance in the direction of their elders, hoping his expression remained impassive. It would not do for her to believe he gave her more than a passing thought.

Sir James, he noted, also stole glances at Miss Bennet as she chatted gaily with Palmer. The initial shock of recognition appeared to be fading, but every line of the old gentleman's face was imbued with sadness; a kind of sorrowful regret for the long-lost past. Darcy could not comprehend what Mr Bennet might think or feel; he had partially turned away from the rest of the company, his attention apparently fixed on Sir James. They were setting up the chessboard.

Darcy surged to his feet. Both Palmer and Miss Bennet looked at him, wearing identical expressions of faint surprise. He bowed. "Excuse me. It appears the gentlemen are to play chess. I thought to observe the game."

"You are a chess player? Do you seek to observe possible opposition?" Miss Bennet glanced beyond Palmer towards Sir James and her father. "Papa will welcome a strong game, but I suspect he is less distracted at this moment than Sir James and will play all the more sharply." Her mouth quirked up into a strange little smile. "He has less to regret."

An odd, knowing remark. No lady of the *ton* would call attention to her quick intelligence by voicing such soft, yet biting, insight... at least, not unless amongst her intimate acquaintance. Miss Bennet's open manners were unsettling.

Darcy bowed and walked across to the chess players. He did not look back, even when she laughed at something Palmer said. Instead, he watched the opening moves of the game, trying to give it his attention, half noticing Miss Iphigenia joining Palmer and Miss Bennet. But when Sir James asked Bennet, "Was she happy at Longbourn?", he concluded that he was too close to one conversation where he had no right to overhear, and too far from the other where he had no wish to. He retreated to the nearest window, to stare out over a lawn silvered by the waxing moon.

Behind him, Miss Bennet was cajoled into going to the piano. It appeared to be an amusing enterprise for her and Palmer, who sat beside her turning the pages of her music. Her playing was adequate. Not a touch on Georgiana's, but not unpleasant. He had heard worse.

Still. An awkward evening. Darcy counted every minute until it was over and the Bennets left, conscious that now he had made his apology, he could breathe again. He bowed Miss Bennet out of the room and allowed his shoulders to relax from their fiercely-held, defensive posture.

What need had he to be defensive? Such folly!

LETTER: Miss Elizabeth Bennet To Her Sister Jane, July 1811

To Miss J Bennet
Gracechurch Street, London

Wenderton Cottage, Wingham, Kent
Tuesday, 2 July 1811

Greetings, oh dearest of Janes!

I am in hopes this finds you as blooming as you deserve to be...
although I thought, when Papa and I stopped in Gracechurch Street
last week, you were a little quieter even than my dearest, most
serene of sisters usually is! Trotting too hard and enjoying the
sights and pleasures of our great metropolis, I expect.

In my last letter, I told you of our pleasant supper with Mary
and our new brother last Friday, and of my amusing encounter with
the gentleman at the dean's summer reception the following
evening. I was pleased to have the chance to deposit that letter at
the postal house yesterday morning before we left dear, kind Mr

Harding's house to travel here to Wingham. Had I not, this missive would be thick enough to cost you too many sixpences to receive. By sending this second letter, I allow you a few days grace between two instances of dreadful expenditure. You must laud my kindness in thinking of your comfort and your purse in such a fashion!

Papa and I had a swift journey here yesterday from Canterbury, and now, I must introduce to you our grand-aunt Iphy.

She is a delight, Jane, and you would like her prodigiously. She is one of those small, fine-boned people whom Papa describes as 'being made in miniature by a watchmaker'. She reminds him of the delicate automata once exhibited in London—you remember how even years later, his delight in seeing their precise and dainty movements was still fresh?—but I see a bird come to earth. Her hands move like small, briskly-beating wings to accompany her every word; she has bright eyes and a birdlike fashion of tilting her head as she speaks, and every movement shows a swift deftness. But her voice, Jane! It has fluting, melodic quality to it, and floats around the room like birdsong. She is almost seventy, but her voice is fresh and young still. She confessed to me, with many a blush and glance around her as if she feared a scolding for the sin of self-pride, that when she was a girl, she was much in demand at evening parties to entertain the guests with her singing. I am not the least surprised. So, most definitely a bird. Something small, and quick, and fluttering. A goldcrest, perhaps. Or a wren.

She was overset when she first saw me, as my resemblance to Grandmamma is marked. It is something in our shared blood, in our great-grandmamma's line, for Aunt Iphy has the look of Grandmamma, and (if I may be so bold) of me. I am built on slightly larger lines than she is, being taller and, I suspect, more robust, but we are alike in other ways. Her hair is thick and white, and still curls naturally—I may look forward to be struggling still with this unruly head of curls in fifty years! Our eyes are the same colour, and our faces and noses have the same shape. By-the-by, while I take note of everything you and Papa say about my eyes being my best feature, I will admit to a certain quiet pride in my nose. It may be an unobtrusive organ, but examined more closely, its rather pert shape speaks of an answering bold quality in my character for which I cannot but be grateful. I am aware that very quality grieves Mamma, but I am sorry to say I am unrepentant.

I am also sorry to tell you Aunt Iphy does not have a great deal of pertness. Her nose has the same tilt and shape as mine, but wants the same impudence. I have good reason to liken her to a quiet hedgerow bird, and not the fierce, darting hawk that was Grandmamma. She is too gentle, sweet and retiring. Indeed, in her, I fancy I see something of you as you will be in more than half a century. She will have all the good effect upon me that you do, my dear!

I fear I would not have liked Miss Cassandra Palmer anywhere near as well. Heavens, but our family here is convoluted! She was Grandmamma's step-sister, and Aunt Iphy's half-sister, and we may be grateful the relationship was no closer. I am sure you are shaking your head and saying "Oh Lizzy!" to mark your disappointment over my uncharitableness, but allow me my feelings. Papa showed you Aunt Iphy's original letter, I know, in which she most innocently showed how much Miss Cassandra dominated her. I have had proof of it myself.

Aunt Iphy, you see, put me into her best guest room. This might be a pretty room if the dark panelling on the walls was lightened, and some fresher, lighter colours used in the appointments. I idled away a moment or two last night before blowing out my candle, imagining away the heavy, dark red brocade bed and window curtains, and a Turkey carpet so gloomy in shade I can discern little of its pattern, and replacing them with something in a pale rose or leaf green. It is a room which is intended to impress a kind of dull superiority over the poor sleeper within its walls, rather than offering welcome and comfort.

I would not suggest of my own accord any changes, you understand, but when she showed me to the room, Aunt Iphy tutted and shook her head, and said "Perhaps this is a little too solemn a room for a young girl. It has been many years since it was refreshed." But then she instantly caught herself up with a "Oh, but it was Cassandra's taste, and she can never be wrong, you know. She had such a proper sensibility and good judgement, which she reflected in all the rooms of the house."

This last is perfect truth, although I suspect Aunt Iphy has made some small changes to the public rooms in the name of greater comfort. I doubt she can ever be brought to admit to such heresy! Still, we can thank the good taste of our forebears who eschewed dark, clumsy furnishings for something intrinsically elegant: it prevents this house from being overwhelming and cowing its residents. I daresay it annoyed Miss Cassandra, who would have doubtless preferred something more dark and lowering, along the lines of Tudor oak.

Poor Aunt Iphy! She has such a horror, too, of me flinging the windows wide this morning to let in the summer and counteract the dour brocade, saying she thinks dear Cassandra would not have quite liked it and would have thought it bold. I was forced to kiss her cheek and use my best wiles to persuade her to allow me some fresh air. She blushed and disclaimed, and called me a pert creature, but I am permitted to open the window so I am not smothered by Cassandra's dour style. Our new grand-aunt requires more light and laughter, and a gentle steer towards freedom from her sister's weighty legacy. I will endeavour to encompass it.

In short, Jane, she is altogether delightful and provokes me to be protective.

Wednesday, 3 July

Papa has been walking with me each morning, exploring the village and the environs, and this morning we walked in the park and took a peep at the Hall. It cannot be more than ten minutes' walk from our aunt's door to that of whatever connection to us Sir James is (our third cousin by marriage? These niceties escape me). The Hall is grand, and its grounds magnificent. It is very old, with beautiful Tudor windows and, Aunt Iphy says, wainscotted rooms with a wealth of old oak panelling, such as Longbourn boasts behind its classical façade. But it must be thrice the size of Longbourn, and is set in the loveliest grounds with formal gardens which shade off into more natural splendour as they merge into the parkland. An imposing place, indeed.

We will visit tonight. Sir James sent word to Aunt Iphy at breakfast that he would be obliged if she brought us up to have an evening's entertainment and drink tea before taking supper with him, his son and his son's guest. His note, while brief, was civil and inviting. We accepted. I have set the maid, Betsy, to refreshing my best evening gown. While it is well enough for Meryton society, I doubt it is elegant enough for the Hall.

But, oh dear! Our encounter in the deanery gardens can be hidden no longer, for the son was with the gentleman who so despised provincials. After our nuncheon, Papa and I told Aunt Iphy what had occurred. She was quite overset, poor dear, that her "dear Gal" could have been so unmannerly, so we hastened to assure her he had not offended, and indeed had tried to restrain his friend. She was relieved "dear Gal" had acquitted himself with honour, but, if the friend at the Hall is indeed the same uncivil gentleman, is also grieved, because the friend has been to Wingham in the past and she had thought him a fine young man. She is now shaking her head and tutting over the lax manners of the younger generation, occasionally holding up her hands at my own impertinent responses to the insult and Papa's indulgence of me, since she herself would never have dared act so. She steals glances at me that are half horror and half, I think, affectionate remembrance of our grandmamma, because, she says, while she should never have dared, her dear Eliza most certainly would. And had.

I must go now and change my dress. Aunt Iphy is all aflutter. I am too prosaic to flutter, as you know, but I will confess to a slight nervousness. The deanery garden was most unpleasant, and I do not know how we shall contrive to get through the evening at the Hall with even a modicum of pleasure.

Midnight (and after!)

Well, my dear, Papa and I were perfect Daniels and survived the lions' den. As you may see from my continuing this letter, we have escaped the Hall unscathed.

I will not tease you with long-winded descriptions of the Hall now, but reserve the subject for a future letter where I have nothing more important to write about. For now, all I shall say is that, were I not afraid of your scolding me for using unbecoming language, it is a very fine place indeed but none of the furnishings are 'bang up to the knocker', although tasteful and chosen for comfort above fashion. Miss Cassandra could have had no hand in them.

The butler announced Aunt Iphy with respectful deference, and Papa and I with indifference. I followed our aunt and Papa into the drawing room where three gentlemen awaited us: my enemy from the deanery, his more courteous friend, and an old gentleman.

I was discomposed for an instant. I may pride myself that my courage is sufficient for any challenge, but I will not deny the incident at the deanery was unpleasant. You have been my confidante for years, my dear, and you will know that though I do not truly care the gentleman found me too unhandsome for him to lower himself to speak, it was hurtful to find a stranger parroting Mamma's views of my deficiencies. I had tried my poor best to look nice, too. Most dispiriting.

However, I found it difficult not to laugh at the astounded expressions on the faces of the two young men. Both looked as if their garments had suddenly shrunk to a size more fitting to two hobbledehoy schoolboys than young men, but I had no time to give either any attention. I told you Aunt Iphy's first response on seeing me was astonishment at my likeness to Grandmamma. I can confirm this is no idle fancy of hers. Sir James—poor old gentleman!—turned so pale on seeing me, I feared an apoplexy. He started forward, ignoring the gentlemen, our aunt and Papa, to grasp both my hands in his. He called me "Eliza", as if I were Grandmamma in truth, and his tone conveyed such a mixture of pain and joy when he spoke her familiar name that I had to blink away tears.

Jane, I am a heedless, heartless creature! Aunt Iphy had told us of the love he once had for our grandmother. I will tell you more some other time, and like all tales of unrequited love, it is both tragic and yet peculiarly commonplace. I am berating myself for making light of it. It is certain, even very many years later, our grandmother still has a place in his heart and memory. The sight of me stirred him greatly. He is, I believe, on the shady side of five-and-seventy, but to think he still holds her in such affection! How wonderful, and yet how sad.

I did not stop to consider a polite response. How I ever prided myself on quick wits, I do not know, for I could think of nothing sensible to say in the face of such emotion. I did not know what I was about, hence pressed the hands holding mine, and, though I had to struggle to keep my tone even, I said only, "I am told I am like my grandmamma, sir."

He gave a queer sort of laugh, half a choke, and agreed that indeed I am, and he hoped I had something of her spirit, too. Since Papa always swears I get every ounce of my impudence from his mother, I was able to give him my sauciest smile and assure him I would do my utmost to prove I was a worthy inheritor of her name. He laughed a sad laugh, and bowed, and Jane! I can barely credit it, but he kissed my hand as if I were the noblest *grande dame* in all of Kent, and bade me welcome to the Hall. It was then he greeted Papa, and introduced his son and friend.

They were indeed the pair you met at the theatre when you were there as Mr Bingley's guest: Mr Galahad Palmer and Mr Fitzwilliam Darcy. They remembered you at once. The atmosphere was more than a little strained, and they were as disconcerted as I. Mr Palmer was pale, and Mr Darcy red across his cheekbones. The introductions were made, and Sir James turned to Mr Palmer and told him Papa and I were to be received as cousins—"For so you are," he said. "Too long sundered, but I welcome family, always."

Sir James, Aunt Iphy and Papa formed a little group together to talk about Grandmamma, leaving me to be entertained by the two gentlemen. I took a seat on a sofa and, after a moment, the gentlemen, looking troubled and confused, came to sit near me.

I cannot reproduce everything said tonight, but I will assure you we parted better friends. Our conversation was laboured and unnatural to begin with, and I will admit I was not kind, but Mr Palmer disarmed my resentment by telling me they had searched the deanery gardens for us on Saturday evening to offer their most profound apologies. He gallantly took some of the blame for pressing Mr Darcy too hard—"Truth to tell, Miss Bennet, he is an unsociable creature at the best of times, and I should have remembered it"—but it had not been he who offended.

As for Mr Darcy... well. I am certain the impetus to make amends came from our new cousin, not Mr Darcy. The gentleman did, in the end, beg pardon for having caused offence, but it is clear he is not in the habit of asking forgiveness for his behaviour. He did it, but he did not do it easily. I do not think he has repented his opinion, but that he had neglected to lower his voice to ensure I did not hear it, since he did not, in truth, apologise for what he said, only that I had heard him. A statue could not be more stiff in manner and attitude. I suspect he was grinding his teeth the entire time!

While our new cousin is an accomplished conversationalist, Mr Darcy is not. He is not a garrulous man, and spoke little, but sat close by and stared at me a great deal in disapproval—or so I must assume, since his expression was grave and forbidding. That he is not enamoured of my beauty, we already knew. I must suppose I am so far from tempting him, he was examining me to catalogue my faults!

He was silent and brooding, abstracted even, until he jerked into life when I mentioned Hunsford. Jane, you will hardly credit the coincidence, but it seems Lady Catherine De Bourgh is Mr Darcy's aunt! She and his mother were sisters, and sisters, too, of the Earl of Ashbourne. His is a very distinguished pedigree. One sees why he thinks himself above his company.

In the midst of our astonishment, we were interrupted by Sir James and Papa finishing their quiet conversation at the other side of the room—I am a curious creature, and chagrined to be excluded!—and settling to a game of chess, while I was sent to the pianoforte to display my meagre musical talents. Mr Darcy retreated to the window to glower out at the fair Kentish evening, Aunt Iphy sat nearby to play duenna, and our new cousin elected to sit with me and turn the pages. Sad to say, his ability to read music was on a par with my ability to play it, hence the performance will never be ranked as the most melodious tribute to Melpomene. However, it amused us both, and went some way to putting me more in charity with him over the deanery affair. Mr Palmer may prove a welcome addition to the family.

I am scribbling this by the light of my candle and must soon retire to my bed. So I will end quickly by telling you Cousin Galahad walked across the park with us after supper, determined to give us escort. Perhaps he feared we would lose our way, although

I am sure Aunt Iphy has forty years more familiarity with the house and grounds than he!

It is a beautiful night, with a warm breeze laden with scent, and we admired a sky coruscating with stars like diamonds against a black mantle. There! That is romantic enough a note with which to end this (all too long!) letter. I shall consign it to the inn in the morning, to be sent up to Canterbury and then to London by the mail coach.

Yours, with love,

EB

CHAPTER SIXTEEN

All Her Manners

Decorum's turn'd to mere civility!
Her air and all her manners show it
— Gray, *A Long Story*

Sir James went early to his bed, soon after Palmer's return from escorting their guests to Miss Palmer's house. Such foolishness. The ladies had Mr Bennet and two footmen to guard them during the short walk across the grounds. They were hardly likely to come to any harm. But no. Despite his customary humour over his own name, Palmer was determined to be a Sir Galahad and act the gallant. Had Miss Bennet's bright eyes bewitched the man?

Sir James did not speak while Palmer was out of the room squiring the Bennets across the lawns, but sat in contemplative silence, the hand resting on the chessboard holding the white queen loosely. He had lost the game.

He stirred when Palmer returned, his smile pain-filled. "Well, Gal."

"They are safely home. I am sorry you had a difficult evening." Palmer went to his father, putting a hand on the old man's shoulder. It was a fine thing to see, such easy affection between father and son. Darcy's own father had been less open in displaying his regard.

"I was shocked when I saw Miss Elizabeth. It is a hard thing, to be jerked half a century into the past." The sad smile grew wry. "Bennet is like his mother, too, and they both have something of her character, I think." Sir James used his free hand to pat the one Palmer had laid on his shoulder. "Well, well. The shock of meeting is over, and we have a few weeks to learn to know our new cousin. Do you like her, Gal?"

"A great deal. She is clever and witty, all fire and steel."

Sir James's smile was that of a man remembering the past with fond indulgence. "Eliza to the life. Some traits breed true indeed. She is as pretty as her grandmother, too." He stood. "Forgive me, Darcy, for involving you in tiresome family matters. I hope you are not too discomfited."

Darcy had been entirely discomfited, but he could hardly lay blame at Sir James's door. He disclaimed any vexation.

"You are very kind," Sir James said in an unknowing irony that Darcy had to leave unacknowledged. "Well, then, I shall retire now. It has been a wearying evening."

"Goodnight, sir." Darcy stood in respect as Sir James left, and bowed his head.

Palmer waited until the door had closed before pouring them large glasses of brandy, and throwing himself into a chair. It was very good brandy. Here in Kent, they thanked the free-trading Gentlemen for the bounty, as much as one should thank smuggling moon-cursers.

"I am glad we were able to offer apologies. It had preyed on me, a little." Palmer leaned back in his chair and cocked an eye at Darcy. "And on you, I think?"

Darcy nodded. "I was... well. I prefer not to dwell on it. She accepted the apology, in the end."

"She is no mewling chip-straw damsel, is she? She would not let it go without she exacted her pound of flesh in payment first, and she did so handily. As I said to Papa, fire and steel."

"Do you like her?"

Palmer raised his glass for another swig of brandy. "I do. She is different in many respects to the generality of young ladies. I found it refreshing. I enjoyed our discussion."

"She is forward."

"You mean she dares show she has a mind, and uses it. Lord, Darcy, if all you want is a simpering *ton* miss, I am surprised you left Town. There are dozens of that stamp waiting for you to crook your finger."

"Not merely her unrestraint. She several times called Miss Palmer 'Aunt', though she corrected herself and tried to cover it."

Palmer frowned at him over the rim of his glass. "She has more right to call her 'Aunt' than I do. Aunt Iphy is indeed her grand-aunt whereas I am a mere cousin, and once removed at that."

"They have just met, and Miss Palmer and Mrs Eliza Bennet were half-sisters."

Palmer raised one shoulder in an inelegant shrug and reached for the brandy bottle, refilling their glasses with a generous hand. "Aunt Iphy would take issue with you. Eliza was a most beloved sister, and Miss Ben— I must practise calling her Cousin! She is still Aunt Iphy's niece, whether they met this week or twenty years ago."

"You accept her as your cousin easily." For the life of him, Darcy did not know why the notion offended him.

"What is to be gained if I deny it? She is my cousin's niece, my grand-uncle's great-granddaughter by adoption. Those are facts. If we choose to acknowledge the familial relationship, where is the harm?"

Darcy acknowledged the sentiment with a slight inclination of his head, but he motioned toward the brandy. "If she does not discompose you, why are you eager to swallow the entire bottle?"

Palmer sighed. "Not her. Her father. Do you realise that if Papa had married Eliza, I would be him? Or he would be me. I am not sure which. Now that I do find disturbing. He is twice my age, at least."

Darcy blinked. It would disturb him, too. "You did say Sir James married late."

"Yes." Palmer threw back the last of the brandy in his glass. "Oh, what nonsense to be uneasy!"

Darcy suspected Palmer was mostly discomposed by the worry that his father would have preferred Bennet as a son, would have preferred any child of Eliza's. He had had similar concerns when it came to his own father's unaccountable fondness for that ne'er-do-well, George Wickham. Would his father have preferred Wickham for his son, given how he had favoured Wickham's amusing character over Darcy's more serious and dutiful disposition? Darcy would never know. The uncertainty galled.

Palmer sighed again. Louder. "The problem with thinking too long on the past, and missed opportunities, and what-might-have-beens, is it throws one into distempered freaks. No more of it. Come. I challenge you to a game of chess. That should take my mind from imponderable absurdities!"

"Your skill at chess *is* an imponderable absurdity. But yes, I would be delighted to take your challenge. We both need to think about something other than the Bennets."

But they could not play. When they sat at the chess table and set up the pieces, one was missing.

Sir James had taken the white queen with him.

It was as if a dam had burst with a vengeance, flooding the world with pert-witted Bennets.

She was everywhere Darcy turned, regarding him through the fine grey eyes he counted as her best feature. He saw her at the Hall each evening either for dinner or to drink tea and amuse Sir James, which she did with unfailing cheer, rising daily in the old gentleman's regard; walking in the park of a morning with her father; in the village with Miss Palmer on their way to the circulating library at the Dog; all three unexpectedly at nearby

Goodnestone Park, as fellow dinner guests of Sir Brook Bridges, a connection of the Palmers. Sir James gave Miss Palmer a mild scold for not demanding a carriage to convey her and the Bennets thither, or at least the loan of horses for Mr Bennet's carriage, since the horses he had hired in Canterbury had, of course, been returned to the posting inn by their postillion.

Miss Palmer blushed and demurred over imposing, but Miss Bennet showed no embarrassment. She had the company laughing merrily over her account of their journey in Miss Palmer's gig, recounting her battles with the horse, Jasper; the three of them compressed into the seat until, after a quarter-mile, Mr Bennet had given up and taken the seat behind the gig's body where the groom usually perched. Miss Bennet had driven, along a road she described as having more potholes strung along a yard of its length than her necklace had pearl beads.

Miss Palmer made faint protest as the company laughed at Miss Bennet's wry descriptions of her experience with the horse. "Dear Jasper carries me to Canterbury for the weekly markets. He is not so very naughty, really, and has not overturned me in years."

"The most recalcitrant creature, determined to have his own way. Papa, however, disclaimed any knack for horses of Jasper's temper and would not take the reins—"

"No, indeed, my dear. You were Amazon enough to manage without my poor help! You had Jasper quite cowed."

Mr Bennet smiled at his daughter's entertaining narration, as did Palmer and Sir James, and Miss Palmer looked on in fond pride. Sir Brook hailed Miss Bennet as family—"You are a connection of my Palmer cousins, child, and I am pleased to claim you as one of us!"—and Mr Austen, his widowed brother-in-law whose estate at Godmersham lay around fifteen miles away, bowed over her hand and regretted that his sister, who appreciated a lively mind and cheerful manners, was not present to greet a kindred spirit.

"Aye," said Sir Brook. "They would get along famously, like two houses afire! You must bring your sister hither from Hampshire, Edward, as soon as may be."

"I look forward to it," Miss Bennet rejoined. "We shall all be able to warm our hands at the conflagration!"

Even Darcy smiled. She had such a light-hearted air she could not fail to amuse, and here, amongst superior company, her deportment was unexceptional. She did not affect to be anything other than herself, with no falseness of manner. Though spirited and open, she gave no offence, everyone appearing disarmed by her sweetness and archness. To judge from the way Miss Frances Bridges hung on her every word, she had a new friend there should she wish for one. Miss Bridges's companion, a Mrs Annesley, looked on in patent approval.

Darcy was close enough the sofa where Miss Palmer sat, to hear Bennet's quiet words to her.

"Thank you, Aunt Iphy, for inviting my girl to stay. This..." Bennet gestured to the company. "This is what I hoped for. My daughters have few prospects in our own county—it is too small and confined a district—and I relish the thought that the best of them has this opportunity to broaden her life and acquaintances."

"It is one reason I wanted her, Thomas. She is a dear girl. A delight." Miss Palmer spoke in the same soft tone, and pressed her hand over her nephew's. "I will do all I can for her. She deserves no less."

Bennet raised his aunt's hand to his lips and smiled. Conscious he was listening to a conversation not intended for his ears, Darcy moved away, engrossed in his own thoughts of his misgivings when Palmer had first told him of the Bennets' visit and his contention that the Bennets would, naturally, seek advantage.

He started as Sir Brook spoke up over the general hubbub of conversation, the kindly man's voice booming from far too near a distance.

"My dears, we have our pretty guest to entertain. We should have some dancing! Come, Miss Elizabeth, you must dance!"

For a moment or two Darcy was silent with mild indignation at the exclusion of all conversation, until one of the Bridges daughters took to the piano and his indignation faded. Instead he had the surprising pleasure of seeing Miss Elizabeth tread a sprightly measure with grace and vivacity.

Still, he was in no mood to dance himself. He preferred to be silent, and observe.

He came upon Miss Bennet in the park on Sunday morning, walking after church. Her father was not present, though a young man in livery was in attendance. She greeted Darcy with civility, remarking that after not quite a week at Wingham, this had become a favourite walk.

"I have ventured here today with Jack, my... well, I suppose I must call him my footman, though he is also our groom. He is from Longbourn, you see, and will remain with me as long as I stay in Kent." She regarded the young giant with the affection of long acquaintance. The footman, after giving Darcy an appraising stare, had fallen back a few yards to give the illusion of discretion and privacy, but Darcy did not doubt the youth would be quick in his mistress's defence should it prove necessary. "My aunt prefers Jack escorts me, since I do not know the country here as well as I do that around my home. She is nervous about allowing me to walk alone. Such a thing was never done when she was a girl."

"I do not allow my sister to walk alone if she goes beyond the gardens. I would be anxious if I thought she was unprotected."

She smiled. "So, a good brother, then! Well, Jack is faithful and true, and his presence eases her anxieties—and Papa's too. I would never wish to cause her any unease."

"Your father leaves for your home tomorrow, I believe."

Her expression changed a little. "Yes. I have left him and my aunt to themselves for an hour or two. They have a great deal to discuss to put to rest the difficulties of the past, and I can do little to help. What is painful to them, was, for me, merely how life was. My grandmother belonged to Longbourn, you see. She *was* Longbourn, as much a part of everyday life as the walls and roof." She laughed softly. "That must sound nonsensical."

"Not at all." Darcy offered his arm, and they continued to walk along a fine elm avenue, the young footman following behind. "I was five years of age when I discovered my mamma had once lived somewhere other than Pemberley and been someone other than my mother. My outrage was acute, and she was quite unable to explain herself to my satisfaction."

"Exactly!" Miss Bennet laughed and waved a hand in the direction of the Hall. "This place was unknown to me, except as a name, not as something of such significance in Grandmamma's life. The significance is for Aunt— for Miss Palmer and Papa, and Sir James. They are best left to resolve it, and today is their last opportunity before Papa leaves for home."

Indeed. She was the future of the Palmer-Bennet connection, not the past. But her tone held a note of mild unease.

"You will miss him."

Miss Elizabeth agreed. "He and I are particular friends, you see. We have a similar turn of mind, something he treasures in a houseful of women. I know he must return home, but I will not repine. I am not made for unhappiness, Mr Darcy. I take pleasure and amusement in many things, and I have found such a welcome here with my aunt, and indeed with Sir James and Cousin Galahad at the Hall, I am sure I will be comfortable."

"Sir James is an affable gentleman, with hearty old-fashioned manners that make his guests welcome and at home."

"What is your connection with my cousin, sir?"

"I have known Palmer since school. We were in the same house at Eton."

She turned a laughing countenance to him. "I suspect he was something of a scapegrace."

"I was a praeposter, and then House Captain, Miss Bennet, responsible for discipline." Darcy made his tone rueful and smiled at her laughter.

"You need say no more, sir! My uncle Gardiner's eldest son is soon to enter the Mercers' Grammar school, and my heart aches in anticipation for the masters and monitors there. He will undoubtedly cause much mischief." She looked beyond him. "Oh, here is Cousin Galahad. He must be searching you out, perhaps to provide some distraction against the *ennui* of a Sunday when there is little amusement to be had."

She smiled a bright welcome at Palmer, who demonstrated his new cousin had taken an excellent portrait of his character. He castigated them both for running away and leaving him to, as he put it, stare at the walls of the Hall and sigh at the want of something to do.

"Come and walk with us," Miss Bennet offered. "I cannot say we will set the world alight, but I am certain we are all more entertaining than a wall."

Those two certainly were. She took Palmer's arm with her free hand, walking between them, and within a few moments they were chatting together, their nonsense and amusements too swift for Darcy to embrace fully. He walked beside them, offering a murmur of agreement when he could edge in a word. It seemed impossible either of those blithe, active creatures knew the meaning of *ennui*.

The Bennets came to dinner that evening, a feast that night to farewell Mr Bennet before his journey home to Hertfordshire. In just four or five days, the tensions of the first evening had lessened. Sir James was easier in manner, jovial and kind.

"I hope we have begun to heal the breach," he said to Mr Bennet, when the two ladies had left them to their port and brandy. "In truth, it should have not been left to fester, and I am very glad that we have reconnected our families." Sir James raised his glass. "Let us drink to many years of proper familial relations, and to building better and stronger ties. I hope we have many years to grow close and know each other."

"Indeed." Mr Bennet returned the toast, and lit his cigar from the candelabrum in front of him. "You have been more than kind and welcoming. It relieves my mind, that I may leave my Lizzy in your care."

"She is already one of the family. It heals old wounds to have her here." And Sir James glanced at Palmer, and smiled.

Mr Bennet's smile echoed that of Sir James; a little knowing and secretive. Palmer, who had his head down over the cigar box as he chose one for himself, appeared not to notice.

Sat the wind in that quarter, then? Would Palmer be matched with Miss Bennet?

Darcy screwed up his eyes against the sting of the smoke from his cigar.

He glanced around the dining room. Could she one day be mistress here, sitting opposite Palmer at the table, and welcoming guests, including Darcy himself? Ridiculous. She did not... she did not fit there.

Not there.

CHAPTER SEVENTEEN

Contentment's Crown

'Be thine the choice' says reason 'where
Contentment crowns a home'
— John Clare

Papa left after breakfast, a week after he arrived. He intended to spend an hour or two in Canterbury and eat his nuncheon with his friend Mr Harding, before pressing on to Hunsford to stay overnight with Mary.

"I may have the great good luck to make the acquaintance of Lady Catherine De Bourgh while in Hunsford," he remarked to Elizabeth as John Coachman brought the Longbourn coach to the front gate, John and a groom having already hitched up the horses hired from the Dog. Out in the roadway, Jack Hill stood ready to load Papa's valises.

"Oh, a consummation devoutly to be wished! If you do, you must write to tell me all about her. I cannot bring myself to believe that Mr Collins's account is quite impartial enough to be trusted."

Papa's mouth twitched. "Has Mr Darcy not discussed her merits?"

"No, indeed. Although I must admit Cousin Galahad had a most peculiar turn of countenance when the lady was mentioned. She must be a curiosity."

Papa took both Elizabeth's hands in his. "As great a curiosity as Wingham?"

"This is closer to us, and hence, of course, more interesting."

"What is your opinion of them all?"

"Aunt Iphy is a dear creature, so sweet and loving I doubt she has ever entertained a cross thought or word in her life. At first she reminded me of Jane, but now I think she is more like Kitty, who is in thrall to a sister who is wilful, stronger-minded and demanding. Aunt Iphy was similarly squashed. I do not believe I would have liked Miss Cassandra."

"I think the lady was most unlikeable. And the Palmers up at the Hall?"

"Sir James is very kind. He loved Grandmamma a great deal, did he not? I fear I look too much like her for his peace of mind, and I hope he remembers I am not her."

"He is a very old man suffering a strong case of nostalgia at present. Continue as you are, and he will come to value you for yourself, I am sure. Young Galahad appears to be a kindred spirit."

"He makes me laugh a great deal. He is not at all a serious gentleman."

"Unlike his dour friend."

"Well, as we know, Mr Darcy is conscious of his social position, but he has been civil these last few days, if not as warm as Cousin Galahad. I am content with civility, but I do wish he would not stare so. I know he considers me barely pretty, and he seems to spend a great deal of his time looking for faults in me to deplore."

"Do you think so?"

"You have seen his expression, Papa; always stern and forbidding. What else could he mean?"

Papa smiled. "We may deduce Mr Darcy never looks at a woman but to find fault."

"True in my case, Papa, but we must be charitable and not assume all womankind fails to meet his notions. There must be an accomplished lady somewhere who can win his approbation."

Elizabeth glanced behind her to check Aunt Iphy was yet inside the house. Her aunt had delayed a few moments, partly to ensure Cook had ready the basket of the best comestibles she could muster—Aunt Iphy being morally certain that gentlemen could not survive even the short journey to Canterbury unless provisioned well enough for a trip to the ends of the earth—and partly to allow Elizabeth time to farewell Papa in privacy.

It would also allow her to prod him into action. A glance at the coach showed both John and Jack were stowing Papa's valises into the imperial luggage carrier mounted on the roof, an awkward task that would keep them occupied for some moments yet. The Dog's postillion stood to one side looking on with a most sardonic expression on his face, being far too superior to lend them his aid.

"Papa, we spoke when we began this journey of Lydia and Kitty. You will take notice of them, will you not?"

Her reminder sobered him, for he had been smiling as they exercised their wit at Mr Darcy's expense. Papa, too, glanced at the coach, and turned to survey Aunt Iphy's house. "This is a richer district than little Meryton, Lizzy, and the company you will keep here is higher. It strikes me that what Meryton accepts—or, at least, ignores—would not be acceptable here, no matter how jovial and unassuming Palmer appears. I would not have your standing put at risk."

Elizabeth was privately of the view that a few days' acquaintance gave her insufficient standing to concern herself about. She raised an eyebrow, and waited.

"Lydia and Kitty would not receive the same attention and welcome here, whereas you and Jane are esteemed wherever you go. You behave exactly as you ought."

"Jane does. I am less quiet and obedient."

"You are livelier than Jane, but your manners are those of a lady, Lizzy. In Meryton, neither of you appear to less advantage for having a couple of very silly sisters. Once I might have said three such sisters, but Mary has surprised me."

"Kitty and Lydia may, also."

He huffed. "I do not suppose the surprise will be pleasant, but I will do as you suggested and observe them closely. Leave them to me. I will bestir myself, I promise."

She smiled. The wonder was he had heeded her at all. Should he remain resolute in the face of Mamma's displeasure and a Lydia who could out-shriek Castle Rackrent's Banshee... Well, the wonder would grow into a miracle. "Thank you, Papa."

"Think on it no more. I would have you enjoy this time of reconciliation with our family." He leaned down to drop a careless kiss on her brow, squeezed her hands and straightened.

Aunt Iphy hurried towards them, followed by a maid with the basket of provender. Jack banged shut the lid of the imperial and buckled all its straps tight, while John Coachman checked every point where it was attached to the coach roof to ensure it stayed attached when rattled over the roads home.

There was no time to say more.

Aunt Iphy was all fluttering good will, kindness and tenderness. Elizabeth had not exaggerated by calling her a dear: she was, indeed, a gentle and loving creature who exulted in having new objects upon which to bestow her affection. Papa stooped to embrace her, reducing her to incoherence by bestowing a hearty kiss on her cheek.

"You will take care of my girl, I know, Aunt Iphy. As we agreed, I leave Jack here. It will ease my mind to know he will watch over Lizzy while she rambles the Kentish lanes! I daresay he will eat your larder bare, but he is a good soul." Papa had raised his voice to be overheard, and now cast a wicked look at Jack, whose face had reddened with embarrassment and gratification.

A few more words of farewell and good wishes, more kisses and a swift embrace, and Papa climbed into the coach. A shout from John Coachman to the postillion, now astride the lead horse, and the coach was off. Slow at first, it reached the base of the hill at a fair rate, and within a moment or two had turned and moved out of sight. Papa could not possibly now see their valedictory waving of handkerchiefs, and Elizabeth let her hand drop.

Three months, at least, until she went home again.

She tucked her hand under Aunt Iphy's arm. "Come, Aunt. I think we deserve some tea, while we plot our course for my stay and decide what we shall do to be frolicsome and gay."

Aunt Iphy stared, her jaw a little slack. Elizabeth suspected the poor thing had never been allowed a frolic in her entire existence.

Well, high time Elizabeth rectified that state of affairs!

Elizabeth led a happy life as July wore on. Perhaps not full of frolic, but full of quiet contentment.

As she had once told Papa, she could always contrive her own amusement. She walked a great deal, practised each day on the square Clementi piano kept in a small room off the dining room, visited Aunt Iphy's friends with her, deepened her acquaintance with Fanny Bridges, and spent quiet hours reading or sewing.

Although she had not expected to have the same duties in Kent as she had at home in visiting the tenants and ensuring their welfare, she found that Aunt Iphy was foremost in the village in the well-meaning efforts to care for Wingham's poorer residents. At least twice a week they ventured forth with the rector's two daughters—rather insipid maidens who had not an original thought between them, but inoffensive enough—and visited the poky little cottages lining the Ramsgate and Goodnestone roads. Elizabeth dispensed food and clothing with cheerful tact, but eschewed preaching. She could leave that to the rector's daughters.

Within a week or two, Elizabeth and Jasper, the stocky bay horse Aunt Iphy adored and feared in equal measure, had reached a state of understanding and mutual dislike. He had a mouth like iron, but Elizabeth was, she boasted, as obstinate as he was. Jasper's cooperation was grudging, but every Wednesday she and Jack pushed the animal between the shafts of the gig and she drove Aunt Iphy the six miles to Canterbury for market day, with Jack perched on the groom's seat behind. Their shopping done, she was happy to accompany her aunt to the little room behind the shop of one Mr Chipperfield, Foreign Fruit Merchant. Mrs Chipperfield supplemented her husband's income, and advertised the excellence of his fruit, by providing a genteel tea room for the ladies of Canterbury. Several of Aunt Iphy's friends were present—their usual arrangement to meet for tea and recover their strength after the labour of shopping. Miss Radcliffe, the archdeacon's sister, was one of the company, and, on Elizabeth's first visit, professed great delight at seeing her again. She made the introduction to the most illustrious lady there: Mrs Andrewes, the wife of the dean of the cathedral, who in turn presented her to the wives of the cathedral's precentor and chancellor.

As Elizabeth wrote to her father later that week, it was satisfying to be received, and approved, by the entire contingent of the Dean and Chapter ladies. Such august company! She was assured now of her place in Canterbury society.

They spent many an evening up at the Hall, either to join the Palmers for dinner or for tea and supper after. Elizabeth could sparkle and jest to her heart's content. Her efforts were a little wasted on Mr Darcy, who never seemed to know quite how to respond to her, and who stared at her a great deal, his expression often cold and remote. Pfft. The man was likely searching still for faults, so he might point and say, "See! I said she was barely pretty!" In consequence, it behoved her to sparkle ever more brightly. Aunt Iphy, bless her innocent heart, thought Cassandra would never have approved of such archness. Sir James, however, greeted each sally with laughter, and could not be more indulgent if she had been a precocious, but beloved, granddaughter. Cousin Galahad was a great man for sparkling in return. Not a rake, but all too aware of his own charm. She would not take anything he said to be serious or in earnest.

She suspected he would be horrified if she did.

Elizabeth and her aunt bonded most deeply over music. The week before Elizabeth arrived in Kent, Aunt Iphy had summoned the tuner from Canterbury to ensure the square piano in the tiny music room was fit for Elizabeth to play, as it had not been much used lately.

"It is one of the greatest sorrows of growing old, Lizzy. My hands are no longer supple and my fingers are stiff. I cannot play with the same ease as I once did." Her aunt's expression had all the wistfulness of a child seeing others getting a treat it was denied, and she looked down at the hands clasped in her lap as if they had betrayed her. "I used to practise every morning before breakfast. I disturbed the house least at that time of day, you see, which is a consideration when one lives with others. But my hands are at their worst in the mornings, and I fell out of the habit of playing, rather than bother everyone with practising later in the day when the stiffness eases."

"Was your sister a skilled pianist?" Elizabeth was certain she could name the 'everyone' with whom her aunt had lived and who had impressed such diffidence upon her.

"Oh, no. Cassandra never learned, though I have no doubt she would have been an excellent musician if she had." Aunt Iphy smiled, perhaps to take away whatever sting her words might leave behind. "She would tell you to practise more, my dear."

Elizabeth looked up from her perusal of Aunt Iphy's store of music manuscripts, bound into large folio albums. Her aunt had told her she had copied them herself. The sheets were so neat and correct, they were as easy to read as print. "And she would be quite right! I am all too easily distracted by the thought of a walk or a book. But I promise I shall follow such good advice now that I am here. I would be pleased to have your help."

Aunt Iphy blushed and disclaimed, but she proved to be a gentle, if exacting, instructress. Elizabeth gave herself up to two or three hours practising a day, with hearty goodwill. It had its effect.

"You will forgive me for saying this, Coz, I am sure," said the aforementioned charming gentleman, leaning on the corner of the piano one evening up at the Hall, as Elizabeth performed a Pleyel sonatina. Mr Darcy, a few feet behind, wore his usual brooding expression. "Your playing has always been delightful, but has a different quality to it now."

Elizabeth agreed, although she suspected from Mr Darcy's dourness that he was unimpressed with her performance. "You mean I have improved! Aunt Iphy has been a boon. She is all encouragement."

"I have not heard her play for years. Not since before my mother died, I think. She says she is too old now." Cousin Galahad frowned. "She played beautifully. Better than my mother, though perhaps I ought not to say it."

Another reason why Aunt Iphy had let her music lapse, perhaps? It would not do to outshine Lady Palmer. Elizabeth glanced across the drawing room to where her aunt and Sir James were meant to be playing backgammon, to find them regarding her instead. Both were smiling. Both looked satisfied.

She smiled back.

She liked her life in Kent.

LETTER: Thomas Bennet Esq to his daughter Elizabeth, July 1811

To Miss E Bennet
Wenderton Cottage, Wingham, Kent

Longbourn
Saturday, 27 July 1811

I would address this missive to 'my dear daughter', but at this moment you are not at all dear. What was I about, agreeing to go to the monthly assembly yesterday to observe my two youngest daughters behaving like a pair of... well, I suppose I should not be more explicit to a gentlewoman, but they misbehaved outrageously. I blame you entirely for the mayhem into which our entire household has subsequently been thrust.

Once, I would have laughed at your concerns, and teased you about squeamish people who cannot bear to be connected with a little absurdity. But I remembered your earnestness, and I am sorry, my Lizzy, that I did not pay heed to you and Jane before now. I may have contrived better if I had.

I have for some time seen signs of behaviour I should not have condoned or ignored, but I took the easy course of doing nothing. I thought those who were offended by a little foolishness, who were missish and vexed by Lydia's and Kitty's silliness, were fools themselves.

Well, such willful blindness was ripped away at the assembly last night. I am wiser, now, and know the depth of my own folly.

As you suggested, I did not announce my attendance, but went there an hour or more after your mother and the two girls left. The scenes that met my eyes were just as you reported. They are indeed more cautious when I am with them and I had not realised how wild they have grown. Indeed, I find it hard to discover where my little ones have gone… the one who brought home every kitten in Hertfordshire to beg me to allow her to keep them, and the other who went nowhere without that disreputable doll clutched in her arms. How many meals did we share where Dolly had to have a place set for her, I wonder? And when did it stop, and Dolly was displaced by a militia officer?

I admit I was appalled at the assembly, my dear. However, I did not cause a disturbance there, but left as quietly as I arrived. I do not believe anyone noticed me.

I awaited the return of your mother and sisters, and— well, suffice it to say I am relieved I decided not to attempt to check their behaviour in public. Lydia, in particular, was so coarse and shocking, and I grew so enraged, that for a moment or two it seemed possible Collins would inherit sooner than I would find convenient. Such a scene in the assembly rooms would have indeed been sport for our neighbours! Kitty took my admonitions without shrieking, but instead is a veritable watering pot. She has not ceased crying since last night and wails aloud every time she sees me. She may also beat her breast in anguish, but I have not seen it for myself so cannot be entirely certain.

I have at last forced myself to compare their behaviour with what it ought to be: I compare it with yours and Jane's. They are wanting in every particular. Consequently, I have returned both girls to the schoolroom, and I have forbidden them to leave the house without my express permission, and without strict chaperonage. I do not consider your mother fit for that duty, hence your sisters may not leave Longbourn for some time. Perhaps they will use this period of inactivity to reflect upon their behaviour. And perhaps not. I doubt either capable of self-examination, and I must think more on my future course. They are almost past amendment, but I must find some way to stave off ruination.

I have found one way to control them. While I awaited their return home from the assembly, I had Mrs Hill empty their wardrobes of everything other than the simplest of gowns, leaving them two each. She has since stripped those remaining gowns of all embellishment, and locked your room and Jane's to protect your belongings. Be assured your sisters cannot raid your closets for whatever clothing you have left behind here. Without my taking that precaution, I do not doubt Lydia would have disobeyed me, but she is too shamed to appear in public in a gown fit only for a schoolgirl. It strikes me, as it must you, that she is shamed for the wrong reason.

Additionally I have banned all male visitors unless they are my own friends. Lydia became hysterical when I gave this order and I had a group of officers turned away from the door. And when I told her she will not be accompanying the regiment to Brighton next month, though the colonel's wife has invited her—! Well. I believe my hearing may take some time to recover. She will remain confined to her room until she can moderate her shrieks. Should she lessen their intensity to emulate Kitty's quieter wails, I will consider allowing her to come down for meals. Otherwise she will stay upstairs so as not to impair my health further. Mrs Hill has shown great facility with locks, and has secured Lydia's door as firmly as your own.

Your mother took to her bed, of course. I have reminded her she does not need to marry you all off immediately, since Mary's marriage to Collins has secured her a home should I predecease her. She may secretly regret the loss of the hedgerows to which she thought she was doomed, but she is calmer than I expected. I have spoken to her of the material advantage that may accrue to the family through association with the Palmers, and the danger Lydia and Kitty pose. Though she has been slow to acknowledge that our two youngest daughters are at fault, she begins to understand the necessity to curb them before they involve us all in irretrievable ruin.

I was surprised at how calm your mother became. She has already risen from her bed and though she remains in her rooms today, I am reasonably sanguine she will be herself tomorrow and join me in attending church. Her nerves, it seems, are not proof against the reassurance of a home when I am gone to my heavenly reward. You need not say anything on that head: I am already reflecting on my own failing to provide such reassurance myself. We must be content Mary has stepped in where I did not, and that is a lowering reflection. I confess myself contrite.

Lizzy, my Lizzy. I did not mean to be a negligent parent. When your mother first placed Jane in my arms, I was filled with such joy, and had so many hopes and good intentions. I am uncertain how that faded over the years. But I must consider how is it that you and Jane, and even Mary, have all grown into estimable young women, and my two youngest, well, have not. I should have checked your mother years ago, assuaged her anxieties for the future. Instead, we now reap the whirlwind. Jane, I am sure, will tell me I ought not to be severe upon myself, but yours is as clear an eye as was my mother's. I should feel my failings as a father, but I fear remorse will pass away too soon. I can only hope for resolution enough to see to the girls' amendment.

I was a little angry with you, my Lizzy, for being so insistent, but now I must acknowledge you were justified in your advice. I find myself thinking sadly of kittens and that benighted dolly.

Enough of this foolishness. Write and tell me more of your doings. Your letters may not interest Lydia and Kitty, but may soothe your poor mother's maternal anxieties. Be sure to mention the high company the Palmers keep, and produce some romantic conquest or other for her edification, and I dare say she shall be quite set up for the rest of the summer.

Your harassed father, at last realising that wisdom does indeed dwell close with folly,

T. Bennet

CHAPTER EIGHTEEN
Without Impudency

...pleasant without scurrility, witty
without affectation, audacious without impudency
— Shakespeare, *Love's Labours Lost*

Elizabeth often walked out before breakfast to escape the summer heat, coming to know both Wingham Park itself and the fields and woods around the village as well as she knew the country around Longbourn. Jack was her quiet shadow, familiar with her love of solitary walking—they had been children together, after all—but also understanding his presence was inescapable, for Aunt Iphy's peace of mind. He undertook his task with great delicacy, walking a few yards to one side or behind her, and speaking only if she spoke first. A better escort could not be found.

Mr Darcy had a similar morning habit, if she were to judge from the number of times she would hear her name called across parkland or meadow and turn to see him striding towards her. Cousin Galahad, she knew, spent this time of day on Hall business with Wingham's steward, so she must assume Mr Darcy had nothing else to occupy him. But why did the man persist in finding her? He had made it plain he did not like her. He did not seem to take any pleasure in her company, and made no effort to amuse or entertain. He never asked permission to join her, but approached, bowed, offered his arm, and was then struck mute. For an educated man who had been out in the world and Society for some years, he appeared to have no notion of how to be agreeable and entertaining, and start a conversation. Elizabeth, forced out of her own quiet peace, would swallow a sigh, and resist the temptation to turn to Jack and roll her eyes. Instead, she must cast around for some topic to engage his interest, otherwise the walk would be conducted in stultifying silence.

What did the man mean by it? Why did he persist in joining her when he did not appear to take pleasure in her company?

"At least he can talk on matters once I have found a subject," she told her aunt over breakfast, following one such encounter. "I do not mean to complain, but have you noticed how much responsibility falls on us females to be polite and engaging, and to smooth along all social endeavours?" The tapping of her teaspoon on the lid of a pot of the honey from Aunt Iphy's own bees made a pleasant little chime of silver on porcelain. "We are expected to apply a great deal of honey to sweeten life, are we not?"

Aunt Iphy's response was surprisingly tart. "I suspect the gentlemen consider it the woman's role to nurture, support and encourage. We are meant to subsume ourselves to the service of others, after all, taught from infancy that it is both blessing and responsibility. Is that not the role of a righteous woman, to influence for good? Gentlemen will not make the effort, when we are trained to do so for them."

"They are idle, you mean."

And they had laughed together, although Aunt Iphy looked a trifle guilty at her heresy. She was named for a sacrifice, after all.

When, one bright morning, Mr Darcy hailed her across a meadow full of daisies and tall yellow buttercups, she greeted him in the smug knowledge that the previous evening she had listed several possible conversational topics in a notebook. She opened her campaign directly.

"I see from the newspapers the government is still hopeful of strategic gains following the battle of Fuentes in May, though it appears to me our armies must have faced a period of considerable frustration given their successes since have been small. Have you read the reports?"

Mr Darcy stumbled. Perhaps he had caught his foot on a daisy root. He should keep his eyes on his boots, then, rather than stare at her with such slack-jawed imbecility. "You read the newspapers, Miss Bennet?"

"I have been able to read for a considerable number of years, sir."

"Ah... I... I did not..." He stopped and blew out a heavy sigh. "Forgive me. I meant no disrespect. I am unacquainted with ladies who read the serious newspapers. Most seem content with the Court Circular and lighter news concerning Society."

"Oh, I read those too. Sir James sends Aunt Iphy the previous day's newspaper every morning, you see. It matters little to be a day behind, considering the slow gentleness of country life. We are almost up-to-date." She allowed a forgiving smile to absolve him. "Aunt Iphy enjoys the Court Circular. I am less fascinated by the doings of our king's numerous offspring."

"Very wise." Mr Darcy coughed. Possibly to cover a choke of laughter, which Elizabeth counted a victory of sorts.

"So, sir, do you have a view of our current campaign in the Peninsula?"

"My cousin Fitzwilliam is with the army there. As you will appreciate, the whole family has an interest in the war, and follows the reports."

Elizabeth repressed the surge of shame for baiting him. "I understand. I first took an interest in the newspaper reporting after the betrothal of a dear friend to our neighbour, who served with General Stuart. Charlotte and I expended our small allowances on the newspapers, that she might soothe her natural anxieties for his welfare. We became quite knowledgeable about the war."

"I expect she would sympathise with my aunt. Lady Ashbourne lives in constant disquiet over my cousin's safety and his health." He added in explanation, "My mother's brother is the Earl of Ashbourne, you see."

Elizabeth was grateful she had stopped short of mentioning Harry Goulding's death in Italy in the year six. Someone anxious about their relative would not want to hear of another's death in battle.

"I am sorry to hear of her disquiet. The earl is active in politics, I believe. Supporting him must take up a great deal of Lady Ashbourne's time and offer some distraction from her anxiety. I have read of your aunt and some of her doings in Society."

"My aunt is one of the *ton*'s leading hostesses, yes. How did your friend— Miss Charlotte, was it? How did she cope with the separation?"

"By making herself busy in the concerns of our town. Her father owns an estate now, and she found great comfort in working with their tenants. It is unlikely a countess and Charlotte would share the same small concerns, but Charlotte did find teaching the tenants' children a sovereign remedy for heartache and apprehension."

"Oh, they are not so very different. My aunt is active on the family estates, and considers it her duty to raise the lot of the poorer classes."

"Any lady or gentleman of worth would, I hope. My sister Jane and I visit our tenants, and Papa established, and supports, the dame school where the children on the estate are taught their letters. It is the least that can be done to help those who are not as fortunate as we."

He nodded and agreed, and for some moments they discussed the care of those upon whom the wellbeing of their estates rested. He was liberal in his attitude towards his dependants: a surprise, considering his apparent contempt for those he considered to be nobodies.

Vexatious man! Could he not be consistent for two days together? To first disdain her as a provincial of no importance. To be so stiff one might think him a statue carved in the attitude of a man staring coldly at the object of his contempt, searching for more proof of her untempting inferiority. Then, apparently, his hauteur could moderate sufficiently to permit him to join her walks—uninvited!—and disturb her with conversation which she, of course, had had to initiate to cover an otherwise painful silence. That he was an affectionate brother, she knew, visiting his sister every week. And now he offered this astonishing insight into a charitable, philanthropic man who could look beyond the needs of his immediate family.

She could not make him out at all. He was exasperating and irksome.

Very irksome.

Elizabeth made several visits to Goodnestone during her first few weeks in Kent. Fanny Bridges often invited Elizabeth to spend a day with her, and her hospitality was returned with pleasure, with Fanny coming to Wingham almost as often as Elizabeth went to Goodnestone. Aunt Iphy allowed the visits to go ahead without her presence, with an indulgent remark that two young things did not wish to have their entertainment curtailed by an elderly aunt.

"I am very pleased, Lizzy," Aunt Iphy would say, disclaiming any inclination to join them. "Fanny is a dear child, and will make you an excellent friend while you are here, and I know Mrs Annesley will take care of you both without needing any oversight from me. I shall be well here for a few hours, do not fret!"

Elizabeth accepted the proffered friendship with pleasure. Miss Bridges was a year or two younger than she, but was pleasant company, and Elizabeth enjoyed their deepening acquaintance. Sir Brook, an affable host, made her welcome on every visit, happy that his daughter and Elizabeth improved in friendship. Mrs Annesley, the companion, was a delightful lady, all common sense and refinement. With Miss Bridges' impending come-out, Mrs Annesley would shortly be looking for a new position. More than once Elizabeth had considered whether she could persuade her father to employ her. Mrs Annesley would do Lydia and Kitty the utmost good.

In the first week of August, Elizabeth raised one such excursion to Goodnestone over dinner at the Hall. Cousin Galahad surprised her by proposing he accompany her. Mr Darcy planned to visit his sister in Ramsgate, leaving Galahad at a loss for something to do. He announced himself pleased to spend time with Sir Brook's youngest brother Edward—the sons of the house being but children—who was home from Oxford and looking for a deaconship before taking orders. Edward Bridges was a keen fisherman, it appeared, and Galahad would happily trade on that to fish Goodnestone's finest lake.

Elizabeth agreed to the scheme at once. "I would be glad of your company, cousin, though I am already partial enough to Wingham to doubt that Goodnestone's waters could be in any way superior to yours here."

This, naturally, gained the approval of Sir James, who raised his glass in salute to her good taste. Mr Darcy looked grave, eying her over the remains of an excellent saddle of mutton as if she were a troublesome maid caught with her fingers in the redcurrant sauce. Elizabeth ducked her head and made a *moue* at her plate. Could the man not put aside his fault-seeking for one dinner?

Galahad, however, only laughed. "'Tis not the very best time of year for pike, but there is one old fellow, ancient in the pike-ish world, who lives in Goodnestone's lake. He is reputed to be enormous, and has been sporting with fishermen for the last dozen years at least. I would be proud indeed if I could take him."

The conversation then became more general, Sir James chiming in with tales of fish he had caught or lost—those he had lost being of supernatural size, it appeared—while Mr Darcy and Galahad argued, with great civility, over the best time to take pike and how to fish a lake the size of Goodnestone's. In truth, Elizabeth and Aunt Iphy lost interest within a few minutes. True to their training as ladies, however, they gave the gentlemen civil attention and, on Elizabeth's part at least, privately resolved never to mention the sport again. Even in jest.

The following morning, Cousin Galahad collected Elizabeth after breakfast in his curricle, his fishing tackle stowed beneath the seat. His poor groom, hanging on the perch behind with one hand, used the other to keep the rods and baskets secure against the uneven road that more than once had them all bouncing uncomfortably in their places.

In between bounces, they talked. While Elizabeth steered the conversation far away from pike and their habits, they ranged over books and plays, before a chance remark had Elizabeth asking about Miss Darcy.

"What kind of girl is she, do you know?"

"Darcy has had guardianship of her these last five years at least, and hence I have met her a dozen times, I fancy. She is but fifteen or sixteen, and seems a shy, unassuming girl."

"She does not have her brother's pride? Young ladies of her age can be difficult, and she may have the true Darcy spirit."

Cousin Galahad chuckled. "Ah, it rankles still, does it?"

Elizabeth grimaced at the toes of her boots. That had been badly done. "I would not deplore his pride so much if he had not pricked mine. Forgive me. In truth, I do not dwell on it, but sometimes my teasing nature gets the better of me."

"There is nothing to forgive, Cousin. Your feelings are right, and just."

"You are kind, but resentment is a fault, indeed. He wounded my vanity, and I acknowledge some small-mindedness on my part in not forgetting it. Let us not speak of it!" Elizabeth frowned. "If she has been his ward for five years, he must have been young when he assumed the responsibility."

"No more than three-and-twenty when his father died."

"Was his mother living?"

"Sadly, Lady Anne died when Miss Darcy was born. He has had a difficult path to tread, with responsibility for an estate the size of Pemberley and the care of such a young child both thrust upon him. Though his cousin, Colonel Fitzwilliam, shares her guardianship, the colonel serves on the Peninsula, and her care falls mostly on Darcy."

Elizabeth turned and studied him. He had most of his attention on the road, which was indeed in need of repaving, and it was a moment before he turned his face towards her to smile and ask, in brotherly fashion, what maggot had got into her head now?

Used to such unmannerly language from the Lucas boys at home, Elizabeth said merely, "I was thinking that you admire him."

Cousin Galahad laughed. "I do. I knew him at school. From the first he was a staunch friend and ally. When my mother became ill in the year two, he was almost at the end of his time at school, about to go up to Cambridge, and I was a graceless hobbledehoy of seventeen. He was kindness itself. He understood what it was to lose a mother, and I do not believe I would have fared as well as I did without his aid. I do not forget his care and kindness."

Oh. Well, Elizabeth's resentments were all the more petty in the light of such intelligence. She swallowed a sigh at yet more evidence that she was a shallow creature in need of a great deal more goodness than she had shown so far. "That was indeed kind. I take it your schooling together is the basis for your close friendship?"

"Yes. He, Bingley and I were a set there. The pair of us were glad to join him in Cambridge later, and our friendship has deepened since then. I am aware he did not cover himself in glory at the deanery, but he truly is the best of good fellows."

"I am sure of it, and that he is the best of friends. I know he is a careful and thoughtful brother, and visits Miss Darcy every week to assure himself of her health and happiness. Miss Darcy doubtless repays his care by being a sweet and tractable young lady. I wish my youngest sister could be so described. She is the same age."

"And is she not sweet?"

"Lydia is neither shy nor unassuming, and most decidedly not sweet. Still, I am hardly sweet myself. I should not complain too much!" Although if she denied herself complaints, she should at least continue to pray Papa held firm in his resolution to amend Lydia's, and hence Kitty's, poor behaviour. "I am far too pert, I know."

"You are perfection, cousin."

Elizabeth beamed. "You are too partial, not to mention too…"

"Flirtatious?"

"Indeed. And yet, such a charming view of my quality quite lifts my spirits. I encourage you to share it with all and sundry. It would be rather grand to be proclaimed throughout the country."

"I will hire a herald as soon as may be," Galahad promised, and on that light note, they turned into the gates of Goodnestone and his discourse returned, distressingly, to fish.

LETTER: Miss Jane Bennet to her sister Elizabeth, August 1811

To Miss E Bennet
Wenderton Cottage, Wingham, Kent

Gracechurch Street
London
Tuesday, 13th August, 1811

My dearest Lizzy,

Your letters from Kent are delighting all of us here, and I can assure you, are most eagerly awaited. We can hear your voice as I read them aloud in the parlour of an evening.

Our uncle sends his thanks for your amusing account of Mr Palmer's attempt on the Goodnestone pike, remarking that pike are tricksy creatures and fearsome opponents to the 'compleat angler'. He sounded wistful. I had forgotten he is a keen fisherman, when he can manage a temporary escape from his responsibilities.

Our little cousins are indifferent to fish, but are most captivated with your descriptions of Kentish smugglers and their dire deeds—

as I have no doubt you intended—and they are, at this moment, playing at evading the excise men. Uncle found one or two small casks in his warehouse and the boys fell on them with delight as perfect for their purposes, which appear to be to smuggle brandy from France as often and as secretly as may be. When he is not in his office, Uncle is cajoled into playing the perfidious excise officer whom they must deceive and rout. Aunt is his deputy when his business keeps him too busy to chase smugglers all over the parlour, while I am the innkeeper's fair daughter who must be rescued by her lover, the chief smuggler, who is, of course, a handsome, charming rogue.

We have been very busy with the children, and attending the summer lectures at the Philosophical Society which have pleased our uncle...

... Well, I can dissemble no longer. You ask about Mr Bingley. I have not seen him since Mary's wedding. More than two months, now. I have called on his sisters, but have missed him every time. Around ten days ago, I received a brief note from Miss Bingley telling me the family were much engaged with friends, and were about to leave London for Bath. They will not be returning for several months. I visited Caroline to bid her farewell. She was not in good spirits, I fear, for she seemed surprised to see me and was quite distracted, and since she was on the point of going out herself, I left after ten minutes.

She told me they expected to stay with friends later in the year, and— well, Lizzy, then she told me she had hopes that one such visit would include the Darcys. I mentioned nothing of your being in Kent in company with Mr Darcy. I had no opportunity. For next she spoke of her brother's prodigious admiration for Miss Darcy, and of his lauding her beauty and accomplishments. Caroline confided her hopes of Miss Darcy being hereafter her sister. For, she said, all the circumstances favour his attachment to Miss Darcy, and it would be a welcome match to both families.

I kept my countenance. I do not know how, for I realised at once she believes her brother to be indifferent towards me and that his heart is given to Miss Darcy. I conclude she intended to put me on my guard, and the lessening of our acquaintance had been one means of her doing so. Nothing was, or could be, said in explicit terms, but I understood her. I wished her Godspeed for her travels, and took my leave. She was somewhat cold throughout my short visit. I understood that, too, Lizzy. She does not wish to further the connection.

Indeed, now I have had leisure to consider it, I am sure she has never wished for the connection at all. She has been mostly civil to me, but her manner in regard to our aunt and uncle has always been cold. It has borne upon me that I have allowed my hopes to blind me to her disdain for our family—and they worthy of the greatest respect!—and for that I am sorry. It was selfish of me to allow them to be mistreated so.

As you can imagine, my thoughts on the carriage-ride back to Gracechurch Street were of regret and chagrin. Thankfully, I was alone, but for the maid our aunt sent with me. I was able to compose myself, and not impose on our aunt's solicitude.

As for Mr Bingley himself, I do not know what to think. I thought he admired me, and I am saddened and mortified to learn that it was not so. I do not hold him to blame in any way. I have nothing with which to reproach him. He has said nothing to me he could not say to the merest acquaintance; made no promises, spoke no empty compliments. He is an amiable gentleman, and the fault must be mine. I misconstrued his affability for interest. Perhaps we have been too cloistered in Longbourn, and with a wider knowledge of the world I would not have made such a mistake. I hope Miss Darcy makes him happy.

Dearest Lizzy, I know you. I can see your mouth thinning down, so like Papa's, and your eyes glinting as you prepare to take up arms on my behalf. You were ever my most stalwart defender. I would not have you hold him at fault, or burn with indignation at what truly is not reprehensible conduct on his part, but my own folly. I have been cast down a trifle, I admit, but I will rally. I am rallying! I will think on it no more, because there is no sense in idle repining.

I can write no more now. My uncle bids me finish my letter and the servant will carry it to the post office with his own business letters and one to you from our aunt, to catch the evening mail.

Do not be anxious, Lizzy. He will be forgot, and I am well. All will be well.

Yours,

JB

LETTER: Miss Elizabeth Bennet to Miss Charlotte Lucas, August 1811

To Miss C Lucas
Lucas Lodge, Nr Meryton, Hertfordshire

Wenderton Cottage, Wingham, Kent
Wednesday, 14th August 1811

My dearest Charlotte,

Your letter is a very welcome pleasure, with all its budget of news and—dare I say it!—gossip. I am endeavouring to decide if I am sanguine or horrified that life in Meryton proceeds just as well without me as it does when I am there to grace it. I am sorry my absence is not more lamented. I had high hopes of reading that all my acquaintance are so cast down, the local shops have quite sold out of sackcloth and ashes, and the populace is having to send as far as St Albans to remedy the dearth of mourning attire.

I assure you that it is no spirit of resentful retaliation I say that, with the exception of missing my family and your own dear company, I am at home here in Kent. Canterbury is a pleasant place. Society here revolves around the cathedral close, giving the city something of the air of a friendly, smaller town where everyone of note is known to everyone else. You would like it here, I believe.

Aunt Iphy grows dearer to me by the day. She is a loving little creature, with such a gentle temperament that she is sweetening mine just as Jane does. I am well served by my friends and relations. You, my dear friend, improve me in the matter of practicality and calm good sense, while Jane and Aunt Iphy soften my acerbity. A much needed corrective on all fronts, I suspect!

My aunt is a little anxious to ensure I am well entertained. Today is market day, and we made our weekly expedition to Canterbury to shop, and join Aunt Iphy's friends in Chipperfield's little tea room. As I mentioned in a previous letter, these ladies are the wives of the cathedral dignitaries. She fears they are all too old for me (the youngest must be the age of my mamma) and that seeing them on every visit to Canterbury has become tedious. I assured her that they are delightful acquaintances, and their gossip is as amusing as listening to your mamma and mine.

For instance, this morning we discussed cathedral affairs (a little lofty for my taste)… the health of the ladies' families… prospects for their daughters, or the lack thereof (a complaint our mammas would share!)… the impending betrothal of the dean's daughter … the news of Miss Bridges at Goodnestone going soon to her grandmother in Town and her companion, who is much respected and admired, seeking a new situation (with most of the ladies wishful of snapping up Mrs Annesley's services for their own girls)… the difficulty of obtaining the exact shade of coquelicot feathers recommended by *La Belle Assemblée* in any place outside of a Bond Street modiste's… the problems with servants… and so on, and so on.

I like Miss Radcliffe the best of them. She is the sister of the archdeacon, and, you may recall, was with me when Mr Darcy failed to cover himself with social glory. She was horrified on my behalf. I have assured her Mr Darcy and I are now on better terms, but she shakes her head sadly if his name is mentioned. So very soothing! One can never have an excess of sympathy.

Aunt Iphy, by the by, thinks it all nonsense, since Mr Darcy walks out with me most mornings. He is a man of deep reserve, and seems ill-qualified to recommend himself in Society. Even after six weeks' acquaintance, I cannot quite make him out. Since I pride myself on taking a character, my failure adds to my chagrin. I am a sociable creature, as you know. I cannot imagine why an educated, sensible man is unable to be agreeable in company and is equally unable to begin a conversation. Also, I do wish he would not stare at me so. It is not admiration, as we know from his own lips. There must be something reprehensible in me, that I draw his notice.

15 August

I had not time to finish this yesterday before going up to the Hall, and since I wished to think about my response to parts of your last letter, resolved to take up my pen again this morning, determined to be honest with you. You will no more break my confidence than would Jane, I know.

You remarked upon the absence of my younger sisters at the Gouldings' dinner and the evening soirée held by the Harringtons. I noted your great restraint in demanding an explanation. I will reward you by confirming that Papa has judged Kitty and Lydia to be too young to be out in company at present.

I do not scruple to admit my relief. Indeed, you have witnessed my mortification often enough when their behaviour has not been what it ought, and have provided solace. You know our situation well enough, and know Mamma's concern is to see us well married before Longbourn passes out of Bennet hands forever, for she fears she will have little to live upon and nothing to spare to promote our interests. Her methods are not always the most refined, and while Mary's marriage to Mr Collins has soothed her fears, my two youngest sisters have grown with the notion that they must marry sooner rather than later. Papa wishes to remedy some of the ills this has wrought on their behaviour. I believe Mamma has agreed this is the best course for the entire family.

The society of a country town such as Meryton is not the *bon ton*, and our manners and ways of going on are not as restrained and refined. Even so, I think we Bennet girls came out before we were ready. Kitty and Lydia will now have the opportunity to learn how to comport themselves properly, and this opportunity must help them find their way in company with more decorum.

Papa is seeking a companion for them, to help them improve their accomplishments and so forth. Particularly the 'so forth'! I hope he finds someone of your stamp, my dear Charlotte, with your resolute and practical nature. You are an excellent overseer of Maria, who is becoming a prettily-behaved young lady. You know how heartily I have wished Kitty and Lydia more like her in their behaviour, and I do not say that merely to flatter you.

Whoever Papa chooses, my sisters cannot but benefit from a good instructress.

They are not philosophical about the change. I have had the most indignant letter from Lydia, so emphatic and emotional that those parts not blotted from what I deem to be angry tears, were so heavily scored beneath the words, she has torn the paper in places. She must have needed to stop and mend her pen frequently.

Whatever else one might think of Lydia, she is no fool. She has guessed that Papa's actions to take her and Kitty to task have been instigated by me, and has no difficulty in stigmatising me as the most horrid and uncaring sister in the whole history of the world. Everything is my fault: that Papa has refused them permission to attend assemblies or anything more than family dinners for the foreseeable future, and, worst of all, has banned all officers from the house.

Well, I am content to bear the stigma, if I may gain younger sisters who are more in the pattern of your Maria!

Oh, Charlotte. How I would welcome your good sense and kind advice at this moment! I was about to seal this and send it to the Dog Inn to be put into the post, when the maid appeared with letters. I had one from Jane.

Poor Jane! I had high hopes of getting the best of news of her progress in London, but instead have the worst. The Bingley family has left for Bath, it seems, with no word to Jane from Mr Bingley. Not one word of leave-taking or regret. He is gone without a backward glance, leaving his sister to pretend concern.

Even Jane remarked upon Miss Bingley's determination to break the connection—we may imagine that every word the creature spoke was designed to flay Jane's sensibilities and turn her aside.

I am half angry, half despondent. More than half angry. Jane is so good, unassuming and gentle! To be used in such a manner! It is beyond anything. Her anxiety must be painful, but we both know she will attempt to hide her distress with cheerfulness and her usual tranquillity.

How detestable and untrustworthy men can be! How callow, weak, and unstable! Yet you will recall Jane's opinion that he is a very gentlemanlike man, educated and refined. It may well be so. She is the sweetest and kindest soul alive, and prone to think the best of everyone whether they deserve it or not, yet her judgement is generally sound. Also, he is a friend of Cousin Galahad and Mr Darcy, and an old schoolfellow. Yet affability and charming manners do not prevent a young man easily falling in love, and just as easily forgetting. How we ladies are taught to blame ourselves! Jane assumes she mistook his affability for more than the gentleman intended.

Charlotte, what am I to do to comfort her?

You know her gentle nature, her modest diffidence. I am aware your opinion has ever been that her reserve might leave a gentleman in doubt about her attachment, but she cannot be more than she is, and if Mr Bingley is unable to see her regard then he is not only inconstant, he is a fool.

And that sister of his, who must be full of malice and duplicity... Well, a lady cannot not speak her opinion of such a person. I should not even think it.

My very great comfort here is Aunt Iphy. She saw at once how I was affected by Jane's letter, and on my telling her the whole, determined that Jane will benefit from a change in society. Jane is to come here, Aunt Iphy says, to consider, and settle herself and, yes, to rally her spirits and remember her own worth, which is more than a thousand Bingleys. I have written to Jane and my Aunt Gardiner to this effect, and as soon as we have Jane's agreement, we will speak to my cousins to arrange her visit.

How I wish you were here to help me restore Jane to contentment and happiness! How I wish, too, I had a greater store of your good sense and practicality to help me. I must rely on my own resources, and am resolved to console Jane to the best of my poor abilities.

Write soon, and comfort us both,

EB

CHAPTER NINETEEN

To Sublime A Sense

Beware of too sublime a sense
Of your own worth and consequence
— Cowper, *Moral*

"Darcy! Are you asleep?"

"What?"

"I thought you must be dozing, you stared so blankly at me. I said, I wish to discuss my cousin's visit and seek your advice."

They were in the room Palmer used as a study or a sitting room. Lined with his Cambridge books and his gun cases, it was the typical retreat of the educated country gentleman. Very like Darcy's own at Pemberley. They sat at each side of the fireplace. Palmer half lay in his chair, his feet propped up on the fender, holding a short-stemmed (and now empty) brandy glass in one hand and tapping on his upper leg with the fingers of the other.

Brought back to alertness, Darcy apologised for his distraction, and added "Advice about what?"

Palmer turned to Darcy and grimaced. "You will have seen, I think, that my father is developing some expectations regarding my cousin."

Darcy nodded. Sir James's approbation was marked now, and he could not be more indulgent and affectionate if Miss Bennet was his own daughter.

Palmer blew out a sigh and straightened, the heels of his boots clattering on the floorboards. "I like Elizabeth. I like her a great deal. But I have not known her two full months yet. Far too short a time to truly consider if we would suit."

Darcy struggled to say, with equanimity intact, "She is an estimable lady."

Palmer shot him a look eloquent of his disbelief. "Well, you have changed that tune. Your opinion at the deanery was sharply different."

"I have apologised for my incivility."

"Yes. I am sorry to raise it again. That was ungenerous of me."

"However, I stand by some of what I said then. Her family is undistinguished, and not of a condition equivalent to yours or mine. Is not Bennet's estate entailed to my aunt's cleric, who has married a younger daughter? Even so, Miss Bennet's circumstances will reduce further on Mr Bennet's death."

Palmer shook his head, his smile faint. "Darcy, we are gentlemen. She is the daughter of one. Mr Bennet's family has held Longbourn as long as we Palmers have been here in Kent. So far, we are all equal."

Darcy responded with a raised eyebrow.

"Yes, there is some disparity in wealth," Palmer acknowledged, "but in birth? Very little divides us. Neither you nor I are anything higher than gentry ourselves. We Palmers pride ourselves on our long history, though we are but baronets. We are not peers. We are merely upper gentry with the right to put a 'Sir' before our names. Your mother was the daughter of an earl, but your father was a country gentleman of substantial means, but no title. Do not disdain her for her birth, Darcy."

"I do not! I meant..." Darcy did not know what he meant. "Very well, I accept Mr Bennet is all that is unexceptionable. He is a gentleman at least, but his wife… Miss Bennet has relatives actively in trade."

"And relatives here. She is one of us, now and forever, no matter whether or not she and I make a match of it. And do not forget how quickly and easily our connections have welcomed her. Sir Brook Bridges, I mean. He is a jovial fellow, but does not claim the entire world as cousins by marriage."

Darcy inclined his head. "That is mitigation, indeed."

And it was. To claim kinship with an old and venerable family, one who had held its baronetcy since Tudor times, did lighten some of the stain of trade. She was less ineligible than he had first considered.

"Moreover, Darcy, Bingley is far closer to trade than she is, yet you count him as a friend and countenance those sisters of his. Elizabeth is a gentlewoman. The Bingley ladies are not, though doubtless their fortunes redress the balance."

"I am not mercenary, Palmer! I do not weigh everything against a man's bank balance or a lady's dowry. A lack of fortune is not a hindrance where there is true affection."

"No, indeed. And I do not need to marry for a fortune, Darcy, any more than you do."

"You imply I am—"

"Top lofty? High in the instep? You certainly can be. I wish you were less closed to the world than you are, my friend. Not every new acquaintance is unworthy of your notice, or to be treated with distrust and hostility. You demand that people prove themselves, but you view their efforts with suspicion and disdain. You may discourage the toad-eaters, but also those who would otherwise become friends and enrich your life."

"I do not disdain Miss Bennet." Darcy's throat felt thick, and he coughed to clear it. "I acknowledge that my reserve may lead me to appear more disdainful than I am."

"It does, indeed. It grieves me, because I know the good man you are beneath."

"Enough of me." Darcy swallowed the last of his brandy. "So, will you pursue her?"

"I will continue to deepen my acquaintance with my cousin, and see where it leads." Palmer rose, and walked to a walnut side table to retrieve the brandy bottle. He refilled their glasses with a generous hand and resumed his seat. "However, matters are complicated by Iphy's request to my father this morning. In two days' time, our coach, two footmen and our housekeeper's niece will be going up to London, to collect Miss Jane Bennet and bring her to Aunt Iphy's for a visit."

"The beauty?"

"Bingley's... well, what should I call her? He has an interest, but I cannot guess if his heart or honour are engaged."

"Why is she coming?"

"I had the impression she is unhappy in London."

"But what of Bingley?"

A shrug may not be considered mannerly, but it conveyed a wealth of feeling. "I know no more than you. Like you, he has a standing invitation to Wingham, and I hoped he might take advantage of it while you are here. I wrote to him to remind him, not long after we arrived in Kent. I have not heard from him, however."

"He is an irregular correspondent, at best."

"Assuredly. I had assumed Miss Jane's company has left him without the time to write to his old friends, but if she is coming here to visit..." Palmer quaffed his brandy in a single mouthful. "What of Bingley? She is indeed a beauty. And altogether, her arrival here is the most damnable complication."

Yes. It certainly was.

What an execrable place to prepare, this cramped room at the Falstaff Inn, with his valet ten miles away at Wingham! Valeting for himself was acceptable in most dire circumstances, but this madcap notion of Palmer's to bring Miss Bennet and Miss Palmer into Canterbury to meet the beautiful sister and then bear them all off to the monthly assembly subscription ball... 'madcap' was the politest way Darcy could term it, certain Palmer was entirely dicked in the nob. He himself must have been bosky when he agreed. Too much brandy, he fancied.

Miss Ben— Miss Elizabeth, that is. With her elder sister's arrival, he must remember to call her by her given name now, and quell the ridiculous pleasure it gave to do so. Well, Miss Elizabeth had quickly fallen in with Palmer's plan, citing the benefits of such a diversion in cheering her sister. No one explained why the elder Miss Bennet required such consideration, but Miss Elizabeth was enthusiastic. Perhaps Miss Palmer had a store of French brandy as potent as the one Palmer kept secreted in his study. No other explanation came to mind when considering everyone's irrationality. They must all have been bosky.

Why in heaven's name had Miss Jane chosen to arrive on the fourth Saturday of the month? August had thirty other days to choose from, none of which were afflicted by Canterbury's monthly assembly. The inconvenience was considerable.

That morning, the day of Jane Bennet's arrival in Canterbury, the party had set out to meet her. She would not be surprised by the attention. Palmer had sent a groom up the London road the previous day to intercept the coach and deliver a letter from Miss Elizabeth explaining all the arrangements. Palmer's plan was comprehensive, and carried out as so:

Miss Elizabeth had driven the gig into Canterbury with old Miss Palmer on the seat beside her and a valise holding their evening gowns strapped on behind. Miss Palmer would act as duenna for the evening's festivities in the assembly rooms. Miss Elizabeth's groom-cum-footman (Jack something-or-other, was it not?) had taken the groom's perch at the back of the gig. Jack was a large addition to a small gig, and Darcy, who rode alongside with Palmer, blessed the carriage builder for ensuring it was well balanced and stable. Jack's task was to take the gig home, leaving the ladies to await Miss Jane at the inn under Palmer's and Darcy's protection. Following the ball, they would all travel home to Wingham in the coach conveying Miss Jane from London, accompanied by two armed grooms. Palmer had hired a dozen link-boys with lanterns, to light their way.

It rivalled one of Wellesley's battle plans for complexity. Such a to-do in order to dance a reel!

He did not know who was the more foolish: Palmer and Miss Elizabeth for falling upon the notion with such delight, or he himself for agreeing to it. It must have been the brandy. He made himself a promise to eschew it for Madeira for the remainder of his stay.

"I am not at my ease at a ball, Palmer." Darcy tugged the sleeves of his coat into place.

"My dear fellow, I could not be more astonished if you told me the sun rose in the east! I am aware that dancing is not your métier. But consider what an opportunity this gives you to mend fences with my cousin Elizabeth. You can atone for your sins by taking her out for the first set."

"Leaving the beauty for you, I take it?"

Palmer merely laughed. Damn the man.

CHAPTER TWENTY
Chasing The Glowing Hours

On with the dance! let joy be unconfin'd;
No sleep till morn, when Youth and Pleasure meet
To chase the Glowing Hours with Flying feet.
— Byron, *Childe Harold's Pilgrimage*

The Palmer coach conveyed them all from the inn to Guildhall Street and the Assembly Rooms as evening fell. The main dancing room was a spacious, stylish apartment. The small orchestra sat in a minstrels' gallery at the far end, and doors below the gallery led, Darcy surmised, to the card and supper rooms. It was elegant in the provincial manner, though not reaching Town standards.

"Rather more genteel than Meryton can boast." Miss Elizabeth surveyed the arrangements with open amusement. "We are quite outshone, Jane! We must be awed in our attitude, to show our appreciation of our good fortune."

Miss Bennet laughed, and Palmer smiled at Miss Elizabeth's affected astonishment. "So I should think, cousin. Canterbury is a rich city. Its citizens expect the best, and enjoy having their taste admired by visitors."

"I daresay if we fail in that duty, we shall be chased from the town by an angry mob bearing flaming-pitch torches— Ah, here is the first!"

"Mr Dowton," Palmer murmured. "The master of ceremonies here. I am sure he means to greet you, cousin, not immolate you."

Mr Dowton was out of character for a baying mob. In early middle age, he was conspicuous for a full head of copious curls of an odd, flat brown shade, as well as a youthful complexion that must owe its bloom to the rouge pot (or the brandy bottle? Kent was awash with the stuff, thanks to the Gentlemen). Mr Dowton greeted them with poised grace, and a conscious politeness. If Miss Palmer's incoherent remarks were to be correctly understood, he was the model of deportment, revered for his elegant, civil manners. He had nary a whiff of pitch about him.

Darcy sniffed the air.

Nor the scent of brandy. The rouge pot it was, then.

"How like Sir William Lucas at home," Miss Bennet observed when their party had returned the greeting and gone on further into the ballroom. The air of serenity Darcy had observed at the theatre, weeks ago, appeared more marked. She met all of Palmer's sallies with a smile, but it had such calmness, such a lack of emotion, it suggested that while her manners were open and engaging, she would not be easily touched.

"Oh Jane, how can you say so? Sir William's manners may be less genteel, but they are genuine and he is sincerely good-natured." Miss Elizabeth's laugh became a slight smirk. "Moreover, Sir William's hair is his own, what he has left of it. I have no confidence we may say the same of Mr Dowton."

"Lizzy!" Miss Palmer's tone held more indulgence than remonstrance, and even this faint rebuke faded into delight at finding an old friend in the crowd of tabbies seated at one side of the ballroom. She bore the Misses Bennet off with her to introduce Miss Jane. Darcy and Palmer followed.

This sort of social occasion was the reason Darcy thought often of building himself a hermitage in one of Pemberley's wilder and least accessible corners. It was a form of purgatory to stand there, forced to listen to elderly ladies twittering and clucking worse than a henhouse under siege by a fox. Palmer was in his element; making the ladies blush and charming them into complaisance, then cleverly cutting out Miss Bennet from the pack and focusing all his attention on her to provoke her smiles and blushes.

Miss Elizabeth turned from the conversation and smiled at Darcy. "You are truly ill at ease in situations such as this, are you not?"

"I have not the talent... My ear is not attuned to catch the tone of the conversation, and hence I do not appear interested in people's concerns, particularly in situations such as this, where the conversations are of, well, little weight. As you know, I can converse readily in other circumstances."

Why did her smile broaden? He had not intended to be amusing.

"You have heard me play the piano," she said.

"And taken great pleasure in it."

Her eyebrows lifted, her eyes widening. Affectation, surely. She must know he enjoyed listened to her music very much indeed. But she answered only, "You are very kind. But the truth is, Mr Darcy, my talents are middling. Aunt Iphy tells me I do not practise enough. She is quite right. I do not. By choice, since I take pleasure in many other pursuits, but the point is I should practise far more than I do."

"And you would have me do the same. Practise to be more sociable?"

"The easier you are in company, sir, the more pleasant it will be for you. People respond in the manner with which they are treated. Be kind and show an interest in small social concerns— feigned if necessary, as long as you do it competently!—and they will repay you with friendship and courtesy. Remain aloof, and they will avoid interaction, partly because they will believe you wish it and partly to avoid being, well, a little frozen by your manner. Your unease makes you a little stiff, you know, and many will misinterpret that and think you consider yourself above your company. So, yes. Practise."

Darcy could only laugh through the sting of her criticism. "My aunt De Bourgh would say exactly the same thing! Well, I will take your advice on the matter, and strive to be more like Palmer, who is always at ease and puts others so. I will begin tonight." Darcy offered her a bow. "May I have the pleasure of the first two dances, Miss Elizabeth?"

She smiled and gracefully inclined her head. "Of course, sir. Thank you."

He covered the unexpected surge of warmth with another bow, somewhat deeper this time, and murmured his thanks for the honour. He stood silent and relieved at her side. Fool that he was. He should take her advice to heart and at least feign an interest in… what were the ladies discussing? Maidservants, and their perfidious followers who came calling after dusk.

No.

He could not feign an interest in that. Not even to win approval in Miss Elizabeth's bright eyes.

He would remain mute and aloof. It was what he did best.

The first of the set was a fast, longways country dance, with the participants organised in groups of three couples. As the third couple in their triplet, they had the opportunity to talk while the first two couples danced. To Miss Elizabeth's amusement, Darcy confessed his disinterest in the evils of maidservants and their followers.

"It does seem a fixed notion in the eyes of the ladies that a maid should not have her head turned by undesirable followers." She quite failed to look solemn, as they waited for the first couple to cast off in the dance and allow them to progress up the set. Indeed her eyes were bright with laughter. "No amount of 'But ma'am, I assure you, he is my cousin John!' appeases a strict mistress. It must be very hard on maids to deny their families, but cousins seem oddly prevalent."

"And hence undesirable."

Miss Elizabeth smirked and nodded. "Perfidious creatures!"

She set to her neighbour while Darcy set to his, and they exchanged sides in a series of small, skipping steps.

"An axiom for all ladies, perhaps," said Darcy, when they had set again and returned to their original side of the dance, "to be careful of having their heads turned."

"And be careful when determining who may or may not be undesirable? Quite right!"

"I am sure it is a source of constant anxiety."

Miss Elizabeth smirked again, and they progressed up the line to take second position, preparing to set and exchange again. "A source of grief and disquiet, sir, in the lives of all. Not only maiden aunts."

He laughed aloud. Would she consider her own words? Cousins could indeed be very undesirable. He hoped she realised it.

He danced next with the beauty. Miss Jane Bennet would bear the palm in Society's estimation: her golden-haired, blue-eyed loveliness was all the rage. And yet, she was not the match of her sister. An honest man must acknowledge Miss Elizabeth did not possess the classic beauty of her sister, though she was a very pretty girl and her eyes were particularly fine. But she was brighter, wittier, more charming, altogether sharper-edged and, well, invigorating. Darcy had no doubt that Miss Jane would prove to be a peaceful, restful companion. Elizabeth, though, was bracing, spirited, and as rousing as a splash of ice water down the back of the collar when a man was least expecting it. She was not dull. Darcy could not imagine a man yawning when she was present to spark the world into animation.

Miss Bennet did not have the same sort of liveliness. They had a careful conversation concerning the splendour of the rooms, the impressive arrangements for supper to be glimpsed through a pair of double doors under the balcony where the musicians sat, the skill of said musicians (although they winced in unison at an unmelodious scrape from the second violin), the number of couples… Altogether, an unexceptional, correct conversation. Its value to him was not that it gave him any insight into Miss Bennet's mind and character, for its very banality failed in that respect, but it undoubtedly could be classed as the practice Miss Elizabeth had enjoined on him and hence could be treated with due seriousness on that head.

He enjoyed two small snippets of their conversation. Palmer and Miss Elizabeth were in the adjacent triplet of the set, and Miss Bennet, watching them dance with a fond smile curving her mouth, said, "How well Lizzy looks! Kent has been good for her, I think." He was able to agree with tolerable composure that Miss Elizabeth looked very well indeed. And when a moment or two later, Miss Bennet added, with a light laugh, "And how she loves to dance! She is the lightest on her feet of all of us. She was always the first to submit to our youngest sisters when they begged her to teach them the steps. I have seen them dance around the parlour many times!", he was assailed with the charming mental image of a younger Miss Elizabeth patiently teaching her sisters, and agreed she was a graceful dancer indeed.

"A true devotee of Terpsichore."

But Miss Bennet looked rather blank, before murmuring something in agreement. He doubted she caught his meaning. Miss Elizabeth, though, would have been arch, and have something witty to say in response. Two sisters, not greatly alike in either looks or character. Bonded in affection, yes, but he could see no other great similarity.

He returned Miss Bennet to the care of their chaperone, feeling a faint sense of relief. Miss Palmer, still occupied with her friends, greeted them with a complacent smile. Palmer and Miss Elizabeth's return elicited a brighter one. For a few moments, they shared their impressions of the assembly so far: company excellent, music tolerable, dancing enjoyable. Commonplace and unmemorable, every word. The enlivening qualities were Miss Elizabeth's eyes, bright with amusement at, Darcy suspected, his discomfiture with such small talk.

"It is a science," she told him, while the others chattered about the fashions on show, "requiring, I grant you, some ingenuity and imagination."

"And a spark to ignite it into a sprightly, bright conversation. Something I fear I lack. I might try to introduce and element of literary or classical lore into conversation—"

"Oh, a very refined approach, sir. Perfectly fitting for a gentleman of fashion and address!" Miss Elizabeth's saucy smile could not be bettered. But such good nature imbued her archness, such implied camaraderie, he took no offence.

"I attempted it. I cannot be certain my meaning was caught, though."

"You are doing excellently well for a novice." Her gaze flickered to her sister, but her smile was unwavering.

"I will continue to practise." When he glanced up, Darcy noted Mr Dowton, the master of ceremonies, making his way towards their group. "But in conversation only. I prefer not to dance unless I am acquainted with the lady."

Miss Elizabeth's smile broadened. "Very well, Mr Darcy. Easy manners, like any skill, must be acquired gradually, I suppose. If you concentrate tonight on conversation, why, by the next assembly, you will progress to allowing introductions to strange ladies in order to escort them into the dance."

"I find myself at a great disadvantage vying with you, Miss Elizabeth. You outmatch me when it comes to polished manners, not to mention brilliancy of wit, repartee, and liveliness. You will be a stern tutor, I fear."

"I am not such a paragon, sir." The faint blush on her cheek was delightful.

He stepped back to allow Mr Dowton to entreat the young ladies to allow him to introduce several gentlemen desirous of the honour of a set. Palmer had already departed to ask an acquaintance to dance, with only a quirked eyebrow in Darcy's direction. He knew better than to importune Darcy.

For an hour or more, Darcy wandered the edges of the assembly room, his attention on the dancers, speaking between sets with the ladies or Palmer, when he could find him. He disobeyed Miss Elizabeth's exhortation to continue his practising. Instead, he weighed another knotty problem, turning it over and over in his mind.

Could he, in all conscience, ask her for another dance without raising expectations he would not, *could* not, meet?

He scrutinised the dancers, all merrily making their way through an energetic cotillion, searching for her. She wore the same pale green dress as at the deanery affair, and had flowers in her hair… There. She was dancing in the first triplet of dancers, stretching out a hand to take her partner's—

Good God.

Wickham.

She was dancing with George Wickham.

CHAPTER TWENTY-ONE

Not Naturally Honest

Though I am not naturally honest,
I am sometimes so by chance.
— Shakespeare, *The Winter's Tale*

This assembly was bigger and more fashionable than those Elizabeth attended at Meryton. The principles were the same: dancing and a little mild flirting were the order of the day. Assemblies were one of the few occasions when young people could learn more of each other. Awaiting their turn in the dance, they could converse in relative privacy, the music preventing them from being widely overheard, and, indeed, their fellow dancers were usually more intent on either their own flirtations or following the figures, than heeding their neighbours.

Elizabeth accepted Mr Darcy's invitation to the first dance. She had come close to scolding him for his manners, and it was forbearing of him to return her impertinence with courtesy. She would repay his generosity with civility of her own, and say no more about his ease, or lack of it, in company.

Jane danced the first with Cousin Galahad. He had so obviously been struck with admiration when Elizabeth introduced them earlier that day, she had preserved her countenance with difficulty. She would have dearly loved to laugh at his gallantries. Jane had met them with her usual composure, but Elizabeth hoped Galahad's honest admiration would soothe her sister's bruised spirits and show her that though one gentleman had proved fickle, the fault did not lie with her attractions and her pure, gentle character. Elizabeth could consign her to their cousin's care with an easier heart.

Not an entirely easy heart, however.

Jane looked well; better than Elizabeth had expected, but of course Jane would put on the best possible face for Aunt Iphy and Cousin Galahad. She would not wish to make them uneasy with a display of feeling, and would show them only her most complacent manners. No stranger would ever surmise she suffered.

But still, Jane's smile was tighter, her eyes a little less bright, her whole demeanour more guarded. Jane's composure and her uniformly cheerful manner hid the strength of her emotions from the notice of the impertinent, but she was more confined and less open even than usual.

Jane was unhappy. And Elizabeth had known it since her sister stepped out of the coach onto the cobbled courtyard of the inn in Canterbury. Jane could not hide from her what she successfully concealed from the rest of the world. Though Jane would never ask for comfort or impose her sorrow on another, Elizabeth determined to soothe her into contentment again. Elizabeth regretted that they must dance, pretending to be blithe and carefree, and kept an anxious scrutiny of her sister until her attention was caught by Mr Darcy and she must turn her mind to watching her steps.

Despite her cares over Jane, she enjoyed the dance more than she had anticipated. Mr Darcy unbent a great deal as they talked, and showed a more light-hearted facet of his character than she would have suspected of him. The second set she danced with Galahad, while Mr Darcy danced with Jane. Subsequent sets were the province of the young gentlemen introduced by the master of ceremonies.

Her earlier partners had been the younger son of a local landowner whose estate was to the south of Canterbury, and the nephew of one of the cathedral's minor canons. Her current partner was, like herself, a visitor to Kent.

"Did I see you dancing with Darcy of Pemberley earlier?"

The abrupt question startled her. Mr... Wickham, was it? Yes. Wickham. Until now, his conversation had been easy and engaging, even charming, and focused on impressions of Kent they might share, both being strangers to its attractions.

Elizabeth did the little skip and jump the dance required of her and delayed replying until she and her partner returned to their places to await their turn in the dance. "Yes. Mr Darcy is the guest of my cousin at Wingham Hall." She eyed Mr Wickham with more interest than she had felt before his unexpected question. "Do you know him, sir?"

Mr Wickham had an attractive smile. It crinkled into the corner of his eyes until his whole face joined in the enterprise. But his smile now and his tone were both rueful. "I do, indeed. I hail from Derbyshire, Miss Elizabeth. Darcy and I were boys together."

"You must wish to greet him. I would be happy—"

"Ah... no. No. I thank you. We... Ah..." He stopped and grimaced. "I am sorry to say our friendship languished some time ago. The disparity between our stations that seemed as nothing when we were boys, is a chasm now we are men. I am not... well, I shall be honest and tell you my father was Pemberley's steward, from which you will understand I am not at all of his sphere. But I was his father's godson, you see. Old Mr Darcy was very fond of me and did a great deal for my comfort and advancement. The current Mr Darcy resented that interest, I believe."

All Elizabeth considered it prudent to say was, "Indeed?"

"And how does Kent find Mr Darcy? I am certain, from my knowledge of him, I can predict with some accuracy how Darcy has found Kent. His good opinion is bestowed but rarely, and he does not trouble to hide his disdain. He does not put himself out to be popular."

Elizabeth did not quite miss her step, although she was a crotchet-beat behind where she should be in the dance.

Not tempting enough for me to give consequence to a provincial nobody. A nobody. Not tempting.

She forced the memory away. Mr Darcy had apologised. She had forgotten it and put it behind her. She would forget it, that painful echo of her mother's constant refrain of "You are nothing to Jane!"

A nobody. Prettyish, but not tempting enough.

Oh, enough! It was nothing then, and must be nothing now. She was not so resentful a creature she could not forget and forgive.

It appeared, though, Mr Wickham did indeed know Mr Darcy well. He had described Mr Darcy's conduct to a fine hair.

Mr Wickham laughed and did not wait for her to reply. "I am persuaded I am right. After all, you do not dismiss my contention that Darcy's manners are not conciliatory! Now, I am a little acquainted with your cousin Palmer, who has always been very gentlemanly. However, I know Darcy a great deal more familiarly. His behaviour does not surprise me. You will have doubtless noted he places a great deal of value on his position in Society, and weighs everyone in the scale against it. They always fall short."

She smiled at the other gentleman in her set, as they made a quarter turn to face each other, reached out and touched both hands together. Chassé, bourette, quarter turn back, full poussette... and she faced Mr Wickham again. She touched her hand to his briefly and they were returned to their places in the set.

She had yet to answer him. "Mr Darcy is a gentleman of some consequence, I believe."

He needed no further encouragement. "Oh yes. His uncle is the Earl of Ashbourne. That relation is the source of his pride and— dare I say it!—conceit. You must have seen it for yourself. He can never hide it for long!" A soft snort, almost unheard under cover of the music of Lady Harriet Clive's Favourite. "We are not at all alike. He thinks my ways too careless. I think his too fixed on his position."

Another chassé and bourette.

"And yet, I have observed Mr Darcy can please where he chooses," Elizabeth said.

"Of course! But how seldom does he choose it! I am grieved to see it if I am honest. He was always a serious boy, but he was kinder in our youth. He has grown ever more severe and judgemental. He weighs everyone and everything in the balance against what he feels is his own worth."

"Do not we all, sir? I know of no other means of judging where I stand. If I have no sense of my own worth and value, how am I to determine the worth and value of others?"

"But you, I am sure, are all kindness! I have no sense in you of overweening pride. A lady such as yourself must view the world with generosity and compassion and goodness. You would not scandalously deny a man his inheritance because he is below you in consequence. And yet—" He stopped and shook his head, sighing. "I will say no more. I had a great deal of love and respect for the older Mr Darcy, and for his sake, I try to forgive the son everything, though it grieves me to the soul that he has been the means of disappointing my hopes and disgracing the memory of his father. For the father's sake, I will say nothing."

What in heaven's name did he expect her to say to such statements? What could he mean by mentioning such matters to a complete stranger, met by chance in a dance? What was the man about? Propriety demanded reserve, for her to meet such odd behaviour with cool dignity, as if Mr Wickham had spoken of nothing more contentious than the weather. Yet, common civility demanded some sort of response.

"Saying nothing, sir, would be the path of wisdom and enlightened self-interest. One does not wish to be such a poor creature as to be constantly complaining against life's reverses."

Mr Wickham's blink and slight recoil suggested he was disconcerted, as if a soft lap dog, from whom he had expected nothing but fawning, had snapped and shown its teeth. Had he expected her to be all complaisance and no opinions of her own? His tales likely won him sympathy and kindness from the ladies, and perhaps he had expected he would win from her the same soft sighs and doe-eyed glances.

When the musicians scraped their way to the double bar of the coda, it was with the sudden lightness of relief that she offered her curtsey at the end of their set.

"Miss Elizabeth." Mr Darcy was behind her.

She turned with more haste than grace, and greeted him. He nodded to her and turned his attention to her partner, whose smirk was now more sneering than ever.

"George." Mr Darcy inclined his head.

The informality wiped away the smirk. Elizabeth understood the slight: Mr Wickham was not worthy of the respectful greeting bestowed upon a gentleman, or of anything that would mark him as Mr Darcy's equal.

Mr Wickham suppressed his grimace quickly, and returned the nod with one of his own. "An unexpected pleasure, Darcy."

"I am sure. You have business in Kent?"

"A friend told me of an opportunity to make my way in life, and pursuing it has brought me briefly to Canterbury. I leave tomorrow." Mr Wickham bowed to Elizabeth. "I must be grateful for the chance to enjoy the great pleasure of dancing with some very beautiful ladies."

Mr Darcy ignored this sally. "Are you for London? I recall you telling me when we last met that you had made your home there."

"I will return to Town soon. And you?"

"I intend to remain in Kent for some time yet. Miss Elizabeth, I should return you to Miss Palmer's care." Mr Darcy waited until she put her hand on his arm. "Safe travels, George."

The two men stared at each other, then Mr Wickham offered Elizabeth an extravagant bow. "It was an honour to dance with you, Miss Elizabeth. Preserve your sense of worth, I beseech you. It is an essential defence against pride and conceit."

Mr Darcy's smile was faint. "Oh, that old gibe! You know my answer. Where there is real superiority of mind and character, pride will always be under good regulation."

"You have not changed." Mr Wickham's smirk was back. He added a nod, and a bow, and an expressive, "Mr Darcy."

"Goodbye, George. I wish you well with your enterprise." Mr Darcy returned a shallow bow, and he and Elizabeth turned away. They walked towards the place beneath the musician's gallery where Aunt Iphy sat with her friends. "I am sorry you were imposed upon by the likes of George Wickham, Miss Elizabeth.

Incidents such as this confirm the risks of public balls where anyone with a modicum of a gentlemanly manners may intrude on the notice of their betters. I hope you are not too discomposed by him."

"No. Not at all." It was a lie, and she suspected he knew it.

"He did not importune you in any way?"

"He… Mmmn… he had some sly observations to share. I could not make out him out."

Mr Darcy's little huff of laughter sounded three parts exasperation. "In that, Miss Elizabeth, you are in good company. I have never been able to make out George Wickham, from our boyhood onwards. Our characters, and manners, and everything about us are too dissimilar in every respect."

Elizabeth smiled. "I had noticed."

CHAPTER TWENTY-TWO

Never Told

Never seek to tell thy love
Love that never told can be
— Blake, *Never Seek*

Elizabeth had to wait for an opportunity to speak to Jane about the encounter. They had been too weary on their return to Aunt Iphy's house after the assembly on Saturday night to do more than embrace, assure each other of their joy at being reunited, and fall into their respective beds to sleep away their exhaustion.

They spent all Sunday after church in company at the Hall. Elizabeth chafed at the lack of privacy to talk with Jane, but delighted over her sister's reception. Sir James had greeted Elizabeth with his usual partiality when they walked up to the house to introduce Jane to him, calling her his Little Miss and tapping her cheek fondly after kissing it in greeting. As she had told Jane, he treated her more and more as a well-loved granddaughter.

"This is your pretty Jane, Lizzy? Aye, and so you are devilish pretty, my dear! Not a whit like your grandmother, though. You must favour your mother."

Jane answered with a serene curtsey and "I am told I favour the Gardiner family, sir. Lizzy is the one most like our grandmother's portrait at home."

Sir James had smiled most lovingly on Elizabeth, and took her hand to bow over it. "Aye. She is Eliza's image. Gal, we should show your cousins Eliza's portrait."

"I will be delighted to show it to them, sir. Darcy and I had some thoughts of seeking the portrait out to show Elizabeth."

"Well." Sir James coughed in a deprecating manner. "I had it returned to a place in the gallery last week. For too many years it was stowed away in an upstairs hall in the guest wing. It is long past time that Eliza came back to the family where she always belonged. Come, now! We should not spend more of this conversation on such ancient history. Tell me of your London adventures, Miss Jane, and we shall decide what we may do while you are here to keep you entertained and happy."

"I am happy to be in Lizzy's company, sir."

And Elizabeth could only laugh, because Jane—dear Jane!—always knew what to say and do to make everyone comfortable and promote harmony, for she could not have said anything more calculated to please their elderly cousin. They spent the day very pleasantly indeed, and Elizabeth hoped that some of Jane's disquiet over Mr Bingley had been assuaged by Galahad's sincere admiration. In any event, Jane spoke more philosophically than Elizabeth had anticipated about her London stay that evening, when they at last had the opportunity for a little private discussion before retiring for the night.

"I am more and more convinced, Lizzy, that I mistook Mr Bingley's affability and his cheerful, sociable disposition for more than he intended. I am glad I have enough presence of mind not to show chagrin or disappointment in public."

"You behave very well. Perhaps you are a little too guarded at times, but no one seeing you would doubt the propriety of your manners."

"I would have done better to show more of what I feel, you mean, and show more clearly my regard? Our dear aunt said something of the same, and Charlotte Lucas believes it too, I know. I assure you, though, I did so as much as I am able."

"I know."

"If I am honest, Lizzy, I am sorriest about the loss of an opportunity to discover if Mr Bingley could be a true prospect for me. The depth of my regard for him... well, I am not certain I know that for myself. I have never fancied myself in love before, you see. I think him an amiable gentleman, to be sure, but I comfort myself with the knowledge I am not in so deep that I cannot find my peace. He will be forgotten, and everything will be as it ever was."

Elizabeth sighed. "I am sorry, Jane. Not only for the loss of Mr Bingley, but the loss of your friend, his sister. I was struck by what you said in your letter, about her taking the trouble to put Miss Darcy's name into your head."

"It was kind of her to warn me."

"Do you think so? I cannot tell how much confidence she should have in procuring Miss Darcy as a prospective bride for her brother, but I will say I have heard Miss Darcy is both very young and very shy. She is but Lydia's age! I cannot think Mr Darcy would countenance a betrothal when his sister is not yet qualified to be a wife."

"Caroline seemed confident as to the state of her brother's inclinations."

Elizabeth hid her grimace. "Well, it seemed from your letter that she was not entirely disinterested in the matter. Her own hopes and partiality may be deceiving her."

"She has known Miss Darcy far longer than she has me. Her partiality is to be expected."

Jane was too good, too blind. Elizabeth had always thought her propensity to seek the good in everyone to be a trait that could not always work to Jane's advantage, but she would not change that aspect of Jane's character. She herself was far more cynical. But then, she was their father's daughter.

They spoke for a short while longer, before Elizabeth bade Jane goodnight and repaired to her own room, where she could pummel her pillows to her heart's content in lieu of looking Mr Bingley in the eye and castigating him for his inconstancy. She slept ill. She could not but wonder if Jane spent as weary a night, but she resolved not to ask. It was best to mention Mr Bingley as little as possible in the future.

Elizabeth did not mention the disconcerting exchange with Mr Wickham until Monday morning. It was of no great import, after all, when set in the scale of comforting Jane for Mr Bingley's defection, and she raised it when she deemed Jane would prefer to speak of something else.

She and Jane took a walk before breakfast, having left Aunt Iphy to her usual early morning consultations with the cook-housekeeper who shouldered all their aunt's domestic concerns. Jane had been introduced to the delights of Aunt Iphy's garden and the vexation that was Jasper, and they had gone into Wingham's park so Elizabeth could show her a favourite walk. As they paced beneath an avenue of lime trees, Elizabeth told Jane of her dance with Mr Wickham at the assembly.

Jane had no more notion than she of what Mr Wickham had hoped to achieve with his odd conversation and hints at improper conduct, though they discussed it for some time. Jane did not wish to think ill of either gentleman. "We know nothing of the causes or circumstances which may have alienated them, and I am convinced it is no one's business but their own. I did not meet this Mr Wickham, and you have a far better acquaintance with Mr Darcy than I. You are better placed to judge them both, but what gentleman would treat his father's favourite in such a manner? Do you truly believe Mr Darcy capable of such dishonourable conduct? Do not forget that in the case of a bequest, it must be difficult to deny it to the legatee and escape censure."

"Mr Wickham spoke of it without ceremony, without—" Elizabeth stopped. "No. That is not quite true. Certainly he spoke without ceremony, but also in a way that was... smooth. It was not the first time he had discussed his history with Mr Darcy, I am sure. The more I consider it, the more I perceive he spoke and acted as if he had indeed taken the Bard's words to heart—we are all players upon the stage, acting a part in the hope of the audience throwing pennies and plaudits our way."

"He was insincere?"

"He did not present insincerity, precisely, but an easy facility with his tale. He was skilled in his discussion. Adept. He did not search for words and ideas. They flowed readily."

"He has told the story before, you mean."

"I think so. He has oft made that particular complaint, presumably to seek sympathy and, perhaps, admiration. He is the hero of his own tale, doubtless. But you are right. We cannot know the truth of his accusations. Yet some of the things he said, about Mr Darcy's pride and his thinking meanly of the world rang true. And then Mr Darcy himself proclaiming that his superiority of mind kept his pride under good regulation! I declare, I almost forgot myself and laughed aloud. It is as well I have some notion of propriety! But in truth, I am cross because this Mr Wickham brought back all my anger at Mr Darcy from our first meeting when he insulted me. I am a poor sort of Christian, after all, that I can hold on to my resentments so."

"So Mr Wickham sought to do Mr Darcy's reputation harm, and happened upon a characteristic you had already noted? If it does not explain Mr Wickham's design, it exposes how he goes about it."

"He named Mr Darcy's besetting sin well enough. There could be no doubt that he knew him well. You know, I wondered at first if Mr Darcy's rudeness at the deanery had been birthed in shyness, and an inability to connect to others. In the weeks since, I have come to believe not that he is shy, but that his reserve and sense of privacy match your own in intensity, if not in how they manifest themselves. You are gentleness personified, Jane. He is all hauteur."

"But you must make allowances for differences in character and upbringing, Lizzy. Much as we love them all, our family is one of moderate wealth and, let us be honest, obscurity. We are not known outside the district of Meryton. Mr Darcy was born to prestige, power and riches. Did you not tell me his uncle is an earl? We cannot hope to understand his sphere. Our lives and experiences have been different. Can you not imagine the demands made on Mr Darcy, the exigencies Society places on one of his birth and breeding? It is not, perhaps, surprising he has retreated into icy reserve as a result."

"You are far more charitable than I! Of course, you are right. Mr Wickham and his sly implications of misconduct shall be forgot— Oh. Here is our cousin and Mr Darcy now, coming to join us. We can speak of it no longer."

The gentlemen were indeed striding across the meadow to meet them, and the flurry of greetings and compliments filled the air. They had come to carry the sisters up to the Hall for a late breakfast.

"Aunt Iphy has already been conveyed thither to preside over the teapot, but my papa is unwilling to allow anyone but you, Lizzy, to give him his coffee. He declares no one else has your touch." Cousin Galahad laughed. "He is a dreadful old flirt, is he not? I came by it honestly."

Jane tucked her hand under his arm. "I hope your father will forgive us appearing at his breakfast table in our old walking dresses. We were not expecting the invitation."

"You are charming, and that is all he will think." Cousin Galahad started off towards the Hall.

"Miss Elizabeth." Mr Darcy bowed and offered his arm.

Elizabeth took it, and smiled after her sister and cousin. "My cousin is a most unserious gentleman."

"Essentially harmless, though."

"I believe you, sir. If I did not, I would guard Jane more fiercely! Now, shall we follow them to breakfast? Walking always gives me such an appetite."

With Jack Hill, Elizabeth's faithful shadow all these weeks, trailing behind them, they walked up the broad avenue to the distant Hall. It glowed gold in the early morning light, a magnificent old place with the sun glinting on the stone mullioned windows. Elizabeth had grown very fond of it, and her cousins.

"Is Pemberley much like it?" She gestured to the Hall.

"Not nearly so ancient. The old house at Pemberley was of a similar age, but was razed to the ground after a fire in 1690. It was rebuilt in the Baroque style and I think it a fairer prospect, set in wilder country."

And with that, Mr Darcy was induced to talk of Pemberley, his every word betraying his partiality for his own home. Elizabeth listened to him, and allowed her irritation over Mr Wickham's words to wash away. They stepped out of the avenue and onto the broad gravel sweep before the front door, and she was forced to give her attention to her surroundings again on hearing her cousin's surprised shout.

A travelling coach had arrived. The horses, blowing and steaming, must have just been brought to a halt, for the coach itself still rocked upon its springs. The door was flung open, and a young man leapt out.

"Bingley!" Cousin Galahad's voice rose. "Bingley! What on earth are you doing here?"

CHAPTER TWENTY-THREE

Tangled Web

Oh, what a tangled web we weave...
when first we practice to deceive.
— Scott, *Marmion*

Mr Bingley, an agreeable-looking young gentleman with tousled brown hair and a harassed expression, could not take his eyes from Jane, who returned his stare with one of her own. "I wrote, Palmer, in answer to your own letter reminding me Darcy was here, and accepting your invitation to stay. Did you not receive my reply? Miss Bennet? What are you doing here? I mean to say, I cannot fathom in the least why you are here in Kent! Here where I am!"

Jane did not answer. Her cheeks were pink.

"I have heard nothing from you, Bing—" Cousin Galahad stopped short, for a woman's hand appeared on the edge of the lowered window of the coach, and the woman, having braced herself thus, put her head out.

"Charles? What are you about? I am waiting! Can you not hand me—"

It appeared no one was capable of finishing a speech, for hers ended as abruptly as had Galahad's. She, too, stared at Jane as if faced with some ghastly apparition. She looked very like her brother—for Elizabeth presumed this must be Jane's erstwhile friend, Miss Bingley. Both sister and brother wore expressions of round-eyed astonishment, but if Mr Bingley's was one of astonished pleasure, Miss Bingley's was most certainly the opposite.

It appeared Miss Bingley, though, was nothing if not socially adept. "Good heavens! Jane Bennet! How... how delightfully unexpected! Oh, Mr Darcy! Such a pleasure to see an old friend again! Mr Palmer, I hope you are well, sir. And... and... mmmn. Charles, do help me down and allow me to greet everyone properly."

Her brother started, and turned, holding out his hand and helping her out of the coach. She smiled at everyone; a practised, facile smile, in Elizabeth's opinion. Both Cousin Galahad and Mr Darcy used their free hands to remove their hats, and swept Miss Bingley a bow. Jane and Elizabeth's curtseys were as slight as Miss Bingley's own, the minimum civility demanded.

Cousin Galahad was rather wild about the eyes. "Bingley, are you and your sister both intending to stay?"

Mr Bingley tore his gaze away from Jane. "Well, yes, as I said when I wrote to you. The Hursts have retired to their estate in Norfolk. Louisa is in an interesting condition, you see, and Caroline finds Norfolk disagrees with her, hence I thought to keep her with me. I cannot think what happened to the letter I sent you, Palmer."

"Your handwriting is so shocking, it has probably been delivered to some hamlet in the Outer Hebrides or is half way to the Americas by now. I had hoped you would visit while Darcy is here, of course." Galahad replaced his hat. "Miss Bingley, you are very welcome. Forgive my consternation, however. Mine is a bachelor household, and I am afraid I do not have a hostess to receive you and see to your care. I must contrive something..."

"Aunt Iphy," Elizabeth said on a soft breath.

Galahad nodded. "I will speak to her over breakfast." His smile was strained, not his customary bright, joyful expression.

"Oh, I am sure we will be admirably cared for," was Miss Bingley's smooth reply. "What a beautiful house, Mr Palmer! So distinguished and ancient a style, so venerable and imposing."

Cousin Galahad thanked her in a somewhat distracted fashion. He waved to the attentive butler and footmen waiting on the steps of the Hall, and drew everyone a few yards away to allow the coach to be unloaded. The butler, giving his best supercilious bow, said he would speak to the housekeeper and arrange guest accommodation, a promise Galahad met with a relieved nod and word of thanks.

Mr Bingley cut into all these domestic concerns by approaching Jane, who still held Cousin Galahad's arm. "Miss Bennet, I am all astonishment at seeing you. Surely you have not followed— I mean..."

This was too much, even for Jane. Elizabeth had read of glaciers, relishing accounts of the huge icy masses of Chamonix and the Matterhorn. She had not realised her sweet, tranquil sister had the ability to impersonate one.

Jane lifted her chin, all the better to show her usual serene expression chilled to ice. "We cannot be very well acquainted, Mr Bingley, and you can have no understanding of my character, if you believe I would follow any young gentleman anywhere."

The frosty steel evidently caught Mr Bingley unawares. "Oh, of course! I did not mean— Not at all! I am merely surprised! Forgive me. I was maladroit. I meant no offence."

"Following, too, suggests the other party was here first, when that is patently not the case." Jane turned her gaze to meet Caroline Bingley's. "It would be particularly difficult to follow anyone to Canterbury when one has been told one's friends are going to Bath."

Miss Bingley's mouth tightened.

"Bath?" Bingley repeated. He frowned at his sister. "Bath?"

"Miss Bingley told me you would be taking your family there, sir."

Miss Bingley, her mouth and eyes pinched with unmistakable annoyance, made a noise that Elizabeth deduced was intended to be a deprecating titter. "Dear Jane! You must have misunderstood."

"You distinctly mentioned Bath." Such unusual firmness had Elizabeth casting her sister an anxious glance. Jane had been more grievously hurt by the Bingleys than she had been willing to admit. "You wrote to me, you may recall, to tell of your planned journey."

"I... Well... It must have been I who misunderstood and made an error. I think I must have done. Bath... Canterbury! How silly of me to confuse the two! But then, they are easily mistaken, are they not? After all, what is the difference?"

"The width of southern England, Miss Bingley," Elizabeth said, all innocence. "Some one hundred and fifty miles."

"Give or take a mile," Mr Darcy murmured in Elizabeth's ear, and she preserved her countenance with difficulty.

Miss Bingley's pinched expression deepened. Perhaps she was in pain? "I do not believe we have met, ma'am."

"Oh, we must remedy that. Cousin, would you introduce your guests?"

"Of course!" Cousin Galahad bowed. "Miss Elizabeth, permit me to bring to your acquaintance Mr Charles Bingley and his sister, Miss Caroline Bingley. Bingley is an old schoolfellow of mine and Darcy's, Lizzy. We bonded in the adversity that is Eton, and we have remained excellent friends. Bingley, Miss Bingley, this is Miss Elizabeth Bennet, Miss Bennet's younger sister. The Bennets are my cousins."

Miss Bingley was definitely in pain. Probably at Galahad's introducing her to Elizabeth, rather than the other way around; the sharp social pang intensified, perhaps, by finding that Elizabeth and Jane had familial connections to the Palmers. "Delighted to make your acquaintance, Miss Elizabeth, I am sure."

"Likewise." Elizabeth offered another shallow curtsey. "Welcome to Kent, Mr Bingley, Miss Bingley."

"We should go indoors," Mr Darcy suggested. "I know Sir James and Miss Palmer are awaiting us for breakfast. Have you have travelled here from Canterbury this morning, Bingley?"

"We stayed at Faversham on Saturday," said Miss Bingley. "A dreadful place! The inn was a bare hovel, with not one speck of real superior comfort. I daresay no one of consequence ever visits the place. Savage, and uncivilised, and unsophisticated! It was dreadful to be forced to stay there for the whole of yesterday, Mr Darcy, since we could not travel on the Lord's Day."

"You will have had an early start indeed to reach us from Faversham at this hour," Cousin Galahad said, "and will need some refreshment. We should go indoors and introduce you to my father."

Miss Bingley touched the bodice of her travelling dress and let out another of those tittering laughs. "I am not dressed for it, sir!" She looked Jane and Elizabeth up and down. "Though customs here in Kent seem more informal. Will Sir James forgive me appearing in travelling dress?"

"Oh, please do not be concerned." Elizabeth returned the contempt with a smile. "I do not suppose Cousin James will notice."

"Indeed not," Cousin Galahad said, heartily. "M'father is not a man to concern himself with things of that nature. Shall we go in? Please follow me."

He patted the hand Jane had still on his arm, and turned to walk up the broad steps to the front door where the butler awaited them. Miss Bingley took a step towards Mr Darcy, but Elizabeth, who had dropped Mr Darcy's arm while the introductions were made, lifted her hand and replaced it.

It really did not seem possible that Miss Bingley's mouth could tighten further without her lips disappearing entirely, but she endeavoured to prove Elizabeth wrong. She took on all the qualities of a poacher's iron trap: rigid, unyielding, and with teeth to savage and tear if only such behaviour were not frowned upon by Society.

It was unlikely Elizabeth and Miss Bingley were destined to be friends. Elizabeth felt she could bear the disappointment.

"Charles, your arm, please."

Miss Bingley's voice appeared to recall Mr Bingley to himself long enough for him to do as he was bid, and offer his arm. He had been staring after Jane and Cousin Galahad, his pleasant features twisting into a frown, although it did not match his sister's for ferocity. Miss Bingley tugged her brother into motion to follow Jane and Cousin Galahad into the house. Elizabeth and Mr Darcy brought up the rear in silence.

Elizabeth did not dare meet Mr Darcy's gaze, lest she lose her composure and give way to unseemly amusement. It would not do to laugh out loud. It would not do at all.

Sir James accepted his guests with old-world courtesy, welcoming them to his hearth and home without once expressing his astonishment at their unexpected appearance in his breakfast room, and meeting Cousin Galahad's anguished glance with no more than a raised eyebrow.

While the housekeeper and two footmen flitted about the breakfast room with more china and cutlery, setting two extra places at table with quiet efficiency, Miss Bingley was all fulsome compliments and pleasantries to both Sir James and Aunt Iphy. Her brother was more distracted. Mr Bingley was composed enough to offer his host greetings and compliments, then, without waiting to seat his sister, sank into a chair halfway along the table and stared at poor Jane. She did not stare back. She took the seat Galahad offered, and fixed her attention, with inhuman intensity, on Aunt Iphy, who presided over the table at its foot. Elizabeth admired her strategy of presenting Mr Bingley with an excellent view of her profile. Jane had an exquisite profile.

It was abominable manners to leave Miss Bingley looking for a chair, and both Galahad and Mr Darcy darted forward to ensure she was seated in a place of honour. She glanced at the empty chair to Sir James's right hand. By rights, as the guest, that was her due, but Sir James beckoned for Elizabeth to join him.

"Come, Lizzy, I have waited for you to make my coffee. You do it so well."

"I merely pour it, sir. Your cook does all the hard work!" Elizabeth took his outstretched hand and bent to kiss his cheek before taking the chair he indicated.

The old man laughed. "Minx!"

They shared a companionable, knowing, smile.

Miss Bingley took a seat two chairs down. With Mr Darcy between her and Elizabeth, and Galahad between Mr Bingley and Jane on the other side of the table, it promised to be an interesting and diverting breakfast.

The housekeeper, an estimable soul, nodded her approval of the footmen's work, and sent them out of the room. She dipped a respectful curtsey at Sir James and promised the guest rooms would be ready directly.

Sir James thanked her, gestured for her to stay, and smiled at Aunt Iphy. "You and the girls had better move up to the Hall, Iphy, if you are willing to act as my hostess while our guests are here?" He ended on a questioning note, but as ever, Aunt Iphy was all fluttery compliance. "Thank you, Iphy. You are a blessing to this house. Now then, which were Eliza's rooms when you were girls here?"

"The Rose suite, James."

"Excellent." And to the housekeeper, he said, "Well, Mrs Webb, can you have rooms prepared in the family wing for Miss Iphy and the Misses Bennet? Make sure Miss Elizabeth has the Rose suite."

The poor housekeeper's bland complacency had taken a battering at having so many extra rooms to prepare, but she promised all would be done as soon as may be. She tottered out. Elizabeth suspected Mrs Webb would need some strong coffee herself, to steady her nerves.

"Oh." Miss Bingley leaned forward to look past Mr Darcy to catch Elizabeth's gaze. "You are not staying here at the Hall? How singular to visit family yet stay elsewhere."

Elizabeth smiled. "Miss Palmer, who is our aunt, has her own house outside the park, Miss Bingley. We have been very comfortable there, and in any case, come to the Hall most days."

"Aye," said Sir James. "And we are glad of your company. Now, my little Miss. My coffee, if you please!"

Elizabeth laughed, and poured Sir James's preferred morning beverage into a large coffee can, adding two spoons of fine-ground Lisbon sugar to sweeten a brew she personally found insufferably strong. She took chocolate herself.

The footmen returned with trays and tureens, and for several minutes everyone's attention was on their breakfasts. Except Mr Bingley, who was seen to pour sugar over his devilled kidneys and stir his tea with the jam spoon.

"I cannot account for seeing you here, Miss Bennet," he said, speaking into a lull in the conversation. "I was sorry indeed to hear that you had left London some weeks ago. Some eight or nine weeks, I think—"

"I left London on Friday last, sir." Jane's tone was flat, a mere recitation of a fact.

"But how can that be? Caroline, you did tell me Miss Bennet had left to visit family in Alnwick, did you not?"

The poacher's trap sitting beyond Mr Darcy did not quite snap its mouth closed with a clang, but Miss Bingley was so stiff, her spine seemed forged of the finest iron. She stared at her brother.

"Where is Alnwick?" Jane asked.

"Northumberland, I believe," Mr Darcy told her.

Jane picked up her tea cup and took a small sip. "We have no family farther north than Stevenage."

Frowning, Mr Bingley turned to his sister. "Caroline?"

The iron mouth curved into a smile. "You misunderstood me, Charles. I spoke of... of Miss Barnett."

"I do not know a Miss Barnett. I am sure I did not mishear."

"Good heavens," said Elizabeth, only half under her breath. "So many grievous misunderstandings abound this morning , and geographical ones at that. It is obvious no library can be complete without the most up-to-date atlas."

Miss Bingley's glare at Elizabeth would have set wet wood aflame. Elizabeth returned it with another innocent smile while the gentlemen on either side of her—Sir James on her left and Mr

208

Darcy to her right—were both fighting to maintain their composure, if the twitching mouths were any indication.

Mr Bingley persisted. "Who is Miss Barnett?"

"She is a connection of... of the Ellsworths." Miss Bingley was as sharp as a lemon. "I am sorry you were labouring under a misapprehension, Charles."

Mr Bingley, who still stared at Jane in mournful fashion, did not grant his sister so much as a glance. "Not as sorry as I am. It must have seemed as though we deliberately neglected our friends, and let me tell you, Miss Bennet"—and his voice grew so loud that everyone at the table looked at him, including Jane (which must have been his object in raising his tone)—"that is something I deeply regret. It was inadvertent on my part."

Cousin Galahad was as guilty as Elizabeth in refusing to mind his tongue. "You were operating on faulty intelligence, Bingley. You need to be more certain of your source."

It was very wicked of him, to say aloud what everyone was thinking. Everyone looked at Miss Bingley, who tried to turn up her iron trap of a mouth at the corners to meet her reddened cheeks. Elizabeth felt a small pang of remorse. That this woman— for 'lady' she could not call her—had schemed against Jane was obvious to everyone, but it was hard she should be exposed to strangers.

Elizabeth glanced around at the others. Sir James was focused now on his breakfast, determinedly looking away, and Mr Darcy looked more grave and remote than ever. No more twitching mouths there, to hide amusement. Jane appeared sorry, her demeanour serious and grave, her teeth caught on her bottom lip. She sat quietly, her hands folded in her lap. Aunt Iphy, too, seemed distressed, her cheeks flushed and her mouth downturned; and the cup she raised shook in her hand.

That would not do. It would not do at all. Neither Jane nor dear Aunt Iphy should be so discommoded.

"Well, it is delightful to make your acquaintance at last, Mr Bingley, Miss Bingley. I believe you have also been introduced to others in our family. The Gardiners spoke very well of you." Elizabeth took a restorative mouthful of her chocolate.

Galahad made a little moue in her direction. Presumably she was spoiling his fun.

"I enjoyed their company a great deal." Mr Bingley did not take his gaze from Jane. "Your uncle is an educated gentleman, easy to converse with."

Miss Bingley sniffed.

"Yes. Well..." Elizabeth was rarely at a loss, but even she found it difficult to think of something to say that would not spark another moment of discomfort. It was evident the Gardiners were as unwelcome a topic to Miss Bingley, as was geography. "I believe you all last met at the theatre. Here in the country, life is simpler and slower, and we cannot offer anything as diverting as Shakespeare. We must consider what we may plan for your amusement. The weather is glorious, and will allow a wealth of things we may do in the way of picnicking, walking and riding. I do not suggest driving just yet, since you have not yet made Jasper's acquaintance and no one should attempt to drive him unwarned."

That drew Mr Bingley's attention. "Jasper?"

"My horse," Aunt Iphy said in a faint tone.

"Ha! A demon in equine form." Elizabeth beamed at Jasper's staunch defender, eliciting an answering, fond smile from her aunt. "He is more stubborn than I am, Mr Bingley, and as all here will aver, that is a boast to be met with trepidation. However, should we subdue his wickedness, we might explore some pretty country by gig or phaeton, while you gentlemen ride. It is not far to the coastal resorts, and if your taste runs to cathedrals, Miss Bingley, we can explore Canterbury together. What other entertainment might we provide, Cousin Galahad?"

"I am sure we can plan a dozen different visits and excursions."

He opened his mouth to say more, but before his besetting imp of mischief could prompt him to suggest they consult the atlas in the library—something Elizabeth was sure he longed to say as much as she did—Darcy joined the conversation with suggestions of nearby attractions such as Goodnestone, or the Old Palace at Bekesbourne, or Sandwich. Thankfully, it was enough to turn the tide of the conversation, and breakfast ended on a far less contentious note.

"Well done, Lizzy," Sir James said, under cover of the party rising from table to allow the Bingleys to be conveyed to their guest chambers, and Elizabeth, Jane and Aunt Iphy to go and prepare for their removal to the Hall. "You are a good girl."

"Not good at all, I am afraid, to allow Jane and Aunt Iphy to be worried so. I should not have provoked the Bingleys."

"It was not of your doing." Sir James called Jane to join them. He stooped and kissed first Elizabeth's cheek, and then Jane's. "It will please Gal and me to have you stay here at the Hall with us, and you will help Iphy, I know, to ensure she is not made too anxious about her new charge. And you will help me spoil and indulge her a little, I hope?"

"Nothing could give me more pleasure," Elizabeth assured him.

She and Jane curtseyed and left, taking Aunt Iphy with them. She turned in the doorway to smile at those new members of her family who had, so quickly, become dear to her. And though they nodded back, faces kind and open and loving, it was Mr Darcy's small, approving smile that surprised and warmed her.

CHAPTER TWENTY-FOUR

Unnumber'd Woes

Unnumber'd woes engender in the breast
That entertains the rude, ungrateful guest.
— Smollet, *Advice: A Satire*

"I anticipate Bingley will join us soon." Palmer neatly potted his first ball, leaning over the billiards table at a precarious angle. "I told him where to find us."

If Palmer had a real character flaw, it was his being altogether too good at billiards. Darcy cast a regretful look at the silver half-crowns lining the table edge, farewelling them in advance of his inevitable defeat. "After he has spoken to his sister, perhaps."

"I had a few words with my father before I joined you. He was already disconcerted by the Bingleys' sudden appearance, and dismayed we must inconvenience Aunt Iphy and the girls. He was not impressed by Miss Bingley's showing this morning, as you will imagine." Palmer stepped back, and gestured invitingly at the table. "His disapprobation deepened when I told him of the other…

shall I call it a misunderstanding? Bath, instead of Canterbury, I mean. A mean trick intended to mislead Cousin Jane."

"As Bingley realises." Darcy leaned over the table, humping his left hand into a bridge to support his cue. He had the yellow cue ball, and Palmer, damn him, had left his own white ball at a difficult angle for Darcy to reach.

Palmer, considerately, waited until Darcy had finished taking his shot before replying. "I understand now why Lizzy was so concerned for her sister, and why Cousin Jane felt abandoned by those she had considered friends. I do not say more than that, because I do not know what sort of understanding she and Bingley may have had, or were developing. I am not yet on such terms with my new cousins that they would speak unguardedly about such private matters. But it is clear she has been wounded by Miss Bingley's inconstancy as a friend."

"Is that why Miss Bennet came here?"

Palmer nodded. "The Bath taradiddle, I believe. Cousin Jane understood Miss Bingley's communication about it to be a severing of relations between the two families. Miss Bingley is not a kind creature, is she?"

"I do not think so. Miss Bingley doubtless delivered the message in a manner characterised more by force than gentleness."

"I wish Bingley had not brought her." Palmer straightened, with a noise sounding very like disgust. "I am in no mood for this game, Darcy. Forgive me if I concede."

"We will call it a draw." Darcy gave the half-crowns another glance at this unexpected reprieve. Cheered, he returned his cue to the wall rack and he and Palmer wandered over to the side-table, where the servants had left coffee and biscuits. "She must have known this was a bachelor gathering and there is no lady of the house to receive her. I cannot imagine why she is here."

"Can you not?" Palmer grinned at him. "I believe her intentions are clear. She has about her the mien of a slavering wolf prowling the sheep pen. You, my dear friend, are a very tempting lamb."

Darcy's fleeting annoyance must have shown, because Palmer laughed outright.

"Your income and Pemberley are quite a prize. She has been casting lures at you these many years."

"I am aware. I have grown skilled at not seeing them."

"Very wise." Palmer poured their coffee and sat back, eyeing Darcy and looking thoughtful, a small crease between his brows. "She is one reason, I think."

"For what?"

"Your discomfort with strangers. She and her ilk, and the good Lord knows, Town is full of women like her. One dance at a ball, and they are off pricing bride goods. You are hunted too much, is that not it?"

Darcy raised one shoulder in a slight shrug. "You are likely right. These last few years since my father died and Pemberley came to me, I have had all too many presume upon a slight acquaintance but who prove to be grasping and out for anything they can get. George Wickham is one such. Miss Bingley is another. Different in essentials, but alike in that they seek to rise by clambering up my coat-tails. It has soured me."

"I have noted it. As I have said to you before, I wish your defences did not manifest as disdain and pride. Those faults—for so I must name them—mask too completely the decent gentleman beneath."

"You have indeed said so. More than once."

"All the better to drum the lesson into your head, old friend. I weary of seeing you hide." Palmer cocked his head, and his expression grew harder. "I do wish I had known Wickham was at the assembly. I would have enjoyed schooling his presumption in imposing on Lizzy. Mind you, she is not likely to be overset by a creature like Wickham. She has too quick a mind for that. But all the same, I cannot like her being his prey even in the smallest sense. You permit him too much freedom."

"He was my father's godson, and a favourite, and has traded upon that these last ten years. He knows how to make himself charming, and is expert at cutting a wheedle. He is angered that I am immune to it, but quick to avail himself of the tolerance I grant him in my father's memory."

"A mistake."

"My tolerance is grown thin. I no longer cover his debts, nor do I speak on his behalf when his creditors seek me out."

"They do that?"

"It has happened. Once it was an outraged father. Oh, no one of great consequence, since Wickham has enough sense to employ his charm with maids and shop-girls, but it did not lessen the father's outrage over his daughter's plight. As boys, we were friends, but now I am weary of him. It has been a pleasant two or three years without his intruding on my notice." Darcy refilled his cup, though Palmer shook his head when he offered the coffee carafe. The strong coffee was a soothing balm to ruffled spirits since it was too early in the day to do more than eye the Madeira bottle with wistful longing. "Miss Bingley's overreaching is of a different sort. She seeks social advancement. Bingley has won friends through his sweet temper and sociable habits. He is an asset at a ball or a rout-party or a musical evening." Darcy huffed out a short laugh. "I am an asset because of my name and Pemberley, but Bingley has earned his place. That is a sobering reflection."

"I am as fond of Bingley as I would be of a brother. But as we have discussed before, his position in Society is equivocal. He needs to make a good marriage into the gentry to secure it." Palmer put down his cup, the coffee almost untouched. Perhaps he too yearned for something stronger.

"Miss Bingley's motive for all she does, I am sure."

"And yet she moves against my cousin. She does not approve of her for Bingley."

"Because Miss Bennet is not high enough to suit her notions. Now, Wickham trades on his education as a gentleman but is less concerned with Society. He seeks a fortune. I will pay Miss Bingley the compliment of saying she is not like him in that regard. She is not seeking wealth, not in itself, but for a certitude of place. Her feet stand on uncertain foundations. It would not need the sort of convulsion that flattens mountains—the merest tremor, and she would see the loss of all their gains thus far. Their origins in trade are not forgotten by them or anyone else."

"Her sister married a gentleman."

"I agree, but Hurst does not possess either a great name or a high position. He is gentry, but no higher. Any reasonable lady of Miss Bingley's kind should find the Hursts of this world a step up. Yet she wants more, pushing her brother to look high for a bride, and harbouring similarly lofty ambitions for herself. Only with an excellent marriage may she feel secure."

"And those lofty ambitions have settled on you. Well, it is true enough that a lady may only raise her status by marrying well, as Mrs Hurst did. They are denied the opportunities we men have to strive for our own advancement. It is understandable, I suppose." Palmer frowned. "While I am glad not to be her object, I will confess to some chagrin that I am not even considered. After all, my wife will be Lady Palmer one day. Please God not soon, mind you! But I would think that is some inducement."

"Be grateful." Darcy sighed. "So. We have Bingley and his sister here for however long, and under the same roof we bring the Bennet sisters. That does not bode well for our peace of mind. Bingley is obviously all-a-mort for Miss Bennet, and presumably worrying about the consequences of his sister's actions. Miss Bennet has a character I find difficult to parse, given our short acquaintance, but on this morning's showing, she is not so compliant as to forgive Bingley easily for the insulting behaviour to which she was subject. Miss Bingley does not favour Miss Bennet and will do everything in her power to destroy whatever regard Miss Bennet had for her brother. I am afraid she and Miss Elizabeth…" Darcy allowed his words to trail away.

Miss Elizabeth had been magnificent. He had rarely seen Miss Bingley so comprehensively and swiftly brought to *point non plus*.

"Lizzy showed her mettle, did she not! So. We will need a battle plan. I will not have poor Aunt Iphy and my cousins vexed when they are doing us such a service."

"Edward Fitzwilliam says a battle plan lasts until the first encounter with the enemy, when all plans are thrown into the air like grapeshot, and the world erupts in chaos, blood and death."

"I had not thought Colonel Fitzwilliam to be such a pessimist. However, I shall persist in trying to prepare some strategy for dealing with Miss Bingley."

"She is not an enemy, Palmer. That is doing it much too brown."

Palmer's frown deepened. "Perhaps. But she is not a friend."

When Bingley joined them, he did not look as though he had spent the hour since breakfast washing the dust of the road from himself and making himself neat. Instead, he wore the same clothes, a little more rumpled, and his hair stood on end. He must have spent at least fifty-nine of the last sixty minutes running his fingers through it in frustration.

While he took the coffee cup Palmer handed him, he stared down into it rather than drink from it, his normal cheerful demeanour altered to chagrin. "I must apologise for this morning's performance." He sounded as though some giant had closed a hand about his chest, squeezing the words from him by brute force. "I am shocked by what I have learned today. And yet, I am not surprised." He replaced the cup on its saucer, untasted. "I should not speak so of my sister, but she has not acted in such a way as to deserve consideration."

"Did she explain?" Palmer asked.

"She maintains it is a series of inadvertent misapprehensions, and that both Miss Bennet and I mistook her. She is apologetic, but unrepentant." Bingley sighed. "I should return to London with her."

Palmer's little mouth twist suggested he did not entirely disagree, but, a good host, he would not hear of it. "I would be loath to forgo your company, Bingley. Aunt Iphy and the girls will be here shortly, and they will lend your sister countenance."

"She does not deserve to stay. I will admit she is a little embarrassed, but I suspect that is because of you both seeing her at less than her best." Bingley stopped and grimaced.

"We understand. The *ton* does not show much mercy, does it?" Palmer's tone was kind.

"No. Any slight imperfection of manner or social grace... No. The *ton* shows no mercy then. She does not like to appear lacking in any way, and, well, you both witnessed her failings today."

"We will not speak of it, Bingley." Palmer patted Bingley's shoulder in consoling manner. "I do not know Cousin Jane as well as I do Lizzy, but I am certain neither will be unkind or uncivil. And Aunt Iphy—Miss Palmer, that is, my father's cousin—well, she is sweetness itself."

"I had no idea you were related to Miss Bennet! You said nothing of it when we met in the theatre at the end of the Season."

"I did not know. I mean to say, I have always known I have relations in Hertfordshire, just as they knew their grandmother hailed from Kent, but the branches of our family have been estranged for many years. In recent weeks we have come to know each other with my cousin Elizabeth's visit to Aunt Iphy. She is their grand-aunt, you see; the younger sister of their grandmother. Lizzy has been here since the beginning of July, and we have grown very fond of her—indeed she is quite my father's favourite—and we are all delighted the breach has been healed."

Bingley's grimace showed he had taken the mild warning about Elizabeth's standing with the Palmers along with the explanation. If he were wise, he would give Miss Bingley a sharp reminder to watch her tongue if she wished to escape Sir James's censure. Although, to be fair, Miss Bingley was not unintelligent. The Palmers were everything she aspired to: a baronetcy, a strong position in Society (both locally and in Town), wealth and a very fine, profitable estate. The Bennets' circumstances were not what she had thought them, and she would likely moderate her behaviour.

One would hope.

Darcy glanced at Palmer, who looked a little glum. How far did Palmer's admiration of Miss Bennet go? The wishes of his father and Miss Palmer notwithstanding, would he pursue Miss Bennet rather than the sister his family preferred? What would that mean for his friendship with Bingley?

Darcy sighed. The relations between Miss Bingley and the Bennets would be difficult enough to navigate. Those between Palmer and Bingley might capsize the boat entirely.

CHAPTER TWENTY-FIVE

Goode Dedes

Dooth somme goode dedes, that the deuel…
ne fynde yow nat vnocupied.
[Do some good deeds, so that the Devil
won't find you unoccupied.]
Chaucer, *Melibeus* (c1405)

By the time a nuncheon was served, everyone had settled in their rooms in the Hall. Darcy went to meet his fellow guests in the smaller dining room, not without some disquiet as to what the meal would bring.

Miss Bingley had exchanged her travelling dress for a day dress of figured silk, which, since it eschewed lace and feathers, she doubtless considered to be 'simple', and hence eligible for country wear. The two Bennet ladies were dressed with more practicality, in pretty muslins. Nothing could more clearly point to the disparity of wealth between the two families.

Bingley himself was quiet and ate little, his attention fixed upon Miss Bennet, who sat close to her sister and picked at her meal. She answered politely, but shortly, every conversational sally he ventured, giving him no more than a flickering glance each time.

Miss Bingley apparently had enough good sense to realise that her brother would countenance nothing but the most courteous of manners. Although she wore a pinched expression around her eyes and mouth, everything was civility and politesse, curtseys and cordiality.

Darcy did not suppose either of the Misses Bennet was fooled for an instant. Still, the light meal—presided over by Miss Palmer, since Sir James kept to his study—passed without too much strain on the enforced harmony.

"We should consider plans for our entertainment today," Palmer said as the meal came to an end. "You will have had a very early start from Faversham, I know, Miss Bingley. I must assume you will not wish to be too active, but allow yourself time to rest and recover?"

Miss Bingley murmured agreement.

"Then let us take a tour of the house, and the gardens later, if the day remains dry," Palmer suggested. "It is a grand old house, if I say so myself, and I hope it will interest you, Miss Bingley. You, too, Cousin Jane, for I know you have not yet seen much of the old place" He grinned at Miss Elizabeth. "I doubt you have seen every last nook and cranny either, Cousin. I hope you will enjoy it too."

"Your cousins do not know the house?" Miss Bingley's tone was sweet. "How singular."

Miss Elizabeth met her with a sweetness of her own. "Well, now we shall repair our lack of knowledge together, Miss Bingley. It is a delightful idea. Will you come with us, Aunt Iphy?"

Miss Palmer refused the invitation, claiming she was too old to promenade around a house familiar to her as her girlhood home and she had seen all she wanted when she had taken Miss Elizabeth over it weeks before. Instead, she would await them in one of the parlours where she would have tea and cakes served in order, as Miss Elizabeth put it, to recruit their flagging strength after their excursion.

Palmer, without a glance at the disconsolate Bingley, offered Miss Bennet his arm. Darcy felt obliged to offer his to Miss Bingley, leaving Bingley and Miss Elizabeth to bring up the rear.

Miss Bingley glanced at Palmer and Miss Bennet, then up at Darcy. A cat with a saucer of cream could not look more satisfied. This particular cat was not so very chastised, then.

At the end of their tour of parlours, drawing rooms, dining rooms, music rooms and library, they walked a gallery the length of the house itself, full of the sorts of portraits Darcy was used to seeing at Pemberley and Rosings. The usual collection adorned the walls: self-satisfied landowners, judges and bishops (several corpulent and ruddy-faced from a fondness for brandy) with their wives (some beautiful and some decidedly not), and assorted children (most seeming bored). The portraits were nothing at all out of the ordinary, although one or two were of exceptional quality. In particular, several miniatures in the collection held in display cabinets on either side of the massive fireplace were exquisite. Darcy coveted those.

Palmer halted before several portraits grouped together at the east end of the gallery. "And here we have an excellent way of explaining how we are related to each other and the Bridges family over at Goodnestone. Good Lord, Lizzy, now I see your grandmother's portrait in a good light, I can understand why my father was so struck on meeting you. You truly are her image."

He spoke nothing but the truth, and they all murmured agreement. Eliza Beeching stared out at them from an elaborate gold frame, one eyebrow quirking up and a smile curving her lips. She may have worn the fashions of more than half a century earlier, with her long dark curls curving over one shoulder in the 'undress' pose popular at the time, but the face was Miss Elizabeth's, from the beautiful, fine eyes to the pert nose and delicately moulded lips and chin. Darcy had seen that smile on Miss Elizabeth's face dozens of times.

"A twin could not be more alike, Lizzy. This is a greater

likeness even than the portrait we have at home," Miss Bennet said to her sister.

Miss Elizabeth nodded, looking away from her study of the portrait. "It seems she had a strong influence on the Bennets. Papa favours her, do you not think?"

"Yes." Miss Bennet smiled. "But not as strongly as you. No wonder Sir James is so fond of you!"

"It is only to be expected," Palmer said, easily. "Let me show you how we are all related. This stern-faced gentleman is Sir Thomas, my father's uncle. He was the fifth baronet…"

Palmer pointed from one portrait to the next. Sir Thomas's sister, Anne, the grandmother of the present Sir Brook Bridges at Goodnestone ("We're a close-linked lot in this corner of Kent, and we claim strong kinship between the two baronetcies."). Palmer's grandfather, old Sir Thomas's brother, dead before he could inherit the baronetcy. Sir Thomas's first wife, Mary, dead now for three-quarters of a century, the mother of the heir who died young, leaving the baronetcy to pass to Sir James. Thomas's and Mary's daughter, the redoubtable Miss Cassandra, scowling magnificently out from her gilded frame, and needing only snakes writhing out from beneath her lace cap to make her resemblance to Medusa complete. A middle-aged Sir James with his wife Cecilia, Palmer's mother, in one of those posed portraits that seemed to show off more of a landowner's house and grounds than his marriage.

The Bennet girls pressed forward when Palmer turned to the portrait of their great-grandmother. Anne Beeching, widow, married Sir Thomas after the death of his first wife, bringing her daughter Eliza with her and presenting him with another, Miss Iphigenia, whose likeness hung beside those of her parents. Looking between the paintings of the second Lady Palmer, Miss Iphy, and Eliza Beeching, no one would doubt they were related: they shared the same dark hair and eyes, and the shape of face and chin, though the resemblance was not as strong as that between Eliza and her granddaughter. Anne Beeching had handed down her looks to her descendants.

"And so we return to your grandmother, Lizzy." Palmer glanced at the Bingleys, and added, in explanation, "She was the child of Anne Beeching's first marriage. Old Sir Thomas took

Eliza as his own, and treated her with the same consideration as he gave Aunt Iphy."

From what Palmer had said privately when he had first related the tale, that was to say not very much consideration at all. Darcy could believe it. The cold-eyed, thin-lipped man of the portrait was the antithesis of kind joviality.

Miss Bingley drew in a long breath. "I see. You are not directly related at all?"

They all glanced at the cat whose saucer of cream now appeared to be overflowing. Miss Bennet's expression remained serene and hence her true feelings were difficult to read, while Miss Elizabeth appeared amused, a sentiment neither Palmer nor Bingley seemed to share.

"We are related through marriage and adoption, Miss Bingley." Palmer smiled, but his eyes were cold. "We are a clannish lot here, as our Scottish brethren would term it. We cherish the links of marriage and family, and foster a powerful loyalty and affection."

"Oh, of course," simpered Miss Bingley. "I was merely trying to understand these complicated familial relationships."

"We have a few of those of our own, Caroline." Bingley's tone was hardly indulgent. "I forget how many cousins we have through marriage, and several of them are step-cousins. No real distinction is made." He glanced at the Bennets. "And unlike the Misses Bennet, they are actively engaged in trade."

"We have little to do with them now!" Miss Bingley displayed an unusual talent for making a sentence completely devoid of sibilants still sound like a hiss of displeasure.

Once more Miss Elizabeth stepped in to ease an awkward moment. "Well, we Bennets are always happy to celebrate our connections, and we welcome new friends also." She smiled at the Bingleys. "And speaking of one connection who cannot be celebrated enough, Aunt Iphy will be waiting for us and she promised refreshments. The cook here makes the most delectable lemon biscuits. Do come and taste them!"

"You are very kind, Miss Elizabeth." Bingley bowed.

"And also right," Palmer cut in. "I can vouch for Lizzy's praise of the lemon biscuits. They are quite exceptional. Let us join Aunt

Iphy." His glance at Miss Bennet was regretful, before he turned to Miss Bingley and bowed. "Miss Bingley? Allow me to escort you." He and she led the way.

Bingley leapt forward to claim Miss Bennet. She put her hand on his arm so lightly, Darcy doubted Bingley felt the weight. They went out of the gallery ahead of Darcy and Miss Elizabeth, Bingley speaking quietly and urgently as they walked in Palmer's wake. Miss Bennet's face was down-turned. Bingley would see no reaction there.

Miss Elizabeth heaved a sigh. Darcy offered his arm. Should he offer his apologies along with it? Propriety and good manners required Palmer give some precedence to Miss Bingley, but that left Miss Bennet vulnerable to Bingley. He suspected Miss Elizabeth was not best pleased. All he could do now was attempt to allay her unease.

"Bingley is a modest, unaffected gentleman, and would be horrified if he gave offence. Indeed, he is horrified by how this sorry situation has come about. I expect he is eager to gain your sister's understanding and forgiveness."

Her mouth twitched, and the glance she gave Miss Bingley's back was inimical. "It appears he is not personally culpable, at least."

"But your sister is discomposed."

"She has had no opportunity to reflect on what she has learned today." Miss Elizabeth cast a sidelong glance at him. "However, my office as a good sister is not to force a confidence or interfere. Hard though it is to resist the temptation."

Certainly too hard for Miss Bingley, though neither of them could say so and remain within the bounds of propriety. Darcy nodded, and they quickened their pace to catch up with Bingley and Miss Bennet. If she had need of it, the latter could have the solace of knowing her sister, and all the comfort that implied, was close at hand.

Miss Palmer served the promised biscuits with the tea she had ordered. Their reputation was well deserved, and they complemented the conversation, which ranged widely from memories of the Bennets' grandmother to the accomplishments Society required of young ladies.

By the time it reached this latter topic, both Palmer and Darcy were ensconced in comfortable chairs with books on their knees. The ladies had taken up their sewing while they talked—something delicate and decorative on the part of Miss Palmer and Miss Bingley, while Miss Elizabeth did something intricate involving small, plain metal rings and strong white thread, and Miss Bennet sewed what appeared to be a plain shirt. Miss Bennet kept her eyes fixed on her task and returned only the briefest responses to Bingley's attempts at conversation. She was, evidently, treating him with great wariness. That latter consideration aside, the scene was one of quiet domestic felicity.

"You ladies are so talented," Bingley burst out. "I am constantly amazed at your skills with paintbrush or needles!"

Miss Bennet favoured him with a glance and an answer. "I have no real talent for fancy embroidery, sir. That is Elizabeth's skill. I do, however, excel at plain sewing."

"Indeed she does." Miss Elizabeth glanced up from her work. "I am not her equal when it comes to buttonholes. Though I will claim I make better buttons!"

She held up one of the rings, through which she had woven and twisted the thread until the ring looked like the tiniest of cartwheels. It was indeed a button, of the sturdy, rustic kind used to close up the neck openings of their shirts by many of those who worked on Darcy's land. She had embellished the woven pattern with embroidered knots. Darcy had never seen one made before, and she had done it quickly and deftly.

The sisters smiled at each other, and Miss Bennet added, "This is for our stock of clothing to gift to our tenants."

Miss Bingley stared. "For your tenants? Truly? That is… well, I do not understand why a lady would do such a thing."

Miss Bennet regarded her, expression composed and sedate. "It is understandable this is beyond your experience." She smiled with all of the serenity and goodness her younger sister claimed for her, though Miss Bingley flushed. "Every country estate, Miss Bingley, is dependent upon its tenantry. Our prosperity is built on their hard work. In return, the part we play as daughters of the estate's owner is to help ensure they and their families are healthy and happy. New clothing is too great a luxury for most working families, and at Longbourn we gift them with clothing each Yuletide as part of their presents on Boxing Day. The whole family prepares for this throughout the year."

Miss Bingley nodded, her mouth tight. Miss Elizabeth unobtrusively pressed her sister's hand and gave her a small, contained smile.

"My cousin is quite correct." Palmer gave Miss Bennet a look the poor fool probably thought was cousinly and did not lay his admiration open for all to see. "All good estate owners care for those with such a claim on them." He turned his gaze to Miss Palmer. "Aunt Iphy is our good angel here, taking care of all on the estate and in the village who need our help."

Miss Palmer blushed and disclaimed, in particular denying any facility at all for making what she called Dorset buttons. Palmer, laughing, suggested they keep Miss Elizabeth at Wingham to remedy their lack of skill.

Before anyone could respond, Bingley struck at another opportunity to compliment the object of his admiration. "It does not surprise me that you ladies turn your skills to such excellent account. You are all goodness!"

Miss Elizabeth smiled. "Our stitchery is our answer to the poet, Mr Bingley, who enjoins us to do good deeds, so the Devil will not find us unoccupied. He meant, I suppose, that we preserve ourselves from temptation by not being idle."

Darcy stared. "You have read Chaucer, Miss Elizabeth?"

"My father has Chaucer's works in his library. I have looked at them, and doubted they truly were written in English. The words are old, and strange, and far from our language now. Hardly surprising, since I believe it is almost four centuries since the poet's time. Papa has translated it for his own amusement, and read it to me while I turned the book this way and that, and attempted to reconcile Papa's words with the poet's archaic English."

Not a literal rendering, Darcy hoped. Chaucer was not genteel enough for a lady to study. Still, he smiled his approval at her enquiring mind.

"Goodness, that sounds a rather masculine pursuit, Miss Eliza. Did not your governess redirect your efforts to more—" Miss Bingley caught her brother's glare and clearly modified her tone and words. "—to the more usual books studied by young ladies?"

"We had no governess, Miss Bingley, though my father was always glad to hand over our education to masters in whatever topic interested us beyond his own learning—or, more precisely, since he is an accomplished scholar, beyond his patience to teach us. Which, I must admit, was most of our education. He would never limit our reading, however. He has little use for a smattering of education intended to be merely ornamental."

"No governess! And so, I suppose, you never went to school, either?"

"No. As I say, we had whatever masters were necessary."

"I see," said Miss Bingley, a world of meaning in her tone. She glanced at the work in Miss Bennet's hands. "I had an excellent education myself, at one of the best ladies' schools in Town. We were taught a great many accomplishments. That is, music, singing, drawing, dancing,"—she glanced at the rough linen shirt in Miss Bennet's hands—"exquisite embroidery, and the modern languages, as a bare minimum of what is required for a lady. To this she should add a distinguished air, a manner of conversing that shows her refinement and delicacy, if she is to be considered truly accomplished."

"And improve her mind through extensive reading." Darcy raised his book, and nodded at Miss Elizabeth. "Even Chaucer."

Miss Elizabeth treated these sentiments with unfeigned merriment. "Well, if ever you should meet such a paragon, I would be delighted to make her acquaintance and enquire how she attained such elegant taste and attainment when each day is limited by our Lord to a fixed number of hours. The poor lady must hardly have time to draw breath!" She glanced at the work on her lap and her smile lit her entire face.

Darcy ducked his head to hide a smile, and returned his gaze to his book. He might point to one or two ladies of his acquaintance who met his notions of accomplishment.

But only one of them could make buttons.

CHAPTER TWENTY-SIX

With Ships The Seas Were Sprinkled

With ships the seas were sprinkled, far and nigh
Like stars in heaven
— Wordsworth, *With Ships*

Darcy was pleased to note that the presence of new guests did not interfere with Miss Elizabeth's usual morning walk. He found her on a favourite path behind the Hall, one winding through the meadows covering the gentle slope of Preston Hill, with the glint of the River Wingham in the valley below. Her faithful groom shadowed her, greeting Darcy's arrival with a nod and slowing his pace to fall behind a little and give them privacy.

She greeted him with her usual unaffected, easy manners, and for a few moments they did not speak of anything of substance, other than make polite enquiries into the other's health. Once assured on that point, they turned to more pertinent matters.

"I wondered..." Darcy paused, and grimaced. "I have no wish to interfere in private matters that are not my concern, but I wondered how your sister is this morning."

Miss Elizabeth matched him grimace for grimace. "As determined as ever to do and say nothing that might discompose others. Nothing in her manner will cause concern."

He took this civil dismissal in good part. Her care for her sister's privacy was exemplary. "I am certain of that. Miss Bennet's manners are very pleasing. However, I have a proposal I hope will lift everyone's spirits a trifle. You may recall some weeks ago I mentioned a cousin who is serving on the Peninsula."

"You spoke of your aunt, Lady Ashbourne, and mentioned her anxieties on his behalf. I hope she is easier in her mind?"

"I am sure she is, if she had the same bounty as I did yesterday. The post from the continent is slow and unreliable. It often happens we get a batch of letters, then nothing for many weeks. I received three letters from Edward—Colonel Fitzwilliam, that is— and I am sure Aunt Ashbourne, too, will have a packet of letters to cheer her."

"I hope he is well?"

"Very well, at the time of writing, and hopeful of soon returning home."

Elizabeth expressed all the good wishes anyone could expect.

"Thank you. It is encouraging news. The colonel shares the guardianship of my sister, and she is very fond of him. I intend to visit her in Ramsgate and take the letters so that she, too, may be reassured. Would you think it convenient and pleasant to make a party of it? Ramsgate would be an interesting visit for everyone, and allow for some lessening of the strained sensations to which we have been recently subjected. I presume we should like to enjoy some tranquillity, to allow feelings to achieve a more equable tone. I hope Miss Palmer will join us for the day, to lend propriety to the exercise. I have no doubt she, and your sister, would enjoy the sea breezes."

"I have never seen the sea!"

Mr Darcy laughed. "Then you must consent to the excursion, and remedy that lack. Besides, I would be honoured to introduce my sister to you. While the Bingleys are already familiar friends, she would benefit greatly from making the acquaintance of you and your sister."

She gave him a sidelong, considering look. Odd. As if she were weighing him in some sort of balance. But in the end, she smiled and agreed. "I would be delighted to meet Miss Darcy, sir, and I am sure my sister will be also. I will speak to her and Miss Palmer before breakfast, to prepare them for the proposal. Thank you, Mr Darcy. You are very kind to think of our comfort so. I am sure our visit will be a most invigorating experience."

In the cool dawn light two days later, Darcy handed Miss Elizabeth and her aunt into the Palmers' most comfortable coach while Bingley and Palmer contended silently for the honour to squire Miss Bennet. Palmer lost the contest, good manners requiring him to ensure his guests' comfort, and he helped Miss Bingley into the coach while a triumphant Bingley offered the beauty his hand.

Darcy, Palmer and Bingley rode alongside the coach. Palmer leaned down often to the opened window to make many a jesting enquiry as to the ladies' comfort or to point out some part of the landscape Miss Bennet must not miss—he named her in particular. Palmer was a dear friend and a clever man, but how could he not realise the great black brute he rode must block Miss Bennet's view of every scene or glimpse of the sea? All the more galling, Bingley was provoked into following suit on the other side of the coach. The poor ladies must see nothing but horseflesh, no matter which way they turned.

Ramsgate was around two hours away, a journey well within the capabilities of the carriage horses and carried out without needing to stop. Miss Palmer bore it well, though noticeably a little stiff in the knees when they alighted the coach in the gravelled sweep before the house the Palmers had leased to Darcy. Palmer was indeed a good fellow. He went straight to help his elderly cousin, allowing her to release the stiffness by supporting her through a slow walk around the coach—though not, Darcy noted, without a dark glance over his shoulder at Bingley, who was engaged in helping down Miss Bennet and his sister. Darcy went to aid Miss Elizabeth, hiding his own amusement even as he noticed hers showing in the dancing eyes and the suggestion of a smile twitching at the corners of her mouth. Good Lord, but Palmer and Bingley were strutting like a pair of cockerels over a pretty hen.

The hen in question came to join Miss Elizabeth, while Bingley was distracted with the task of handing down his own sister. Miss Bennet seemed serene enough. Miss Elizabeth slid a hand into hers, and together they turned towards the sea.

The cottage, sited on the cliffs, had nothing but a greensward between the low hedges marking the garden and the drop to the sea beyond. Miss Elizabeth gave a faint gasp.

He followed the direction of her gaze, to the great heaving mass of green-grey-blue water—what colour *was* it?—filling the entire world to a far, misty horizon. Ships, small as toys, sped across Ramsgate Bay. The low whish and hiss of water against land was a constant in his ears, and his nostrils filled with that indefinable smell so characteristic of the sea. "Miss Elizabeth?"

She started and stared.

Darcy smiled at her wide eyes—those lovely eyes made even lovelier when bright with delight and wonder—and the gleam of white teeth seen through her parted lips. "A breathtaking sight, is it not? I was awed when first I saw it."

"I… Yes. I mean… Yes…" She sighed and shook her head. "Good heavens. Such inarticulate fumbling destroys my little reputation for always having a merry word at my fingertips!"

"Do you like the sea, my Lizzy?" Miss Palmer's slow perambulation had brought her and Palmer to join them.

"It is beautiful. More than beautiful. What words can encompass such piercing glory?"

Darcy allowed his gaze to return to the sea. "Very few men, or women, could weave such words."

She laughed and agreed. "It is beyond my poor talents."

Miss Bennet leaned in close. "I never thought to see the day, Lizzy! But you are quite right. It is beautiful."

The Bingleys joined them. They were both familiar with seaside resorts, but joined in the murmurs of appreciation of the beauty before them.

Miss Elizabeth drew in a deep breath. "I had not realised ships move so swiftly. They are small and sure, are they not?"

Darcy glanced out to sea again. "There is a brisk wind today, driving them south."

"The fishing fleet, I fancy. They will have been out since before dawn, and now, early in the day as it is, will be returning to shore with their catch. If you have never had fish fresh from the sea..." Palmer laughed at the ladies' head shakes and demurral. "Ah, then, we will have a treat later. I will send one of the servants to the fishermen's shacks and bespeak our supper from them. With your consent, Darcy? They are temporarily your servants, after all."

"An excellent idea. You will not believe the difference in taste, ladies. Even in London, with fast boats bringing a catch upriver, the fish is never as fresh."

"Oh, a treat indeed." Miss Palmer leant more heavily on Palmer's arm.

"I look forward to it." Miss Elizabeth pointed. "That is not a fishing boat, surely?"

"A frigate, do you think, Palmer?" Bingley shaded his eyes with his free hand.

"Aye. It is small enough, and fast enough."

"One of the home fleet, likely, guarding our shores from the Corsican." Darcy watched it race before the wind, white sails belling out, its sharp prow breaking the glassy sea into foam to mark its passing.

"The French coast is not thirty miles from here," Palmer told them, tone sober.

"Oh, so close?" Miss Bingley shuddered delicately. "How horrid!"

"We owe them much, those brave men. We are lucky indeed to be so well defended." Miss Elizabeth's mouth curved up into a smile as she watched the frigate. If ever an artist were commissioned to paint the epitome of pure delight and pleasure, he would paint that smile. "Does she not move with a... a kind of hard grace? I have rarely seen anything so free and lovely, and yet so deadly and purposeful. I have seen ships close to, cargo ships, in the docks at London. But there they moved slowly, sails furled, pulled by lighters and barges into their place at the wharf. It was fascinating to see, but it is only now I realise how restrained and cramped they were. They were meant for this"—with a wide sweep of her arm at the waves below—"not a wharf."

The docks? Oh. Doubtless some venture of her tradesman uncle's. Darcy, thus sharply reminded that although she was a gentlewoman, she had some deplorable connections, lost the thread of the conversation for a moment and when he regained it, it had ranged beyond the ships to the assault the sea made on the nose. Palmer was explaining what gave the air its characteristic piquancy.

"Salt, of course. I always fancy it can be tasted in the air. Also, brown sea weeds tossed up and left to dry at the high tide mark on the shore below. They are strange plants, and some, I am told, are edible." He laughed at the expressions turned towards him. "I have never tried them for myself. We shall see the shore later, when we walk, and you may taste them if you choose."

"Oh no!" protested Miss Bingley.

"No, I thank you. I am not so adventurous. I am the sort of simple soul, cousin, who prefers a plain dish to a ragout. You may keep your sea weeds." Miss Elizabeth wrinkled her nose. "So, salt and weeds, and a very elderly fish or crab cast up on the sands?"

Miss Bingley's nose had been identically wrinkled since Miss Elizabeth had mentioned the London docks. "Not to feature on our menu, I hope!"

"Indeed, not. And talking of refreshments, I think Aunt Iphy has stood long enough." Palmer patted the old lady's hand as she made some demur. "No, my dearest aunt, I will not let you tire yourself needlessly, waiting for our raptures over the sea to abate a little. You require some rest, I believe."

"Of course." Darcy glanced at Miss Palmer to assure himself his lapse in hospitality had caused no lasting harm. She was pale and looked a little tired. "Come inside to refresh yourselves, ladies, and meet my sister. Afterwards, I hope, we will have every opportunity to explore the town and sea shore further. Palmer, I know, has plans for walks and explorations aplenty."

"I certainly do!"

Palmer and Bingley would likely have strutted against each

other once more, but Miss Bennet prevented it by taking a step towards Palmer, who offered his free arm with nary a glance at Bingley. They started for the house, going at Miss Palmer's slow pace. Bingley, poor fool, started after them, looking so fretful and annoyed that his sister hurried to catch him up, for once not attempting to claim Darcy's attention.

Miss Elizabeth laid her hand on Darcy's arm and allowed him to lead her inside, although not without two or three swift glances over her shoulder at the sea's magnificence. He would ensure she had the opportunity for exploration later. He would not curtail any pleasure of hers, but for now would indulge his own pleasure in introducing her to his sister.

Seeing them together, Miss Elizabeth and Georgiana... He took in a sharp breath.

Georgiana was taller than Miss Elizabeth, and built on more generous lines. Indeed, in form and colouring she was very like Miss Bennet, although even to Darcy's loving eyes, not Miss Bennet's match for beauty. Few were. She was, in fact, a softer, girlish version of himself. While Georgiana had inherited their mother's fair hair and he was as dark as their father, they both had the intensely blue Fitzwilliam eyes that were their legacy from their mother, and had something of the same look around the cheekbones and mouth, too. No one could doubt they were related.

But when had she grown so womanly? His little sister seemed to be a child no longer, and she had more than once hinted she felt more mature and she was almost grown up, that she was lapping up Mrs Younge's training and precepts as a cat laps up cream. He was not prepared to see her grow away from him. She was all he had.

Georgiana greeted the Bingleys demurely as old friends, bearing their fulsome greetings with grace. She was, as Darcy expected, quiet and restrained with the Bennet ladies and Miss Palmer at first, and it was several minutes before she could look up from her apparent study of the Persian rug and try, timidly, to enter the conversation. Darcy was pleased by her efforts, and wished he could thank Miss Elizabeth, who was all smiling friendliness and gentle encouragement. Georgiana responded as a bud opening in sunshine, clearly more at ease. A quiet word from the estimable

Mrs Younge, a nod and a slight smile, and Georgiana rose to her office as hostess to offer and distribute refreshments.

Mrs Younge, to whom Darcy quietly granted a few hours holiday after assuring her that he would support Georgiana, slipped away to carry out some errand of her own. A discreet and thoughtful woman.

Miss Bennet had seated herself near her aunt, and looked on in near silence. She glanced once or twice at the Bingleys, but her attention was mostly for Georgiana.

"Goodness." Miss Palmer looked from her eldest niece to Georgiana. "I am astonished how alike Jane and Miss Darcy are! I can hardly credit it."

Miss Bingley turned red. "Oh, I see no real like—"

Her mouth clacked shut when Darcy, who had started speaking at the same instant, agreed with Miss Palmer. "You share my own thoughts, ma'am. They are alike."

"It is the colouring, and they have the same tall slenderness." Miss Elizabeth glanced at her elder sister and smiled. "Jane's eyes are a softer blue, but the resemblance is otherwise quite remarkable."

Miss Bingley huffed, and looked away.

Miss Elizabeth had taken a seat beside Georgiana's and now addressed her directly. "I understand you have been unwell, and are here to restore your health, but I must say the mayor of Ramsgate should consider using your image as a prime example of how the air here is a sovereign remedy!"

Unused to such raillery, Georgiana blushed and looked to Darcy for guidance, but before he could speak, Elizabeth smiled and added, "You appear to be very well, Miss Darcy. Your brother must be greatly eased by your improved health."

How quickly she perceived his feelings and his heart! It must be obvious how his anxieties were assuaged, seeing Georgiana more her old self than she had been in weeks. And how kind of her to say so.

His timid little sister found the courage to respond. "Yes. Yes, I hope… He is very good to me. Although I cannot think he will like the mayor using me as an example."

"No, indeed!" Elizabeth's expressive face showed only kindness and merriment when she glanced at him, and her smile grew brighter. "I imagine he has that delicacy of mind, a mix of family pride and the sense of what is proper, to make him reluctant to allow your image to be exposed to the public eye."

Georgiana smiled back. "He is best of brothers."

"He is, indeed." Miss Bingley's look at her own brother lacked Georgiana's guileless partisanship.

Elizabeth gave Darcy a saucy glance. "Oh, but stern, I am sure!"

"Oh no, I assure you. He is indulgent, and very kind." Georgiana's expression lacked sauce of any description, her earnestness sweet and unforced.

"I envy you. We are five sisters, you see, and we have always wished for a brother, have we not, Jane?"

Thus appealed to, Miss Bennet broke her silence, and smiled. "I am sure you deserve every kindness, Miss Darcy."

"No one could deserve it more!" Miss Bingley was as effusive as ever. "Why, we have known *dear* Miss Darcy this age, and none can compare to her for elegance, beauty, and sweetness of temper. She is the epitome of all the graces! Do you not agree, Charles?"

Bingley had no opportunity to reply, though the look he gave his sister bore an air of faint astonishment. Elizabeth laughed before Darcy could speak, and turned the conversation to music, admiring the piano he had hired for Georgiana's use.

Darcy watched them, pleased. Elizabeth glanced at him again. What had she thought of Georgiana's loving partiality? Had she agreed with Georgiana's shy praise and compliments?

But all she had said was, *I envy you… we have always wished for a brother.*

It astonished him that what he felt most was chagrin.

CHAPTER TWENTY-SEVEN

Yellow Sands

Come unto these yellow sands,
And then take hands
Shakespeare, *Ariel's Song from The Tempest*

"Well, Jane. Are you satisfied that Caroline Bingley does no more than voice her own wishes with regard to Miss Darcy, rather than there being any real inclination on her brother's behalf?"

Elizabeth kept her voice low, for her sister's ear only. She tilted her parasol to shade her from the hot late-August sun and hence preserve her from Mamma's laments about freckles, but principally to help ensure their privacy. They were a few yards behind the rest of their party, ostensibly drawn to study the wares of a shop selling all manner of things created from seashells, with the excuse that they must seek out unusual keepsakes to take home to their sisters. The others were no strangers to the delights of a seaside resort, and had strolled on to allow her and Jane to relish the novelties appearing at every turn.

Aunt Iphy had remained behind at the cottage, on the grounds she was too old now to be rambling about, adding, in response to

Elizabeth's comment that the sea air would put roses in her cheeks, "A mere sea breeze is fifty years too late for that, my dear! No, you go and explore with Galahad. He knows Ramsgate well, and I am certain he will be delighted to show you all the shops and walks." She had, pointedly, not looked at either Jane or the Bingleys as she spoke, and Elizabeth had escaped post-haste, avoiding her cousin's gaze and reflecting that not even her Mamma could have been more unsubtle. It had taken some little while for the roses in Elizabeth's own cheeks to cool, but she put her discomfort aside, taking this opportunity to speak quietly to Jane.

"It is difficult for me to tell you my mind. I do not know what to think." Jane, her free hand tucked inside Elizabeth's elbow, tightened her grip. "I cannot laugh myself out of ill-temper, or talk myself out of anxiety or a megrim, the way you do. I do not have your ease with words to explain what my feelings are. Indeed, I barely know, myself. It is all too fresh, too immediate, and much of my time must be spent in their company. I have had little opportunity to reflect upon everything that has happened in the last few days, or ponder over every utterance Mr and Miss Bingley make. I am all confusion."

It weighed upon Elizabeth, that Jane had been reluctant to talk to her since the Bingleys' arrival. It was typical of her sister's reticent nature, but her heart ached for Jane's unhappiness. "I wish I could do more to help. I will say in reassurance that it is clear Miss Bingley orchestrated her brother's apparent desertion. Just as her words about his so-called devotion to Miss Darcy are patently false."

"Do you think so?"

"Jane, he has made no effort whatsoever to single her out. He greeted her kindly, as a man greets a girl who, though on the cusp of womanhood, is yet a shy child. He shows no symptom of any particular regard. No. His regard is all for you, and Miss Darcy being his object is all Miss Bingley's fancy. Another tarradiddle to rank beside those she told him about you."

"Yes. That seems true."

"But does not allay your unease?"

Jane looked along the street, Elizabeth following the line of her gaze. Their companions had paused outside a confectioner's shop, evidently in deep discussion over the delights for sale inside. Miss Darcy held her brother's arm, Miss Bingley was on their cousin Galahad's. Mr Bingley, with no lady to demand his attention, stared gloomily down at his feet.

"I believe the misunderstanding—for so we must call it, and remain polite—was of Miss Bingley's contrivance. But Lizzy... Lizzy, do you love our sisters?"

"I beg your pardon?"

"Our sisters. I love them dearly, and I want always to believe the best of them. But Mary is pedantic and heavy. Not in features or form, but in her mind."

"The perfect wife for a clergyman."

"She will do well there. It is the ideal sphere for her good qualities, too: her desire to help and teach. Kitty is indeterminate and fractious, but wants something that is hers alone at which she can excel. She will bloom when she finds it. Lydia is bold and often unkind, and ruthless in getting her own way. She wants nothing but admiration."

"And me?"

"You leap to judgement, Lizzy, and you sometimes use too sharp a tongue to show your cleverness and quickness." Jane gave her a slight smile. "What matters more is that your heart is good and you are kind, loving and generous. You are my dearest Lizzy, who is all the sweeter for the occasional tartness!"

Elizabeth laughed. "Jane!"

"You are all very dear to me. But though I seldom speak of our sisters' characters, I hope I understand them. I want to believe they are good and any faults in them can be explained away. I have to believe that, and be true to what I believe the church requires of us in loving our fellow men. But I am not so blind I cannot see where they err. I love them, so I forgive them."

"You are always kind to them. And to me."

"You are all in my heart. Doubtless Mr Bingley holds his sister in the same great affection, but he does not see what we have. He is blind to what she is about. He seemed astonished, did he not, that she had contrived and schemed, and told untruths. I presume she acted to part us because we Bennets are not prominent and rich, and I do not have a good dowry. All of that weighs against me in the scales she holds dear. How did he not see that? Does he know her so little, or have no notion of her character and ambition, and hence not doubt the intelligence she gave him? He is an amiable man, sweet natured and good tempered, but evidently not a man of discernment, resolution, or deep reflection. Is he too easy? Too facile and credulous?"

Elizabeth tightened her lips against the question she longed to ask. It would be for Jane to reveal the state of her heart when she wished to do so. If at all. Instead, she contented herself with asking, "And that is what you must reflect upon?"

"Yes. To be at ease in my own mind."

Elizabeth could only sigh and nod. "I agree. You must take your own path to knowing your heart and mind. You will prevail, I know. Your understanding is excellent, your principles strong, and kindness the very foundation of your character. When I first arrived in Wingham, somehow a conversation arose in which I said as much about you, and if you had a fault, it is your wish to believe the best of people. Mr Darcy, I remember, remarked that people rarely merited such faith."

"His upbringing and situation must make him more wary, I suppose, and suspicious that acquaintances must be seeking something of him. His caution is understandable, if unfortunate."

Elizabeth's smile broadened. "There! The perfect example of what I told them of you. You will always pity and explain failings in others, and never condemn them." She sighed. "I suppose we must rejoin the others. We have tarried here too long already, and the gentlemen are looking at us. Doubtless to hurry us along!"

Jane nodded and agreed, and they turned to follow the rest of their party.

"I would add, Jane, that of those gentlemen who await us, I would never consider our cousin lacking in resolution. Let his admiration be some balm and solace."

"I suggest, Lizzy, his family's ambitions lie elsewhere."

"Not his, though, I am certain. I do not think he believes he is bound to redress a romance that went awry half a century ago. I do not, you may be sure."

"Lizzy!"

But Jane could say no more, for they were already within hearing distance of the others, and so they must hurry, and smile, and beg pardon for being distracted by all the unusual goods for sale. They had not intended to keep everyone waiting on their pleasure.

"I, for one, cannot believe how inventive these artisans are with a sea shell, once its former occupant has no more use for it." Elizabeth infused her tone with as much merriment as she could. "That must be my excuse for delaying you. I am sorry!"

After the *not-at-all* demurrals, which were of varying levels of sincerity, Mr Darcy nodded towards Fairfax's Tea House. "My sister tells us this is the best confectioner in Ramsgate, with an excellent reputation for ices and iced creams. Is that not so, Georgiana?"

Miss Darcy blushed at being appealed to directly, but agreed in a burst of eagerness. "They make many fruit ices, and they are very prettily done. They put them into moulds, you see, so you may choose to have your ice shaped as a swan, or a shell, or... oh! all manner of things! It is very clever. They bake the most delicious little almond biscuits to eat with your ice, and all kinds of candied fruits and sugar drops. Mrs Younge discovered it when we first explored Ramsgate, and we have visited often."

"How do they contrive to make ices in this hot weather?" Jane said kindly, to encourage Miss Darcy's eloquence. Her usual pleasant mask was in place, hiding all behind its serene smile. "We used the last of the Longbourn ice house's bounty at our sister's wedding in June."

"There are caves tunnelled deep into the cliffs east of the harbour, where shopkeepers like Fairfax keep their store," Cousin Galahad explained. "The ice lasts all year round, until more can be brought in winter. From Norway, I believe."

"Norway," murmured Miss Darcy, with a small frown.

Elizabeth made a face at him for discomposing the girl. "If I were modest about my accomplishments, I would deplore my lack of competence in the use of the globes. But since I am made free with my father's library, and he is fond of those gentlemen who

242

travel the world and publish what we must hope are truthful accounts of their voyages, you cannot bamboozle me, cousin." She smiled at Miss Darcy. "A country in the far north of the world, and parts of it subject all of the year to snow and ice."

Cousin Galahad laughed and bowed. "And months of darkness, I have read, where no man sees the sun in winter."

"How chilling." Miss Bingley tipped her parasol to better shield her face.

The parasol was not one whit prettier than Elizabeth's own, though Miss Bingley had undoubtedly bought hers at some exclusive shop while Elizabeth had been given hers direct from her uncle's warehouse. Pettiness was its own reward, sometimes. Elizabeth tilted her own parasol against the clear blue sky and the heat hammering down upon them. "I agree! Although a little coolness now would be welcome."

Mr Darcy gestured to the shop. "Then let us sample these miraculous ices. We should not visit Ramsgate and forbear to taste the best it can offer."

To this proposal the entire party consented. The day was hot, the ices cold, and each of them welcomed the refreshment.

"Oh!" Miss Darcy had all the enthusiasm of the nice child she was. "I do hope they have peach ices! They are my favourite!"

Elizabeth laughed, tucked her hand under Jane's elbow, and followed the Darcys in.

The ices were indeed very good. Elizabeth's had been flavoured with strawberry and moulded to look like one, complete with stalk and leaves, and she was still savouring the remembrance of its cold sweetness an hour later as their party explored the sandy shore east of the harbour.

The sands were busy with crowds of visitors, walking and bathing. The bathing wagons, with peculiar canvas projections curving out and down at the rear (which, Cousin Galahad explained, allowed the bathers to enter the sea without outraging modesty and discretion) plied back and forth to the water, pulled by sturdy horses.

"Fascinating!" Elizabeth eyed the contraptions with a touch of envy.

"I have sea-bathed every week since I arrived," Miss Darcy said. "My doctor thought it would help improve my health. The water is very cold, even on a day like this."

"I would not like it." Miss Bingley gave a fastidious shudder.

"I wish we had time to try it." And Elizabeth sighed for a lost opportunity.

"I have arranged for a sailing trip around the bay for later today, which may mitigate your disappointment." Mr Darcy pulled his watch from his pocket. "I agreed to meet the boat's owner at two, leaving us time for a walk here and a light nuncheon at the cottage first."

"Then do let us walk! I do not wish to miss anything this day." Elizabeth, hoping Jane would forgive her, singled out their cousin Galahad and tugged him along the shoreline.

The tide was still out, and they walked along the firm, still-damp sands that, in an hour or two, would be underwater again. Elizabeth searched for bounty in the seaweed strewn along the line marking the closest the sea would come to the lands. She enlisted her cousin's aid, making use of the more capacious pockets with which a gentleman's clothing was equipped, and filling his with shells and smooth, frosted pebbles of white or green or amber. Glass, perhaps?

"Yes. Fragments of glass worn to smoothness by the sea," Cousin Galahad said, when she asked. "Perhaps from a shipwreck, or from some drunken sailor casting his rum bottle overboard."

Elizabeth laughed. "Well, they are pretty, however they fell into the waves." She glanced around. They were a little distant from the others, who were engaged in trying to make out which hedge visible on the cliffs above belonged to the house inhabited by Miss Darcy, an enterprise involving much pointing and walking backwards to peer upwards while shading their eyes with their hands. She determined to speak while she had the chance. "I told Miss Darcy that my sisters and I have always wished for a brother. Allowing the use of his pockets would not be the least of his charms."

He gave her a searching look, studying her eyes and face. No fool he. But then she had never thought him one.

She smiled. "I hope you do not object to me thinking of you as I would my brother if I had one?"

He huffed out a laugh that started in something very like chagrin but ended in genuine amusement. "No, I do not object." He took her hand and raised it to his lips. "I will gladly carry your shells and glass, cousin, and be a useful brother."

They had reached an understanding without having to say more. She smiled again. "Thank you! I will try not to exceed the limits of your patience." She glanced towards the others, who had turned back and were making their way towards the path to the harbour and from there, she assumed, intending to return to the cottage for the promised noon repast. Both Jane and Mr Darcy were looking towards them, and she raised a hand, to reassure them their intentions were understood. "We had better catch up the others before they wonder what we are about."

She put her hand on the arm he offered, and they walked briskly across the sands in the wake of the rest of their party.

Cousin Galahad laughed again. "I suspect that when you marry, Lizzy, you will do more than fill your husband's pockets with shells. You will lead the poor man the merriest of dances!"

"But that is what marriage should be, do you not think? A dance, where both know the steps, love the tune, and can sing it in harmony." Elizabeth laughed up at him as they toiled up the rough stone stair to the top of the harbour's east wall at the point it met the cliffs. The road to the cottage was to their right, their companions walking up its slope. Her eye caught by a movement to their left, and she half turned towards the harbour itself, which was fronted by shops and small houses.

Miss Darcy's companion, Mrs Younge, stepped onto the road from a shop. Behind her, a shadow moved. Stopped. Retreated. The shopkeeper, no doubt, seeing her from his premises.

Mrs Younge, without a glance behind her, dropped a curtsey. "Mr Palmer. Miss Elizabeth. I hope you are enjoying your visit? Ah, I see the rest of Mr Darcy's party are ahead of us. May I join you, if you are returning to the cottage?"

"We would be delighted." Cousin Galahad offered his free arm with a flourish. "How are you finding Ramsgate and the cottage, Mrs Younge? Miss Darcy's health appears improved."

"Oh, she is. I am very pleased by the changes in her." Mrs Younge's smile was demure and restrained, as became a young lady's companion. "I impute it all to Ramsgate, the sea air and regular sea bathing. Our stay here has been to everyone's great advantage. The companion's smile broadened. "Miss Darcy will have no cause to repine. I will make certain of it."

CHAPTER TWENTY-EIGHT

Playing The Painter

Mine eye hath play'd the painter
— Shakespeare, *Sonnet 24*

Elizabeth was a little late joining the party when it convened in the yellow parlour after breakfast the day following their Ramsgate excursion. She hurried in, concerned she had left Jane too long at the Bingleys' mercy. But no. Jane was safe, ensconced on a sofa with Cousin Galahad at her side living up to his namesake's chivalry by being ready to rescue the fair maiden and banish marauding dragons.

The dragon in question sat beside Mr Darcy and could not have been more smug if she had put several small villages to the flame and was now resting, replete, from her labours. Well, as smug as those dragons were who had the habit of sitting and leafing through the copy of *La Belle Assemblée* held on their laps, making *moues* at some of the fashion plates and approving little nods and murmurs at others. Mr Darcy's expression was unfathomable. Not so that of Mr Bingley, who stalked around the room with a mien both disconsolate and vexed, looking always between his sister and

Jane, as a man trying to solve a conundrum beyond his understanding.

"Forgive me! I was delayed." Elizabeth took a chair near Jane. "Aunt Iphy is more wearied by our journey yesterday than she would admit to at first, but I have coaxed her into returning to her room for the rest of the forenoon. I made a promise to her on the behalf of you all that none of you would think any the worse of her if her maid drew the curtains, and she were to close her eyes for an hour or two."

There was a general murmur of concern, such as most people would express for someone little known to them. Cousin Galahad, however, looked away from Jane quickly, turning to Elizabeth with all the solicitude born of true affection.

"She is not ill, is she? Should I send for our doctor?"

"Oh no, I assure you. She is tired, but I do not believe it is more."

Galahad's genial face twisted into a grimace. "She is almost seventy now, and though she wears her years well enough, I should have been less conscious of my own pleasure in the outing yesterday and more solicitous of her comfort. You will watch over her, Lizzy, and tell me at once if we need do more?"

"Of course. Do not distress yourself, cousin."

"It was an arduous journey and a long day for an elderly lady," Mr Darcy said. "I am sorry indeed she is suffering some ill-effects from gratifying a whim of mine. That is far from what I hoped the day would give us."

He was swift to take responsibility onto himself. Indeed, he seemed grave and concerned.

Elizabet granted him a reassuring smile. "You intended us to have a day of pleasure, Mr Darcy, and you achieved that with ease. My aunt told me how much enjoyment she took from both meeting your sister and seeing Ramsgate again. Please do not take any responsibility now for her indisposition. I promise you she is merely a little more tired than usual. Do not blame yourself."

"Oh!" Mr Bingley's manner was somewhat insouciant. "It is Darcy's besetting sin, Miss Elizabeth, to take responsibility for others. He was the most diligent praeposter at school, you must know, and quite the luminary among the House Captains."

Elizabeth smiled a little, but did not otherwise respond. She fancied Mr Darcy was a little offended, and he had shown such pleasing concern for Aunt Iphy, he did not deserve to be laughed at. "I will look in on her often. In the meantime, she urged me to tell you we should consider our next amusement and not allow this to affect our plans." She shook her bag of shells and polished glass pebbles into her lap, to sort through them. The maid assigned to her had had them cleaned, and had returned the bag to her as she left Aunt Iphy's chamber. What was she to do with them?

"We might spend the day quietly," Jane suggested. "I do not wish to leave Aunt Iphy unattended, in case she has need of us."

Galahad agreed. "I agree. I had thought we might drive across to Goodnestone after our noon meal, but we may reserve that for another day when we know Aunt Iphy is recovered. You will like Sir Brook Bridges, Bingley. He is an excellent fellow."

Elizabeth picked up a shell, the outer casing broken to show the convolutions within, and examined it. What a lovely thing it was, with the pink sheen over its smoothness. "Goodnestone is a pleasant place, but yesterday's amusements will be difficult to surpass. I thank you again, Mr Darcy, for the treat. I will never forget my first sight of the sea, though I will endeavour to forget sailing around the harbour. While my courage rises whenever something conspires to daunt me, I was not entirely at ease on that ship!"

Mr Darcy smiled, while the others laughed or, in Miss Bingley's case, stared in surprise. Perhaps she was marvelling at Elizabeth's pert tone. Who could say?

Mr Darcy inclined his head. "The pleasure of the day was mine, Miss Elizabeth. You seemed at ease enough, though. I did not notice any greenish tinge to your complexion."

"I must have hidden it too well. I am used to a form of locomotion that, even on the most poorly-maintained roads, is usually in one direction. One that also moves up and down with such vigour and, well, enthusiasm..." Elizabeth lifted her hand into the air and used it to imitate the boat rising and falling on the swell of the waves. "I can appreciate it in a philosophical sense, and reserve my wonder for those gentlemen whose joy it has been to wander the seas and oceans to explore this great world of ours. My admiration for the gallant sailors protecting our shores is increased tenfold."

Mr Bingley's laugh was the loudest, while his sister produced a tight-lipped smile. Good heavens. Would nothing induce the Friday-faced creature to unbend?

"What is more," Elizabeth added, "I am grateful to you for the opportunity to meet Miss Darcy. You must be very proud of her."

This provoked a response from Miss Bingley. "Oh yes! Such an honour, Miss Eliza. Dear Miss Darcy is the most elegant and refined lady of my acquaintance. Mr Darcy is very careful of her. It was so kind of him to permit the introduc—"

"Not at all." Whatever else Mr Darcy would permit, it seemed it did not include allowing her to finish what was likely to be another of her insults. "I was honoured and pleased to introduce her to the Misses Bennet. But you are correct, Miss Elizabeth. I am indeed very proud of her."

Miss Bingley sniffed. Perhaps she had a cold.

A short silence fell. Jane examined her shoes with some assiduity. Although she had eventually agreed with Elizabeth's conclusion that Mr Bingley's supposed preference for Miss Darcy was all in his sister's fervid imagination, she had been discomfited by the young girl's presence. Elizabeth still had no deep understanding of Jane's thoughts and inclinations where the Bingleys were concerned. Jane was more reserved even than usual, but Elizabeth hoped Miss Bingley's manners were teaching Jane that she should not regret the distance that had grown between them.

After a moment, Cousin Galahad gestured to Elizabeth's shells. "You certainly made the most of our visit, cousin. What do you intend to do with your treasure trove?"

"I have not the least notion! I fear my admiration for the trinkets we saw in Ramsgate generated an ambition my poor artistic talents cannot realise. I thought of decorating a plain picture frame with them, to enhance some nautical painting or other, although I might do better covering a plain box. I have no talent for drawing or painting, you see, and finding a seascape would be another difficult problem."

She and Jane between them had bought shell-bedecked boxes for their mother and sisters, and she would like to produce something of similar ingenuity and beauty. She doubted her capacity for such artistry.

"Miss Darcy's skills in drawing are the equal of her musical abilities," Miss Bingley put in. "It is a great shame we did not have the opportunity to examine her sketchbooks yesterday. You would be amazed at her talents, I am sure."

"She is as modest about her drawing as she is about her gift for music." Mr Darcy raised his eyes from examining Elizabeth's collection of shells. "But she is talented. She inherited it from our mother, I fancy, who was an excellent artist. Sadly, Miss Elizabeth, I have no ability myself in that direction."

"Then she would have much in common in that respect with my youngest sister, with whom she is of an age. Lydia is by far the best artist amongst us."

Miss Bingley put aside *La Belle Assemblée* as Elizabeth spoke, with a sharp, dismissive gesture. Presumably one of the fashion plates offended her beyond endurance. "Are you comparing your sister to Miss Darcy, Miss Eliza?" Miss Bingley's smile was all sweet malice. "I intend no offence," she went on, in the sort of dulcet, cloying tone that meant she intended to be extremely offensive indeed, "but Miss Darcy is the granddaughter of an earl. She has been very highly educated and very delicately raised. Her tastes and accomplishments must be very different to those of your sister."

"Caroline!" But Mr Bingley's tone was one of more weariness than force.

Elizabeth had pressed her lips together for an instant against the angry words she would like to unleash. Now she found a tone of such honey, matching Miss Bingley dulcet note for dulcet note, she surprised herself. "I am all astonishment, Miss Bingley. I was unaware you had met my youngest sister and were familiar with her drawings."

Miss Bingley flushed scarlet. It did not complement the pinkness of her dress.

Elizabeth did not give her time to speak. She kept her voice and mien mild with an effort, allowing her fingers to tighten on the shells and release her irritation on their unyielding hardness. "It is true that Lydia's interests have, these last few months, been restricted to depicting elaborate and intricate decorations for her bonnets, but she has some facility with pencil and paint, nonetheless. I am uncertain what a lofty lineage would do to confer such a God-given talent upon an individual. They either have it or they do not."

Mr Darcy could not hold himself more stiffly if he had looked full in the face of Medusa herself, his expression pinched, his jaw so tight it must have ached. "Miss Bingley—"

But Miss Bingley was in no mood, it appeared, to allow even the object of her solicitude to finish. "Oh, please do not misunderstand me! You have already informed us that your parents' approach to education has been... unconventional. Miss Darcy, by contrast, attended one of the finest schools with the best masters. I am sure your little sister's work is very creditable considering she did not have the same advantages, but still I cannot see how she might rival Miss Darcy's achievements."

Jane could not look at anyone, and returned to studying her shoes. Galahad was as tense as Mr Darcy, with an alarming red over his cheekbones, his eyes narrowed and his mouth a hard, whitened line. Mr Darcy, in contrast, was pale. Both gentlemen were, of course, constrained by civility, and both turned to look at Mr Bingley, who alone had the authority to silence his sister. Mr Bingley, though, turned away, rubbing one hand over his face.

Most of the honey had been swept from Elizabeth's tone, but still she strove to keep it lighter and less biting than Miss Bingley deserved. "I am sure there is no misunderstanding. I will agree that training and practice are most necessary to develop the gifts God bestows upon us. I do not dispute that in all probability Miss Darcy has had finer masters than my father could provide, but we are hardly untaught savages. However, this is a discussion we will be unable to resolve, since I have never seen Miss Darcy's drawings and you have never seen Lydia's. We had better change the subject, Miss Bingley, and cease the argument."

Miss Bingley's brother turned back and struck in with "Aye.

Arguments are too much like disputes. We are here for a pleasant visit with friends, and I would prefer it, Caroline, you find something else to discuss." He bent, picked up the copy of *La Belle Assemblée* and thrust it at his sister. "Or return to your reading."

Miss Bingley opened her mouth, but again she had no chance to speak.

Jane rose, elegant and lovely, and only her heightened colour spoke of her distaste for the scene. "I am going to see how Aunt Iphy fares. Come with me, Lizzy?"

"Of course." Elizabeth stood, tossing the bag of shells amongst the cushions of her chair.

"I will come too. I wish to satisfy myself our aunt does not require the services of the local doctor. Cousin?" Galahad held out his arm for Jane to take and escorted her to the door. Elizabeth, with a mere glance at the Bingleys and Mr Darcy, followed.

As she closed the door behind them, an explosive snort of derision came from the Bingley woman—for 'lady', she could not be rightly termed.

"Well! What a scene!"

They had not gone more than a few yards down the wide hall towards the stairs before Elizabeth let out the breath she was holding in a loud whoosh. In other company she would have refrained from such unladylike behaviour. But Jane was safe, and Galahad, she thought, would sympathise rather than condemn. She was right.

He gave her a wry smile, one that twisted up one corner of his mouth. "I could not agree more, cousin dear, but let us get to some haven before we discuss it further. I do want to assure myself that Aunt Iphy is not dreadfully unwell, and then we can go somewhere to recover our equanimity."

Elizabeth nodded, and followed on. Her pulse slowed. When she had been fencing with Miss Bingley, her heart had been pounding harder than a blacksmith hammering a horseshoe on his anvil. She had hardly noticed, intent as she had been on besting that horrid woman. Had she shown her agitation? She hoped not. She did not wish to give Caroline Bingley even so little gratification.

They had reached the top of the stairs when something behind them banged. Elizabeth spun around, catching her balance against the banister rail. The door to the parlour had been thrown wide open and Mr Bingley was already half-way along the hall, his boots clattering and thudding against the marble. He did not look towards them, but rushed towards the front door so precipitously the footman on duty barely had enough time to leap up and open it for him. Mr Bingley thundered past and out onto the portico without acknowledging the poor man. Behind him, Miss Bingley could be heard but not seen, her voice seething with annoyance. Elizabeth could not make out the words. She could imagine them.

"Good heavens," Elizabeth said as they continued on. "What cakes we are making of ourselves today! It is rather like living in a Cheltenham tragedy."

"I prefer my tragedies on the stage. They are less wearing on the nerves." Galahad ushered them into Aunt Iphy's suite.

He waited in the little sitting room, his gaze fixed on Jane, while Elizabeth peeked into the bedroom leading off it and held a soft-voiced conference with the maid.

"She is sleeping. Let us not disturb her." Elizabeth went to Jane, who stood by the window, twisting a handkerchief in her hands. "Jane, dear…"

"He did not stop her. He does not censure her behaviour. He allows it." Jane nodded, the movement uncharacteristically sharp. "Well. There it is."

"Jane."

"I am very fond of Bingley," Galahad said. "But he is not the most resolute of fellows. The best of good friends, but…"

"Yes." Elizabeth closed her hands over Jane's for comfort's sake, before releasing them. "He is amiable and cheerful, and I am sure he is generous and good hearted. But more is needed. Cousin, I apologise to you now, and I will do so to Mr Darcy as soon as I am able. I am angry with myself for allowing Miss Bingley to provoke me into such ill-humour. She has been here not five full days yet, and to have reduced me to such distemper! Her assertions are nonsensical, but a lady should refrain from pointing that out to her. I am sorry. I should not have contributed to the discord. I was uncivil and unladylike."

"Nonsense, Lizzy. You did nothing requiring an apology. You were far more restrained than I would have been in your place." Galahad joined them near the window and took Jane's hand in his, saying, gently, "I think you and Lizzy should have some moments of peace. If Aunt Iphy is sleeping, she will not object to you staying here in her sitting room until you feel more composed. I will go and see Darcy, and we will decide what must be done to restore harmony."

He kissed her hand, bowed and left. He acknowledged Elizabeth's approving smile with one of his own. What an excellent man. They were lucky indeed this reconciliation with their grandmother's people had brought them not only the delight that was Aunt Iphy, and Sir James's kindness, but also such a man as their cousin. Elizabeth was sorry indeed for the estrangement that had robbed them of this closeness for so long.

She turned to Jane to say so, but Jane was raising the handkerchief to her eyes to dab at them. "I am sorry, Jane. This distresses you."

"Oh, Lizzy." Jane sank into the long sofa set in the window embrasure, with more weariness than ladylike grace.

Elizabeth sat beside her, and took her hand. "What may I do?"

Jane smiled, but her eyes remained downcast and shadowed. "Your being here is enough, dear Lizzy. I am sad Mr Bingley has shown he will not check his sister's misbehaviour." She looked up at last, blinking as if to force away tears. "I am resolved not to marry where I cannot be certain my husband is strong enough to manage our household and family, to guide and discipline where that is needed. I would not have a marriage like our parents."

"Is it the same? You and Mamma are very different, as are Papa and Mr Bingley."

"Yes, we are different, but for one striking resemblance in character. I know you are Papa's favourite and you love him dearly. So do I. But Lizzy, his recent action to restrain the excesses shown by Lydia and Kitty is the first I can recall in my entire life where he did not give way, did not deplore the noise and commotion disrupting the quiet life he craves, did not retreat to his book room and leave the house in chaos, where he did not sit back and laugh at what he perceives to be folly. Can we be certain he will maintain his resolve with regard to our sisters, and ensure some true amendment in their behaviour?"

"I do not know. I hope so, but I do not know."

"Nor I. I do not wish to live with that sort of uncertainty. No." She dabbed at her eyes again, and straightened her shoulders. "Mr Bingley shows a similar disinclination to deal with ill temper and high emotion, to stand firm against his sister's poor behaviour. Where are his principles? Where is his resolve? Mr Bingley is an amiable and pleasant gentleman, but if he were on his knees now before me, I would refuse him. I would pity any distress he feels, but I will not become Mamma, desperate for guidance and strength but discovering my husband does not have either to offer me."

Elizabeth took her first breath for several moments. Jane's quiet, even voice had held her captive, every nerve straining so she did not miss a syllable. "I understand." She nodded. "I do. You are all prudence and good sense, and you are right. You have thought long on this, have you not?"

"Since I visited Caroline Bingley and realised she is no friend to my acquaintance with her brother. Their arrival here sharpened every thought, but brought no new sensation. I had no understanding with Mr Bingley. There never will be one."

Elizabeth kissed her cheek. "I am sorry this has hurt your heart."

"I will be well. If he had been the sort of gentleman I seek, it would be harder. But all will be well, Lizzy. All will be well."

Elizabeth drew her close, and for a long time they sat in quiet contemplation. She glanced more than once at the door, remembering their cousin's firm step and expression, and Galahad's care for Jane.

Perhaps all would be well, after all.

CHAPTER TWENTY-NINE
With Friends Possessed

Wishing me like to one more rich in hope,
Featured like him, like him with friends possessed
— Shakespeare, *Sonnet 29*

"I do not know at all what has possessed my brother, Mr Darcy. Poor manners appear to be contagious!"

Darcy turned—he had been contemplating following Bingley to safety and had already taken steps towards the door —and regarded his friend's sister. She had always been there, an adjunct to Bingley's life; a gawky young miss, all jutting elbows and ungainly inelegance when he had first met her some eight or nine years earlier ... yes, sometime in the year two. He and Bingley had been much involved with Palmer following Lady Palmer's untimely death, and he had met the rest of Bingley's family during a visit to Town, when he and Bingley had sought to divert Palmer from his grief. Miss Bingley would have been twelve or thirteen.

Nowadays, her elbows were under perfect control. She was fashionable, forged in the school old Mr Bingley had chosen to educate the taint of trade out of his daughters and turn them into elegant, accomplished ladies. She was *polished*, as glossy and impervious as if she were waxed to a shine by her maid each morning, perfecting the façade she presented to the world. She was not deficient in intelligence either, and made the most of the opportunities open to her to advance her position. While on their own account the Bingleys would never be seen as top drawer, they had access to many of the larger Society events and anyone could attend the theatres and the opera where all the *ton* went to be noticed. Miss Bingley went everywhere she could, cultivated every acquaintance whose company could be said to add lustre, and ensured her brother hired a box at all the principal theatres for the duration of the Season.

But that by no means justified the superior airs she took with the Bennets. By no means.

She had been on the hunt for a husband these three years at least. Her elder sister had married a gentleman, but not one high enough for Miss Bingley. Her ambitions far outstripped her sister's. She had one eye at least on Pemberley, but Darcy had perfected his own armour against such pretension. He strove always to be oblivious to any lady's arts and allurements. He was polite, always, but careful not to see the lures cast at him. He was not fond of dancing, but that careful sidestep to avoid entanglements was his favourite. He practised that dance assiduously.

"I cannot believe Miss Eliza sought to compare her sister with yours, sir! It is all of a piece with the ridiculous notion that there is some superficial resemblance between Jane Bennet and dear Georgiana. It is unconscionable, how the Bennets grasp for position and consequence." Miss Bingley threw aside her magazine.

"I do not believe she made any comparison. She said her sister had a similar interest."

"Really! Does Miss Darcy spend all her time drawing embellishments for bonnets? Good Lord, they might as well be in trade, drawing the designs for the less discerning dressmakers and milliners!"

How in heaven's name did she leap to that conclusion?

"I cannot agree. I think you have misunderstood what Miss Elizabeth intended." Darcy paused, and added, his tone wryer than he normally permitted himself in company: "We seem beset by misunderstandings recently, do we not?"

She comprehended his meaning at once, if her heightened colour was any indication. Her mouth tightened. "We should not quarrel over such inconsequential people. I am sorry my brother's temper is a little uncertain today. I assure you he has been quite content these last weeks without the company of those whose condition is far beneath ours."

"They are a gentleman's daughters, Miss Bingley."

She lifted one shoulder in a movement that should have been vulgar, but which she sought to make elegant. "With strong links to trade, sir. Have you forgotten meeting those mushrooms at the theatre, and the woman who implied she knew Pemberley? I was never so mortified by the pretensions of such people, and being forced to be seen in their company. And worse, imposing them on you at the theatre! How foolishly thrusting that woman was. How could a Cit's wife know Pemberley?"

He had forgotten, it was true, and it had irked him at the time. Now, he merely inclined his head to acknowledge the truth of Miss Bingley's recollections. "Nevertheless, Longbourn estate has been held by the Bennets for generations. They are gentry."

"A provincial estate of no great consequence, and I have that from Jane Bennet's own mouth. It is barely a fifth of Pemberley in eminence and worth, and entailed away to a distant cousin somewhere. The Bennets will sink, mark my words, when the cousin inherits. My brother should look higher."

"One sister has married the heir, so I doubt the Bennets will sink below their present position." Darcy kept his tone even with an effort. Had he been free of societal constraints on a gentleman's behaviour, he would have made it biting. "As for your brother, ambition is best tempered with practicality. A gentleman's daughter is a step up, as was your sister's marriage to Mr Hurst."

Her colour deepened. She understood him, he had no doubt of that. "We are well educated and considerably wealthier than the Bennets—" She bit off whatever else she would have said. In a more temperate tone, she went on, "Our father's last wish was that we enhance the Bingley name, and move in the best circles we can attain. This we have done, and my brother deserves better than a wife whose links to trade will pull him back again. You must help me persuade him, sir, that he must act in his own best interests."

Darcy suspected there would be little need for persuasion. Despite his occasional misgivings about the Bennets' place in Society and what that meant for their ambitions, Jane Bennet had done nothing to try and attach Bingley since his arrival. She was quiet and distant. Darcy could read little from her serene countenance, and if she favoured his friend, she was wary of showing it. In Darcy's reckoning, Miss Bingley had triumphed indeed, and her brother would likely need to look elsewhere. Whether that should be higher than a gentleman's daughter, though, was for Bingley to resolve.

"Should your brother seek my advice on any topic, I will offer, I hope, an unbiased opinion. Now, forgive me. I must seek out Palmer."

Darcy offered her a jerky half-bow, before leaving the room. He closed the door, blew out a loud sighing breath, and made haste to the sanctuary of Palmer's study.

He did not quite run.

He had no need to send a footman in search of Palmer. The man himself appeared in his study several minutes after Darcy reached it. They exchanged a long look, before Palmer went scrabbling about in the drawers of his desk. He straightened, clutching two cigars and an instantaneous light box.

He joined Darcy in the armchairs near the fireplace. "It is most vexing that it is too early in the day to open the brandy bottle. One would not wish to appear to be a drunken sot at eleven in the morning, no matter the provocation."

"Very vexing."

"This will have to suffice." Palmer proffered a cigar, and laid his own on the arm of his chair while he operated the tin light box. It held a dozen acid-dipped matches, one of which he slid into the tiny vial of vitriol in the box. The match head exploded with what Palmer, who tried to pass off his flinch by laughing, described as a jolly little conflagration.

"Smoking cigars in summer is a risky business." Palmer tossed the match into the empty fireplace, where it could finish its tiny blaze without taking the house up with it, and with careful deliberation, closed up the light box to prevent accidental infernos.

Personally, Darcy would have sent for a tinderbox from the kitchen fire. It might be dull, relying on such age-old devices rather than the modern methods the natural philosophers of the Royal Society invented, but Darcy had no wish to be the subject of such experiments. As Palmer said, it was risky.

"Easier with a fire and taper," Darcy agreed. Tobacco was not one of his vices, but the cigar was of excellent quality and a mouthful of mellow smoke an acceptable compensation for the lack of brandy.

"Bingley?"

Darcy nodded towards the window. Palmer stood to look outside.

"He is stamping about my Mamma's garden as if the roses have given unforgivable offence." Palmer resumed his seat, shaking his head. "Whereas, we all know that is his sister's office."

"Your cousins?"

"In Aunt Iphy's sitting room, where it is quiet and no one will disturb them. Jane is somewhat distressed. She does not relish discord and disharmony, whereas our fiery Lizzy is primed and armed for war." Palmer smoked quietly for a few moments, before adding, "Darcy, I would like some advice."

"Regarding Bingley?"

"And my cousin Jane. Miss Bingley's delight in provoking discord is past bearing. I am glad Papa did not witness this latest outburst. He would be furious. He likes Jane, and Lizzy is the delight of his life. He would not sit quiet and allow them to be disdained. It sits ill with me, but I must ask Bingley to take his sister back to London. It galls me to be inhospitable, and to a dear friend."

"I agree. It is necessary."

"Then what remains is whether or not I should suggest he returns here alone to make his peace with Cousin Jane, or give him the opportunity to do so before he leaves. I cannot tell if she would welcome that."

"I have been thinking on it, too. I find her inclinations hard to read. She is so serene. Looked at in a rational light, one would expect her to welcome any advances from him. We are both aware the Bennet girls have little in the way of expectations, and he is an eligible prospect for her."

"They are not mercenary, Darcy! I would have thought this two months' acquaintance with Lizzy would have taught you that. Not everyone pursues an acquaintance for personal gain. They are not all Wickhams."

"No, but there are many Miss Bingleys."

That had Palmer laughing. "Aye, I must grant you that. All too many young ladies are willing to marry for position and wealth. However, to put your mind at rest about my cousins and their aspirations, I will tell you Lizzy delicately made it known yesterday that I make a fine brother-like figure in her life. I was half relieved I had not raised her expectations, and half chagrined that my father's wishes are so obvious, she felt the need to reassure me."

Most unaccountably, Darcy's heart thumped, one big beat, then pounded so loudly Palmer ought to be able to hear it. Palmer was still speaking, but the sound was muffled and far away, muted, as if someone had filled his ears with candle wax. He took a deep breath.

Palmer's voice was clear again. "… not in the least grasping, or like Miss Bingley in thinking entirely of her own advancement."

Darcy swallowed. The mad pounding slowed to its normal pace, and the prickling of sweat on the back of his neck eased. What in heaven's name was amiss with him?

He found voice enough to answer, though even to his own ears he sounded a little choked. "I assure you, Palmer, I do not consider the Misses Bennet mercenary, and I apologise if I gave that impression. I am thinking of practicalities. Bennet himself revealed his daughters have few prospects back in Hertfordshire."

"He did?" Palmer frowned. "I do not recall it."

Darcy frowned back at him. He was sure Bennet had said so, at some point. "Well, I cannot recall the circumstances now. My point is, though, that marriage is the best—indeed, the only—provision for young women who are in want of a fortune, to preserve them from hardship. Any sensible lady of Miss Bennet's circumstances must consider prudence in marriage. Bingley is amiable and gentleman-like, and his fortune, though from trade, is excellent. Many a peer would envy his income."

"If not envying such a sister as Bingley will provide."

"True. Miss Bingley must live with her brother until she marries. That is something of a drawback."

Palmer nodded. "What you are saying is that in essence I must allow Cousin Jane to make her wishes plain. And, I suppose, not cavil if she chooses to be practical, as you put it." He sighed. "I could ask Lizzy, but I suspect she is too fond of Jane and too accustomed to being her sister's defender to view the Bingleys in an impartial light. She will be no champion of permitting Bingley a chance at redemption. I doubt, too, she will betray any confidences Jane has bestowed on her. However, the decision must be Cousin Jane's, loath though I am to put her in such an embarrassing position."

Darcy had no opportunity to respond. Bingley flung open the door and marched in, his face pink from his exertions in the rose garden. He returned their gazes for a moment, blew out a sigh, turned, and carefully, softly, closed the door to shut out all the world's noise and confusion.

"I had hoped for brandy." Bingley pulled up a chair to join them around the hearth.

Palmer squinted through his cigar smoke at the mantel clock. "A trifle early, for three sober young men who have eschewn the worst Town vices. I try not to be in my cups before noon. Cigar?"

Bingley shook his head. They sat quietly for a few moments, then Bingley sighed. "Palmer... Gal, dearest of good fellows, forgive me. I had not expected Caroline to be so impossible. Indeed, this entire imbroglio has me set on end. I could not have foreseen Miss Bennet's being here... Well, that is no excuse. I have sent word to have my coach prepared, and as soon as Caroline is packed, we will leave for Town. I am sorry we have cut up your peace here."

Palmer put his free hand on Bingley's arm. "It is not I who am most offended, my friend."

Bingley winced visibly. "No. I would be glad of a word with Miss Bennet before I go. I owe her the courtesy. Will it be possible?"

"More to the point, is it advisable?" Darcy put in.

"Necessary." Bingley paused, grimacing. "I do not believe my honour is engaged, but I singled her out in Town and as a consequence, exposed her to Caroline's ire. She deserves the opportunity to ring a peal over my head for my thoughtlessness. I would like to beg her forgiveness. If I am wrong about the extent of the injury done to her, and honour demands I repair it, I would prefer to discover it immediately, and make the proper amends. I would not hurt her further for the world."

"And your feelings for her?" Darcy asked.

"I shall never know, shall I, if partiality could develop into deeper affection? Caroline has dished me up completely in that regard. I will ask for nothing from Miss Bennet but forgiveness. I would like to apologise, most sincerely." Bingley made a soft huffing noise. "We all know Caroline will not."

"Can you not send your sister to the Hursts, and return here? You are always welcome." Palmer's tone was kinder than Darcy could produce himself if he had been the host ill-treated by an uncivil guest.

"Hurst will not allow it. I told you Louisa is increasing, I think. Hurst will not mind me confiding that her condition is precarious, and Caroline is not conducive to the quiet life Louisa needs to carry the babe to term. No." Bingley had the oddest expression of wry amusement on his face, warring with his undoubted distress. "No. I will make my apologies to Miss Bennet, if you will broker the opportunity for me, Gal. And then, since Caroline was so eager to mislead Miss Bennet as to her true destination by telling her we were for Bath, that is exactly where I shall take her. The waters are famous for healing everything from leprosy to gout. Let us see if they can cure a sour disposition."

Palmer's smile was all amusement.

Darcy reverted, as Bingley had done, to the familiar names of their boyhood, all the better to convey his approval for this course. "Well done, Charles."

A fitting response to Miss Bingley's nonsense! Bingley was stiffening his spine against his sister's rule, and not before time. Too late for Miss Bennet, perhaps, but it suggested a more hopeful future.

"Fitz." Bingley managed a faint smile. "You know, I almost regret the day we claimed not to be boys any longer, and we changed to more formal names for each other. Know you are always Fitz and Gal in my heart. I am a lucky man, to have such good friends. I do not tell you that often enough."

Darcy and Palmer both murmured something embarrassed but sincere in response, and for a few moments, they sat in companionable silence to allow Bingley time to screw his courage to the sticking point and seek out Jane Bennet.

Bingley would have their support. He would always have their support. Darcy had included Miss Bingley and the Hursts in most—if not all—invitations because, well, he was always pleased to champion Bingley. He could continue to give his backing to his friend, but he was not required to have anything to do with Bingley's sister in the process.

It was a curiously liberating conclusion to reach. Most satisfying.

An hour or more later, Darcy stood in a part of the garden that gave him a sideways view of the high walls surrounding the stable yard. The high arching gates that gave out on the gravelled drive before the Hall's magnificent frontage were flung wide. Beyond them, the grooms bustled to prepare Bingley's travelling coach.

"So, they are leaving." Miss Elizabeth spoke from behind him, making him start.

He spun to greet her, feeling his face flush with the surprise of her being there. He bowed as she dropped him a quick curtsey. "Yes. I believe Bingley wished to speak to your sister first."

She nodded, her expression as she watched the grooms rather hard and unforgiving. He preferred to look at her rather than the stable yard. She wore a light spencer over her day dress, and her bonnet swung by its strings in one ungloved hand. She looked as though she had left the house in haste. She looked angry. She looked pretty. More than pretty: she looked glorious, with dishevelled curls, pink cheeks and eyes brightened by anger. After a moment she took a deep breath and, glancing at the bonnet in her hand, placed it where it belonged.

A shame. He liked the curls the bonnet hid.

"Forgive me. I am not usually so ramshackle." The look she gave him was part-amused, part-shamed. She tied the ribbons into a jaunty bow under one ear. "A lady, I am told, must always be seen properly attired, and neat as a pin." Her mouth turned up at the corners. "Ah well, I do my poor best."

"You are charming."

"And yet, I am a shrew. I was less than civil with Miss Bingley, and I beg your pardon, sir, that it was in your presence, and involved your poor, innocent sister in our argument. It was unconscionable."

"But not of your creation." He offered his arm. "Shall we walk, and leave the grooms to continue?"

She smiled, and put her hand under his elbow. "Thank you. I am sorry I allowed myself to be provoked. My excuse must be that I love my sister dearly."

"I can sympathise."

Her smile broadened. "Yes, indeed. Your affection for Miss Darcy is marked. You will understand why I am a trifle out of sorts. Jane agreed to speak with Mr Bingley, you see, and it distressed her."

"I know he wished to see her." Darcy had to prevent himself from patting the hand on his arm. It was too familiar a gesture. "We had a discussion this morning. He is very aware of his sister's unkindness and wishes to make amends."

"He made a very handsome apology, and was a perfect

gentleman. I was present, though I sat at the other end of the room to give them as much privacy as I could. I can say no more, since it is not my tale to tell. Mr Bingley is a good friend, I believe?"

"If I had brothers, he and Palmer would be the ones I would choose."

"I thought so. Then, sir, I will say only that Mr Bingley would likely appreciate the sympathy of his brothers at this moment. Jane was saddened and affected by the whole interview. Our cousin is with her now. He has persuaded her to take some air and allow the Bingleys to leave unimpeded." She stopped, and frowned up at him. "Is that why I am so discomposed? That she has chosen to walk with Cousin Galahad rather than accept my sympathy? How dog-in-the-manger of me!"

Darcy, who was certainly aware of Palmer's interest in his beautiful cousin, could not think what to say. Instead, he smiled at Elizabeth's consternation. How delightful that she trusted him enough to show him the workings of her heart and mind. How—

"And why do you smile at me so, sir? I am a wrongheaded, contrary creature, and I acknowledge it. Does that amuse you?"

The face turned up to his was bright with amusement, those eyes—those eyes!—gleaming with laughter, and one riotous curl escaping the confines of her bonnet. She swept it back with her free hand, but it sprang loose again to bounce merrily against her temple. Her face when she pursed her lips to blow the curl away! Charming. More than charming. And to add to her manifest beauty, she was clever, witty, genuine, unaffected. Unspoiled by the pointless 'education' offered the young ladies of the *ton*, her intelligence shone. And she was loving. Her clear affection for her sister, her wholehearted championship... Georgiana must long for such a sister. In all, Elizabeth Bennet was lovely. So very lovely.

He let his smile widen. Something unaccustomed—joy, perhaps—rose in him, as warm and nurturing as the sun whose rays were pleasant on the back of his neck.

"No. I do not think you contrary. Your concern and affection for your sister is admirable. You are admirable. You are beautiful, and all that is lovely, kind and generous. You must know how much I admire and love you."

CHAPTER THIRTY
Repenting In Thorns

And he repents in thorns, that sleeps in beds of roses.
— Francis Quarles (1592–1644)

Elizabeth's lips parted in an audible gasp, the rosy colour leaching from her cheeks, leaving her pale and staring. "Aahh…"

Darcy was almost as astonished as she appeared to be. He had not at all intended to make any sort of declaration, but his tongue, usually under excellent regulation, had run away with him. He could not regret it, though his heart repeated the peculiar convulsions it had undergone earlier that day when he was talking to Palmer. It once again began a curious hammering and pounding, and he had the most extraordinary sensation that he was the frigate they had seen the day before, running pell-mell before the gusting wind with little control over his speed or direction. It left him breathless.

Could she hear his heart beating? Perhaps she could, for she stared at him as though she were seeing him for the first time, her eyes so wide only a grey line ringed the darkness of her pupils. She stopped walking so abruptly her hand fell from his arm, and he took a step without her before he realised it. He turned on his heel.

Frowning, he tried to gather his thoughts into a coherent whole. He had to speak now. He had committed himself too far to withdraw with honour. What an idiot to speak before he had thought about it, considered it, weighed every word before he spoke it! He hoped he would not make a mull of this.

It was important she understood this was not a mere simple attraction, or mere animal passion. She was worth more than that. She had to know, to understand, that he had learned to value her above everything he had once held as immutable truths about marriage and what it meant for one of his position and connections.

Coherence was beyond him. But he tried to express to her what was in his heart, to explain the cataclysm she had wrought upon his careful, considered life.

"I have always known, you see, it is my duty to marry well. As you know, my holdings are extensive, and my family is of some consequence. While the earl, my uncle, does not exercise control over me, he has certain expectations. He is prominent in government circles and values connections that will bring support and influence, and, of course, you cannot... So you must see that my duty, my expectation, was to marry in a way to promote the Darcys' prosperity and reputation. I am putting that aside. For you."

He paused, to give her the opportunity to respond. She appeared to be affected beyond the power of speech: although her mouth opened a little, nothing emerged. It was likely, since she was a clever, sensible woman, that she had never expected him to offer for her. Knowing his position and connections, she could never have considered she would be a suitable match. How pleased she would be, when she had mastered her surprise!

"You cannot deny there are some impediments we must overcome, some disadvantages, my uncle's likely misgivings... To the matter of wealth, I am indifferent. It is not a primary consideration. But the position of your family, your mother's in particular, is, you must agree, objectionable."

"Objectionable?" Elizabeth's voice was higher and a little weaker than usual. The wind bearing him along had robbed her of breath and force, it seemed. It had brightened her eyes, though, and her colour was returning.

"One uncle in trade and the other a country solicitor are not eminent connections. I do not hold it against you, Elizabeth, believe me! If I did, I would not stand here now. But those scruples imbued in me by my excellent parents... well, I must set them aside. I am aware that by offering for you, I am not connecting myself to a family of consequence, as I once expected I should— and indeed, consider myself to be entitled, taking into account my own position and the unimpeachable connections to the nobility brought by my mother. It is a difficult undertaking to ally myself with those whose condition is far beneath my own, as I am sure you will appreciate." He saw her mouth tremble, and hastened to put her mind at rest. "You may be certain your own worth, your own consequence, outweighs these concerns. You are all that is charming."

"Mr Darcy. Allow me to speak, please." The paleness was ebbing away. The tip of her tongue darted out to moisten her lips. It was enchanting to see. "Are you making a declaration?"

Of course he was! He held out both hands wide in a supplicating gesture. "But, yes."

"And yet, you consider your position in relation to mine is very high, and your declaration therefore contradicts all those scruples and expectations you mention. I gather you have struggled to reach this point where you can tell me of your feelings?"

Once again, her bright intelligence had cut through to the nub of the matter.

"Yes. I must admit—"

"May I ask you a question, sir?"

"Anything."

"Your cousin, the colonel. Why did he join the Army?"

If he had been walking, Darcy would have missed a step. He almost jerked, as a man did on the edge of sleep when his foot kicked suddenly. What? Why in heaven's name did she want to talk about Edward? At such a time, when she had just received the most eligible declaration! "The colonel?"

"Yes. Why did he become a soldier?"

Darcy frowned. "He is a younger son."

"So I presumed. Thank you for confirming the supposition. It is the way of the gentry, is it not, and even, as in your cousin's case, the nobility? Elder sons inherit through the mere circumstance of being born first, no matter their abilities or merits. Younger sons inherit little or nothing, and must find their own way in the world—the army, the church or the law."

"Yes? I do not quite underst—"

"My mother's father chose the law. He was a third son of a man who owned a large estate near Colchester; my mother's second cousin owns it now. My grandfather Gardiner ate his dinners in Lincoln's Inn, as did many a gentleman before him, and was called to the Bar. He was very successful, but the air of Town was injurious to his health, and on his doctor's advice he settled into a country practice. Until his death, he dined half a dozen times each year in his Inn, as was his right as a gentleman and a barrister. It is true his wife was but the daughter of the local solicitor and not a gentlewoman. It is also true his elder daughter married my uncle Phillips, who is a member of a mere Inn of Chancery rather than being a barrister. You will think my uncle an insignificant country solicitor, no doubt, but his work and that of those like him is the backbone of the law of this land, even if he is not a gentleman born. So, you see, my mother's family is not so very low—"

"Elizabeth—"

She frowned. "Miss Bennet, sir."

He bowed his head to her reproof. When had she become Elizabeth to him?

"My grandfather's only son, my uncle Gardiner, did not choose to follow him into the law. After studying at Oxford, my uncle discovered his talents lay elsewhere. I do not dispute he is in trade, but he is the scion of gentle families and an educated, successful man."

Darcy's face burned. "Miss Bennet—"

"You have met him, Mr Darcy. He and my aunt were with Jane at the theatre when you were first introduced."

"I remember. He… he was very civil."

"Yes. Hardly savage at all in company."

Darcy grimaced.

She did not permit him to respond. "My aunt Gardiner's father, likewise a younger son, chose the church. You must be acquainted with him."

"I... How?"

"Mr Ross, the rector of All Saints in Lambton. I understand from my aunt, who was raised there, that Lambton is near Pemberley."

Darcy's stomach clenched. Sweat prickled on the nape of his neck, beneath his cravat. "At the theatre your aunt mentioned Pemberley. I had not realised... I do know Mr Ross. I know him well. An excellent man. I knew he has a daughter married in London... I did not recognise her, I am afraid. She must have left Lambton while I was yet at Cambridge."

"Well, I did not expect you would know her. Your families are not intimate acquaintances. I am merely trying to show that while you are a gentleman, I am a gentleman's daughter whose forebears were also gentry. I have no earl to claim as an uncle, but in all else, sir, we are equal."

They stared at each other. Darcy's face must show every iota of his shame and consternation. Her expression was cold, and she blinked rapidly.

"Forgive me," he said. "Forgive me. I meant no offence."

"Did you not? Mr Darcy, I had no notion of your admiration, I assure you."

But how could she not? How was that possible? They had walked together every day, talked together... he had shown her more of himself than ever his friends had seen. How could she not see it? "But—"

"You made your opinion of my charms clear that night in the deanery garden."

"I have apologised! I hoped you had forgiven me. We have been on such terms these last weeks, I thought that, at least, was behind us."

She smiled. She actually smiled. A small curve of the lips, it was true, and there was something uncomfortably cold about it. But it was a smile. He breathed a little easier.

"As I recall, you apologised for speaking so loudly." Her tone was brittle, as though she spoke through sheets of breaking ice.

"But put it aside, for now. I have tried not to dwell upon that night. I have enjoyed our walks and conversations."

His next breath still felt as though he were being strangled. "Every walk, every word, has been the delight of my time here."

"I had no thought of love. I did not think you admired me. That must have been blindness on my part. I am sorry."

"I do love you. Most ardently."

"But you do not respect me, Mr Darcy. No man who did could speak of my family so, with such disdain. No gentleman could speak so, and to the lady he professes to admire. It is unfathomable. You have astonished me because I thought you more the gentleman than that."

"Miss Bennet! Elizabeth!"

"No, sir." She dabbed at her eyes with ungloved fingers. "Your friend Mr Wickham—"

"He is no friend of mine!"

She made a dismissive gesture with one hand. "He knew you. He told me to remember my worth, a defence against pride. Well, I do remember it. I am worth more than condescension, Mr Darcy. I am worth much more."

"Elizabeth, I beg you! Let me explai—"

"No. No more. I am sure that after this... this discussion, any feelings you have, those you have bestowed so unwillingly despite my manifest drawbacks... well, I am sorry if this causes you some little pain. I did not consciously mislead you or use some art to lure you. You will excuse me, please. I must return to the house."

She turned and fled. Literally, fled from him. The first few yards she moved at her usual brisk pace, then she picked up her skirts and ran along the path bordering the wide lawns, leaving him staring after her, as shocked and bereft as if she had snatched the heart from his breast and taken it with her.

Which, indeed, she had.

He had given his orders to Harris, and his valet was working swiftly and, after one look at Darcy, silently. Harris packed with his usual efficiency. Darcy himself sat in the small sitting room attached to his bedroom, and stared his folly full in the face.

He felt… he did not know what he felt.

He had cast up his accounts behind one of the bushes in the shrubbery, until his gut settled and he could return to the house. He hoped that if he met anyone, he could pass muster and escape questioning. He had ached with misery every step of the way, and he ached now. He could not ache more if he had gone ten rounds with Gentleman Jackson himself, and, naturally, had the worst of it. Darcy was no more than a decent pugilist. Jackson would never say of him, as he did of some who displayed to advantage, that he could make a prize fighter of them if they had not been gentlemen.

I thought you more the gentleman than that.

He put his head in his hands, both to hide what must be written on his face for all to see, and to try and quell the resurgence of sickness. He would welcome Jackson's iron fist jabbing past whatever poor defence he could make to remind him that he was a thrice-damned mutton-headed fool.

He lived a life of quiet rectitude, governed by rationality, duty and the hard work needed to care for Georgiana and Pemberley. His had not been a life where his passions outran his intellect. He had thought he was a gentleman.

She did not share his opinion.

He clearly had no idea how to approach a woman of worth. Whatever his notions of what a Darcy of Pemberley was due, she had shown her scorn of them. He had wounded her pride. How many times had he wounded her pride since that first instance in the deanery garden? How had she borne his company since? What an addle-pated simpleton he was! No matter how justified he was in his expectations of a good match, no matter his consequence and position, he had sailed in, expecting her to be overcome with gratitude at his giving her any notice at all. He did not know if he were more surprised and angry than hurt that she was not grateful at all. Or both.

Both.

Dear Lord, how had he come to this?"

"You, I suppose, are the reason for my cousin Elizabeth's ranting around Aunt Iphy's sitting room, pummelling cushions and flinging the remains across the room in a passion?"

Palmer's voice startled him, as hers had earlier, making him jerk upward from where he had been bowed over his knees. He let his hands drop and turned.

Palmer's look of mild amusement vanished in a trice. "Good God, Darcy! Are you ill?"

"No. No, I am quite well."

"You do not look it."

Palmer glanced at Harris, who must have let him in without Darcy noticing, and gestured to the decanter set on a side table. Harris hurried to pour two glasses of brandy. Palmer waited until Harris had served the glasses and returned to his work in Darcy's bedroom. Harris closed the door between the rooms to give them privacy.

"Lizzy would say little, but I gather you spoke?" Palmer sipped at his brandy. "I have watched you these last few weeks, you know. I have never seen you act in like manner with any lady, and I do not mind telling you I derived no small amusement from seeing the impervious Fitzwilliam Darcy brought to his knees at last."

"Was I so obvious? She did not think so."

"I know you very well, do not forget. So. From her reaction, and yours, I assume it went ill?"

"She handed me my head in a basket." Darcy tossed back the brandy in one. "I do not understand it. I am Darcy of Pemberley!"

Palmer coughed. It was possible the brandy had burned on the way down, or that he was trying not to laugh. "And she is a Bennet of Longbourn, and hence inferior to a man who looks for a wife with connections and fortune and a position in Society? Good God, man, you had better take your own pride for a wife. A cold bedfellow, but one you cannot cavil at."

Not a laugh. That was anger in his friend's tone.

"I do not ask for the impossible, Palmer! It is not pride. Not just pride. I have some right to expect a wife with those attributes."

"Town is full of young women from impeccable bloodlines, with good dowries and accomplished enough to keep a man in painted screens and tables from now until his dotage. What you mean, Darcy, is that one such young lady is as good as the next, provided she possesses those longed-for connections and can further your wealth and position. If you think my cousin would meekly accept any man who measured her against those terms, you are indeed a fool."

"Head in a basket," Darcy said again. Perhaps he deserved it.

Palmer had no such uncertainty. "Good girl. With a sharp word, I hope."

"Several."

They eyed each other for a moment, then Palmer went for the brandy bottle and refilled their glasses.

"Darcy... Fitz. You have money, position and connections enough for you both. But I cannot understand why you persist in thinking her deficient. She is a gentleman's daughter. You are a gentleman. What more can you ask for? Connections? We have already discussed, you and I, that she is now and forever a Palmer in all but name. A baronetcy is a reasonable enough connection for most men."

"One I would welcome." Darcy had seen for himself how swiftly she had been gathered into the Palmer fold. Why had he discounted it?

"As for wealth... well, Aunt Iphy has some fortune of her own."

It was as well Darcy was merely lifting his glass to lips, otherwise he would have choked on the brandy in it. "Are you serious?"

Palmer tilted up one shoulder. "It was her mother's money. Anne Beeching was a widow, you may recall, and she brought a tidy sum into the marriage with my grand-uncle from her first husband's fortune. By rights, Eliza should have had at least a goodly portion of it, if not the whole since it came from her father, but my grand-uncle cut her out and her own mother seems not to have protested. He was a hard man, and her defiance likely cost her dear. But it has never been Palmer money, and my father has always said Iphy could name whomever she pleased as her heir."

"That is disconcerting."

"I never had any expectations of Iphy. I suspect, and my father does too, that she originally intended it for Mr Bennet, considering it restitution for old hurts and returning her mother's fortune to the line to which it belongs. But if he one day inherited, Bennet must need to divide the sum between all his daughters and it would not materially improve their prospects. But Papa says, and I must agree, that it would not be surprising if she leaves Elizabeth every penny, since she is the Bennet daughter closest to Iphy's own sister. It would give Elizabeth a better prospect in life, at least, and Iphy might calculate it would help raise the other sisters' prospects more indirectly."

"I see."

"It makes no difference, because it is not material. Neither you nor I need to wed for a fortune." Palmer regarded him steadily. "I take it Lizzy refused to hear you because you made all your requirements for a wife plain to her."

"I merely intended to show her what I was putting aside for her sake."

"In other words, you implied all the advantage would flow from you—your name, your connections, fortune, and estate. King Cophetua to the life, condescending to the peasant girl. The basket is entirely understandable."

Darcy grunted.

"You know," Palmer said, tone a little more gentle, "instead of thinking of what you bestow upon her, consider what she will gift the man she marries. That brightness of hers, that laughter, that light. Those joys alone are a fortune to be savoured."

Darcy grimaced.

"What will you do? Harris appears to be packing."

"I cannot stay. I need some time to think. Gal, I never intended to speak to her, not until I had thought through everything of significance. I surprised myself more than I did her. And now I must consider, most carefully, what I do wish for in my life. I cannot do that here, not with her in every room, at every meal. It would be excruciating for both of us. She does not consider me much of a gentleman at present, but I am too much one to impose my company on her after today."

Palmer made no effort to dissuade him. "Do you go to Georgiana?"

"No, I would not impose my temper on her, either. I am for Town, and then to Pemberley. I will write to Georgiana when I reach Town. You will care for her?"

"Of course. She may send for me at any time, day or night, and I will go. Ramsgate is but an hour away on a good horse." Palmer hefted the brandy bottle and raised an enquiring eyebrow.

Darcy sighed, shaking his head at the notion of more brandy. His glass was yet half-full and he felt befuddled enough without more. "I had better take my leave of your father. But the ladies?"

"I think not. Leave them to me. Lizzy is still stormy, Jane all-a-mort over the Bingleys, and poor Aunt Iphy is trying to soothe them both. I will make your excuses. Lizzy will understand why you have left."

He had no doubt of it. Despite her blindness to his attraction to her, she was a clever young woman.

"Bingley has been gone no more than an hour. You might come upon him and travel with him."

"I would gladly travel with him. Never with his sister." Darcy managed a faint smile when Palmer laughed and nodded. "Thank you, my friend. I will write... at some point. When I have conquered this."

Palmer's smile held fondness, and a touch of amusement. "Conquered what, Fitz? Your heart or your pride?"

Darcy tossed down the last of the brandy in his glass. "I'm damned if I know."

Thrice damned.

CHAPTER THIRTY-ONE

Brighter Than Glass

Brighter than glass, and yet, as glass is brittle
— Shakespeare, *The Passionate Pilgrim*

Elizabeth stared across the sun-bright garden. Its gravelled pathways wound between roses whose heavy heads drooped in the heat under the weight of drowsy bees. The air was thick with their perfume, and she breathed it in, drawing it in deep as she kicked at the leg of the stone bench on which she sat.

"My poor Mamma's rose garden is being ill-used today." Galahad's voice startled her.

How had she not seen him until he stood before her, his shadow falling over her? She looked up at him, and blinked.

"Bingley marched along these paths as if they had given him mortal offence, and now you kick my favourite bench to flinders." Unasked, Galahad dropped onto the bench beside her. "At least with those stout boots of yours, you will not break a toe. That is something to be thankful for."

His solemnity made her smile, though it probably looked as wan as she felt.

He returned the smile and leaned back, supported by the trellis and pergola that gave the bench its welcome shade. For a moment or two he remained silent, his gaze on the roses, then said, "He is gone to Town, Lizzy."

Floundering for her usual quick wit, Elizabeth said what she thought. "Oh." Another moment's silence, and she found enough words to add, "With the Bingleys?"

"He may see Charles in Town, but does not intend to journey with them. He will avoid her when he is back in Brook Street, I suspect. What little countenance he gave her was for her brother's sake. It will be less now."

He reached for her hand, and she was surprised to find she was wringing her fingers in her lap. They ached. While he took the hand nearest him, she shook the tingles out of the other.

He patted the hand he held. "You have him reeling, you know."

"I do not know. I am sure those sentiments he had to fight before he could speak will soon overcome what little chagrin he may feel."

"That is more ungenerous than I ever suspected of you, Lizzy. He told me he had made a mull of it."

"I had no notion. I did not think he admired me, you see. What did he say in the dean's garden? I am only prettyish, and not tempting enough. I had not realised he had amended his opinion. Yet, despite that rude behaviour, I did believe we had become friends of a sort."

"He hurt you."

"Galahad, you have seen my sister. You admire her, do you not?" And when he grimaced and looked apologetic, she went on, not allowing him to speak, "And so you should, because Jane unites beauty with a gentle spirit and a generous, loving character. She is peerless and I love her dearly, but it was pleasant for me that night to attend an occasion where I hoped I was in good looks and no one was there to tell me, as Mamma does, that I am nothing to Jane. Yes. He hurt me. Mamma is one thing. A handsome man speaking her words in his own voice is quite another." Her face grew hot. What a fool she was! "I am sorry. That is vanity speaking, and ridiculousness, and it is the least of my objections to Mr Darcy's conduct. I have other provocations."

"I am certain he made a complete cake of himself, Lizzy."

"I would not cavil at a mere inability to speak charmingly, as long as sincerity and esteem laid behind it. But he offended and insulted me, even as he declared himself."

"Lizzy."

"Galahad, he chose to tell me that he liked me against his will. That he had weighed every reasonable objection to the lowness of my position and connections, and decided, in his munificence, to overlook them. He expected me to be grateful. To fall at his feet. Pfft. It was my family he insulted. He objected to my having such deplorable connections. I have a father who is a mere country squire; a mother who though descended from gentle families, was born to a man who pursued the legal profession in a country town, having given up the Bar. I should be glad he has never met my two youngest sisters, who are a pair of silly geese. His disgust would be complete."

"Oh, my dear girl—"

"My true demerits consist of having one uncle-by-marriage who is a country attorney, and another, my mother's brother, who is in business in London. Yet Mr Gardiner descends from a long line of gentry who have been owners of their estates as long as the Bennets have held Longbourn. Does Mr Darcy disdain the Bingleys so? They have as strong a connection to trade, yet they are acceptable and I, the daughter of a gentleman, am deplored. Mr Darcy may have some passing admiration, but he does not respect me. He has been rude, and unmannerly, and most definitely not the gentleman."

Galahad was grimacing by the time she came to a stop. "I think it more than a passing fancy, Lizzy, but he has a propensity for sticking his foot in his mouth, and is an idiot deserving of your ire. But for all that, he is a good man."

"Mmphfh."

Galahad ignored the soft snort. "I have been astonished at the change I have seen in him, these last few weeks. I will not deny his first reactions were to keep his habitual distance, if not to say suspicion as to the motives of others. He is ever thus, and, from his point of view, with good reason. But he did indeed change. Your company, your brightness, changed him. You drew him in. I have never seen him as open with a lady, so undisguised and willing to put aside the reserve he dons as a knight dons armour. Lizzy, I have never seen him so happy."

"It was not consciously done." She kicked again at the bench, and a curious desire to understand better prompted her to say, "You have known him many years."

"And lamented what Society has made him, yes. I went to Eton not long after my twelfth birthday. It was Charles Bingley's first day, too. We were in Drummond House, and the master gave to the older boys of his house the task of helping us settle in. Darcy was not two years our senior, but had already impressed the masters with his sense of duty and responsibility. Mr Drummond assigned Bingley and me to his care. Never was there a better, luckier decision!"

He should be grateful that school and an active life was his lot! Though to be sent away from home so young... Elizabeth glanced at his hands. He should be grateful. He did not have the delicate fingers needed for the needlework she had been set to at twelve. She would have preferred school. "He took good care of you?"

"Yes. I was grateful for it, and it was the saving of Bingley. You will appreciate that at Eton, the son of a Yorkshire mill-owner was at something of a disadvantage. Darcy prevented the worst of the bullying..." Galahad paused and frowned. "Do you know, that may be the root of Bingley's need for more resolution and decisiveness. Of course, we should not have allowed him to be mistreated, but perhaps our protection slowed his growth in that regard."

"Some things must always be prevented." Elizabeth spoke soberly, to respond properly to the confidences Galahad shared with her. "I know boys are brought up to be the heads of their households, be responsible for their families, work in the world, and be strong against adversity, but a life of being hectored and intimidated must breed misery, not strength."

"I agree. The adversity of our schooldays bred a very deep friendship. Gal, Charles and Fitz... we were proof against anything, both at school and later at Cambridge. Darcy was open and cheerful. Five years ago, when he was barely two-and-twenty, his father died, and he was suddenly master of the second-largest estate in Derbyshire and responsible for his ten-year-old sister. A great burden for young shoulders."

"Yes. I suppose."

"Then the *beau monde* went to work. His cousin the colonel would tell you the attacks came on two fronts. First, from those who would gull a young man out of his fortune: every Captain Sharp who regarded him as a pigeon for plucking, every wastrel and ne'er-do-well sought advantage and to live well at his expense. Darcy was proof against this, because he is a good man, given good principles, and not tempted by the vices they offered. The small exception was his father's favourite, Wickham, and it is filial piety and respect that has stayed Darcy's hand there."

"The man at the assembly last week?"

"He is an immoral leech and shockingly loose in the haft." Galahad laughed at the glower she gave him. "I am sorry for my language, but you are not so missish you do not know what I mean. The man leaves debts and other encumbrances wherever he goes, and Darcy cleans up after him out of respect for his father's partiality for the rogue. My point, though, is for more than five years he has been the target of people whose intent is to relieve him of some of his wealth, or at least take advantage of it and him. It has made him cold and suspicious of those he does not know well, and he holds strangers at arms' length. More, he has come to believe that those who are less well-positioned than himself are always seeking advancement at his expense."

"A propensity I have shown at every turn, I suppose?" Elizabeth frowned. "And the second reason?"

"Ah, the ladies. Now, I will not pretend he is the most sought-after bachelor in London, because of course he is not. He is rich and well connected, but others are richer and titled. But to the ladies of the *ton*, he has one advantage—he is already his own master. No need for them to marry a son who is still dependent upon an allowance from his father, where they must be sweet and obliging to the old man while waiting upon his demise to reign over the estate."

"He is hunted, you mean."

"By some. It is often most unsubtle, too, with their mammas speaking in his hearing of their daughters' virtues and good points." Galahad's tone was all amusement. "I talk of my horses in the same terms. Or Bessie, my best pointer bitch."

"It seems my mamma is not as singular as I hoped."

"All mothers with daughters to marry off must live with anxiety." Galahad's gaze turned to his mother's garden. "In response to that sense of being assailed by Society on both fronts, Darcy has grown his armour in the form of reserve, of a reluctance to engage with those he does not know well. I have observed he has worsened over the years, with an increasing tendency to think meanly of those outside his immediate circle."

"And so nurtured a natural propensity to treat people who are his inferiors in Society with pride and disdain. He is rude, Galahad."

"I am not denying that he spoke ill to you, both in the deanery garden and, worse, here. He knows it himself. But I also firmly believe his affections are engaged in a way I never thought to see. Believe me, if he had treated Miss Bingley for one day in the manner he has treated you for the last two months, she would have ordered her bride clothes before the noon bell rang. He could barely take his eyes from you."

"I believed he looked to find fault, since I was not to his taste."

"My dear girl, if a man does not like a lady, he does not stare at her in such a mooncalf-y way. He does not stare at all."

"Then the deficiency is mine, that I do not recognise mooncalves." Elizabeth stared at the pavement at their feet. The soft red of the paving stones, set in a clever herringbone pattern, was a pleasing contrast to the white rose petals the breeze had pulled from the arch above their heads. She tapped a toe over a petal or two, crushing them against the stones and releasing their perfume. "I am sorry if I have driven him away. You enjoy your friend's company, I know."

"He will return, I am certain, when his head is clearer. He told me he intends to take some time to reflect on your reproofs. You have given him much to think upon, shown him how little a woman of worth appreciates his views and attitudes, and that if he is to win her regard, he must meet her ideals and standards. I hope and pray he will be a better man as a result."

"I expected him to be angry."

"He may be, a little. But mostly with himself. He is aghast at what has happened, and questioning all he has said and done. That is a good thing. He should do so. Because you are right, Lizzy. His behaviour, always reserved, has degenerated into a rude disdain ill becoming a gentleman. He knows that. We have both laid the charge at his door." Galahad paused for a moment, frowning. "The deanery garden set both of you marching on the wrong foot. You have harboured some prejudice against him, while he is proud. I hope at least I have been able to explain him to you, and that if he is to spend a few weeks in reflecting on his wrongheadedness…"

"You wish me to reflect on mine?"

"I do not believe you to be wrong-headed. There is nothing amiss with having a sense of your own worth. But self-reflection, we are told, will bring nothing but good. When he returns, Lizzy, all I ask is that you give him a fair hearing. Neither of you deserves less." He pressed her hand. "Enough portentous talk! Will you come into the house?"

"Later, perhaps. I need to walk." Her mouth felt tremulous, wanting to pull down at the corners, and it was an effort to curve it into a small smile. "I manage all my distempered freaks through long walks. I will be the better for it, rather than impose on you or Jane and Aunt Iphy."

"I will send Jack out to you then. Please do not go without him. I would go with you myself, but I would like to see how Cousin Jane fares. The Bingleys distressed her."

"That is normally my office." Elizabeth grimaced. "I am failing her."

"Nonsense. Go for your walk and leave me to comfort my other cousin." Galahad laughed. "I am becoming most proficient at it."

"Yes. You are." She waited until he had patted her hand and bidden her not to walk herself into exhaustion. He was several steps away when she called him. "Cousin! I will not break a confidence, but it is my firm belief that Jane has no expectations of Mr Bingley and seeks none."

He had stopped, but not turned. Now he did, but only to give her the sweetest of smiles before resuming his walk to the house.

She smiled after him. Such a brother would be a boon indeed.

But such a brother's friend? That, she did not know. She was all confusion, still a little angry, all wounded pride and hurt.

She was hurt.

And that was the most surprising and confusing thing to deal with. Jack should hurry, although she suspected Mr Darcy was one freak and distemper that would refuse to be dismissed by a brisk walk across Kent's summer meadows.

Such a contrary, disobliging, infuriating man!

September was now upon them, bringing the last of the harvest with it. The weather remained warm and clear. Though Galahad was busy from dawn to dusk each day, overseeing the wheat and barley being brought from the stooks drying in the fields, the harvest brought little change to the ladies' daily avocations.

The next weeks were spent in their usual quiet amusements. Elizabeth, Jane and Aunt Iphy returned to Wenderton Cottage soon after all the guests left the Hall, although Sir James more than once said, "I shall miss you, my Lizzy." Since they still met at the Hall every day except those given over for visits to Goodnestone, Elizabeth was at a loss to know what opportunity Sir James would have to mourn her leaving, but she forbore to say so. She had grown very fond of the old gentleman, and though she could not acquiesce in what she suspected was his design for her and Galahad, she hoped for a strong familial bond with the Palmers.

She rejoiced in the slow dance between Galahad and Jane; Galahad gentle and giving Jane time to know her heart and mind, and Jane serene and happy in her tranquil pleasure at his notice and solicitude. It plainly disconcerted Sir James and Aunt Iphy. Both could be seen in the evenings with their heads together, observing

Galahad and Jane, then turning to regard Elizabeth at the piano with expressions that spoke of chagrin. But since Elizabeth was at pains to be her usual self with them to show them she was not in the least disappointed, they were kind and welcoming to Jane. It would not take long for them to value Jane for her own sterling virtues.

Their days were quiet. Elizabeth read a great deal, taking her book to a low bough in one of the apple trees at the bottom of Aunt Iphy's garden, which provided her with an admirable bower to help soothe battered spirits. She took up her needle, and between practising on the piano and aiding Aunt Iphy with her visits to the tenants and the poor of the village, she worked a pair of embroidered slippers for Sir James, her contentment returning with many quiet hours spent creating something beautiful. She walked mile upon mile with Jack as her willing escort, and if, on her morning walk, she sometimes looked about her as if searching for a companion who was no longer there, only Jack witnessed such weakness.

She did all the self-reflection Galahad had wished, and came to the realisation that she had not known Mr Darcy anywhere nearly as well as she had thought. Galahad's explanation of Mr Darcy's behaviour did not excuse his conduct, nor did Galahad condone it, but she now understood him better. Her own flash of anger had left her uncomfortable regarding her manners and comportment, but she forbore to speak to Jane about it. She would not disturb Jane's peace. Her sister's growing happiness meant more than her own selfish desire to demand comfort, and the reassurance she was not as vain and nonsensical as she felt she was.

It was her own folly and nonsense, to be suppressed and forgotten in her pleasure at seeing Jane restored to peace and happiness, blooming under Galahad's attention.

That must be her solace.

Each Wednesday, they went as usual into Canterbury to shop at the market and take refreshments with Aunt Iphy's friends in the little tearoom at the back of Chipperfield's, the fruiterer's shop. The Ladies' Dean and Chapter were welcoming of Jane, charmed both by her beauty and her manners. On this, the third such September market day, Jasper and the gig were stabled at the Rose Inn, which stood most conveniently on the corner of Rose Lane and the Parade, close to the stalls in Longmarket. Elizabeth would welcome retreating to Chipperfield's but Aunt Iphy and Jane were intent on shopping for bargains, apparently oblivious to the unusual number of people about.

Heavens, how crowded it was, how many men, carriages and horses were milling in the streets. Mostly young men, too; loud and boisterous, and none too careful about knocking into innocent ladies intent on their marketing. And the heightened colour on some of them, and the way they lurched unsteadily on unsure feet, or touched their hats with exaggerated care... well, inebriation this early in the day was not encouraging. She hurried to catch up with Jane and Aunt Iphy. It would not do for them to be importuned by young men whose characters were unknown but whose behaviour was disorderly.

"Jack, do I imagine the crowd is greater than usual, and rather unruly?"

"Leave me to discover it, Miss Lizzy." Jack darted off to enquire, while Elizabeth caught up with her sister and aunt. He returned within minutes. "Seems there was a boxing mill nearby at dawn today, Miss Lizzy, from what these men be saying. Out in a field someplace Chartham Hatch way. Some say Tom Cribb himself was there, but that's not too likely, for if he were displayin' his skills, the town'd be full of swells to watch 'im. Naught here but Cits." He added, quickly, "None of them the quality of your uncle Gardiner, I fancy, Miss. Just a lot of men with more blunt than sense and too few of 'em with the means of leaving the place. Every chaise is hired and every stage full, they say. The inns are full of these men, drinking and gaming."

"It is most disagreeable. Let me gather my aunt and Miss Jane, and we will go to Chipperfield's and get out of this crowd. Stay close, please, Jack. I would not wish Miss Jane to be made uncomfortable and with these sorts of men about..."

Jack, who had already diverted one red-faced lout with a well-placed elbow to the ribs, nodded.

It took her a moment or two to make her relations aware of the bustling hordes, though Aunt Iphy did peer around and say that she'd thought there was a larger throng than usual. She readily agreed to go to Chipperfield's and remove themselves from the fray. "I would be glad of some tea. If you recall, Mrs Chipperfield promised some of her ginger cake this week."

The High Street teemed with people. Progress was a case of taking ordinary steps and shorter ones, as the flow and ebb of the crowd demanded, and sometimes feinting right or left to pass by a group of rowdy young men while being deaf to anything said to them or called after them. Thank the good Lord for Jack. He was so large, few attempted to accost the ladies in his charge, no matter how many whistled or called at seeing Jane. Jack shepherded them along, his grim expression making him seem older than his years.

A collision, though, was unsurprising. Someone bumped into Elizabeth, jostling the basket on her arm and making her take a little jump to avoid losing her balance.

A girl, hurrying through the crowds with her head down. The first glimpse showed Elizabeth little beyond an expensive-looking blue pelisse, thick with gold, military-style braiding, and oh, what a wonderful hat! A tall mirliton cap in a matching blue adorned with magnificent white swan plumes... she had never seen anything like it outside the pages of *La Belle Assemblée.* Very fashionable, and distinctive. Not a costume for going unobserved.

Then the girl looked up.

Elizabeth almost dropped her shopping. "Miss Darcy!"

Georgiana Darcy, ashen-faced, her expression twisted in fear, her breath coming in and out faster than if a blacksmith's bellows had replaced her lungs. Georgiana Darcy recognising her, reaching for her. Georgiana Darcy clutching her with hands that shook as if palsied.

"Oh, help me. Help me! I do not want to go with them! I do not want to go. Please help me! Please!" A shuddering breath, and a softer, "Please."

CHAPTER THIRTY-TWO
Evil Claws

Twixt evil claws
The mouse had fall'n
— Dante, *The Divine Comedy*

Elizabeth stared. "Miss Darcy?"

"Please." The girl's fingers dug into Elizabeth's arm with such force, she would leave marks.

Elizabeth swiftly surveyed the street. Aunt Iphy and Jane had stepped to one side, to stand outside a milliner's. Jack was behind her and Miss Darcy, sheltering them from the press of people with his sturdy frame, making the Canterbury crowd go around them. A man stumbled past, cursing as Jack shouldered him to one side. They had to get out of the stream of pedestrians.

"Here." Elizabeth caught Miss Darcy's hand with her free one, and tugged her towards the milliner's. "Where is your companion?"

"No, no, please! She says I should go with George, that there is nothing amiss and I am a lucky woman—"

What? What had this girl so frightened, and who, in Heaven's name, was George?

"Do not let them take me, Miss Elizabeth. Please do not! I do not want to go to Gretna!"

Gretna? Gretna Green? Good God! The silly child was eloping?

The girl's finely-clad shoulders shook as the bellows started up again. "I am sorry, I am sorry! I know I am bad, and wicked, and... and... but I do not want to go!"

Elizabeth glanced from Miss Darcy to Jane, whose mouth was round with astonishment. Aunt Iphy held onto Jane's arm as to a lifeline. There was no time to think. Miss Darcy was a scant inch from dissolving into full hysterics on Canterbury's main shopping thoroughfare.

She took a step nearer Miss Darcy, and forcibly turned her towards the hats and bonnets on display in the window. The girl was a stringless puppet, obedient under Elizabeth's hands.

Elizabeth dropped her voice. The last thing they needed was to be overheard by any passing drunkard. "Not another word! Do you hear me? Not one word, or you will have everybody in Canterbury privy to this."

Miss Darcy took in a soft, whooping breath. Shock, perhaps. It wasn't likely many people commanded the Miss Darcys of this world in such a manner.

"Good girl. Am I to understand your companion and a man brought you here, en route to... to the north? And you have escaped them?"

Miss Darcy nodded vigorously. Aunt Iphy let out a soft whoop in echo to Miss Darcy's own.

"They will be looking for you."

Miss Darcy nodded again.

"Then we must remove you from sight as soon as may be."

Dear God, the girl's reputation would be in tatters if she were known to be running around the city without an escort. Worse still, the place was rife with drunken louts fresh from the excitement of watching a boxing match, and the child was without protection.

Did she have no thought of her danger? And if Gretna were mentioned! No amount of noble breeding and riches would prevent Miss Darcy's utter ruin.

Elizabeth raised her voice a trifle. "You are quite right. That hat would not suit me at all. A shame, for it is vastly pretty! Let us go and seek refreshments to mollify our disappointments." And in a lower tone, "To Chipperfield's, everyone. Jane, do you and Aunt Iphy go in front, as fast as you can. Jack, stay close. Miss Darcy—" Oh, that ridiculous hat of hers stood out like a beacon! "Keep your face turned down and duck your head. No questions now. Let us be off."

They all obeyed her without hesitation. Jane, it was true, glanced over her shoulder, eyes wide, but hurried Aunt Iphy along, taking most of the old lady's shopping in her free hand to aid the enterprise. Jack was close behind, a comforting, familiar presence. She left him to see to their protection, while she cudgelled her brains for ideas for dealing with this conundrum. What on earth was she to do to rescue this child's reputation along with her person? How to account for her not being in Ramsgate where she belonged, but in Canterbury—*sans* brother, *sans* companion, and sadly, *sans* propriety? How to counter whatever rumours might arise? How?

It was but a few minutes' walk. Elizabeth had her arm through Georgiana Darcy's and hauled her along with all the speed they could muster. The girl scurried beside her like a little mouse, keeping her head so low her eyes must have been trained on Jane's boot heels.

They dashed into the haven that was Chipperfield's, past Mr Chipperfield, who bowed and waved them through. Elizabeth waited until they were in the short corridor at the back of the shop leading to the tiny tearoom and the private garden behind. A room to one side had been delegated to the use of accompanying servants. She stopped everyone there.

"Can you keep an eye open, Jack, for anyone else coming in?"

"Both of 'em, Miss Lizzy." Jack collected the rest of their baskets. "I'll be nigh to the door, and I'll keep it ajar."

He slipped into the room. There was but the one entrance to the tearoom, thankfully, and now Jack had secured it.

Elizabeth took another deep breath. Three pairs of eyes fixed on her in pained enquiry, awaiting her instructions. Lord. Must she do *everything*?

She nodded towards the tearoom door. "When we go in, you will hear me tell some necessary small falsehoods. Please pretend that I speak nothing but the truth. Miss Darcy— No, if we are to be successful, you must be Georgiana, and we are Lizzy and Jane. We cannot hide your presence in Canterbury, but we will try to explain it. If you are to escape ruin, you will smile and curtsey, and greet the ladies to whom I will introduce you. Nod and say as little as you can to them, and agree with everything I say. Do you understand?"

The poor child nodded as if she were one of those charming porcelain figures from the Orient, whose heads were on pivots. But colour was returning to her face.

"Good." Elizabeth exchanged gazes with Aunt Iphy and Jane. Both nodded back at her. "Let us go in. Aunt Iphy, if you will lead the way?"

Elizabeth linked arms with Miss Darcy and forced a smile onto her face. The tearoom was very small, and, as she had hoped, the Ladies' Dean and Chapter were already in attendance. They occupied both tables in the room, which Mrs Chipperfield had pushed close together, with enough chairs and space for the Wingham contingent to join them, as usual.

The greetings were cordial. Elizabeth waited until the usual courtesies were over, and Aunt Iphy was seated comfortably, before standing before the tables with her arm still linked with Georgiana's. She had noted already more than one speculative look at the stranger. They would be admiring Miss Darcy's strikingly fashionable ensemble and mentally pricing it to the last farthing.

She glanced at Mrs Andrewes, the dean's imposing wife, and smiled. *Come, Mrs Andrewes! You are the leader of this little coterie. You know your office…*

That lady nodded in magisterial grandeur, knowing what was asked of her as well as if Elizabeth had been able to prime her in advance. "Would you introduce your friend, Miss Elizabeth?"

Excellent.

"I would be honoured, ma'am. Ladies, I am pleased to present to your acquaintance Miss Georgiana Darcy of Pemberley in Derbyshire. Miss Darcy is the sister of my cousin Galahad's close friend, and niece to the Earl of Ashbourne, and to Lady Catherine De Bourgh of Rosings Park near Westerham."

Miss Darcy's distinguished pedigree thus established, Elizabeth turned to her. "Georgiana, I am honoured to make you known to Mrs Andrewes, the wife of the dean of the cathedral. The lady beside her in blue, is Miss Radcliffe, whose brother is the archdeacon. The lady on the other side is Mrs Benton, the wife of the cathedral's precentor... Mrs Peel, whose husband is chancellor... Mrs Tiverton, wife of the treasurer... Mrs Quentin.... Mrs Maisey...."

Georgiana Darcy had been well brought up. She dipped into a curtsey on each introduction to the wives (and one sister) of every official in the cathedral, murmuring polite greetings. Her pink cheeks and obvious shyness were taken as signs of modesty, and Elizabeth noted more than one approving nod from the assembled matrons.

Within Canterbury society, none ranked higher than those who lived within the cathedral close. They would be the saving of Georgiana Darcy, even if neither she nor they knew it. Now for the rest of it.

"Georgiana is a dear friend, and has come to spend time with us in Wingham. Her companion has been called away suddenly, you see." Elizabeth ushered Miss Darcy to a vacant chair, clamping a hand on her shoulder and encouraging her to sit. "Georgiana has come to us from Ramsgate, where she has been staying at our family cottage." She gave the girl a look she hoped conveyed fond affection. "She has been recuperating there after a severe illness, and we are all pleased at how well the healthful air of Kent has restored her. Mr Darcy consigned her to our care and oversight when he had to return to London, and we are more than delighted to have her stay with us in her companion's absence."

Georgiana squeaked out something about it being a great pleasure.

"You are overrun with girls, Miss Palmer." One of the lower-ranking ladies as wife to a mere canon and apparently resentful of her position, Mrs Quentin was noted as the sharpest tongue present.

Aunt Iphy—oh bless her, the darling aunt that she was! Aunt Iphy found enough spirit and good sense to smile. "It is the delight of my life to have my Lizzy here with me. To have Jane and Georgiana is the gilding on the gingerbread."

The ladies all laughed, even Mrs Quentin, for at that very moment Mrs Chipperfield arrived with tea in her best porcelain teapots, and several plates of the gingerbread for which she was renowned. The talk turned to the usual topics, and during a particularly lively discussion of the problem of finding good abigails for the ladies' growing daughters, Elizabeth relaxed and sipped her tea.

Excellent start.

Under the table, Georgiana Darcy caught her free hand and squeezed it. Elizabeth turned and smiled reassurance at her.

"All will be well," she said in Georgiana's ear. And louder: "You must have some gingerbread. There is nothing like good cake to revive oneself after a morning's marketing!"

Which was an incontrovertible truth. She eyed the plate of gingerbread nearest her. She had no need of revival, but what of that? She would still have two slices.

If not three.

The ladies did not linger long, thankfully. They dissected the servant problem, considered fashions—with much admiration for Georgiana's dashing ensemble—and deplored the number of strangers in town who had come for one of those shockingly vulgar sporting events afflicting the country.

It was the presence of the strangers that persuaded the ladies to return to the sanctuary of the cathedral close. Thank heavens they were going. The gingerbread had been delicious, and an excellent aid to planning and reflection, not to mention decisiveness. Elizabeth had only one course open to her: she needed to spirit Georgiana out of Canterbury. The sooner the ladies left her to carry this out, the better.

As soon as they were alone in the room, she turned to Georgiana. "Well? Will you tell us what has been happening to bring you here today?"

As she suspected, the tale was unedifying. Georgiana liked Ramsgate, but it had been dull to be always following doctor's orders, and when an old friend of her brother's appeared in the town, she was ripe for something more novel and exciting than demure walks along Ramsgate's sands. "I have known George all my life, you see. He was always kind and attentive—"

"Who is he?" Jane asked in her usual gentle tone.

"Oh, George. George Wickham. He lived at Pemberley. He was my father's godson, and very close to our family."

Elizabeth replaced her teacup in its saucer with great care. "George Wickham? I met him a few weeks ago here in Canterbury. I have seen him with your brother, and all I will say is if they were once friends, they are not any longer."

"George told me that they had some disagreement. He said my brother thought he—George, I mean—had forfeited all claim to friendship by some boyish folly or imprudence... George said, in short, it was anything or nothing, but his warm, unguarded temper meant they quarrelled. I was sorry, for I have very happy memories of George at Pemberley when my Papa was alive. It was pleasant to walk with him and recall happier times."

"You met him often?" Aunt Iphy's eyebrows were so high they had almost disappeared under her lace cap.

"Every day."

"And Mrs Younge?" Aunt Iphy had not the sort of countenance that took easily to showing disapproval, but she showed it now.

"Oh, she did not think there was anything objectionable in seeing George. We are such old friends, you see. She let us walk together, and once we all had ices at the confectioner's." Georgiana's smile had nothing now of the terror she had shown not an hour since. She blushed a rosy red. "He... he said he could not believe I had grown... and he thought I was pretty... he said, oh, many things that were nice to hear! Then he admitted he loved me, but he said my brother would object to our marrying."

Elizabeth would have put her head down on the table in despair, but the thought of removing sticky gingerbread crumbs from her hair dissuaded her. "And so he proposed the flight to Gretna."

Georgiana nodded.

"Oh dear," said Jane. "That was wrong of him."

Which was the greatest condemnation ever to fall from Jane's lips. Aunt Iphy tutted.

Elizabeth exchanged pained glances with her sister, and returned to extracting this sorry tale from its heroine's lips. "So you chose today for your elopement? You must have left Ramsgate very early."

"At dawn. Mrs Younge was with me in the coach, while George rode beside us. It was all most proper."

"Georgiana, an elopement is never proper." Elizabeth softened her tone when the girl's chin trembled. "But I assume you came to that realisation yourself, and changed your mind."

"I... I could only think, as we travelled here, how my brother... how it would distress him... I could not but think of how grieved he would be, how disappointed... how little he would like for me to be settled in such a way. I felt we should go to him and seek his consent. I desired to tell them to turn back, but George was so... so ebullient and Mrs Younge so convinced we were doing right, I could not see how to persuade them. When we arrived here, the postillion would go no further and insisted on being paid before returning his equipage to Ramsgate. George was upset and angry to find not one conveyance for hire in the whole of Canterbury. He took all our funds and went in search of something, anything. A coach, a gig... whatever he might find. I was... I was..."

"Frightened?" Jane suggested.

Georgiana turned to her and nodded. "Yes. I *was* a little frightened. I have only seen George be gentle and kind, and indulgent to me. I was... I realised I truly did not want to go to Gretna. I wanted to go to my brother honestly, and openly, and seek his approval. Mrs Younge, though, is so much George's champion, I did not think she would countenance my abandoning the scheme."

Elizabeth imagined not, if Mrs Younge and Wickham were in some sort of confederacy. "You are correct about your brother's dismay, and that you were not on the right course. How did you escape Mrs Younge?"

"We were at the Falstaff Inn, and I said I must go to the necessary. It is in the garden. A great many people came in as we walked through the public rooms and we were separated. I slipped out and got away, although I did not quite run."

"No, indeed. Running would have attracted attention. It is lucky Canterbury is crowded today. She must have lost sight of you quickly." Aunt Iphy gave the child a kind look. "Miss Darcy, forgive me asking a personal question, but I assume you have a good dowry?"

Georgiana admitted she had thirty thousand pounds.

Aunt Iphy and Jane spoke in unison and the exact same intonation. "Oh, dear."

Elizabeth would have considered herself rich with one tenth that amount. "Did you say Mr Wickham took all your funds?"

"Yes."

"You were paying for your own elopement?"

Georgiana went a fiery red and muttered something about necessity and George being very short of funds.

"How ungallant. If a man wishes a lady to toss her bonnet over the windmill and elope to the anvil with him, the least he ought to do is pay for it." Elizabeth sighed. If the girl had no money, that ruled out one possible avenue of getting help. "I doubt we will have money enough for an express rider then…?"

Jane and Aunt Iphy shook their heads, and Elizabeth knew her own purse was too light.

She sighed again. "We must contrive something else."

She rose, and went to the door to call in Jack and to ask Mrs Chipperfield if there were paper, pen and ink to be had. The lady was pleased to provide writing materials, and Elizabeth resumed her seat when it arrived. Ink so old it was water and sludge, and the pen needed mending… Still, it would suffice. While she scribbled a note to Galahad, she told Jack that Miss Darcy had been imposed upon by her companion and a rogue, who were in pursuit of her fortune. She trusted Jack, and he was no fool. Better he understood what they were dealing with.

She ignored Georgiana's faint protests, and spoke aloud to explain her reasoning to her companions. "We must get Miss Darcy to safety. The rogues will be seeking her, but we cannot approach any of the town constables for aid. That might cause a commotion and undo all the good we have achieved, since we cannot explain away the circumstances. We must be discreet if we are to save your reputation, Georgiana." She scrabbled in the pen box Mrs Chipperfield had supplied, and found the penknife and a narrow red cotton ribbon. While she cut slits in the folded missive and threaded through the ribbon, she continued her explanation. "So, we must take you to Wingham with us as soon as we can, where you will be safe. The gig is too small to convey us all. It was a squeeze enough for the three of us coming into Canterbury, and will not admit of a fourth, even if none of us are very large. We cannot use the groom's seat, you see, because that is Jack's, and his protection will be vital. This"—she brandished her letter—"is to tell Galahad to bring the coach post-haste. We ought to be safe enough in here until he can reach us, with Jack as protector. I hope we can convince Mrs Chipperfield to allow us sanctuary here." She glanced at Aunt Iphy. "You will have to be overtaken with fatigue, aunt, and be our reason for sending for the coach."

A variety of murmurs signalled everyone's acquiescence to this plan. Elizabeth turned her attention back to her letter while Jack fetched a lit candle for the sealing wax, to seal the ribbon ends to the parchment. She had no sealing ring, but the back of a fork pressed the wax into place well enough for it to hold.

She handed the letter to Jack. "Please find someone to take this to Wingham, Jack. They must understand it is urgent. One of the boys from the Rose, perhaps? Return as quickly as you can."

When Jack had left, she turned back to find Georgiana— No, not Georgiana. This cross damsel with the tilted-up chin and the arms folded over her breast was most definitely Miss Darcy again.

"George is not in pursuit of my fortune! He told me he would gladly marry me if I were a pauper!"

Aunt Iphy's jaw dropped. "And you believed him?"

Georgiana gasped and stuttered and stared.

Aunt Iphy sounded sterner than Elizabeth had ever heard her. Perhaps her late, indomitable sister Cassandra spoke through her lips. "Child, a penniless, conscience-less rogue took advantage of your brother's absence to try and get his hands on your dowry, with the connivance of your companion. That much is plain."

Elizabeth was struck with a memory. "Mr Wickham—and you must stop calling him George, Miss Darcy. He is not worthy of such familiarity. At the assembly last month, Mr Wickham said he was here because a friend persuaded him to pursue an opportunity to make his fortune. He must have meant Mrs Younge."

"He loves me!"

"He had no right to say so." Jane was mildly stern. "Miss Darcy, it was wrong of him to approach you without the consent of your guardians. It does not speak well of his principles or character. You should not have listened to his protestations."

"It was exciting... and romantic... and..." Georgiana looked from one to other, and blushed scarlet to the roots of her hair.

"Yes, but we are glad you thought better of it, for your sake and your brother's. If you and Mr Wickham are in earnest, and show how responsible you are, your brother may come around to the idea. Far better to have his sanction. You made the correct choice today." Elizabeth tucked the writing supplies back into their japanned box, reached for the teapot and shook it. It did not swish with the promise of enough tea for all of them. "I shall send for fresh tea. In the meantime, we should all have more gingerbread. We will have a while to wait."

Jack returned within the half-hour, and with ill news. "There is not a lad at the Rose to spare for the job, Miss Lizzy. Nor at the other inns on the High Street. The innkeepers have so many people demanding service, they are near run off their feet. More'n one told me as how these sporting men were trying to get every gig and horse in this part of the county, so the stable lads are all employed in guarding their charges. Ted Heard, him as keeps the Rose, might spare someone at teatime, but I thought you wouldn't want to wait that long."

"Oh." Elizabeth took back the letter and thrust it into her reticule. "I wish I were a man, and could swear with impunity!"

"I could take the gig and go, Miss. It'll take me a good hour or more to get there, and at least that back."

"If you go, we are left with no protection here. We cannot risk having no recourse if we are found. No. I must contrive something else."

Elizabeth was a lady. She had been taught never to slump in her seat, that her body must be straight as a ruler, and a good inch visible between her spine and the chair back. What a relief it would be to throw herself back in her chair and drum her heels on the floor in frustration.

Jane was as serene as ever. She was never—

Oh.

Elizabeth's gaze went from Jane to Georgiana, and back again. "I have an idea…" When everyone looked at her expectantly, she gestured to Jane and Georgiana. "When we met in Ramsgate, we were all struck by how alike you two are in figure and colouring. Jane may be a little taller than you, Georgiana, but she could otherwise be a relation. So, this is what we will do. Give Jane your hat and pelisse, and take hers. Aunt Iphy, do you know your way to Mr Harding's house at Boys's Hospital?"

"From here?" Aunt Iphy pursed her lips, then nodded. "Yes. To Guildhall, then into Palace Street, and from there, turn into Northgate, where the Hospital is. It is some little distance. I will be slow."

"Take as long as you need, dear aunt, but you and Jane must go to him for sanctuary. Jane, you must be Georgiana Darcy for a while, and she will be you. I am sorry to ask this of you, for you may be importuned."

"You mean, this Wickham person or Mrs Younge may see me and think me to be Georgiana? We will be in well-populated streets, Lizzy. They cannot harm us." Jane smiled. "It will be our adventure, while you and Jack take Georgiana to Wingham."

Elizabeth could only pray Jane was right. "You will be safe when you and Aunt Iphy reach Mr Harding. I will send help back as fast as I can do it. Jack will go with us on the back of the gig." Elizabeth gave a decided nod. "Yes. This is our chance. There is no time to be lost. Change clothes. Quickly!"

CHAPTER THIRTY-THREE
False Borrowings

Fairing the foul with art's false borrow'd face
— Shakespeare, *Sonnet 127*

It went well. Better than Elizabeth had feared.

They parted from Jane and Aunt Iphy inside Chipperfield's, Aunt Iphy deciding to wait a quarter hour before leaving for the walk north to Mr Harding's house, to give Elizabeth a little lead to reach the Rose and start for home. Wickham would be looking for Georgiana Darcy's distinctive blue pelisse and hat, not Jane Bennet's unremarkable, unfashionable brown ensemble. The longer that blue pelisse remained out of sight, the longer Elizabeth and Jack would have to spirit Georgiana away.

"Keep your head down." Elizabeth linked her arm with Georgiana's. "The Rose is not far from here, but I would not have any passerby see your face."

Georgiana obeyed. The hand resting on Elizabeth's arm

trembled, and her breath came harsh again—whatever small sense of security the child had gained from their respite in the tearoom was dissipating in the open streets. She must fear that at any moment a hand would reach for her, and Wickham's voice would call her name. All Elizabeth could do was hurry along to the Rose, and try to keep this time of danger as short as possible.

The streets remained busy. Men lounged on the corners or bustled about in loud-voiced groups. Jack, who had left their shopping with the Chipperfields for later collection, likely relished his role as knight protector. As children, they had ranged Longbourn's lands playing at Camelot, Jack armed with a wooden sword that Elizabeth had envied greatly. But if he was borne back in memory to their childhood games, he made no mention of it. He was all wary readiness.

Two of the Rose Inn's lads were in the stables, protecting the horses and carriages. It was the work of minutes for them to help back Jasper into the traces and buckle him into his harness. Jack gave the boys some coin and handed Georgiana up into the gig's seat. Elizabeth joined her a moment later, and as soon as Jack was perched on the backward-facing groom's seat, his arms outspread to clamp his hands on the iron stanchions coupling the seat to the body of the gig, she flicked the driving whip to crack over Jasper's ears and started him out of the stable yard.

Georgiana did not need to be told to keep her face hidden. They were far more noticeable now they were perched in a moving gig than they had been as two ladies walking along the street. She half-turned towards Elizabeth and huddled in closer than was consonant with the ease of driving, but Elizabeth let her be. It would have been better if Jane's bonnet had a veil, but it did at least have wide slat sides. Very little of Georgiana's face should be visible to the people in the street.

Not so far, to get out of Canterbury. Up Burgate, and along the road past the ruins of St Augustine's Abbey, then out of the city bounds on the east road to the coast some twenty miles or more distant. Elizabeth was a fair whip and Jasper surprisingly tractable, but the sheer number of people milling about in the roadway made driving a more exacting task than usual. Many of the pedestrians were heedless of the other users of the roads and streets, and Jasper was upon them before they noticed a small, heavy-set horse was about to run them down. They leapt aside with Jasper's frothy snorts sounding in their ears.

Once on the coast road, the crowds melted away and Elizabeth breathed easier. Wingham was an hour's journey at Jasper's best speed. But still, they were clear of Canterbury and on their way home. Perhaps they were safe.

"Is it far? I know my brother was staying with Mr Palmer at Wingham Hall, but I am afraid that I have not quite fixed the scheme of the place into my mind. I have no mind for maps." Georgiana had straightened up once they left the city. Now they were out in the open country, she seemed to be more at ease.

Elizabeth smiled. "It seems our most noted ladies' schools do not teach proficiency in geography!" At Georgiana's enquiring look, she added, "Your friend Miss Bingley showed a similar lack of aptitude, though I am sorry to say hers was deliberate. However, to answer your question, Wingham is around seven miles from Canterbury. A one-horse gig, though, is not the fastest equipage, and Jasper hardly the swiftest of steeds—he is old and obstinate and does not like to hurry himself. At least an hour."

Georgiana sighed in a wavering sort of way, and fell silent. Elizabeth concentrated on keeping Jasper at a reasonable speed that would not exhaust the old horse. Georgiana looked about her, speaking now and again to point out something of interest as they passed. Jack was quiet, but Elizabeth had no doubt his attention was riveted on their surroundings and particularly on the road behind them.

They had travelled past the turn-off for Littleton and drove through Bramling without meeting anything more alarming than two farmer's carts and a flock of geese that had wandered from their pond to crop at the clover growing on the verges on each side of the road. Jasper had stamped his way through with a fine disregard for ruffled feathers and the indignant snapping of beaks. On any other day, Elizabeth would have laughed.

At Bramling, the road bent to the north east. A bare two miles now to Wingham, the road winding through mainly open fields with a few scattered copses. Over to the right, a thin, twisting line of smoke rose from the distant chimney of the farm at Wingham Wells, greyish-white against a cloudless sky.

Jack's hissed intake of breath warned Elizabeth before he spoke. "Rider behind us!"

A little gasp escaped her, while her heart gave one enormous thud then raced along, juddering as though running from an earthquake. Georgiana took in one enormous breath, and clamped her hand onto Elizabeth's arm, fingernails digging in like talons.

"Chasing us?" Elizabeth demanded, and her voice had risen to a pitch that she did not recognise. She cleared her throat.

"He's coming up on us fast, Miss Lizzy. He's just clearing Bramling now. He's got that horse coming at us all out."

"It must be Wickham. Bother! We are so close." Elizabeth cracked the whip over Jasper's head, but after five miles in the September warmth, the old horse had little left to give.

"I'll jump down and—"

"No! Stay where you are. He will not hesitate to run you down, and we would be lost. He will likely manage to stop us. Look for a chance then!"

Georgiana bent double on the seat. Only her grip on Elizabeth's left arm held her in place.

Elizabeth could hear the horse now, its hooves loud on the packed stones of the road. A glance behind. No time for more.

A dark horse coming at a full gallop, a man bent low along its neck. She could see little of his face. Nothing of him but a shape wearing a top hat, and a gleam of teeth where he had drawn back his lips in a grimace. He was close. Very close.

The road was clear ahead. Not even a goose in sight, much less anyone who might have helped. The fields were all empty, golden with stubble. She would have given worlds for a shepherd or a reaper. She gripped the whip tighter in her hand and called out to Jasper. "Get along, Jas! Get along!"

Perhaps it was the desperation. Perhaps the fright. But something in her voice had Jasper leaning into his harness and picking up his normal trot into something faster.

Not fast enough. Not fast enough.

Oh God, he was on them!

The horse flashed past, to be pulled into a scraping turn in front of Jasper that had the horse rearing in fright and Jasper veering off towards the ditch. She just managed to pull him away before they would have capsized, leaning back her whole weight, her hands shaking on the reins, fingers white. The horse was turned again, and the rider grabbed at Jasper's nose harness and pulled him back. The gig came to a stop in the middle of the road.

Elizabeth gasped again, but Georgiana screamed. Frightened out of her wits, no doubt, by their near escape from the ditch. The rider's expression showed bitter anger, his teeth still bared. It was the man from the assembly. It was Wickham.

The gig rocked as Jack dropped from the back. She had to help Jack. She had to do something. Do some—

Elizabeth surged to her feet, raised the long driving whip over her head and brought it round with all her strength in a crack of leather. Wickham yelled, and pulled back his horse, but not fast enough. She lashed at him again.

His head snapped back, the top hat tumbling off. Wickham's face, white with fury and fright, turned towards her and she lashed out again.

The horse. Get the horse.

Another snap of the whip, and the dark horse reared. Jack was in there now, leaping up to pull at Wickham, to get him down.

Get him down. Get him down—

The horse screamed. Georgiana screamed. Wickham yelled, and fell backwards out of the saddle. Jack was on him in the same instant, his arm pulled back and smashing forward, again and again.

Georgiana's scream died in her throat, the grip she had on Elizabeth's arm slackening. Elizabeth spun around, caught her as she fainted, and bundled her back into the gig seat somehow. Wickham was groaning and twisting, but Jack… Jack was a fury.

Another flashing blow and Wickham lay still. His horse had fled a few dozen yards up the road towards Wingham, but its trailing reins brought it to a halt beside the roadside hedge. Jack, astride Wickham's chest, sat back.

"Oh." Elizabeth fell back into her seat, panting harder than if she had run the distance from Bramling herself. "Oh. Jack?"

"Broke his nose for him." As Wickham stirred, Jack raised his fist in threat. "Stay down, you!"

What to do now. What to do.

Georgiana stirred and groaned, put a hand to her head. No time for her now. No time.

The road was still and deserted. High hedges hid the empty fields on either side. Bramling was quiet behind them, Wingham still out of sight ahead.

No help there. No help anywhere.

She glanced at Georgiana. Wide blue eyes stared back at her, but the child was at least able to sit unaided. "Hold on tight to the seat, Georgiana, and do not let go."

Georgiana nodded, near senseless with terror, her hands on the iron of the seat arm. Elizabeth did not blame her. The last few moments had been shockingly violent.

Despite its earlier fright, Wickham's horse was a phlegmatic creature. It was cropping the grass of the verge now. Elizabeth slid out of the gig to collect it.

"Miss Lizzy?"

"Do not let him move." Elizabeth sidled past Wickham.

He stared at her but did not seem to see her, his eyes showing little of the man who dwelt behind them. His nose and cheek bled freely. Horrible sight! She darted up the road to escape it.

The horse threw back its head as she neared it, and danced away a step. Jack would murmur nonsense at it, and hold out his hand for the horse to sniff. He had taught her that years ago, when he was first learning to care for Longbourn's horses. She tried it now, though her voice was anything but a soothing murmur while she begged pardon over and over for frightening it. The creature rolled its eyes to show the whites, but it allowed her to gather the reins and went along meekly enough to the gig. She tied it to the seat stanchion. Her fingers, weaving the last knot, shook and shook like leaves in a gale.

She clambered back up into the seat, forcing her knees to stop trembling and obey her will. Swallowed the bile threatening to burn its way up into her throat.

Jack turned his head. "Miss Lizzy?"

"I am well, Jack. I promise you. Just out of breath." She glanced behind them. "Is there anywhere in Bramling he can get a horse?"

"Not likely. There's only the one farmhouse and a few cottages, and the farmer don't welcome strangers. He'd run him off, 'specially the way he looks right now."

"Good."

From her seat, all she saw of Wickham was his boots, and feebly-kicking legs. The rest of him was under Jack's large frame. She frowned. She should do more. They had to hamstring this rogue further. What to do? What to—

His boots.

"Jack, take his boots and stockings and toss them up here. Search for his pocket book, too, and see if he has Miss Darcy's purse. If he has no money, he cannot hire or buy another horse."

Jack's face cracked into a wild grin. "Clever! It's done."

By the time Jack had stowed boots and a pair of grubby stockings behind the gig seat, Wickham stirred, trying to sit up. Jack let him be, and handed up a pocket book and a lady's purse. The knuckles of Jack's right hand were burst and bleeding. It must have hurt badly, but Jack did not show it.

Georgiana found her voice when Elizabeth dropped the flat purse into her lap. "I had thirty pounds in here!"

Elizabeth took a quick peek into the pocket book. Almost empty. Wickham must have given the money to his confederate. She took a deep breath. It would be such a relief to give way to hysterics, but as her mother always said, Elizabeth did not know what it was to have weak nerves. Mamma did not mean a compliment.

"Mr Wickham."

The man ran a hand over his face, and groaned aloud when it came away scarlet and dripping. He glared at her. He looked as if he were at a masquerade and a red half-mask had slipped down over his nose and mouth, to reveal the angry glitter of his eyes. "You damned bitch!"

"Here now!" Jack took one step forward, and Wickham shrank back, throwing up a hand as a frail shield. "You'll keep a civil tongue in your mouth around Miss Lizzy, you bloody rogue, or I'll do more than break your nose!"

Wickham, breathing hard, glared and gave black looks. Then his gaze fell on the girl in the gig. "Georgiana!"

Georgiana gasped and stared at him.

Wickham snarled like the feral beast he was. "I will ruin you, you bleating simpleton! Do you hear me? I will ruin you! One word of Georgiana Darcy eloping with the steward's son and that damned brother of yours will pay me every penny of your thirty thousand pounds to keep me quiet! I would not touch you otherwise, you ninny! You boring little mopsy! But I will have my pound of flesh. You just see if I do not!"

Georgiana squeaked, possibly too shocked to speak.

Elizabeth was not. To her own surprise, she let out a peal of laughter. "Mr Wickham, I should like to see you try."

Georgiana squeaked once more. Wickham stared, his mouth hanging open to show its ruin. Jack must have loosened a tooth or two.

"Miss Darcy took tea this morning with the wives of every single member of the dean and chapter at Canterbury Cathedral. Every one of them will swear that Miss Darcy is my guest at Wingham, and has never been out of proper chaperonage. Every single one of them, Mr Wickham, will proclaim you for the liar you are. Who do you think will be believed? You? Or the wife of the dean of England's premier cathedral?"

He opened his mouth. Closed it again. Scowled.

"You false, deceitful man! Who would believe you?" Elizabeth blew out a soft breath to calm flutterings her mother would have envied. "We are little more than a mile from the Hall, where I may call upon a dozen large grooms and footmen. Were I you, you... you mountebank, I should start walking and as quickly as I could do it with no boots and no money. I should run, were I you." She glanced at Jack and gestured with her head to the back of the gig.

"Get out of my way, Wickham."

She clucked to Jasper, who started off the instant Jack swung back onto the groom's seat behind. Wickham's horse trotted alongside without baulking. Wickham yelped and rolled to one side. Georgiana turned in her seat, bent double, ducked under Elizabeth's left arm and buried her head in Elizabeth's lap.

Elizabeth twisted in the seat and handed Jack the pocket book. "Wait until we reach the bend, then hurl this as far as you can into one of the fields. He will watch us out of sight. He will not be able to help himself, and he may waste enough time hunting for his pocket book that Galahad might catch him. But he shall not claim we stole and kept it. Toss out his boots farther on."

"Yes, Miss." And Jack smiled widely.

Behind him, Wickham had come to his feet, bloodied face twisted with rage and hatred. He glared after them as if he could strike fire from them and burn them to ashes.

She turned back to urging the best speed she could from old Jasper. For once, the contrary creature did as he was bid, and the gig rolled along merrily. Jasper snorted, likely scenting his home stable. He was not a bad horse, after all. She would be sure to find him an apple later.

By the time they reached the stable yard at the Hall, Georgiana Darcy was insensible. At least it was easy for Elizabeth to hold onto her, since the girl still lay face down in her lap and she could press one hand hard onto Georgiana's shoulder to keep her from falling from the gig. The other was engaged in making Jasper turn right into the Hall's grounds, rather than left into his own stable in Aunt Iphy's garden. She had to use both hands to persuade him, but luckily Georgiana did not fall.

As Jasper, blowing hard now, came to a stop, Jack leapt from his seat, shouting to the grooms to "Fetch the master! Hurry!" even as he reached up to take Georgiana from Elizabeth's grip.

"Careful now. Careful. I have her." Jack stepped back, while one groom jumped to Jasper's head to take control. Another ran hard, already out of the stable yard gates and racing towards the house.

Habbauld, the head groom, had come running from the tack room, and raised his hands to help Elizabeth out of the gig. He frowned when she could not prevent her own hands trembling in his warm grip. "What the devil?" Then to Jack, "The mounting block, Jack. Sit her on it, and push her head down onto her knees to get her out of that swoon."

Jack, carrying out some odd contortions to get the girl secure in his arms, started for the nearby mounting block. Elizabeth, weariness flashing over her like a river bursting its banks, tottered after him, her hand on Habbauld's supporting arm.

"Can you manage, Miss Lizzy? Jack'll need help."

She nodded.

Habbauld darted forward to help Jack seat Georgiana on the mounting block. He stilled for a second, then used his broad hand to push the girl's head down and held her in place, splaying his strong brown fingers between her shoulder blades. "Thought t'was Miss Bennet."

"Do not say anything. Do not let anyone see." Elizabeth reached them, and sank onto her heels to peer up into Georgiana's stark white face, steadying herself against the mounting block with one hand. It was rough and gritty under her fingers. Georgiana's cheeks showed no sign of returning colour. Elizabeth needed a vinaigrette, but she was not her mother and never carried one. "Do we have someone to send for the apothecary?"

"Aye. Can you hold her, miss?"

She nodded, and put her hand where his had been. She felt every shallow breath Georgiana took. At least the child was still breathing.

Habbauld was back within a minute or two. "Jim'll take that nag you brought, miss. If he has to go lookin' around the district for the 'pothecary, it'll save him having to run back here for a horse."

"Good. We need to get her into the house."

"Lizzy! Lizzy!" It was Galahad, pounding through the stable yard gate at a speed that surprised her. "Liz—" His voice went up several notes. "Jane! Good Lord, Jane!"

Elizabeth pushed to her feet and caught hold of him, making her tone as urgent and as compelling as possible. "Not Jane. It is not Jane." She straightened and raised her voice. "We met Miss Darcy in Canterbury as agreed, but there was some misunderstanding about her carriage and we were forced to use the gig. We could not all fit. So my sister and aunt are waiting at Mr Harding's until you can go and collect them."

Gal stared at her, looking quite wild.

"They are safe with Mr Harding. We need to get Miss Darcy indoors. She has been taken ill."

"Wha—"

"Please, Gal, let us go inside."

"Jane is safe?"

"She and Aunt Iphy should be with Mr Harding."

But Wickham or Mrs Younge must have come upon Jane dressed in Georgiana's clothes, recognised her and made the connection to Wingham. He had said at the assembly that he knew of Galahad, had he not, and of Wingham where Darcy was staying? And Mrs Younge would recognise them at once. Good Lord—

Galahad swore, words she did not know. Wickham had sworn at poor Georgiana like that, too. Better not to know exactly what either had said.

"Get the coach ready, Habbauld," Galahad ordered. "And mount every groom you can. Be ready to leave as soon as may be." He stooped over Georgiana, lifting her with Jack's help. "Oof. Lizzy, do you need help?"

"No. I am well." Elizabeth turned to Jack.

She had no words at first, but he nodded. He knew. He knew how grateful she was, that without him things would have gone ill indeed. She held out her hand, and Jack took it in his.

"Thank you, Jack. I am sorry you had no sword today, as you did when we were children. You were always the best of protectors."

He smiled at her. "We managed it, Miss Lizzy! We managed."

He made a good knight. He always had.

CHAPTER THIRTY-FOUR
An Army With Banners

Who is she that looketh forth as the morning...
terrible as an army with banners?
Song of Solomon 6:10

It was awkward, carrying the girl indoors. Light as she was, she was a great burden for one man to carry any distance. Elizabeth, having found some new vitality now they had reached safety, hurried along beside Galahad, supporting Georgiana's lolling head.

The side door to the gardens was the closest, and it was already flung wide. Sir James waited there, with Mrs Webb, the housekeeper.

"We need to put her to bed," Elizabeth gasped out.

Galahad blew out a hard breath, but kept on going. Through to the main hall and up the stairs, with Sir James and a footman behind him, to prevent his falling should he lose his balance. Mrs Webb ran on ahead, with Elizabeth bringing up the rear.

"In here, sir." Mrs Webb threw open the door to a bedroom.

In a moment more, Georgiana was stretched out on the bed, with pillows under her head. Galahad, blown from the effort, walked out to the hall where Sir James gathered Elizabeth in close, the way her father would have done. He was warm, and safe, and she leaned against him as Mrs Webb settled Georgiana, her forehead resting on his waistcoat. He smelled of mellow snuff, familiar enough that she had the comfort of knowing it was him and Wickham could not harm her now. He murmured the same kind of soothing nothings Jack would use with a horse.

"I must see to Georgiana." She tightened her grip on him for an instant, and pulled free. "I will be down as soon as possible."

She closed the door on their anxious faces, and ran to help Mrs Webb. That admirable woman had already divested Georgiana of Jane's bonnet and was easing her limp body out of the pelisse. It took but a moment to help, and, while Elizabeth chafed Georgiana's hands, Mrs Webb, whose silver chatelaine at her belt included the much-needed vinaigrette, waved sal volatile under the girl's nose.

Georgiana's nose wrinkled at once. She coughed, flushed a deep rose pink, and her eyelids shot open. Her face wrinkled too as she murmured a complaint about the sharp smell, and Elizabeth held her hands when she tried to push the small bottle away. She stared around the room wonderingly, since she could have no notion of where she was, but the moment she saw Elizabeth, she burst into a shock of tears and sobs, and flung herself into Elizabeth's arms.

Elizabeth patted her back until Mrs Webb could put aside the sal volatile and come to gather the girl up against a bosom far more maternal than Elizabeth's. Mrs Webb rocked and soothed and stroked tumbling-down hair.

"All is well, Georgiana. You are safe now." Elizabeth took the girl's hand and squeezed it.

Georgiana sobbed out her disillusion with her erstwhile lover, with many a broken word about how horridly Mr Wickham had spoken to her. How cruel he was! Why did he say such things? Why? What had she done? Oh, what had she done?

"I am sorry you have had such proof of his perfidy." Elizabeth tucked a loose lock of hair behind Georgiana's ear. "I am sorry. But you are safe here. Do not think on it now. Think later, when you feel a little more yourself."

She kissed a cheek that was more flushed than it had been, and glanced at Mrs Webb. "Mr Habbauld has sent a man for the apothecary. I pray this is merely overwrought nerves, for our journey was not without incident, but the apothecary must be told she is recovering from a dangerous illness she had in the late spring. A putrid sore throat, I believe. She has been slow to regain her full strength."

Mrs Webb grimaced as if she had taken a hearty sniff of her own sal volatile, but nodded. "I'll see to her, Miss Lizzy. If you ring that bell on your way out, I'll get one of the maids to bring up a nice cup of tea. We'll have the little miss right as trivet in no time."

"Thank you." Elizabeth smiled. "Georgiana, I must go and talk to my cousin and ensure we retrieve my aunt and sister. Mrs Webb will take very good care of you. I will return as soon as possible."

She left Georgiana in Mrs Webb's capable hands, and slipped out of the room. The footman stationed at the bottom of the stairs awaited her with a message to join the gentlemen in the blue parlour. She reached the door just as Jack came in from the stable yard.

"They sent for me, Miss Lizzy. Is all well with the little miss?"

"I think it will be." Elizabeth put out a hand as he went to open the door, stopping him. "Jack, I am so glad you were with us today. We have always been friends, have we not? I could not have a better one."

Jack, redder than a soldier's jacket, made a jerky bow. "Honour's mine, Miss Lizzy. The master said I was to take care of you. It's my job, see?"

She smiled, looking on his honest, familiar face with deep affection. "Thank you, Jack. Let us go in."

Jack opened the door and followed her in. Galahad and Sir James were near the fireplace, Sir James seated in a wing chair, while his son paced the room in a fine show of impatience.

"Lizzy! At last. Miss Darcy?" Galahad bounded forward to meet her.

"In Mrs Webb's care."

"I grew so impatient, I sent for Jack." Galahad led her to the sofa before the fireplace, and helped her out of her pelisse, draping it over a chair arm. A moment later, he pushed a glass into her hand. "Drink this, my girl. Slowly! And for God's sake, tell us what in damnation is going on!"

She forgave the strong language. "Jack knows all, and has been stalwart in our defence. He will say nothing to anyone else about today's adventure."

"Of a certainty I won't," Jack said, stoutly. "Not a word."

Elizabeth loosened and tossed aside her bonnet—caked in dust, it would never be the same—and took a welcome sip of brandy. "Well, it all began when we met Miss Darcy in Canterbury. There is a great crush of people in town today."

"The mill outside Canterbury, sir," Jack put in. "Place was full of Cits and sporting gents."

"I had forgotten about it. I would have gone with you, had I remembered." Galahad nodded. "Go on, Lizzy."

"Miss Darcy left Ramsgate at dawn this morning with her companion and… and George Wickham."

Galahad said something very profane. How marvellous to be able to say such things, to be able to relieve her feelings in like manner!

"Gal, my boy," Sir James offered a mild reproof. "You know the man?"

"He has leeched on the Darcys for years. He has left a trail of debt and ruined women behind him since his Cambridge days." Galahad swallowed whatever bile-filled epithet had come to mind, and after an instant of pressing his lips together, went on, "Such a one should not allowed within a mile of a lady. Elopement, Lizzy?"

"Yes. Mrs Younge—the companion, Sir James—appears to have helped Wickham work on Miss Darcy's sensibilities. Georgiana has known this man from childhood, and has fond memories of him. She can have known nothing of his real nature, and she was preyed upon. However, because of that boxing mill, when they reached Canterbury no carriage was to be had for them to journey onwards."

"Thank God!"

"Yes. It was the greatest good luck, or she would be lost, halfway to London by now. Anyhow, Miss Darcy had remembered better herself, and was full of doubts and regrets, but naturally such a pair would not permit her to turn back. The delay allowed her to escape Mrs Younge while Wickham hunted out a carriage of some sort, and she met us. She was very distressed."

"Aye," said an unsympathetic Galahad. "And so she should be. But nowhere near as much distress as one day's marriage to that wastrel would deliver."

"I believe you. A most unconscionable rogue!" Elizabeth pushed aside the memory of hate-filled eyes above the half-mask of blood. "Well, we knew they would be searching for her, so we hurried to the tearoom at Chipperfield's to hide until I could hit on a way of removing her safely from Canterbury. By another stroke of great good luck, all the cathedral ladies were there. I used them to quell, I hope, any rumours that may arise in Canterbury. It is well known now in the town that she is our guest here at Wingham because her companion was called away. The ladies are unimpeachable. They will be believed."

"Good girl." Sir James had risen from his chair and now leaned over her, and kissed her on the brow. "You are a very good girl to think of that."

"I was a very good liar, sir."

"In a righteous cause."

She smiled slightly. "We had not enough money for an express rider, and there was not a boy to be had to bring a note out here to you. I did not want to send Jack away with a message, since he was all our protection. We hit upon another scheme. She was wearing a distinctive pelisse and hat, and she and Jane are alike, as you know. So Jane put on Georgiana's clothes, and went with Aunt Iphy to take refuge with Mr Harding. And we came back here in the gig."

Oh dear. Now, they must be told of Wickham.

"Wickham caught up with us this side of Bramling. There was an... an altercation."

"The devil there was!" Galahad who had relaxed enough to lean against the mantel, straightened in one convulsive moment, his face reddening and his hands curling into fists.

Sir James drew in a sharp breath. He sat beside her, put a hand over her free one. Why did he... Oh. Why was she shaking?

"She hacked at him with the driving whip," Jack burst out. "I never saw anything like it, sirs! Miss Lizzy stood there in that little gig, hacking away at the man until his horse pitched him off and I could get at him."

Elizabeth took another sip of the brandy Galahad had given her, while the two gentlemen stared at her with astonishment writ large on their slack-jawed faces. She wished she could smile, but her hands were shaking again, and it was all she could do not to rattle the glass against her teeth.

Galahad laughed. He really, truly, laughed. "I am sure I do not read my Bible as I ought, but I remember verses celebrating a lady who was as terrible as armies. I do wish I had seen that. Wickham must have been very taken aback."

"He seemed a trifle surprised," Elizabeth conceded.

"He won't find it so easy with the maidens now. Broke his nose for him, I did." Jack added, looking at her, "You've always been a good'un, Miss."

Her face grew hot. "I was too incensed and, in all honesty, too frightened to think clearly. And far too stubborn to allow him to take Miss Darcy. I had to do something to help you get the man down, Jack, and it was the only weapon I had. You are the real hero, you know! You saved Miss Darcy and me. If you had not been there..."

"I will buy you a pistol for your reticule as soon as may be." Galahad came to kneel at her side. "Lizzy, you could have been hurt."

"We were not."

"Thank God for that. We'll send the men out after the rogue. Did you chase him off?" Sir James looked grey, and every inch his age. The hand he put on Elizabeth's arm shook as badly as her own.

"He must be somewhere on the Canterbury road. I cannot think there is anywhere else for him to go, and he left his accomplice there with most of his money. We took his horse, his boots and stockings, and the money he carried. He will have a painful walk. He may still be searching the fields for his pocketbook and his boots, since Jack pitched them over the hedge." Elizabeth smiled at her accomplice. "Jack has a strong arm."

"Different fields." Jack smirked in patent satisfaction. "On both sides of the road."

"He is on foot and penniless. Excellent. Best news all day." Galahad turned to Jack. "I owe you great thanks, Jack Hill, for the care you have taken of my cousin today, and I trust, as she does, to your promise to say nothing of it. I will talk to you later, and show my gratitude better when we are done with today's business. In the meantime, well done, my lad. Very well done. Mr Bennet will hear of it, and I am sure will be as grateful as we are. Now, go and see to your hand. Wickham is a poisonous brute, and I would not have you gangrened by him."

"Yes, do, Jack," Elizabeth said. "And thank you."

Jack, red about the ears, sketched out a bow and left. Given his speed, Elizabeth suspected he was glad to escape their gratitude. His parents would be so proud of him. Elizabeth would ensure they were told.

Galahad waited until the door closed, before giving her a sharp look. "Could she be with child, Lizzy?"

What? Wha— Oh. Oh dear Lord. She stared at Galahad, unable to prevent the slackening of her jaw.

"While all I know of Wickham has involved maids and tavern wenches, and not a lady, he would risk it if it means she has no escape from him. We need to know before I send for Darcy."

"Oh, good Lord. The notion never crossed my mind." Elizabeth choked down her protest that Society expected her, a maiden, to know nothing of such things. No one else could take on the office; not even Mrs Webb, trusted as she was. "I will go and speak to her."

The entire world was her burden that day, it seemed. Was there nothing it was not her responsibility to do? Was there no respite? Elizabeth gulped the rest of her brandy. Coughed at the burn. And went to determine if they had more than today's misadventure to deal with.

Georgiana had more colour in her cheeks and was sitting up against a stack of pillows, the counterpane spread over her legs. A porcelain tea cup and saucer stood on a table beside the bed. Mrs Webb may well have been correct about tea's efficacy.

Elizabeth smiled. "Mrs Webb, I must speak with Miss Darcy. Would you wait outside for a moment, and give us a little time together? Thank you."

Mrs Webb gave her a knowing glance, but curtseyed and left, closing the door quietly behind her. Georgiana eyed her with obvious trepidation, her eyes large and wide. Elizabeth took the girl's hands in hers.

"It pains me to ask this, Georgiana, but I must. Is there a possibility of a child?"

She might as well have enquired if Georgiana regularly danced the quadrille atop the waves of Ramsgate Bay in the moonlight, the girl stared at her with such dazed incomprehension.

"Did you lie with him? Allow him into your bed?"

"Nooo!" wailed Georgiana, high-pitched and wavering.

Elizabeth had never seen a face twist so. If she had used both hands to pull the soft flesh first one way, and then another; to crumple it into creases and folds as she might an old, unwanted letter, destroying its smooth shape before tossing it into the flames… Georgiana's face was so distorted, her loving brother would not know her; mouth opening in a soundless, grimacing wail, brows coming down and eyes screwing up in some sort of horror.

"You allowed him no liberties? Did not anticipate the vows you thought you were to make?"

Georgiana's mouth was wide now, moving in a silent demand of *How can you ask me this?*

"I ask because I must. Georgiana, if you are old enough to contemplate an illicit marriage with such a man, you are old enough to face the questions and the consequences. Did he... did you...?"

"No! No!"

Elizabeth sagged where she sat. She blinked a great deal for a moment, then she embraced the poor girl, speaking softly into the ear near her lips. "I am sorry. I am sorry. We had to be sure."

Georgiana turned her face towards Elizabeth. A whisper. Agonised and almost voiceless, husky with tears. "I let him kiss me once... this morning, before we left. That is all. I— I swear it. I swear it."

"Oh, my poor girl." Elizabeth gathered her up and cradled the child as she sobbed, rocking back and forth. "Hush now. Hush. Take courage, Georgiana. You have been foolish, but not the worst sort of foolish. You will likely escape this with no more than a severe scolding from that imposing brother of yours."

"He will be so angry."

"If there is one thing I am sure of, it is that he loves you very dearly. He will be disappointed at your imprudence at putting yourself into the power of a man like Mr Wickham, but if you explain all and confess your fault— for you do know elopements are not proper and that you should not have listened to Wickham's blandishments. Seek his forgiveness. I am certain he will give it."

"George— Mr Wickham said such cruel things. Horrible, horrible things. I cannot believe he wants to ruin me."

"He will not. Not if I can help it. I have done too much hard work today to prevent it. We have more to do yet, but we will see you safe. I promise."

"I thought he loved me. But he did not, did he? Not if he could say such things."

Elizabeth tightened her lips. "He is not a good man, Georgiana. He is not worth your tears." She gave the girl a little shake and allowed her to lie back against the pillows. "Now, I must go and arrange to bring Jane and Aunt Iphy home. Would you like more tea?"

Georgiana nodded. She looked very woebegone, and very

young.

"Excellent. I will ask Mrs Webb to keep you company until I can return. Until then, try and sleep a little. You will feel better for it."

To her surprise, the girl lifted up her arms for another embrace and clung to her most desperately for a moment, before releasing her and lying back. Elizabeth patted her cheek, the way she used to do with a ten-year-old Lydia crying over wanting more stories or treats, and had a shaky smile in response. Mrs Webb asked no questions, but appeared to take heart at the smile and nod Elizabeth gave her as she left the room.

Elizabeth returned to the parlour with more speed than propriety, eager to relieve everyone's mind. Galahad had been busy. He had donned an outdoor coat, and a footman held open a pistol case while he checked the two guns inside. He cast a quizzical glance Elizabeth's way.

She shook her head, and said as much as she could with the footman present. "I think all is well."

"Good. I am for Canterbury, to retrieve Jane and Aunt Iphy. The men will go with me. We'll keep an eye open for him." Galahad smiled. "May I borrow your horsewhip, Lizzy? Should we catch him, I'll skin him with it."

"Oh, do! But I am coming too."

"You're fagged to death, my girl. Stay here and rest."

"I could not. I must be sure they are safe. You and the men will be with me, and I will be riding in a coach. I cannot stay behind. I cannot." She caught his hand. "Gal, one of those two rogues must have seen Jane and Aunt Iphy in Canterbury, or why else would he have known to follow us here? I must go with you. I must be sure."

Galahad stood stock still. He closed his eyes for a moment. "I should have thought of that myself. Very well, Lizzy." He turned to the footman, closed the case of pistols and took it from the man. "Get word to Habbauld to bring the coach around to the front door, Peter. Quickly."

"I cannot like you going, Lizzy. You have done enough getting the child here." Sir James came to her as soon as the door closed behind the footman, and delivered another of those crushing hugs.

"Gal will take good care of you, but still."

Elizabeth reached up and kissed the old man's cheek. "Of course he will. Come and see us off. On the way we will decide what to tell Mr Darcy, and then Galahad will need to ride to Ramsgate when we return."

"I will write an express to Darcy when we reach Canterbury. But Lizzy"—and there was a note of complaint in Galahad's voice—"why the deuce do I need to ride to Ramsgate?"

Elizabeth pulled on her pelisse, found her bonnet and jammed it back onto her head, heedless of the dust and dirt. "We quelled the rumours in Canterbury. You will need to do the same in Ramsgate. We will devise our—"

"Lies?"

"Well, yes. More lies. We will consider what you must do and say in Ramsgate while we are in the coach."

"I believe," said Sir James, "that the Bible verse you were thinking of, my son, did not talk of any army, but of one with banners. Rather more magnificence."

They had reached the front steps, and the coach could be heard coming around the house. But Galahad was not looking that way. He stared down the main drive.

"Jane! Jane! Thank God! Jane!"

He leapt down the steps and ran to meet the shabby two-horse landaulet, light and fast, bowling up the drive. Mr Harding sat on the box beside the driver, with Jane and Aunt Iphy safely ensconced on the seat behind.

"Oh!" Elizabeth had forgotten about the landaulet Mr Harding kept at the Mill Inn. What a ninny she was! "Oh thank heavens! They are safe! They are safe!"

She paused in the act of picking up her skirts to run to join them, then let them fall again. No. Let Jane and Galahad greet each other.

The landaulet came to a halt beside Galahad, who reached up for Jane and—

Goodness! Jane was not usually so precipitate. She did not usually throw herself out of a carriage into a man's arms like that. Oh.

Jane disappeared into Galahad's embrace. Georgiana's expensive hat was torn from its place and tossed, quite literally tossed, onto the drive for the horses to nose at. Was Galahad kiss—

Oh. He was.

Elizabeth laughed. Jane did not appear to protest or complain. But what a shame about the hat. It was a beauty, and one of the horses had just trodden it into the dust.

She turned to Sir James. He was ruddy-faced, his mouth pulled tight. She slid a hand into his. "It is for the best, you know. She will grace your home, and they will be very happy."

"I wanted it to be you, child."

"I know. And Gal and I would likely have dealt well enough together, but not so well as that." She nodded towards the two on the drive who were oblivious to anything but each other. Neither noticed the landaulet starting up again. Mr Harding, the pillar of rectitude, looked forward, but the driver and Aunt Iphy frankly stared.

"I want to keep you in Kent. The way I wanted… the way I wanted her to be here always." His smile was pitiable. "I failed her too."

"I will stay for a while longer, and I will return. Often." She took his other hand, too. "It is not failure, sir. Jane is as much her granddaughter as I am. A part of Eliza will be home again, and all will be well."

He pulled her into a warm embrace, and if he said, very quietly, that it was not the same at all, Elizabeth could pretend she did not hear.

All would be well. Jane and Aunt Iphy were safe. Georgiana Darcy was safe. She and Jack had come through the encounter with Wickham unscathed, bar Jack's skinned knuckles. Jane and Galahad would be a blessing to this house.

All would be very well.

Which did not at all explain why her chin trembled, and her chest ached, and her eyes filled so suddenly with tears that she had no time to prevent them.

CHAPTER THIRTY-FIVE
Glass-Headed Men

And for-thy, who that hath an heed of verre,
Fro cast of stones war him in the werre!
— Chaucer, *Troilus and Criseyde (1385)*

Darcy had left Wingham mid-afternoon on Friday. By dint of having a groom ride ahead of him to bespeak a change of horse at each stage and have the new team waiting when the coach reached the posting inns, and not stopping for more than a few minutes to bait himself and the grooms, he was in Town early Saturday morning.

It was a miserable journey.

He spent it staring out at fields full of reapers, their sickles bringing down the golden wheat in swathes, and, later, at a gloomy darkness pierced by the pole braced in the lead groom's stirrup, a thick mass of flaming oil-soaked rags fixed to its upper end. His mind was as blank as he could wish. So blank, indeed, it took him an moment or two to realise they had passed the turn-off for Sevenoaks, and Westerham beyond. One moment the wooden post loomed large as they bowled over the crossroads, barely lit by the groom's link-light, each long arm ending in a rudimentary pointing finger to show the way. The next, it was gone. He regarded its passing with a shrug.

Lady Catherine would grumble if she knew he had passed by Rosings and not paid her the deference she expected from a dutiful nephew, but what of it? In her own words, she was celebrated for her sincerity and frankness: she would not offer understanding and sympathy. She would be too intent on showing her astonished contempt that he ever tried to declare himself at all.

He spent that Saturday night in his own bed, sleeping badly and waking from each short doze unrested and over-heated, with his bedcovers twisted into knots around his legs to show the extent of his discomfort. He ate without relish or appetite, and pushed away more food than he consumed. He had constantly to remind himself to be courteous to the staff. It was not their fault that Elizabeth Bennet did not consider him to be worthy of her. As it was, his valet walked quietly around him, as if fearing to tread on a tiger's tail.

Overnight, August gave way to September. Town was yet a desert: hot, airless, parched and desolate. Everyone of any note had left for the country weeks since in search of more wholesome air. Even if they had not, Darcy was in no mood to be convivial. He did see Bingley, who called on Sunday evening, after Darcy sent around a note with firm underlining to ensure he was not misunderstood: ... *would be glad to see you on your return...*

Bingley arrived alone, remarking after they had greeted each other that Caroline was in a foul mood and unfit to meet either man or beast. He eyed Darcy over the glass of brandy handed to him. "I had no notion you intended to leave Kent."

Darcy turned away to replace the brandy bottle on the mahogany side-table. "It is several months since I was last in Pemberley. Not since the spring planting in early April, before Georgiana was taken ill." He turned, smiling. "Far too long! While I trust my stewards, it is a poor estate owner who abandons his responsibilities for months on end."

"Perhaps I should reconsider buying an estate someday." Bingley sighed. He tossed back his brandy. "You must have left soon after we did. Did you see Miss Bennet?"

Darcy shook his head.

"Oh." Bingley sat back. "She allowed me an interview to offer my apologies, and she was kinder than I deserved. Well, there is nothing more to be done. Caroline's machinations have destroyed whatever small pleasure Miss Bennet may have once had in my company. I do not blame the lady in the least." He cast a glance at Darcy, and for a moment there was the flash of the old, ebullient Bingley. "I fancy Caroline might have been brought to accept Miss Bennet once she was aware of the connection to the Palmers, but for her antipathy towards Miss Elizabeth."

Given how Elizabeth had bested Caroline Bingley at every turn, Darcy could believe it. "I do not think their characters are much in sympathy."

Bingley snorted out a laugh. "No, indeed. Caroline has never done well, seeing others gain what she desires for herself." The smile he gave Darcy was sweet and yet held slight mockery. Then the smile died, and he sighed with a dolour Romeo would envy. "Gal admires her. Jane Bennet, I mean."

"I believe he does."

"He is the best of good fellows. She deserves no less."

"Will it pain you, if he pursues her?"

"Yes, a little. But… Well, I do not know if I love Jane Bennet. She is beautiful and gentle, and I was pleased to be in her company and receive those smiles. I do not know if more would have come of it, had we been left to ourselves to discover it. Caroline's interference has ensured I never will know. I have no claim."

And Bingley went on his way to Bath, repining.

Darcy could not blame his ills on a sister so intractable and vicious, she thought nothing of cutting at other ladies the way the Saracen had used his scimitar on Christians, and with as little remorse. Bingley was to be pitied—but also blamed for not acting to curb his sister ere now. He had lost Jane Bennet's good opinion but did not intend to fight for her.

Darcy took another sip of the brandy that had constituted his dinner. He was in no better case than Bingley. What had Chaucer had said about men with glass heads? That they should beware of stones? Well, what right had he to cast stones at Bingley when he himself had not stayed to fight for Elizabeth, but had fled just as incontinently? Was he as irresolute?

Why had he not stayed to argue his case? Mortification at being refused, certainly. Shame at having offended the woman he professed to love and admire? He should be ashamed. Why would he accept Bingley in friendship, yet decry her lesser links to trade? Hypocrisy and hubris were painful bedfellows.

In the distance, the bells of St George's chimed out another sleepless hour.

No solace here. Time to go home.

He had not been to Pemberley for months. He had not been prevaricating about the responsibilities of a landed gentleman in possession of an estate. He could be resolute in that, at least. Some may not think him a good gentleman, but he was a good estate owner.

So. He was for Pemberley.

"Tomorrow," Darcy spoke aloud. "I will leave tomorrow."

Pemberley. All russet-mellow stone glowing on a golden afternoon, the setting sun dipping behind the distant hills drenching the house and lake and land—his house, and his lake, and his land—in a kind of natural gilding. The spicules in the sandstone glinted like glass. The world was still and heavy, and the air smelt of warm hay.

Home.

For the first time in days, the hard fist clenching in his chest and gut finally relaxed its hold, and he could take a deep breath. He managed a small smile when the coach rolled to a stop in front of the steps, and Mrs Reynolds rushed to greet him with a smile and deep curtsey. Darcy was borne into the house on a wave of familiarity. The hall's vaulted ceiling, festooned with gilded cherubs and held up at the corners with the caryatids whose naked breasts had been the undoing of the boy of twelve or thirteen, who knew he should not look but could not take his eyes from them despite the heat in his face and groin... The chequered marble floor leading to the great sweeping staircase—he had slid down those banisters many times, to the great detriment of the seat of his nankeen breeches... Mrs Reynolds's pleasant voice with its flat Derbyshire vowels, that had been a part of the sound of this house since he had been first breeched at four years old.

All familiar. All *home*.

Here he would find the peace of mind to think and reflect, and to decide what he was to do about himself, to find the resolution to amend his faults, and to return to the fray.

To stop being so glass-headed.

A fortnight after Darcy's return, Colonel The Honourable Edward Fitzwilliam appeared at Pemberley's door to claim sanctuary. Darcy, hearing the well-known voice from his study, hurried out to the hallway to find his cousin bending over Mrs Reynolds's hand and raising it to his lips as a courtier might kiss the queen's.

"Edward! I did not know you were home!"

Darcy sprang forward, hand held out, and for a few moments they indulged in a reunion that, while it involved a great deal of manly reserve and calm expressions of delight at each seeing the other to be well, he knew was genuinely felt on both sides. They had been brothers-of-the-heart all their lives. Neither wore said hearts on the sleeve for the world to gawk at, but he held Edward in the highest esteem, confident Edward returned it. Indeed, Edward often claimed he was far fonder of Darcy than he could ever be of the jugbitten rakehell who was his elder brother, Viscount Carsington. Not an excessive compliment, considering Carsington's manifold failings.

Now Darcy held Edward at arms' length and looked him over. "You are unhurt?"

"I am well. I wrote to tell you I was home, but I sent the letter to Kent. I had no notion you were here at Pemberley until your steward mentioned it to ours. I have been in England these last two weeks." Edward followed him to the sitting room, Mrs Reynolds's flustered promises of refreshments following them. "I landed at Dover, but I was carrying despatches to Horse Guards and could not take the time for a side trip to Ramsgate to visit Georgiana or to Wingham to call on you. I was sent straight to London, and from there went home to Ashbourne."

Edward was unharmed. Well, uninjured. Darcy was too wise to think that the fact Edward had a whole skin meant his cousin would not crave the quiet peace of his childhood home to help heal the wounds of the spirit that war imposed on those trapped within it. He was not surprised Edward hastened to Ashbourne. He was surprised to see him at Pemberley so soon.

Edward's appearance was laid at the door of his loving mamma. He had endured, he said, as much mollycoddling and mothering as he could stomach for now. "I do understand she was anxious for me, but Mamma forgets I am nearer thirty than three. I swear she checked herself several times from rushing to kiss all my scrapes and bruises better."

Mrs Reynolds and a maid bustled in with fresh coffee and plates heaped with cakes and Cook's best almond biscuits. They paused their talk to allow her to serve the refreshments and exclaim her delight again, and resumed the conversation when the dear old soul had bustled herself and the maid out again.

Darcy took a slice of cake before Edward could claim the entire plate. "Now then, you will stay for a while, I hope? As long as you wish."

"I would be delighted." He eyed Darcy. "You are worn to a thread, man. It has been a hard time for you, with Georgiana's illness. I should have enquired earlier, but your letters assured me she was recovering, and Mamma says the same. I am not wrong there, am I?"

"No. I do not deny we had an anxious time with her, but she is doing well now. I saw her three weeks ago, in Ramsgate. The good air and sea bathing have set her up nicely, and in a few more weeks, perhaps after the harvest home, I will go and collect her, and bring her home for the winter."

"So what has you looking as though you have a fit of the blue devils?"

Darcy froze. He had thought he had presented nothing but his usual self. Leave it to Edward to see through any dissimulation! And no number of innocent statements along the lines of "Why, whatever do you mean?" or "I do not understand why you should think such a thing!" or "I have been riding the estate since dawn with my steward, and only just returned to the house" deterred the colonel for a moment. Darcy attempts to brush off his cousin's concerns were unconvincing. Evasions had Edward pouncing, as if plotting his way across a battleground and parrying every stroke the enemy made at him.

"You have been in Kent for weeks, I know, with Galahad Palmer. I doubt he is the one making you so down at the mouth. Bingley? Oh lor, William, you have not made an offer to that sister of his, have you? She has been setting her cap at you these three years, at least—"

"I have not."

"Well, that is a great relief to my feelings, I can tell you. If you were in Kent, I doubt you escaped Aunt De Bourgh's coils. You have not offered for Anne, either, I hope and pray?"

"I have not," Darcy said again. He added, thinking to divert Edward, "In fact, when Georgiana and I called on her on the way to Ramsgate, I told Lady Catherine I would never do so."

"And I did not hear the shrieking in Spain?" Edward raised his voice in a strident, womanish falsetto. "I am most seriously displeased!"

Darcy laughed. It was their aunt to the life. "She was indeed displeased, but accepted it in the end. Anne's health is still poor, and I cannot marry without some thought to an heir." He needed a counterattack. "You always deal well with Anne."

"But not with Lady Catherine."

"Anne's husband would have the authority to remove Lady Catherine to the dower house."

"Which is much closer than Spain. The poor man would be unable to escape the shrieking." But for all that, Edward pursed his lips.

The seed was planted.

"Who is she, William?"

Damnation. The man was indefatigable. Darcy stared. Serpents swayed and hypnotised their prey into immobility, and while Edward may not sway, those brilliant Fitzwilliam-blue eyes of his were both kind and compelling. He trusted Edward more than he trusted himself.

"I made a mull of it. I was the most complete nodcock."

Edward nodded slowly. "I thought so. Who is she?"

"A connection of Galahad Palmer's, by marriage."

And to Edward's nods and encouraging murmurs, he spoke of Elizabeth Bennet's brightness, her beauty, the fine eyes that had first attracted his notice and the light of intelligence that they displayed, the way she laughed, the joy of every conversation with her, her kindness, her charm, the sharp wit, and, chuckling at the recollection, the glorious way she set down Miss Bingley at every turn: in short, that she was the flame burning his mothwings to ash.

He spoke of the history of Eliza Beeching and the Palmers, and what he knew or had gleaned of the Bennets and their position in the world, their links to trade and his belief that they had little with which to dower their five daughters. He held back nothing of his own conduct, from the deanery garden onward, to his growing esteem for Elizabeth and its deepening into true admiration and love, only to suffer her indignant refusal to listen to his declaration.

"I do not deny that my first response was disbelief. I could not fathom why she considered I was unworthy of her acceptance. I am Darcy of Pemberley! Few establishments are more desirable than the one I offered her. My situation in life, my connections, and Pemberley itself are all circumstances highly in my favour. She would never receive a more eligible offer." Darcy groaned. "Those were my thoughts, Edward. That was the proud, arrogant, disdainful attitude she protested against."

"Ah. Your nodcockiness."

"In part. There is worse. I was abominable when we first encountered each other, as I told you, basing my supposed superiority on the differences between our situations. I was suspicious of the Bennets to begin with. Everyone wants something, was my credo. Influence, connections, a stake in my or the Palmers' wealth… I thought them capable of anything because, I believed, anyone lower than me must be looking to better their situation and would use any means to do so. I made plain to her that in my view, she stood below me. That her own situation in life, her connections, were inferior, and she could not expect me to be pleased with acquiring relations whose condition in life is so decidedly beneath my own."

Edward's jaw sagged. "Surely you did not say that?"

"Not in those precise terms, but that is what I meant and what she understood. She refuted the assertion, telling me all the relations I scorned were, in fact, descendants of a landed family in Essex. Still, you understand, below…" He trailed off and grimaced. "One thing I did not mention earlier, but I met her elder sister at the theatre with the Bingleys in June. Jane Bennet was at the point of being courted by Bingley, and she attended with the aunt and uncle in trade whom I so deplored. I doubt I was barely civil, and I remember thinking at the time how magnanimous I was in allowing the introduction at all."

"Nodcock is the mildest term I would use."

"Do you know, I keep hearing Lady Catherine's voice in my head. Can you imagine what she would say?"

"About Miss Elizabeth?" Edward used the strident, high-pitched tone again. "Have you lost your senses? An alliance to a woman of inferior birth and standing, one without family, connections, or fortune, would be utterly scandalous! Such a dishonourable, imprudent connection with one so far outside our own sphere must disgrace you in the eyes of everybody connected to you, and involve us all in your degradation. You cannot expect your family to offer such an upstart anything other than censure and disdain."

This time, Darcy could not laugh at Edward's impersonation of their imperious aunt. "My imaginings have not been those exact phrases, but entirely those sentiments. And although Elizabeth has never met Lady Catherine, I suspect that sort of intemperate censure was what she heard, but delivered in my voice. I do not like who I have become. It is right to have some proper pride in our family and what we have. It is right to think of the good of Pemberley and endeavour always to leave more for my son than I inherited for myself. It is my duty to my name, as my father made clear. I truly believe my parents gave me good principles—"

"They were all goodness."

"Yes, but they allowed me to live by those principles in pride and conceit, until I became selfish and overbearing. I do not mean to cast blame, believe me. The faults are all mine. I have come to care for none beyond my own circle—you, your parents, a few friends like Palmer and Bingley. I looked down upon the rest of the world, deemed the positions and worth of most people I met to be far below the value of my own. I became too much like Lady Catherine, demanding that the differences in rank be preserved. Elizabeth was not pleased. She told me what she thought of my pretensions with every turn of her head and curl of her lip. She was right. I am not worthy of her. And *that* is the conclusion I have reached, these three weeks later. I was proud and disdainful, and infinitely deserved the peal Elizabeth Bennet rang over my addle-pated head."

"So what do you intend? What good can you do here, at Pemberley, while she remains in Kent?"

"I have been asking myself the same thing. Another aspect to this story involves Bingley, Miss Jane Bennet and Galahad Palmer… I will tell you more later. The pertinent point is that Miss Bingley is implacably opposed to any alliance that may pull them back the few steps they have made into acceptance by the *ton*, and Bingley, deciding his suit was hopeless, has not the resolution to fight for Jane Bennet. Another conclusion I have reached, is that hiding myself away here at Pemberley makes me as irresolute as Bingley."

"What have you decided?"

"When I go to collect Georgiana, I will speak with Elizabeth again. If she has left Kent and returned to her home, I will follow her. This time I will whole-heartedly beg her forgiveness and her charity, and for the opportunity to show her a better Fitzwilliam Darcy than she has known hereto. I do not have the pretty manners of Galahad Palmer, or Charles Bingley's easy amiability, but I hope I may show her a principled man who is reasonable enough to allow the justice of her reproofs of my conduct and manners. More than that, her reproofs of the failing in my moral character, which were well deserved. I will prove, I hope, that I can be a man worthy of her good opinion."

"Good man! If you can show her you have learned from your errors, that you have improved yourself in order to please her and she is a woman worthy of such effort, you will go far to mitigate her ire." Edward smirked. "I understand the ladies like to think they can change us at will. Well, from our side, I will be glad to see you happy and for Georgiana to gain a sister to support her. I believe my mother will, too. M'father will likely grumble at her lack of dowry."

"She is herself a dowry." Darcy managed a smile he felt was frail as gossamer. "As Shakespeare said, who had a word for every human condition."

"Well, she is the daughter of a gentleman, and he will be pleased with the connection to the Palmers, who are solid enough. Carsington's opinion is not worth a farthing, but Lady Catherine…" Edward's voice trailed away and he winced.

"Indeed. But to be frank, her opinion is not worth any more to me than is Carsington's."

"Good man. Well, have at it, William. Faint heart never won fair lady, or so we are told." Edward frowned. "Was that Shakespeare too?"

"He and everyone else." And for the first time since he left Kent, when Darcy laughed, he meant it.

They dined late. Darcy ate better than he had in weeks, soaking up the comfort Edward's presence instilled in him. Having someone with whom to discuss the matter eased his spirits. He was able to speak of other things that had happened at Wingham, telling Edward of the Bingleys' visit and seeing Georgiana in Ramsgate. They both laughed over the number of times Miss Bingley had been schooled by Miss Elizabeth.

"Like a puppy having its nose tapped with rolled up paper," Edward said appreciatively. "I wish I had seen it. Bingley is an amiable fellow, but his sister considers herself higher than a duchess. That she disdains the Misses Bennet, who are not only gently born but connections of Bingley's host! It is beyond anything."

"The tone of Miss Elizabeth's voice when she informed Miss Bingley that the difference between Canterbury and Bath was the width of southern England! I preserved my countenance with great difficulty. She—" Darcy broke off, as the dining room door was thrust open and Wilkes, the butler, hurried in with a sealed letter on a small salver.

"An express, sir, from Kent. It has just this minute arrived."

LETTER: Galahad Palmer to Fitzwilliam Darcy, September 1811

To Fitzwilliam Darcy, Esq,
Pemberley, Derbyshire

Wingham Hall, Wingham, Kent
Wednesday, 18 September 1811

Fitz

We are all safe and well. I will repeat that as many times as I must to prevent you flying into the boughs, since I am sure you think that if I am sending expresses to Pemberley, ill news must be their burden. Not at all, I assure you. Merely, I wished you to have this news promptly, and the normal mails are slow to travel from one end of the country almost to the other.

I am bid by my cousins to tell you they are enjoying hosting Miss Darcy here at the Hall. She is rapidly becoming a fast favourite with both Aunt Iphy, who already clucks over her like a hen with one chick, and my father. My two cousins are considering what they might do during her stay to ensure her amusement and happiness.

Doubtless, you are wondering why Miss Darcy removed to the Hall from Ramsgate. When you consigned her to my care in your absence, we had no notion that circumstances would compel her companion to give up the duty herself. Mrs Younge, escorted by an old acquaintance of ours, has been obliged to leave Kent. I did not have the opportunity to speak to Mrs Y myself, but it seems urgent business of some sort required her instant departure from Ramsgate this morning. Mrs Y's travelling companion is G W, whom you will remember. The two took Miss Darcy to Canterbury where she was met this morning by my cousins and Aunt Iphy, and brought safely to Wingham for her visit. We are delighted to have her here. We believe Mrs Y and G W have travelled on to Town, assured that we have taken full responsibility for Miss Darcy's welfare.

Miss Darcy is very well, although her spirits are a trifle affected by the upheaval. She will be kept diverted, I am sure, by Lizzy's cheerful company and Jane's gentle kindness. You may have every confidence that they are taking good care of her, and are looking forward to spending the next week or two together.

I am bid by all here to say you are very welcome to join your sister's holiday when you are free to do so. It will give us all great pleasure when you return to Wingham.

Yours ever,

Gal. Palmer

CHAPTER THIRTY-SIX
Proud Grief

> I will instruct my sorrows to be proud;
> for grief is proud, and makes his owner stoop.
> — Shakespeare, *King John*

What the devil? Who in hell had kicked him in the gut and stopped his breath? His heart, though, had not stopped. No, it lurched and stuttered, and then bolted like a mad horse thundering away in his chest and kicking the inside of his ribs to sharp, stabbing splinters.

Darcy read the express again. Georgiana had left Ramsgate without his knowledge and consent. Had been abandoned by Mrs Younge and G W.

G W.

"Oh, hell and damnation! Wickham!"

"What?" Edward shot bolt upright in his chair.

Darcy gave the express into Edward's eager hands. His own shook. "Wickham! I saw him in Canterbury, the week before I left Kent. Spoke to him. He said something about an opportunity to improve his circumstances, but I understood him to be leaving

Kent for Town. That this 'opportunity' involved Georgiana! Dear God! Dear God."

He put his hands over his face. Wickham had smiled, watching him escort Elizabeth back to Miss Palmer. All Darcy had been concerned about then had been to ensure she had not been imposed upon by Wickham's easy charm. And all the time that festering, stench-ridden bastard had been scheming against Georgiana! And Mrs Younge? What treachery was hers?

Georgiana. Dear God. Georgiana.

What had she done?

No! What had *he* done, leaving her at the mercy of Wickham? Why had he not been more suspicious? Had a few years of not seeing anything of the bastard blunted Darcy's guard? He had failed Georgiana utterly. The thunder of his heart was smothered by a rising nausea burning its way up into his throat like lava.

What had he done? Oh God, what had he done leaving Georgiana in Kent while he ran to Pemberley to lick his wounds?

"Palmer said nothing that might harm Georgiana if his letter fell into the wrong hands. Clever. He paid well for this to reach us in two days." Edward returned the letter, his hand a great deal steadier than Darcy's own. "An abduction, or an elopement."

The words fell like hammer blows to a farrier's anvil. "I pray to God Georgiana has more sense than to elope!"

"She is fifteen. No one of fifteen has much sense. No matter. Wickham is the one who needs to pray. If he has touched her, I will tear his hands off." A slight twist of Edward's lips. "And other sundry parts of his odoriferous body."

It would be a relief to put his head down onto the table. No time. No time. He had to reach Georgiana. "I must get to Kent."

Edward, so calm he might be discussing a book or a play, glanced at the clock on the mantel. "Almost seven. The moon is on the wane, but it is a clear enough night to give us a little light. We could reach Derby tonight, rest your horses overnight and start the journey south at dawn tomorrow. Except..."

"Except?"

"Except Palmer has taken great pains to assure you there is no need for that sort of haste. He made it plain that he has Georgiana safe at Wingham Hall, that she is well, if conscious of whatever folly was in hand that day, and that Wickham and Mrs Younge are no longer in the vicinity. It appears to me he has done everything possible to avoid talk and rumour. What does it achieve to rush away pell-mell tonight, except to undo whatever good work Palmer has taken to quell gossip? Do not allow your concern to override your good sense."

It had all the good effect of a glass of cold water dashed into his face. The rushing thoughts and tumultuous sensations stopped dead, and Darcy found enough self-possession to draw breath.

"My first idea was to leave for Kent at once." Darcy took Palmer's letter and folded it carefully. "But you are right. It was panic speaking. Now is not the time to indulge in histrionics."

"You are not usually prone to panic, but this has been an exceptional year." Edmund reached for the wine carafe and refilled both their glasses. "Have your coachman get the light travelling coach ready—"

"It would be faster to ride."

"The distance is far too great, and you are not accustomed to riding so hard and so long. You would be half-dead by the time we got there. *I* would be, and I am the dragoon in the family. No, the coach is best. We will start at dawn and get in at least one clear day of travel before the Lord's Day... not that I suggest we stop on Sunday. I would brave several finger-pointing sermons on the evils of not keeping the Sabbath, if at the end of my journey I can rectify the sin that is Wickham still breathing."

"You are coming?"

"Of course. I daresay my company may not be entirely unwanted—" Edward laughed at Darcy's hasty assurances, because the Lord knew Darcy would give anything to have him at his side. "Besides, I will kill Wickham the instant I see him. After tearing him into small pieces." Edward's smile would not be out of place on the face of the wolf met by Perrault's Little Red Cap.

Darcy nodded. "Then let us go to my study and write a reply to Palmer, and plan our route."

Wilkes awaited them in the hall. Mrs Reynolds stood to one side wringing her hands in her apron. The express had evidently overset his most senior staff.

He gave his orders quickly. "The colonel and I are leaving for Kent in the morning. Wilkes, send word to the stables, please, to have the light travelling coach ready at dawn. Tell them to mount two grooms and to bring a spare horse each for them, along with the second coach for Harris and the colonel's man. Is the express rider still here?"

"In the kitchen, sir, catching a bite to eat. We'll house him in the servant's quarters overnight." Mrs Reynold would not stop wringing out her apron.

"Excellent idea. When he has finished his meal, send him up here. I will have a letter for him to take back to Kent, and a purse to fund his journey." Darcy forced a smile. "Do not be anxious, Mrs Reynolds. It is not ill news. Miss Darcy is safe in the care of friends, and the colonel and I intend to join them for a short holiday."

"I have not seen her these two years," Edward put in, tone hearty and cheerful. "As her more charming guardian, it behoves me to visit her before I am sent back abroad!"

Mrs Reynolds smiled in relief, and Darcy dismissed the two servants with a nod of thanks to Wilkes and, for his housekeeper, in the kindest tone he could muster, a "We would be glad of some coffee now in my study, Mrs Reynolds, and would you speak to Cook and arrange breakfast for us for tomorrow at five?"

They both hurried off to see his bidding done. Darcy led the way into the study.

"You are a lucky man, to have such faithful servants." Edward closed the study door.

"I know it." Darcy sat behind his desk, and reached for paper and pen.

Edward looked at the ceiling as if calculating, his lips moving. "Wingham is what? Two hundred miles from here?"

"A little more. The roads are generally good."

"In that case, the greatest potential for delay will be horses."

"One groom will ride on ahead to bespeak them at each stage, but it cannot be guaranteed they will be available. We may have to wait, or allow the ones we have to rest." Darcy tapped his quill on the paper. "I am anxious to reach Georgiana, but I trust Gal Palmer. If we were needed urgently in Kent he would say so, without equivocation. So, you are right about not travelling with reckless haste. We will make a reasonable journey, and endeavour to arrive at some point on Monday. An extra night on the road, if she is truly unhurt and safe, does no harm."

"Except to your peace of mind."

"I have none anyway, Edward. It is not to be expected, under the circumstances. I must do as best I can, and hope I find my peace when I see my sister safe and sound." Darcy bowed his head and scribbled a brief reply to Palmer, telling him they were on their way, the scratching of the quill against the paper the only sound for a moment or two.

"This Mrs Younge," Edward said. "Who is she?"

"A clergyman's widow. From Sussex, I believe. I took Georgiana from school in April— Did you receive that letter?" On Edward's nod, Darcy continued, "The school was of limited value, unless all I wished for in a sister was another vacuous young lady whose only achievement was netting a purse or painting a table while simpering. A range of masters would do better to give her a real education. Mrs Younge came to us a week or two before Georgiana was taken ill at the beginning of May. Her task was to oversee Georgiana's establishment and guide her as her education continued. Of course, Georgiana's illness interfered with those plans."

"She had good references?"

"The best. You think they were false?"

"From Palmer's hints, she was working hand in glove with Wickham and you were deceived in regard to her character. Let me have copies of whatever information you may have on her, if you please. If she and Wickham are indeed in Town now, she may be a way to find him."

"You mean Wickham may have planned this for months? He is untrustworthy and profligate, but this is beyond anything."

"I think you have underrated his hatred all these years. He has resented you ever since he was old enough to realise who was the young master, and who the steward's son. Georgiana comes with thirty thousand sweeteners to soothe his bitterness."

"He was angry I would not give him the Kympton living, flinging aside the fact I had paid him to resign his claim to it. I never considered that he would plot against his godfather's daughter, even if he wanted revenge for my refusing him."

"Perhaps he has grown desperate. He has not followed any profession…"

"Not that I am aware."

"Then her dowry alone would be an inducement, if it brought him the income to which he feels entitled."

"Though sweetest of all must be knowing his revenge on me would be complete indeed." Darcy sealed the note to Palmer and sanded the superscription to dry the ink. "Money. We will need money."

He unlocked the cast-iron safe set into the wall behind his desk. Yes. Plenty to stuff into his pocketbook to ease their journey, pay for new horses at every stage, and get them to Georgiana quickly. He added some guineas to a small purse for the express rider's use. He did not bother to count any of it. He could balance the books later. A great deal of accounting may be needed later. And, when it came to accounting… He took the packet of Wickham's vowels he had kept there since his father's death.

"What is that?" Edward asked.

"I have cleaned up Wickham's sins for years." Darcy closed up the safe and dropped the papers onto the desk. "More than a thousand guineas of debt is recorded here. Another weapon against him, should we need it, and one I should have used years ago. I have been too indulgent of my father's memory, knowing how fond he was of his godson."

Edward's laugh held no amusement. "Good. When I am finished with him, we can toss the scraps into the Fleet or the Marshalsea. Or better yet, have him transported."

A fitting consequence for Wickham's misdeeds, if Edward did not kill him. Edward was a soldier who had seen battle, who had killed before now, and would not baulk at dispatching the rat. Despite his calm, practical exterior, Edward's hatred for anyone who may have hurt his little cousin and ward would be absolute.

Darcy would not stop him, if he caught up with Wickham before the debt collectors could.

Darcy would not think of stopping him.

Pemberley to Northampton on Saturday, and the Black Horse Inn. Foul beds with so much life in them, Darcy spent the night sitting sleepless in a chair on one side of the window while Edward dozed in a chair on the other. At least Cooper and the grooms reported their quarters over the stables to be decent enough, although Harris shuddered delicately when asked about his.

Northampton to Brook Street on Sunday, arriving in London in a smoky, humid dusk. Not as far as he would have liked. He had hoped they might get as far as Dartford, or even Rochester, but the infrequency of Sabbath travelling meant fewer horses were available, and they lost three hours at St Albans resting the ones they had hired from the inn in St Neots. Still, after the uncomfortable night in Northampton, it was a blessing to sleep in his own bed and he rose like a giant refreshed, as the Psalmist had it. Again, they were away just after dawn.

"Some sixty-five miles," Edward noted, rolling up the map he had brought with him from Pemberley's library.

They rattled over Westminster bridge, the river all mists and steams that early in the morning, the dawn fogs wreathing around the lanterns placed across the bridge's span, not yet burnt off by the new-rising sun.

"What is sixty miles of good road? A little more than half a day's journey. We should have less trouble finding fresh horses at each stage today than we did yesterday. An easy distance."

"And that is your eagerness to see Georgiana speaking." Edward used the rolled-up map to poke, disrespectfully, at Darcy, and turned away to look out of the window to stare at the stews of Kennington as they passed them. When he bent to ensure the coach pistol was within easy reach in its pocket on the coach door, he mumbled something about "Or eagerness to see someone else."

Darcy ignored him. It was the safest thing to do.

Faversham. The last stage before Canterbury and Wingham beyond. The Sun Inn, ancient walls freshly limewashed, windows gleaming, the sign bearing a jovially-faced celestial being with improbably fiery hair, swinging in a mild breeze.

The courtyard, with his groom standing ready. Eight fresh horses, four for each coach, being brought out of the stables by the inn's ostlers and postillions.

And Galahad Palmer, sitting on the mounting block with a tankard of ale in his hand, and a welcoming smile upon his face.

CHAPTER THIRTY-SEVEN

Scorpions

Full of scorpions is my mind
— Shakespeare, *Macbeth*

Bless the man, but he had tankards of ale ready for everyone, from Darcy and Edward to the postillions from Rainham who were unhitching their charges from the traces to allow the Sun's horses to be put into place.

It should have been the most welcome benison, and Edward gulped his down with grateful thanks. To Darcy, it tasted of rust and dust, guilt and failure.

He drank it anyway, to moisten his dry mouth.

When Palmer had greeted them both, he had held Darcy's hand an instant longer than usual, and his familiar irreverence had been chased away by the kind heart living beneath it. "All is well, Darcy. I had your express this morning, and thought I would meet you here. We can talk in the coach."

Darcy agreed, although grudgingly biting back demands to know how his sister fared. He stood to one side, the tankard half-forgotten in his hand, while Edward and Palmer carried out some desultory conversation as the horses were changed. He roused to give the Rainham postillions their tips.

Palmer's grey was taken in charge by one of the grooms and they were off within ten minutes. It felt like hours.

Palmer settled into the seat facing them, and did not wait to be invited to speak. "Let me reassure you. Miss Darcy is well, and in the care of my cousins. Our apothecary says she has taken no physical harm. He was told of her illness in the spring, but, after examining her, did not discover any lingering weakness. He pronounced her to be generally very well, although discomposed and subdued by her adventure—he was told she became separated from her companions in Canterbury and had been overwhelmed by the press of the crowds. He gave her a composer and said he had no need to visit her again." Palmer winced at Darcy in sympathy. "I am sorry, Fitz. It was a planned elopement."

Darcy bowed his head. The air was so thick to breathe he must put all his attention to that, while beside him Edward sighed loudly enough for all to hear.

"The saving grace, beyond her coming upon my cousins who offered aid, is that she thought better of it. Forgive me, Darcy, but I had Lizzy—my cousin Elizabeth Bennet, Colonel. I had Lizzy question her gently about the extent of her contact with Wickham… well, you understand. I do not think you need worry. Forgive me if we overstepped."

"There is nothing to forgive." Edward spoke before Darcy could unclench his jaw. "It is a natural concern."

For a moment Darcy had to hide his face, fearing it would betray his terror and disgust. Mortification had his gut roiling. That Elizabeth was privy to Georgiana's folly was ignominy enough. But this! He stared out of the window, so rigid that his neck and shoulders shot pangs of discontented aching at him, and forced his voice out of a throat threatening to close up entirely. "It is a relief to know she is unharmed. No word of Wickham?"

"Nothing since it happened. I sent grooms searching for him on the Canterbury Road, hoping we might take him since Lizzy had deprived him of his horse and boots, but he doubtless hid in the hedge every time anyone passed."

"Horse and boots?" Darcy and Edward spoke in disbelieving unison.

"Let me tell you the tale from the beginning," Palmer protested, "else I lose its thread. At dawn last Wednesday morning, Miss Darcy and her two companions left Ramsgate, with Wickham on horseback and the two ladies in a hired coach. By the time they reached Canterbury she had a complete change of heart but was, rightly, convinced they would not listen or allow her to turn back. She was in their power, and knew it. The hired coach would go no further. I know these Ramsgate coaches, and they are not built for anything other than short excursions, plying backwards and forwards between Ramsgate and Canterbury. Miss Darcy's stroke of luck was that Canterbury was full and there was not another carriage to be hired."

Palmer's tale was uncomfortable hearing. The danger into which Georgiana had been placed; the crowds of men unregulated by any sense of propriety and with their spirits elevated with the excitement of the boxing match; the good fortune that had Miss Palmer and the Bennet girls in Canterbury at the precise moment Georgiana needed help; the awful, awful consequences if they had not met—

The sheer happenstance that had saved his sister had Darcy swallowing hard to avoid throwing up his accounts. The risks, the what-if-Elizabeth-had-not-been-there possibilities... His stomach roiled again, awash, it seemed, with lava. He wanted to bend over his knees and put his hot, sweaty face into his hands, but he forced himself to remain upright. His cousin placed a hand on his knee. The weight was comforting.

He owed his sister's salvation to Elizabeth Bennet. Her quick thinking to take Georgiana along with them to a place of safety off the streets, to introduce her to the cathedral ladies, to use the superficial likeness to Miss Bennet to exchange clothing and allow Elizabeth to get Georgiana away to Wingham...

"A clever stratagem. I am impressed by the action she took to preserve my cousin's reputation, too, with so little time to think about it. I will be pleased to meet the lady. I have heard much of her already." Edward's hand pressed a little harder before lifting away.

Everything hurt and withered in on itself, like paper shrivelling in a fire. But these flames were of ice. Darcy drew his shoulders up until they were hunched under his ears. "Go on, Gal. Please."

Palmer nodded. He leaned forward to squeeze Darcy's shoulder, before resuming the story.

The 'escape' from Canterbury, with Elizabeth driving Miss Palmer's small gig with Jack Hill on the groom's seat behind. The encounter, two miles short of Wingham, when Wickham caught up with them—

"How in hell did he find them?" Edward demanded.

"Miss Darcy's pelisse and hat were distinctive. He found Jane and Aunt Iphy at the bottom of Northgate, a few hundred yards from the friend's house for which they were making." Palmer laughed. "Jane told us the instant Wickham caught at her arm, coming at them from behind, she flung him off and her 'Unhand me, sir!' rang from the rooftops. Naturally, the street around them came to a standstill, and, taken aback, Wickham was at a loss. Mrs Younge was with him, and must have recognised both Jane and Aunt Iphy at once. She pulled Wickham away. Without a word, they rushed away back into the centre of Canterbury, leaving our two ladies to carry on and claim sanctuary with Mr Harding. It is clear that having recognised Jane and my aunt, our villains deduced the connection with Wingham and reasoned Georgiana was on her way to the Hall. Wickham set out in pursuit on the horse he had ridden from Ramsgate."

Palmer went on with his tale. The small, one-horse gig had not been—could never be!—a match in speed for a rider who would risk everything to catch them; the fright Elizabeth and Georgiana had being almost run off the road; Elizabeth with the gig's whip in her hand, laying it about Wickham and his horse until the latter threw him, allowing young Jack Hill to pummel the villain into submission.

Darcy stared, his mouth dropping before he recollected himself and closed it with a snap. He glanced sideways at Edward, who could not look more astonished if Napoleon himself had leapt up in front of him, having lain in ambush under the seat squabs.

"Are you serious?" Edward demanded.

"Indeed. Jack broke Wickham's nose and cost him a couple of teeth, and Lizzy caught him on the cheek with her whip. Between them, they have spoiled his pretty looks."

Edward's smile was a sunrise. "What an Amazon!"

"Is she not! Do you not wish you could have seen it? I do not doubt Jack would have protected the girls, for he is a giant of a lad, but the advantage must always be with the rider when one combatant is afoot. Lizzy's actions evened the field and allowed Jack to subdue Wickham quickly. She was marvellous." Palmer smirked, and added an obscure, "With banners."

What did Darcy not owe that indomitable girl? The girl, he learned, who tied Wickham's horse to her gig and, while the blackguard was yet dazed and moaning from being pulled from the saddle and thoroughly beaten, had Jack Hill remove Wickham's boots, stockings and pocket book.

"Lizzy abandoned Wickham in the road, and got Miss Darcy safely to the Hall. We were about to set off for Canterbury for Jane and Aunt Iphy—and to search for Wickham en route—when they arrived in Mr Harding's old two-horse landau, safe and sound. I then rode to Ramsgate to quell any rumours there, and to collect Miss Darcy's maid. I made certain to spread the tale that with her companion called away suddenly on some urgent errand, Miss Darcy was our guest at the Hall. No hint of impropriety or scandal. It seems to have been successful."

Darcy could not speak, his throat too thick and constricted. He had to look away again. What a fool he was! An idiot, leaving Georgiana unprotected while he ran away to Pemberley because he had been a different kind of fool over Elizabeth Bennet. How weak of him! How could Georgiana ever forgive his neglect and carelessness? He, who knew Wickham was in the same county!

"We cannot thank you enough for that," Edward said.

"It was little enough to do, I assure you. To conclude… since Wednesday, we have neither seen nor heard anything of Wickham. I assume he made his way back to Canterbury and found Mrs Younge. I considered making enquiries with the magistrate, but decided it might undo our work to protect Miss Darcy's reputation, and Lizzy agreed. We were content to have her safe."

Edward straightened, so brisk and competent that it made little difference he had left off wearing his uniform. Every inch the colonel. "I will undertake that office, and employ other reasons for seeking him out that will not cast doubtful glances Georgiana's way. William, will you entrust me with Wickham's vowels? I can use those as an excuse with the magistrate, and we will see what may be discovered."

"Yes. Of course."

"I will send a footman into Canterbury to arrange a meeting with the magistrate, Colonel." Palmer's mouth twisted into a wry smile. "Wickham would not have been inconspicuous. The thought of him hobbling barefoot into Canterbury, bearing Lizzy's justice on his face for all to see, is some recompense for his actions."

Edward guffawed. "I would give a guinea to have seen George's feet after a five-mile walk. Five guineas! He probably had to buy someone's old boots at a pawnbroker's or a slop shop. Delightful." The smile on Edward's face did not falter. "I hope he gets gangrene in each foot. I should like to be there when the surgeon chops them."

"We may hope." Palmer leaned back. "And that, gentlemen is all the tale."

"Dear God." Darcy wanted to curve his spine and bury his face on his knees. It was an effort to square his shoulders and lift his head. "She was prey to them, like a doe with wolves. I cannot fathom the wickedness that would have a man exploit and... and mould to his purpose a fifteen-year-old girl he has known all her life."

"She would have only fond memories of him," Edward pointed out. "As you say, he knew her from babyhood, and he treated her with kindness."

"But that was before my father died. She cannot have seen him these five years."

"So her memories of him were those of a child," Palmer said with a nod. "If she remembered him fondly, it was a weakness he was quick to exploit. I take it she knew nothing of the real Wickham?"

Darcy bridled. "Would you tell a child of the maids and tavern girls? No woman, no matter her age, should know of such selfish dissipation. My disapprobation for him should have been enough."

Palmer grimaced. "I cannot agree. Ignorance is not innocence. It is not even a shamming sort of innocence, no more true gold than pinchbeck is. It is merely ignorance, Darcy. How can anyone defend themselves or choose their course wisely, much less a girl inexperienced in the world, if they are not taught to understand other people's true characters, if they are so shielded and protected they do not recognise the wolf when they see him?"

Heat flashed through Darcy. But before he could find enough breath to speak, to protest, Edward had nodded agreement.

"You are right, Palmer. No one expects William to delineate every one of Wickham's sins to Georgiana, but it is sensible to armour her against such men. No, William! I do not blame you, and nor does Palmer, I am sure. What little wisdom we have now has come from retrospection. We have looked more deeply at Wickham to better understand his nature, and must conclude Georgiana was fine prey for one such as he. We have learned a hard lesson."

"Harder for her." Darcy forced the words through a jaw clamped tight upon his grief and guilt. "I cannot easily excuse my own culpability, leaving her unprotected and vulnerable to their wicked game. The fault is mine. I knew Wickham was not a trustworthy man. I knew he was in Kent. I should have protected her better."

"Nonsense. Listen to me." Palmer leaned in and stared hard until Darcy met his gaze. "We have all known Wickham to be a leech, to be the sort of man who wishes to be a gentleman without the means to pay for it or the consequence to carry it off. Your father paid for an education that should have given him entry into any profession he wished, but Wickham is the sort who works harder at avoiding real work than he does at being of use in society, a man always with his hand held out for another to pay for his support. He is gamester and a rake, but a rake only without the risk of angry fathers. He uses doxies and servants. Had you ever heard of him attempting anything with a lady of quality? Had you any inkling that such a course would be one he would pursue?"

It was hard to speak past whatever large rock had lodged itself into his throat. "No."

"Nor I. Nor Fitzwilliam, I'll be bound. Why should you have anticipated Georgiana would be in danger from him, or even that he knew where she was?"

Defeated, Darcy shook his head. He would not—could not—absolve himself of his failure. Not yet.

And certainly not an hour later when he walked into one of the small sitting rooms where Georgiana sat with Elizabeth, and his sister, making the mewling noise of something injured and agonised, leapt up to hurl herself across the room into his arms.

It took some time to soothe Georgiana into a semblance of calm. Or at least enough calm that he could talk to her.

He half walked, half lifted her over to the sofa set opposite the one she and Elizabeth had occupied, and sat with her. She clung to him with a fierceness that had him apprehensive of what she had to say, twisting in the seat beside him and wrapping her arms around his chest, cleaving to him as fast as a limpet on the rocks of Ramsgate Bay.

"You will wish to talk in private." Elizabeth's expression and tone were full of sympathy.

"Oh no! No! Stay with me. Please!" Georgiana's hold slackened and she pulled away, making swift, half-aborted, jerking movements as if she wished to throw herself onto Elizabeth, but couldn't let Darcy go. "Please, Lizzy. Do not go!"

Elizabeth met Darcy's gaze. She had risen, but now hesitated. "You must talk with your brother, Georgiana. He needs to understand what has happened, and discuss it with you in order you both may heal from the injuries inflicted on you."

"Please! Please do not go. Nothing can be private about it that you do not already know. Please." Georgiana stretched out a hand. "You have been so good to me, so truly my friend when I never had a friend before. It helps me, to have you close."

Elizabeth had worked wonders indeed, to have his shy sister come to depend upon her so completely in only a few days. It was both blessing and curse. Darcy could not but rejoice that Georgiana saw Elizabeth's worth, but her clinging to Elizabeth caused a pang. He was no longer the sole lodestar.

He managed a faint smile. Georgiana was all that mattered. "I have the utmost faith in you, Miss Elizabeth, and know you will keep our confidence. It eases my heart that my sister, too, has learned to trust you."

She took Georgiana's hand, and allowed herself to be drawn to their sofa to take a seat on Georgiana's other side. She kept hold of Georgiana's hand, and her gaze did not leave him for a moment. "I will stay, but I will not speak." She dipped forward to press a kiss on Georgiana's cheek. "This is Georgiana's tale, and we have talked about how she must have the courage to tell it."

That was so very Elizabethan a statement, it warmed his heart. He turned his sister back to face him, wrapping her in his arms, and slowly he drew forth the story. Georgiana spoke in a voice so tiny, so breathy and feeble, fainter than a candle-flame in the bright noon sun, he strained to hear her as she spoke of Wickham's first approach one day, when she and Mrs Younge walked along the shoreline on their way to the bathing machines.

"It was the day after you brought everyone to visit from Wingham. He was surprised to see me! He said he would not have been sure he recognised me, but that I look like my mother." Georgiana lifted her head. "Do I? Really?"

"Yes. You are very like Mamma as I remember her."

"Well, he said..." Her head drooped again. "Oh... that I was as beautiful as she was. He said... he said he could not believe how grown I was, and Mrs Younge thought he was gallant and..." And now Georgiana's face crumpled back into its former desolation.

"Mrs Younge?"

"When I explained who George is—"

Darcy snapped, before he could moderate his tone. "Mr Wickham, Georgiana! Never George. It is improper for you to call him anything else!"

Elizabeth winced, but held true to her declaration that she would not speak.

"Uh." Georgiana's mouth worked, and he cursed his folly for

discomposing her.

"I am sorry, Georgiana. I should not be so sharp. I am angry with Wickham, not with you."

She had more resolution and strength than he anticipated. She pressed her lips together, though her chin wobbled, nodded, and in that breathy, faint voice she told him how George Wickham—may he burn in every circle of hell for all eternity—had courted her and convinced her that the dispute between them would melt away when they could greet each other as brothers.

And on and on. Meetings and walks, and once joining Georgiana and Mrs Younge for ices at Fairfax's. Georgiana's pitiful assertions it was all very proper, that Mrs Younge was always present. Proper! When what she described was Mrs Younge subverting every aspect of the charge she had over his sister to prepare her for her come-out, and telling Georgiana over and over that a woman's role was to marry the handsome man who loved her, and none was so handsome and eligible as George Wickham, surely! Wickham himself, plying his gilded, lying tongue to persuade Georgiana she loved and was loved, dazzling the shy child with his attentions and his charm.

The one saving grace was her fervent swearing that nothing more improper happened. That she was not ruined and disgraced. By the grace of God and Elizabeth Bennet, she was not ruined.

All of this twisted Darcy's heart, for it was his role to be both brother and father. To listen, to comfort, and to condemn her conduct where it fell short of what it ought to be. She knew better. She knew much better than to listen to any man's sweet-voiced murmurings and risk herself and her reputation the way she had. She—a Darcy!—behaving so improperly, so... so immorally! It was his duty to correct her behaviour, to convey his disappointment at her breaking his trust.

Gentle as he was, it left Georgiana in tears.

He petted and consoled, murmuring that she was safe, he was here, she was forgiven, while she cried and protested she was sorry, that she had been naughty and would never misbehave again.

Elizabeth made a soft sound, not quite words, and rose. She

stooped to drop a kiss on Georgiana's bowed head and slipped away, walking behind the sofa towards the door. His heart leapt when, as she passed, she rested her hand on his shoulder for the briefest of moments. He twisted his head to glance at her, trying to keep his voice calm and gentle as he offered Georgiana solace and, he hoped, absolution. The smile Elizabeth gave him pierced him with its sweetness, and his heart leapt again.

But now was not the time for thinking of Elizabeth. Now was the time for his sister.

He stroked her hair, rocking her as he had rocked the motherless babe in Pemberley's nursery. Then he had been an awkward, ungainly lad of twelve, all scuffed knees and elbows, holding the baby out from his body with arms so stiff they might have been carved from wood, hardly daring to breathe lest he dropped the squirming little creature his mother had consigned to his care. It was his last memory of Mamma, her face whiter than the pillows behind her head, the trembling hand she held out to him almost too heavy for her to lift. She had listened intently to his promise to be the best brother it was possible to be, his voice cracking, while she fixed her too-bright eyes on him. She had nodded and smiled, and his last ever sight of her had been that smiling gaze following him to the door as he had been gently ushered out, until his father had moved from the corner of the room where he had stood, mute with anguish, and blocked Darcy's view of Mamma with his tall, broad body. She had died before nightfall.

He had never forgotten her, and never forgotten his promise. Until now, though, he had not realised how completely he had broken it.

CHAPTER THIRTY-EIGHT

Knocking

"Go to your bosom;
Knock there, and ask your heart what it doth know."
— Shakespeare, *Measure for Measure*

Jane found her in the garden, sitting on the same bench under the rose arch where Galahad had comforted her after Mr Darcy's ham-fisted proposal. This time, at least, Elizabeth was not kicking at the bench in angry frustration.

"Galahad saw you from the window. He said his mother's garden seems to be a potent balm for perturbed spirits, but I thought I had better come and see if you wished to talk." Jane glanced around at the roses, fewer now and less heavy-headed as autumn approached, but still filling the air with perfume. She took a seat beside Elizabeth. "You were with them longer than I anticipated."

"They asked me to stay. I left when I deemed it time to leave them to comfort each other, while he assures Georgiana that she is loved and cherished, and nothing is irretrievably lost, that all will be well. They had no need of me for that."

"But to have you stay during such a private moment! What a mark of confidence in your honour and integrity!"

"I felt the compliment, I assure you. He was very good with her, Jane. He would not allow any evasion until she had explained herself to him and acknowledged her mistakes and fault, and yet he was so kind and loving. He chastised her folly gently, and then comforted her bruised spirit. I was most impressed by his whole demeanour."

"Yet it has you overset."

Elizabeth huffed out a little sigh. "Not exactly, but it set me thinking that a lady cannot truly know a man until moments like this." She reached out, and Jane clasped her hand in an instant. "Our social lives are so beset with rules and conventions, it is a wonder any lady can say she has discerned a gentleman's character, or she has clearly delineated his moral worth."

"But surely, talking to him, spending time together, cannot leave a lady in complete ignorance of a gentleman's character?"

"You are right, of course. I mean only that the mores of Society place constrictions upon her behaviour and his. She wears her best company manners, and so does he. They are both of them performing to strangers, with little opportunity for private conversation and reflection. All a lady might be able to say is that she has danced four dances with him, or dined with him in company so many times, or they have walked together about the estate with her footman present to give respectability to the exercise."

Jane laughed. "For many couples, Lizzy, that must be sufficient."

"Oh, it may be well enough if she prefers to know as little as needs be about a man, other than he is generally known to be respectable and of good character. Knowing that though a gentleman may not anticipate a ball with enthusiasm, he has learnt his steps well enough to be a competent dancing partner; that he prefers vingt-et-un to commerce, or plain dishes to French; that they both enjoy walking, and he is an engaging conversationalist once an agreeable topic of conversation has been found... If ignorance is her object, it might be sufficient to apprehend nothing of more significance."

Jane's smile was gentle. "So, to take this philosophical point from a general to a particular example, what have you learned of Mr Darcy, now and in all your weeks in Kent, and is it full enough to content you?"

Jane knew her far too well.

"I have been thinking that the gentleman I danced with in Canterbury, or conversed with over dinner or when walking the estate—or, even, the surly gentleman I encountered at the dean's summer reception—is no more the true man, than I show the true Elizabeth. I must always present the polite, civil, amenable façade demanded of a genteel lady in public. I cannot allow people to see impatience, or weariness, or boredom when in company. I must always be the perfect lady."

"Yet those of us who love you, dearest, are not deceived, I assure you!" Jane's smile broadened at Elizabeth's rueful laugh. "But, I understand you. Ladies are always expected to nurture and smooth social discourse."

"Yes! You have it, Jane. We must show elegance of manners and grace in our deportment—"

"Behave with courteous dignity to all, be complaisant and uncontentious, show a meek docility to our elders and betters, and converse with lightness when we are required to amuse or with seriousness when that is called for."

Elizabeth laughed again. "Have you been reading Mary's copy of Fordyce's Sermons? But Fordyce and his ilk would never wish us to express our real opinions, or even admit we have them. Faugh! What stuff and nonsense it all is."

Jane sighed now. "And yet, if she is not to be considered vulgar and ill-bred, those are the rules by which a lady must live."

"We are sadly put upon." Elizabeth leaned up against her sister's shoulder. Jane had been her rock and respite all her life, the source of comfort and understanding. "You comprehend me, Jane. Few do."

"It gives me an advantage I am not slow to press. What does this mean for your opinion of Mr Darcy now?"

"For a gentle creature, you can be obdurate." Elizabeth grimaced. "As I said, he too must perform to strangers by presenting a polite façade to the world. It follows I cannot perceive the real man until he is shorn of all pretence, of all the shifts and evasions being out in Society demands of him. Until he trusts me to see him as he truly, fundamentally, is."

As Fitzwilliam Darcy had trusted her.

"He is so much more than the well-bred gentleman who shared my walks. Far more than the supercilious creature who disdained me in the dean's garden. He feels deeply, Jane. It was both touching and uplifting to witness his affection and gentle care for Georgiana. I have no doubt he would treat everyone for whom he felt he owed a duty of care with the same solicitude and consideration."

If he was committed to a lady, if he loved her, he would make it his life's work—not just a point of honour, or duty, but pure, unalloyed love and inclination—to ensure his wife would have such extraordinary sources of happiness she could have no cause to repine her choice.

As, she suspected, he loved her.

She turned to look Jane full in the face. "To be loved by such a man, to be able to trust oneself to his care and enduring solicitude, would be something, indeed."

Jane pressed her cheek against Elizabeth's. "I cannot wish better for you, Elizabeth. It eases my heart that you have realised it at last." She smiled and straightened. "Galahad did ask me to fetch you. We have refreshments waiting, and Colonel Fitzwilliam is all afire to meet you."

"And you are already missing Galahad's company. Admit it!"

"I am grown a little too used to having Galahad with me constantly."

"You cannot always be together so."

"I know it. When we are married"—and Jane's smile was so contented, Elizabeth was tempted to hurl something at her head, except no one could do that to Jane and, in any event, she had no convenient missile to hand—"we will both have different spheres of work and duty, that will necessitate some separation. It is not to be deplored, since it is the natural state we both long for: a good, strong marriage. All I am saying, my dear sister, is that this period of courtship is very sweet, and to be savoured as much as possible until it reaches its best, happiest, wisest, most reasonable end. As you will soon learn, I hope."

Elizabeth stood, preparing to go into the house. She smoothed her skirts, and considered Mr Darcy's character. She understood his disposition better. He improved upon acquaintance. "Perhaps I will."

Colonel Fitzwilliam was undeniably a relation of the Darcys. He shared Georgiana's fair colouring, his thick blond hair cut *a la Brutus* above a face so gold-tanned by the Iberian sun, his blue eyes were all the brighter and more piercing. Those, too, were a family characteristic. The resemblance in figure between Mr Darcy and the colonel, and in the shape of their faces, was unmistakable. Both were handsome men.

The colonel was, however, a great deal more charming than his taciturn cousin. He bowed over Elizabeth's hand when Galahad introduced them, and raised her hand to his lips as if she had been the grandest of *grandes dames*.

"I have not the words to thank you for what you did for Georgiana, Miss Elizabeth. I will always be grateful. And if our family knew of your kindness and your quick-witted defence of our girl, I should not have merely my own gratitude to express."

Elizabeth's face burned. "We are glad and thankful we were there when Miss Darcy needed us."

"You cannot be more glad than my cousin and I." The colonel, to give him his due, kept his attention on her, with a mere flickering glance at Jane, whom he had undoubtedly admired the instant he set eyes on her. "Your sister has told me of her part in Georgiana's rescue, and Palmer has recounted your own tale. I am told you put Valkyries to shame. How I wish I could have seen you bring Wickham down!"

"I did not set out to do so. As I have told everyone, it was three-parts fright to a mere one-part bravado! We were fortunate. Jack—the groom—did the most."

"I have been in many skirmishes and several full battles, Miss Elizabeth. Every act of courage I have ever witnessed was three-parts fright to one-part bravado. And ofttimes, that grossly overstates the bravado." He raised her hand, which he still held in his, and kissed it again. "You are in very good company."

And with that, and a promise to seek out Jack Hill later to convey his gratitude, he turned the conversation away from what Elizabeth had done and onto his plans to try and bring the villain to book. That he did it to spare her blushes was clear. It was very gallant of him.

Elizabeth settled on the sofa beside Jane, and drank a welcome cup of tea, while the gentlemen turned their attention to considering how to gain intelligence of Mr Wickham and Mrs Younge. Her cousin and the colonel examined the satchel of papers the colonel had brought with him—a tally of debts, it appeared, they hoped would give them a pretext for approaching the Canterbury magistrate.

"Darcy began covering Wickham's debts when his father was taken ill. He did not want my uncle's peace to be cut up over Wickham's profligacy, and considered it a price worth paying if his father were not unduly disturbed." The colonel glanced at Elizabeth and Jane, and explained, "Wickham was a favourite of my Uncle Darcy's, you see, who did a great deal for him in the way of ensuring his education and giving him opportunities to prosper. As we know, Wickham chose not to profit from this kindness in the way it was intended. However, the fact remains that Wickham's charm and outwardly cheerful disposition meant my uncle took pleasure in his company, and Darcy would never deny his father whatever comfort was available, particularly in his last years."

"I am sure he was a dutiful son and did what he could to preserve his father's peace of mind. I know him to be an affectionate and attentive brother." Elizabeth saw him in her mind's eye again, his head bent over Georgiana's, all his attention on her account of Wickham's perfidy; all his focus on love and protection.

"Yes." The colonel's smile was a trifle strained. "He is. It is kind of you to say so, after all that happened."

"It does not change what we know of him." Elizabeth considered his discomfort and sought a diversion. "So, Colonel, now that you have a plan of action against Mr Wickham, let us put the distasteful topic aside for now. I understand from your cousin that you have been lately in the Peninsula. I know little of the region beyond what can be gleaned from geography books, and one or two letters from a friend's betrothed who served there years ago. I do not beg you for tales of battles, but do tell us something of the countryside and its people. Does it differ greatly from England?"

He gave her a smile that spoke of his gratitude, and talked of the people and countryside of Portugal and Spain, speaking of everything from their dress to their food in such a lively manner that Elizabeth found herself well entertained. Galahad and Jane were more caught up in gazing at each other. Beyond an occasional murmured "Indeed!" or "How singular!" from one or other of them, the colonel must have known he had an audience of one. But he was a convivial and cheerful man, and Elizabeth made every effort to show she, at least, was sincerely interested in what he had to say, provoking him into greater detail by questions and comments.

He was describing to her the excitements and dangers of a night ride through the rugged hills south-east of Badajoz when Mr Darcy, face pale and drawn, walked into the room. The colonel's voice faltered into silence.

"Fitz?" Galahad came to his feet.

"My sister is gone to her room, to rest."

Galahad and Jane exchanged glances. Nothing needed to be said, other than a gentle "I shall go to her for a few minutes," from Jane, who rose and left quickly.

"Is all well?" The colonel's expression showed his concern.

Mr Darcy nodded. "Yes. I think so. She is discomposed, and sorry, and sad. And so am I." His gaze caught Elizabeth's. "Walk with me, Elizabeth. Please."

She rose, and took the hand he held out to her.

CHAPTER THIRTY-NINE
Wise Man's Son

Journeys end in lovers' meeting—
Every wise man's son doth know.
— Shakespeare, *All's Well That Ends Well*

They barely spoke for the first two perambulations around the lake lying to the south of the Hall. A quarter around a third circuit of the lake, he stopped and said, simply, "Thank you."

"I am glad I was there."

"I, too. I cannot tell you how much." He paused, his mouth working as if he were dealing with toothache. "Georgiana is distressed, as you know, but I think we have an understanding. We were both at fault, I deem, and we must both endeavour to rebuild trust in the other. She knows she should not have listened to his blandishments, that even contemplating an elopement was wrong, and for my part, I should not have left her vulnerable to his schemes. I have coddled her, to her detriment, and left her in too much ignorance of the world."

"I am pleased you did not excuse her conduct. I feared you

would." Elizabeth gestured to the path and they walked on. "Not that I am offering censure, you understand, but because it is the nature of anyone who loves to hold the object of our affection as something very precious, and we wish to protect them and blame others when they are hurt." She tucked her hand inside his elbow. "I have talked with your sister a great deal over the last few days, as has Jane. Jane is comforting, while I am more bracing, and prone to mopping Georgiana's tears with one hand while using the other to prod her into reflecting on the mistakes she made. In fairness, I think Mrs Younge did a great deal to soften her, to make her more susceptible to Wickham's smooth tongue."

"I do not understand how."

"Oh, in a myriad ways, I expect. Mrs Younge was well placed to gain influence. I have no doubt every one of those lessons on deportment, or how to arrange a dinner table, or how to deal with morning callers, was twisted to serve her purpose as she worked on Georgiana's sensibilities. I gained the impression that Georgiana has led a sheltered life." She ended on an interrogative note.

Darcy agreed. "Very sheltered. Too sheltered, it seems. I have erred in keeping her in swaddling bands. Gal had it right, when he said that ignorance is not innocence. There is such a difference in years between us, you see. I have been more father than brother, and am too accustomed to thinking about her as a child to be protected, and not a young woman who should be prepared for the world."

"She is also shy."

"She has been reserved from childhood. She has had few companions her own age, and it has left its mark on her. She is used to being the youngest and most helpless, reliant upon others, her elders, for direction and approval."

"I thought so. I suspect Mrs Younge understood that, and subtly larded every lesson on, for example, how to pour and present refreshments, with 'you are full-grown now, a woman at the age for marrying... a girl cannot marry soon enough, and handsome man will be your fate, I am sure... look to those you have trusted from childhood to guide you...' And Wickham positioned himself as just that person—older, wiser, able to see what would be best for her. As soon as they sprang the trap with the supposedly accidental meeting in Ramsgate, Mrs Younge must have directly encouraged her to repose her faith in an old friend who also happened to be a handsome man who professed to love her."

He frowned. "On two or three occasions recently, Georgiana asserted her adulthood. Not in a hectoring or demanding manner, because that is not her way, but claiming she was grown up and yet still treated as a child in too many ways."

They paused at the far end of the lake, and for a moment Elizabeth admired the vista across the placid waters, with the Hall set in its gardens. A pair of swans and their grey-plumaged cygnets floated past, the young ones almost the size of their parents now. The cob stared at them with a hint of belligerence in his hot, yellow eyes, spreading out his wings in warning.

"What do you plan to do with Wickham when you apprehend him?" She turned hurriedly and added, with a smile, "Do not answer unless you wish it! I am aware most gentleman would not discuss such things with a lady."

"With whom else can I speak of it, if not with you? Our plan is simple enough. Wickham owes me a great deal of money, and my cousin intends to seek a writ for debt. If we can catch hold of him, he will rot in the Fleet or the Marshalsea for the rest of his life."

Elizabeth nodded. "Your cousin mentioned the debt, intending, I believe, to use it as the pretext for his enquiries with the magistrate in Canterbury. I am happy the debt also gives you a weapon to wield, a defence for Georgiana that is apt to your hand. I have no compassion for Mr Wickham. He deserves none."

He looked away, seemingly watching the swans as they moved towards the reeds fringing the shore. "I am concerned about what he may do or say while he remains at large to blacken Georgiana's reputation."

"Out of revenge?"

"Yes. Or to extort payment to ensure his silence."

"I hope he will see the folly of attempting it, with all we have done to ensure no rumours exist for him to build upon."

Darcy smiled a little then. "You have been so good for her, and I can never repay your kindness and good sense." He gestured to a path leading out into the southern meadows. "Shall we go that way?"

"Of course." Elizabeth took his arm again, and they left the lake path, passing under a belt of trees and out into the sunlight.

"I will search for a new companion for Georgiana, though it may take some little time to find someone suitable." Mr Darcy's smile was a little strained. "In the meantime, it may be wise to take her home to Pemberley for a little while to help her recover, and to rebuild the relationship between us. Do you agree?"

"I agree she needs a companion you can trust to help prepare her for her come-out, and a settled home cannot but help secure her footing until she recovers some confidence in herself. I am loath to interfere more than I have already, but I have heard the lady who is companion to the Bridges family at Goodnestone may soon be seeking a new situation. Mrs Annesley is estimable, and if Fanny Bridges is an example of the sort of girl she can turn out, then she is a worthy lady indeed."

"I shall look into that. Thank you." He shook his head with a little grimace. "What of yourself? What are your plans?"

"Galahad will escort us home to Longbourn at the end of the month. Aunt Iphy goes too, to meet my mother and other sisters, and will stay until the new year. Galahad and Jane need to speak to my father, you see."

"Sits the wind in that quarter?"

"The wind blows very strongly, and Jane and Galahad are bowled along like a pair of leaves caught up in the breeze." Elizabeth laughed. "I own myself astonished, since they have known each other only a few weeks and Jane is hardly noted for her impetuosity! They make a fine couple however. Jane is very happy, and Galahad is just the sort of determined gentleman to suit her."

"A fine couple, indeed. I am happy for them."

"I hope it will not affect Galahad's friendship with Mr Bingley."

"Bingley will understand, and I am certain will recover any lost spirits. He is a gregarious creature, and at a time of life when friends and engagements are continually increasing. He will be well, I am sure."

"Good. I liked Mr Bingley."

He nodded, and for half the width of a meadow they were silent, before he spoke again. "I had determined to return, even before all this. I spent a great of time reflecting on myself and my behaviour. I had to come back. For several reasons."

"Oh?"

"First, to make the deepest and most grovelling of apologies for my behaviour, from the dean's garden onwards. I was greatly at fault, I know. I took no pains to disguise my belief in my superiority to all. I was so sure of myself. I am Darcy of Pemberley, I said; I can have a wife of high birth and great riches merely for the asking... and then you showed me how all my pretensions were as naught in the estimation of a woman worthy of being pleased, worthy for her own sake, and for her own innate value against which more worldly values seem as chaff and dust. Until that moment, I had not realised how very disdainful I had grown. From the first, my conduct towards you was unconscionable. My manners were execrable and completely deserving of the reproofs you offered me. I cannot think of my actions, my beliefs, my comportment towards others—and you in particular—without abhorrence. To treat you as if I were conferring inestimable honour by merely being no more than ordinarily civil!" His mouth twisted. "We both know I was often uncivil. I deserved every iota of your disapproval, and I am heartily ashamed of myself."

His sincerity was unmistakable.

"If the behaviour of both were closely examined, neither of us would escape without criticism. I was unkind, and for that I am sorry."

"I do not deserve your kindness."

She stopped him, and when he turned to face her, she smiled. "Everyone deserves some kindness, Mr Darcy. Galahad helped me understand you, to understand the forces that helped mould you into the man you are. It allowed me to see how unkind I had been."

"He is a very good friend."

"He loves you as dearly as he would a brother. He showed me

the man he knows, rather than the armour you present to Society. I am grateful for the insight."

"Then I owe him a great deal. His wedding present will have to be something quite extraordinarily grand."

She laughed, and the smile he gave her in return was wider and happier than she ever remembered seeing on him. "I will add that observing you with Georgiana just now, I believe I saw more of your character and principles than I would think possible under normal circumstances. I was touched, deeply, by your care and tender consideration for her. I approve of that man highly. Your tenderness, your honourable conduct with her, proved Galahad right, and that my own vanity and resentments had prevented me from perceiving you clearly."

"No. Do not blame yourself for our misunderstandings. I am wholly at fault."

"I will strike a bargain with you, sir. If you will forgive my sharpness and unkindness, then I will forgive your less sociable traits. We will both strive to see the best in each other."

"Done. Thank you." He gestured towards a distant copse. "Shall we walk there?"

She acquiesced, and they strolled across the meadow.

"I said I had several reasons to return. After begging your forgiveness, my second reason is to beg for the opportunity to show you the man I should be, and wish to be. I will never be as gregarious and easy in company as Gal Palmer or Bingley, but I do want to lessen your ill opinion by showing you your reproofs have been attended to."

"I do not think, Mr Darcy, that you ought to be different in principle or in essentials. You are a man of sense and education, with an excellent mind and strong morals. Your understanding and opinions are mostly pleasing. All those things are admirable. You need only a little liveliness, you know, and a little more patience with the world."

A tinge of red appeared on his cheeks. "It is courtesy I lack and I know it, but I am endeavouring to better myself, that I may be more the sort of man who is worthy of your good opinion. Will you grant me the opportunity to show you that I can do better?"

"Gladly."

"Thank you." His smile warmed her. "Well, my other reasons for returning must now wait upon the success of these first two."

His meaning was clear to her. Her face burned, and she could do nothing but incline her head and look away, so he should not see her confusion. After a moment, she gathered enough composure to ask, "What would you have done if we had already returned to Longbourn?"

He gave her a look that was part surprise, and part sweetness. A great deal of sweetness. "Why, followed you, of course. What else could I have done?"

She blushed.

He reached for both her hands, holding them in his own, his thumbs lightly smoothing over the backs of her fingers. If he noticed them trembling, he made no mention of it. "Elizabeth, I made many mistakes with you, from the very beginning of our acquaintance, but the one error I have not made is that of knowing my own heart and inclinations. I confess at first I wished to deny it—you know very well what wrong-headed ideas I had—but I knew what I felt and what I truly wanted. I cannot believe I have known you only these two or three months, because my life is so very different now. You have come to fill it entirely, and fill it with light, and that laugh of yours, and the brightness you cast over everything... The writer of Proverbs has it right, for your price is above rubies."

Her face was aflame, and she had no hands free to press the heat and colour from her cheeks. "Mr Darcy—"

"I will not importune you now, I swear. I merely wish you to know that though I expressed myself in ways that bring me nothing but shame and self-reproach, the feelings I had then are still the same. My affection for you, my wish to have you as my wife, are as strong now as then. Stronger. I ask to be allowed to prove it to you."

"I— I do not know what to say."

"An unusual state of affairs!" He stooped to look her direct in the eyes. "I will not repeat the question I asked last month. Not yet. It was premature, and I had not then—nor have I yet—earned the right to ask it. Will you, though, agree to a courtship, to the opportunity for us to know each other better? Let me have that privilege, at least: to call on you, and show you a man who is not yet worthy of you, but is endeavouring to be so."

"I am not the sort of lady you expected to marry. I cannot offer the dowry, or connections, or—"

"Rubies, Elizabeth. You are beyond them. I do not need a dowry. I have more connections than I care to keep up. As I said, you bring light and brightness, wit and kindness, and a great heart. I do not want more. No man could—or should!—ask for more. If I were lucky enough to gain you, I would gain the most worthy woman of all."

Heavens. Where had the reserved, rather silent Mr Darcy learned to speak with such ardent charm? What was it she had thought while speaking to Jane in the rose garden? That he would strain every nerve and sinew to ensure the woman he loved could never repine her choice, that he would ensure her happiness and well-being. Something of that nature.

He offered it all to her. His entire world, he offered to her.

She blinked to clear the blurring of her sight. There was no impediment to seeing how well the expression of heartfelt delight happiness became him when she nodded, and pressed the hands holding hers She could not quite quell the quivering in her voice. "I would welcome a courtship, very much indeed."

Mr Darcy did not smile, the way Galahad and Jane were always smiling. No, indeed. Reserved, cold-mannered, remote Mr Darcy threw back his head and laughed, as loudly and as unrestrainedly as a boy. So loudly, a clamour of rooks rose from the treetops in alarm, and the glade they stood in echoed with it.

And Elizabeth, her breath coming fast and hard, her entire body as light and hot as the sun, laughed with him, while he raised her hands to his lips and rained kisses upon them.

No. She did not think she would repine the choice she had made. She did not think she would repine at all.

LETTER: Mrs Elizabeth Darcy To Miss Iphigenia Palmer, May 1816

Miss Iphigenia Palmer
Wingham Hall, Wingham, Kent

Pemberley, Derbyshire
Monday, 20 May, 1816

Greetings, my dearest, dearest aunt!

This has been a sad time for you all in Kent, as it has been for me here in Pemberly. I hope these last few weeks have brought you some ease from the first shock of grief, and you are finding solace with Galahad and Jane. I wish I could fly to Kent to be with you! But I am sorry to say I am recovering only slowly from the birth of your namesake, and cannot yet encompass such a long journey, even if this unseasonable, cold, wet weather would allow for easy travel. William is quite firm in that regard, and I cannot but give way.

William has been comfort itself to me, and I have found great consolation in remembering what a good man Sir James was, and knowing he is now at peace with God. He was as a grandfather to me—the dearest of men! I have been prone to giving little Thomas James many an embrace as I tell him of his namesake, and how kind Sir James was.

Papa and Mamma came to Pemberley, as Mamma wanted to be with me for Iphigenia Anne's arrival, and, as you will realise, they were here when the sad news came. Papa was much affected by our shared loss. He and Sir James developed such an excellent friendship over the last five years, and played many a game of chess through their exchange of letters. Papa laid down his king in Sir James's honour, in great sadness. They left Pemberley a fortnight ago, and Papa has roused himself to write to assure us that although the roads were execrable, they arrived safely at Longbourn. Mamma has taken great pleasure in making the rounds of the neighbourhood to boast of her stay here, and to assure friends like Lady Lucas that her grandchildren are far superior to theirs! Dear Mamma. Even Kitty's marriage to John Lucas has not tempered that rivalry!

Letters from you and Jane have been another source of comfort. In her last letter, Jane rejoiced that you have agreed to live with her and the new Sir Galahad up at the Hall. Such excellent news, Aunt. This terrible spring— I do not recall one so cold as this! Georgiana, who is enjoying her second season under the aegis of Lady Ashbourne, mentioned in her latest letter that hail fell in London last week. In May! William says it does not augur well for the planting, with nothing sprouting in this cold wet earth, and he fears for the harvest this year, with all the dreadful effect that will have on people's livelihoods. We are already planning with our neighbours and the local clergy how we might support the families of the poor if need be. With this in mind, I am pleased you are safely ensconced in the Hall.

Jane and Gal's little ones will be glad to have you, their grandmother in all but name, closely associated with them. I know I benefitted much from my grandmamma's companionship and teaching. You will be no less beloved, I am sure, by young James and Cecy. I should warn you, though, that I do not wish you to become too settled and comfortable! If, as I hope, we succeed in our plans to meet later this year, be warned I fully intend to steal you away to Pemberley with me when we return here, to allow you to fulfil the same grandmotherly office for Thomas and little Iphy.

What plans, you ask? Well, Papa has announced his wish to host us all at Christmas, and Mamma is eager to fix the scheme before Papa can consider what he has set in hand, and retreats to his book room. There will be many letters winging back and forth, I expect, as we fix our plans.

I hope by then Miss Iphigenia Darcy will be old enough to tolerate the coach journey. A journey with an infant is no sinecure, and keeping Thomas James amused for two or three days' journey is no task for the faint-hearted! When we gathered together last Christmas at Wingham, Papa took great delight in noting William's expression when he entered the coach for the journey home to Pemberley with Thomas in his arms. Papa wrote to suggest that should I prove to be my mother's daughter and offer him half-a-dozen pledges of my affection, William had better determine to ride in the box beside the coachman for the rest of his life. It will, Papa says, be more comfortable than a seat inside. More than once since Papa's letter, I have seen William eyeing the coachman's seat in speculative fashion!

Now, I have an entire budget of news of the family. Jane will have her own sources for news, but I hope to have all the joy of at least being first with that part of it relating only to the Darcys.

William is fretting mightily: Georgiana has a suitor in the form of a scion of the Spencer family. The young man is a barrister with a very easy income, and though unlikely to succeed to any of the illustrious Spencer titles, his career at the bar is very promising. The Spencers look high for brides, but we are confident that not a breath of her Ramsgate adventure has attached scandal to our girl—with Wickham and Mrs Younge in Van Dieman's Land, thanks to Edward Fitzwilliam's efforts, she is safe.

Of course, no gentleman, Spencer though he may be, can be quite up to the mark when it comes to William's sister, and he is torn between wishing to be there to protect Georgiana's interests and knowing his place is here with his wife and children. Georgiana is happy in the Ashbournes' care, and Edward has gone up to Town from Rosings to ensure young Mr Spencer and all his relatives appreciate his good fortune.

Edward is out of his deep mourning now, but as a result of his loss and his absence from Rosings, the Collinses are visiting Longbourn. Life in Hunsford was difficult for them when William married me. While old Lady Catherine's initial resentment abated when her daughter Anne wed the colonel, as he was then, it flared anew in January with Anne's sad demise. Edward is not at all amenable to his mother-in-law's resuming her former role as mistress of Rosings Park. Lady C is incensed and beyond all reach of reason, blaming poor William for what she calls his "dereliction of duty". She has sent many intemperate letters since Anne's death. William consigns them unopened to the fire. He relies upon his cousin to let him know if there is anything of real import that he must deal with.

Lady C's ire having thus been reignited against me for daring to take her daughter's place, it has landed upon poor Mary and Collins, since they were conveniently to hand to bear the brunt of it and their being related to "that perfidious Bennet chit". In consequence, they and little Cathy are visiting Longbourn for a month or two. I was greatly amused to hear from Mary that Lady C's strictures caused so much shock and sorrow, my brother Collins has remembered his family pride. He considers reverting to the Bennet name resigned by his grandfather almost sixty years ago. Papa says he is encouraging the change, as it would gratify him to pass Longbourn on to a Bennet, after all.

The Collinses will stay at Longbourn at least until Kitty is confined in July. Mamma writes to say Kitty's girth has everyone suspecting she may be bearing twins. Though there are none in the Bennet family, they are prevalent among the Lucases. Charlotte Lucas-as-was presented her husband with a second set of twins a month ago. You will recall meeting Charlotte at my wedding, I am sure. She is a dear friend, and I know I spared no one my smug self-congratulations when my bringing her to Pemberley resulted in her marrying the rector of Kympton. William assures me the living is a good one, but I do think that, as its patron, he must consider increasing Mr Gibson's stipend. Otherwise the good reverend will be doomed to be the very pattern card of country parsons: rich in offspring, and poor in every other worldly consideration. Charlotte is very happy, but it seems to me contentment may be as easily purchased by welcoming one little stranger at a time, as opposed to two.

You will be astonished to learn I have had a letter from Lydia. It seems she and her new husband are somewhere near the Azores. I am grown as deficient in geography as was our old acquaintance Miss Bingley, and had to resort to the atlases in the library to find where the Azores may be. Lydia's constancy in her determination to have a uniformed man is to be applauded, I suppose, but the comfort is that the Navy breeds splendid officers, and Captain Harville seems to be keeping her in tolerable order. William liked the captain a great deal, and they keep up a lively correspondence. I live in dread of being asked to visit the Harvilles in the Caribbean, where they will settle for some years. William may relish the adventure, but ever since first stepping foot onto a ship at Ramsgate, I have been an indifferent sailor. I cannot anticipate such a journey with anything other than horror.

As an aside, Miss Bingley is married at last, her brother tells us—he is staying with us while considering purchasing a nearby estate. She married a baronet from Somersetshire, a widower whose two elder daughters are older than she, and who leases out his estate to live off the rent. Despite gaining her dowry, Sir Walter will not return to his estate, being little enamoured of country life. I am a sad, petty creature, I know, but my delight was boundless when I learnt the new Lady Elliot's home is a rented apartment in the city of Bath.

...

The small break in my letter was the result of a cool sun poking its way through the cloud cover at last, and my having to run to keep a promise to my son. Although only three, he has all William's tenacity of purpose. His mamma promised him that the first fine day she would take him and his sister to hunt for frogs along the edges of the lake, and this gleam of sunshine had him and his nurse at my sitting-room door, all aquiver with excitement to ensure his mamma did not disappoint. Of course, I could not! We made an expedition of it, processing across the lawn in grand style. We persuaded William to abandon his study and accompany us, so our procession went something like this:

William, holding Thomas by the hand to try and prevent him joining the froglets in the muddy water. He did not succeed.

Me, carrying various small nets and jars for catching froglets and toadlets, to allow Thomas to examine them with more scientific exactitude in the nursery later.

Nurse Ellen, carrying Miss Darcy, who may be too young to care about frogs, but who has a fine pair of lungs with which to make clear her disapprobation at the notion of being left behind.

Nurse Sarah, carrying a small basket provided by Mrs Reynolds, which Thomas decreed should contain a great deal of cake. Frogs, it seems, are sad creatures who almost never have good things to eat, and Thomas, who has a kind heart, felt we should endeavour to remedy the lack.

A footman, trying hard to control his expression, which was half-amused, half-apprehensive. I expect he suspected who would be carrying Thomas back again, and a sturdy young man who is full of cake is no light burden. His other task will be to return the froglets to their native milieu once Thomas has succumbed to sleep later.

We had a splendid time. Thomas fell in twice, once by accident, and was carried home in triumph on the footman's shoulders. William baulked at the amount of mud on Thomas, you see. My husband has unbent greatly over the last few years— another sin laid at my door by Lady C, that I have induced my husband to put aside his dignity and act as if he were some common sort of father, and not a stiff-necked Darcy—but he has some way to go still when it comes to accepting mud with complaisance.

I do not complain, Aunt Iphy. He accepts his wife, bothersome creature that she is, with more than complaisance. He likes me a little, I daresay. And certainly he is the most loving and indulgent of husbands. I remember thinking, the day he returned to Wingham, that he is just the sort of gentleman who, when he loves his wife, will ensure she experiences such happiness, she can have no cause to repine. I am pleased to say I was correct.

This evening, as the fugitive sun vanished again and we reversed our procession over the lawn—Thomas all muddy happiness, Iphy still sleeping, my petticoats six inches deep in mud following Thomas's first excursion into the lake, and William's boots squeaking with water following his second—I can honestly say I have not repined one instant. I am indeed blessed.

I owe it to you, dearest of aunts, and your brave notion to heal the breach in our families. Without you, I would never have met William or Galahad or Sir James. Without you, neither Jane nor I would be so happily settled. What can I say, but that Kent is the place to get a husband, it seems, and without you, I should never have known it.

With all my dearest love and gratitude

Lizzy

~end~

The Bennet-Palmer-Bridges Family Tree

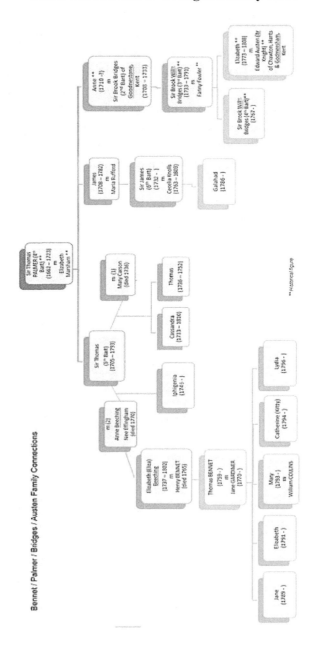

ABOUT THE AUTHOR

 Once I used to do communications work for the UK government, in a variety of departments that saw me do things as diverse as managing national TV campaigns and an internal TV service delivered through everyone's desktop PC. These days I live a much quieter life with my husband in a pretty Georgian vicarage deep in the Nottinghamshire countryside, and I am writing full time. I'm supported in that endeavour not only by the tolerant Mr Winter (bless him!), but also by the lovely Mavis, a Yorkie-Bichon cross with a bark several sizes larger than she is.

I have been a lover of Jane Austen's works for most of my life. I know it is appalling cheek to use even a fraction of Jane's 'little bit of ivory', but I hope she will forgive me. My only excuse is that of all literary heroines, Lizzy Bennet is the one I wanted to be. Writing Pride and Prejudice variations is the closest I shall ever come.

Julia

Contact me: juliawinterfiction@gmail.com
Website: https://juliawinterfiction.com
Twitter: https://twitter.com/fiction_julia
Facebook: https://www.facebook.com/JuliaWinterFiction

GLASS HAT
PRESS

Made in the USA
Las Vegas, NV
02 March 2024

86602135R00216